Critical Acclaim for
Song of the Silent Harp
Book One of An Emerald Ballad

This popular novel of the Famine period glows with love and faith amid the hardships, and even cruelty, of life under absentee landlords in nineteenth-century Ireland.

The author has created a cast of complex characters in a panorama that stretches from County Mayo to Dublin, London, and eventually New York where the Kavanaghs are to work out their destiny.

All the color and imagery of a film enliven this story as it unfolds against a background of aborted revolution, disappointed love, and the elemental struggle for life fulfillment in a harsh society.

Rarely has a novel captured so authentically the enduring faith of the Irish peasant that sustains Nora Kavanagh through the tribulation and struggle of that harrowing period.

This is a compelling and uplifting read that adds to an understanding of Ireland in the last century.

Eoin McKiernan, Founder
Irish American Cultural Institute

An Emerald Ballad Series

Song of the Silent Harp
Heart of the Lonely Exile
Land of a Thousand Dreams

LAND of a THOUSAND DREAMS

B.J. Hoff

BETHANY HOUSE PUBLISHERS
MINNEAPOLIS, MINNESOTA 55438

With the exception of recognized historical figures, the characters in this novel are fictional, and any resemblance to actual persons, living or dead, is purely coincidental.

The suffering that took place throughout Ireland during the Great Hunger of the 1840s was all too real, and has been documented in numerous journals. Nevertheless, it is depicted herein by fictional characters.

Manuscript edited by Penelope J. Stokes.

Cover illustration by Dan Thornberg,
Bethany House Publishers staff artist.

Copyright © 1992
B. J. Hoff
All Rights Reserved

Published by Bethany House Publishers
A Ministry of Bethany Fellowship, Inc.
6820 Auto Club Road, Minneapolis, Minnesota 55438

Printed in the United States of America

Library of Congress Cataloging-in-Publication Data

Hoff, B. J.
   Land of a thousand dreams / B. J. Hoff.
     p. cm. — (An Emerald ballad ; bk. 3)

   1. Irish Americans—History—19th century—Fiction.
I. Title. II. Series: Hoff, B. J. Emerald ballad ; bk. 3.
PS3558.034395L36   1992
813'.54—dc20   92–13051
ISBN 1–55661–112–9   CIP

For Dana and Jessie,
Two very special dreams fulfilled—
My daughters

Acknowledgments

My continuing thanks to Dr. Eoin McKiernan of St. Paul, Minnesota, founder of the Irish American Cultural Institute, for his encouragement and assistance. . . .

And to Patrick Mead, Lancaster, Ohio, a true Gael and a great help.

As always, my heartfelt thanks and deepest appreciation to all the special people at Bethany House Publishers. In the eye of this beholder, you form a beautiful reflection of God's grace.

A special note of gratitude to Carol Johnson and Sharon Madison for their ongoing encouragement, support, and ideas . . . and to Penny Stokes, my editor, who happens to be the real genius behind Sandemon's creative inventions, and whose challenge to excellence rings true because of her own untiring efforts and commitment.

About the Author

B. J. HOFF, novelist and Christian poet, has authored numerous books, including historical novels and mysteries, as well as poetry and devotional collections.

A direct descendant of Irish ancestors who came to this country before the Revolutionary War, B. J. brings years of dedicated historical research and personal involvement to her present work. Her love and understanding of the Irish people—their history, their struggles, their music, and their indomitable spirit—lends to her writing all the passion and power of her rich Gaelic heritage.

B. J. holds memberships in Authors Guild, the American Conference for Irish Studies, the American Irish Historical Society, and the American Irish Political Education Committee. She and her husband make their home in Lancaster, Ohio. Their family includes two daughters, an Irish dog named Casey, and Abigail the Arrogant Cat.

B. J. enjoys hearing from her readers. You may write to her in care of:

Bethany House Publishers
6820 Auto Club Road
Minneapolis, MN 55438

Contents

PART TWO
DREAMS ABANDONED • NIGHT SHADOWS

PART THREE
DREAMS FULFILLED • NEW TOMORROWS

Pronunciation Guide

Aine . . . . Än´ya

a gra . . . . a grä´
                                               (my love)

alannah . . . . a län´uh
                                            (my child)

asthore . . . . .a stor´
                                        (my treasure)

Drogheda . . . . Draw´he guh

Killala . . . . Kil lä´lä

Sandemon . . . . Sanda mōhn´

Seanchai . . . . .Shan´a kee

Tierney . . . . Teer´ney

Build houses and dwell in them;
plant gardens and eat their fruit.
Take wives and beget sons and daughters;
and take wives for your sons and give your daughters
to husbands, so that they may bear sons and daughters—
that you may be increased there, and not diminished.
And seek the peace of the city where I have caused you
to be carried away captive, and pray to the Lord for it;
for in its peace you will have peace. . . .
For I know the thoughts that I think toward you,
says the Lord,
thoughts of peace and not of evil, to give you a future
and a hope.

JEREMIAH 29:5–7, 11, (NKJV)

PROLOGUE

The Hanging of Brian Kavanagh

Well, they fought for poor Old Ireland,
And full bitter was their fate;
(Oh! what glorious pride and sorrow
Fill the name of Ninety-Eight!)

JOHN KEEGAN CASEY (1846–1870)

Castlebar, Western Ireland
October 1798

"It seems the day of Brian's hanging should be dark and stormy, not a day such as this," said Peggy Kavanagh.

The doomed man's wife lifted a trembling hand to her lips. Heavy with child, her skin ashen, she looked acutely uncomfortable and somewhat ill. Her stricken gaze was riveted to a paper—one of many—nailed up outside the courthouse.

Dan Kavanagh glanced down at his brother's wife, then up at the fair Mayo sky overhead. He took Peg's meaning well enough. This golden harvest day, clear and sweet-scented and deceptively calm, did not seem a fit day for a hanging.

The sky should be black with thunderheads. A raging gale would be far more suitable than the soft and clinging mellow autumn breeze. No man should meet the hangman on a honeyed

13

day like this. Certainly not a man like Brian Kavanagh.

Again he stole a glance at his sister-in-law. " 'Tis not right, your being here, Peg," he muttered. "What sort of woman watches her husband die so?"

Immediately he regretted the gruffness of his tone. He had not thought to chastise, only to protect.

"The kind of woman who would be faithful to her vows." Peg's voice was as brittle as dead leaves. "Faithful unto death."

Her chin jutted up, and Dan saw a glistening of tears in her eyes. "Brian might be the great fool for what he did, but I'll not be abandoning him at the end. He is still my husband, and father to my sons." She paused, shooting Dan an accusing look. "And who should understand that better than the man's own brother?"

Chastened, Dan shoved his hands deep down in his pockets and stared at the dusty street. "Sure, I do understand, Peg. I only meant to spare you a measure of the grief."

"Don't I know that?" Peg softened her tone. "But this is a grief not meant to be spared, Dan. 'Tis for me to feel the very depths of Brian's pain this day, I'm thinking. Perhaps it's all that will bind us together at the end, don't you see?"

Dan nodded, his own heart bowed beneath a heavy sorrow. Brian had been the hero of his life, ever since he was old enough to speak his brother's name. Wasn't it Brian who had taught him to sit a horse before he'd even learned his letters? 'Twas Brian who had first showed him how to plow a field, to fell a tree, build a wagon. He had even attempted to teach him the mystery of the Kavanagh harp, though to no avail; his own big knobby fingers had ever been too clumsy for all else save working the land.

Dan's stomach knotted at the thought of the harp. He had grown used to falling asleep in the back room of his brother's cabin, listening to the harp scatter its golden tones over the floor like singing shells. Now the harp would be silenced, Brian's music only an echo in the memory of his family and friends.

Beside him, Peg stirred and moved closer to the courthouse wall. Reluctantly, Dan followed her. This side of the building was checkered with numerous pieces of foolscap on which were printed the names of those recently hanged, or those about to be.

It had rained during the night, washing away some of the names, smudging others. But his brother's name could still be clearly read:

BRIAN KAVANAGH. Tenant farmer. Rebelled against the Crown, fought with the French. Guilty of treason. Death by hanging.

Was this his brother, then? Brian, with the rolling laugh and the sunburned face and the freckled hands? Brian, who was known to dance to the fiddle until sunrise, then go directly to the fields without so much as stopping for a bite in between? Was this dangerous wild rebel the same tenderhearted man who brought his wife bouquets of wildflowers and carved wee animals out of tree stumps for his children?

"I pray it does not rain for days," murmured Peg beside him.

Jarred out of his thoughts, Dan stared at her. "Why would you say such a thing, Peg?"

"I would not have his name washed away like the others," she answered dully. "I would have it read and remembered by all those who turned and ran when it counted most."

Dan's throat tightened. "Do you blame me, then, Peg," he asked, clenching his calloused hands at his sides, "for not fighting alongside Brian?"

At last she dragged her eyes away from the foolscap to meet Dan's miserable gaze. "Ah, no, Dan," she said softly. "Not at all. Haven't we always understood the killing way was not in you? Brian himself said it would wither your very soul to lift a pike against another man—even a soldier. No," she repeated, turning back to the courthouse wall, "my bitterness is toward those who made their great boasts and then scattered like scared chickens when the bullets began to fly!" Her mouth pulled down. "Fools such as Feary MacNulty and Michan O'Dowd, who accepted the Frenchmen's weapons and pledged to use them to free Ireland. 'Tis said they nearly blew each other's toes off in their frenzy to drop their guns and run."

"They are but simple plowboys, Peg. What do they know of battles and dying? Don't be too hard on them."

She swung around to face him. "Had they and the other blathering cowards not deserted their own men, our Brian might not be about to swing!"

Dan shook his head, knowing there would be no reasoning with her this day. Nor could he argue the truth of her words. But what had they expected, after all? The outcome of this latest failed rising could have been predicted by all but the most dull-witted.

Somebody—a man named Tone, they said—had worked to convince the French that a united Ireland was ready to rise and throw off its shackles, that thousands of strong-bodied men were eager for muskets to set the land free from England's tyranny. So the French had sent their soldiers to aid and abet. But instead of the full-fledged army they'd been led to expect, they had found only straggling bands of untrained peasants who had never held a weapon more deadly than a blackthorn stick.

Many, like Brian, had fought with a fury right to the end, when they were finally captured or slaughtered. Others, fearing for their lives or the punishment that would fall to their families, had fled the battle for the shelter of the hills.

It was but one more vain attempt to turn farm boys into warriors. There had been other endeavors in the past—visionary plots by well-intentioned patriots and ludicrous schemes by dark-souled pirates. All proved futile. For Ireland was no country of gentleman soldiers, but rather a land of poor, uneducated farmers. Its true gentry had been destroyed by England's greedy colonization, its scholars and professional men mostly scattered and persecuted. The nation's military force consisted of farm boys with borrowed muskets and homemade pikes, homeless poets, and frieze-clad fishermen.

Yet every few decades a rebellion would erupt to further deplete the already weakened peasantry. Just so with this latest. Both the rumors and promises had proven false, and Ireland was once again defeated. Brian was but one of the unfortunates to be captured by the scarlet-coated scorpions, and today his hasty sentence would be accomplished.

Dan looked around their surroundings. He was sickened by the curious crowds, the swaggering soldiers filling the streets of Castlebar. Business was brisk for the taverns and the shops this day, he noted angrily. Sure, and there was nothing like a proper hanging to draw the crowds.

Looking back to Peg, he determined once more that she must not witness what was to come. The babe was due any day now, and she was already failing from her despair.

She did not realize the hideous torment that awaited poor Brian. Somehow he must get her away before the hanging.

Dan had seen men hang before today. The cruel and grisly act—even when the victim was a stranger—was a gruesome sight to behold. And the rope was not the worst of things. After the hanging, Brian's body would be taken down, tarred, and hung up again for the crowds to view.

It would destroy Peg entirely. He could not, he *would* not allow her to watch.

Hadn't Brian made him promise to take care of his Peggy and the lads? Dan had given his word that he would see to them, had sworn to do his best for Brian's wife and for his sons and the unborn babe.

The thought of the child made him even more determined to get Peg away. "We will find us a less crowded place, Peg," he said, taking her arm. Giving her no chance to protest, he led her off from the courthouse into the dusty street.

They tried to squeeze through the noisy crowd, only to become entangled in it. One middle-aged woman with a red petticoat and a loud mouth swore at them; beside her, a big, florid-faced youth, who looked to be her son, grinned as if he were well in his cups.

At last, two soldiers, one of whom shot a look of contempt at Peg's swollen middle, backed off just enough to let them pass.

When they reached the fringes of the crowd, Dan took both of Peg's hands, making her face him. "You will hear me now, Peg. I promised my brother to see to you and the family, and I will do so. I would fail him in the worst way altogether were I to let you stay in this terrible place a minute longer."

When Peg attempted to protest, Dan tightened his grip on her hands and raised his voice. "You will do as I *say*, Peg! I may be an unmarried man, but I know well enough that you'll risk the babe and perhaps your own life as well if you insist on watching our Brian's final misery."

She attempted to wrench away, but Dan held her. "No, now you will hear me! Sure, Brian could have no doubt—none at all— as to your devotion. You have been a faithful wife. You have made him a happy man—you have blessed him. But I heard him last night, Peg. I heard him plead with you, before we left the cell, not to come to the hanging! Isn't that so, Peg?"

Her mouth trembled, but she gave a small nod. "Aye, he did," she admitted softly. "But, Dan—"

"Oh, Peg, don't you see how it is? No man would have his wife

17

watch him die—especially by the rope! Don't we both know what a proud man is Brian? Your being here today would give him more grief than the hanging itself! He would fear for you, and for the babe—and wouldn't he be shamed? Would you heap still more sorrow on the man's heart, Peg? Isn't it enough that he must hang like a common felon? Must he also have the pain of knowing you will witness his disgrace?"

Peg's shoulders sagged, her hands went limp, and all the light went out of her eyes. Dan could have wept for the terrible bleak anguish that looked out at him.

Squeezing her eyes shut, Peg gave a soft keen of despair. "Oh, Dan . . . Dan . . . what am I to do? I will have no husband, no home . . . oh, didn't they even burn our *home*, Dan! What am I to do without Brian?"

Dan put an arm around her shoulders and, sensing her submission, began to lead her off, one step at a time. "You will lean on our Lord, Peg," he answered quietly. "And you will lean on me. We will take shelter with the Old Man and the Mother for now— they have already opened their door to us. We will work hard and honor Brian's memory. We will do all we can to give his sons a better world. A better life, in a free Ireland. It's what he would want, now, isn't that so?"

Peg stopped, turning to face him. Her eyes were almost calm now, deep, unstirred pools of sorrow and defeat. "That is a noble thought, Dan, and I know you do mean well. But today I give up my husband. Tomorrow it may be my sons. Somehow I count the price of Ireland's freedom too dear. Too dear, indeed."

The sound of drums rolled over the street, hovering between them. Sick at heart, Dan led his brother's wife away.

Behind them, the eager crowd waited to see the hanging of Brian Kavanagh.

PART ONE

DREAMS CHERISHED

——

Bright Promises

How sweet are your promises to my taste.

PSALM 119:103

1

The Five Points Celebration Singers

How happy the little birds
That rise up on high
And make music together
On a single bough!

ANONYMOUS (Nineteenth-century Irish)

Five Points, New York City
Early October 1848

Inside the Big Tent in Paradise Square, Evan Whittaker faced the ten youthful, expectant faces turned toward him with the numbing admission that he hadn't the vaguest idea what to do next.

Knowing he had brought this present dilemma upon himself only compounded his sense of failure. The entire situation was bizarre beyond imagining: a one-armed British immigrant playing choir director to a mix of black and Irish boys. And in the middle of the vilest slum in New York City!

Today marked the third official rehearsal of the Five Points Choral Society. Evan had chosen the name himself; not particularly inventive, he conceded, but at least it supplied an identity to the singers.

Not that the singers cared very much about their identity.

21

Evan wished he had not been so hasty in responding to Jess Dalton's plea for help. If only he had stayed home from last month's mission department meeting. If only he had stayed *silent* at last month's mission department meeting!

He winced at the memory of his own impulsive behavior. It was totally unlike him, completely out of character, to offer an unsolicited opinion or suggestion. And yet he had done just that.

Pastor Dalton had begun the meeting by voicing his concern about the church's efforts in Five Points: "It's not that we haven't made progress," he said. "The health clinic is an indisputable success. The worship services are growing by the week, as are the Bible studies. But I'm beginning to despair of bringing about any real difference in the lives of these people unless we can somehow get them to stop *fighting* one another! The Negroes hate the Irish—the Irish hate the Negroes—they both hate the Polish—" He broke off, running a hand through his full head of curly hair. "There must be something that would bring them together instead of tearing them apart!"

"Music," Evan had said quietly, without the slightest hesitation. "There's nothing quite like music to b-build a bridge."

The words had slipped so easily from his tongue. Why, he'd scarcely even stuttered! Jess Dalton had shown immediate interest, and, swept up in the pastor's enthusiasm, Evan impulsively agreed to give the matter some thought.

The next thing he knew, he had been put in charge of organizing—and directing—a choir! Their first rehearsal had been an abysmal failure, the second no less a disaster. In addition to Daniel John, Arthur Jackson, and Casey Dalton—all of whom showed up, no doubt, solely to lend their support—only a token number of Irish and black youths had returned for the second and third rehearsals.

And these few faithful, Evan admitted grimly, appeared anything but enthusiastic. Still, they were present and, for the most part, willing. He could not simply walk out on his responsibility.

With a sigh, he tapped his baton on the makeshift wooden music stand. Doing his best to ignore his feelings of inadequacy, he turned to the challenge at hand, that of rendering "Praise God From Whom All Blessings Flow" as a song of praise rather than a funeral dirge.

During a break halfway through rehearsal, the three friends in the back row held a hurried conference.

"Appears to me Mistah Evan needs some help," suggested Arthur Jackson, his voice low.

Daniel Kavanagh and Casey Dalton nodded agreement.

"Mother says Evan is discouraged," admitted Daniel. "At first he was excited about the choir, but now he's feeling inadequate. He's wondering if somebody else couldn't manage it better."

"There's nothing wrong with Mister Evan at all!" Casey Dalton stepped closer to the other two. " 'Tis the *music* that's wrong!"

Daniel regarded Evan with a troubled look, taking note of the slight slump of his shoulders. "Still, I think Mother's right. He's blaming himself."

"S'pose he wouldn't want no suggestions from boys like us," Arthur said, shoving his hands into his pockets.

Daniel looked at him. "What sort of suggestions?"

The black boy shrugged, looking from Daniel to Casey Dalton. "Seems like there ought to be some way we could tell him the truth."

"I'd not want to hurt his feelings," Daniel said quickly. "He's trying his best, after all."

"That's true." Arthur shrugged. "But his best ain't ever gonna work down here if he don't do *something* about the music!"

Casey Dalton nodded in agreement. "I'm afraid that's so. What do you think, Daniel? You know him best. Would he be wanting our opinions or not?"

Daniel thought for a moment, his eyes on Evan. "Aye," he said uncertainly, "I expect he would." Shouldering his harp, he added, "We might as well give it a go, I suppose."

———

Evan saw the three boys coming toward him and resigned himself to the fact that they were going to quit. He couldn't blame them. So far, today's rehearsal was proving still another failure. Most of the boys seemed to expend more energy yawning than singing. Obviously, they'd rather be anywhere else but here.

Lifting his chin, he forced a smile as he watched the three approach. Daniel, the tallest, was flanked by the other two boys. Arthur Jackson's enormous dark eyes looked everywhere but at Evan. The small, thin-faced Dalton lad wore his usual lopsided grin; as always, his hair was an unruly tumble of red curls.

"Well, b-boys," Evan said, thinking to delay their desertion if at all possible, "it's g-good to have you here today. You're all wo-working hard, I can tell."

Daniel looked acutely uncomfortable. "Evan? We were wondering . . . could we speak with you? Just for a moment?"

Evan nodded, making no reply. His heart sank even further.

"The thing is—" Daniel stopped, darting a quick glance at Arthur Jackson. The black boy merely raised his eyes and began studying the top of the tent with excessive interest.

"Yes, Daniel?" Evan prompted halfheartedly.

Again the lad hesitated. Evan pretended not to see the Dalton boy nudge Arthur, who still appeared intent on his examination of the canvas roof overhead.

Obviously, the black youth had been appointed spokesman, albeit a reluctant one. In spite of his disappointment, Evan could not stop a faint smile. "Was there so-something you wanted to ask, Arthur?"

Arthur lowered his gaze from the tent top to Evan. He pursed his lips, still hesitating. "I wouldn't want you to take me wrong, Mistah Evan," he finally said.

So they *were* quitting. Evan took a deep breath. "You m-may say whatever is on your m-mind, Arthur."

The boy dug his hands even deeper into his pockets, shifting from one foot to the other. "The thing is . . . we was thinking that if you was to use—maybe a different kind of music . . ."

His sentence died away, unfinished. Evan frowned, puzzled. "A different k-kind of music?"

The black boy's eyes brightened. "Uh-huh, that's right. A different kind." He paused, shooting a look at the other boys before going on. "The kind of music you been using is just fine, Mistah Evan—for old folks."

Evan winced. He saw Daniel frown and poke Arthur in the ribs.

The black boy gave Daniel a puzzled look, then turned back to Evan. "Oh, you're not old, Mistah Evan! I just meant to say that maybe the music is . . . well, kinda stuffy." He stopped. "Maybe."

Evan blinked. "St-stuffy?"

"Uh-huh. That's right. Stuffy."

Evan looked from the black boy to Daniel, who was now examining his shoes intently. The Dalton lad had his head down as well.

They weren't quitting, after all!

"I see." Evan cleared his throat, delaying his reply. "Well, then—what sort of m-music would *you* like to sing, Arthur?"

The boys looked at each other.

"See here, b-boys," Evan said gravely, "I would very much like to hear your opinions. It's p-perfectly obvious that things aren't g-going well. If you have suggestions, let's have them."

Daniel looked at him closely. "Truly, Evan?"

"Truly."

Too eager to be tactful, all three boys began speaking at once. Evan quickly caught their point: The music was dry. The music was dull. The music was boring.

"We need to sing more *movin'* music," Arthur Jackson put in.

"*M-moving* music?" Evan repeated.

The black boy once again took the initiative. "Uh-huh, *movin'* music. Music that makes you feel like you just can't stand still, like you just gotta *move*, maybe even shout a little! That's what kind of music we'd like to sing."

"Arthur knows a lot of grand music, Evan," Daniel put in, "the kind of music they sing in . . . in—"

"Miss'sippi," Arthur finished for him. "Where I come from."

"Sure, and there's a great deal of lively Irish music as well," Casey Dalton quickly pointed out. "Mother plays it on the flute, you know. Jigs and reels and the like."

"We could even sing some of the sea chanties the sailors and dock workers sing," suggested Daniel.

Evan raised an eyebrow.

"Without the curse words, of course."

"We could maybe use different instruments, too, Mistah Evan." The black youth's dark eyes danced with enthusiasm. "I can play the harmonica, and Daniel, he's learnin' how to fiddle. He could save the harp for the slow songs, if you still want to sing some of them, too."

Evan considered the three with guarded interest. "It sounds fine, b-boys. But I'm afraid I d-don't know very much about other kinds of music. I'm familiar only with the traditional music of the church."

The three boys exchanged disappointed glances.

"Still," Evan said firmly, straightening his shoulders and giving the lads a smile, "even old folks like me can always learn something new."

He paused. "With a bit of help, that is."

———

Michael Burke was on his way out of Five Points when he spotted the crowd at the church tent in Paradise Square. Fearing trouble, he turned back and crossed the square to have a look.

As he approached, the singing from inside the tent grew louder. Much louder.

He had heard this kind of singing before. Loud and spirited, with an irresistible rhythm, it was the music of the freed blacks in the city.

He parted the spectators at the entrance to the tent and went inside. The scene that greeted him made him stop and stare in amazement.

At the front of the tent, a number of youths, mostly black, were singing and swaying to the music. Their faces were creased in good-natured grins, and as they sang, they clapped their hands to the rhythm.

Leading them was Arthur Jackson, the young black boy the Daltons had taken into their home a few months ago. He seemed to be having himself the fine time, stamping one foot and pounding his hands together as he led the others in song.

Up until now, Michael would have thought he could no longer be surprised. Presumedly, after fifteen years on the New York City police force, he had just about seen it all.

But he had not seen the likes of this, and that was the truth! Black and Irish stood shoulder to shoulder, singing together, swaying together, grinning at each other—almost as if they had forgotten their bitter enmity. Even as he watched, two boys moved out of the crowd of spectators and went to the front to join the other singers.

But the most astounding sight of all—the sight that made Michael blink and gape in disbelief—was not Arthur Jackson or the unlikely choir. Somewhat off to the side, but still very much in the thick of things, stood the always correct, somewhat straight-laced Evan Whittaker, rapping his baton on the music

stand and tapping his foot to the beat. The man was beaming a
wide, boyish smile.

Michael knew for a fact that the Englishman's idea of great
fun was a night at the opera or the lecture hall. Yet here he was,
clearly enjoying himself as much as his singers!

"Ain't that somethin', Captain?"

Michael turned to look at the big black laborer who had moved
in next to him. Skipper Jones stood, his cap pulled low over one
eye, his thick-muscled arms crossed over his chest, nodding in
time to the music.

Michael looked from the black man to the singers. "Aye," he
said, shaking his head in slow wonder. "That is something indeed." Evan as he spoke, his own foot took up the irresistible
rhythm with a sharp tapping.

———

By the end of the day's rehearsal, the recently established Five
Points Choral Society had a number of prospective new members,
the beginning of an entirely new repertoire—and a brand-new
name.

With the consent of their somewhat dazed director, the singing
group would henceforth be known as the *Five Points Celebration
Singers*.

As he started across Paradise Square to his borrowed carriage,
the always correct and somewhat straight-laced Evan Whittaker
had all he could do not to click his heels in the air.

He could not *wait* to get home to tell Nora!

2

Shadows on the Heart

Pulse of my heart,
What gloom is thine?

From WALSH'S *IRISH POPULAR SONGS* (1847)

Nora Whittaker stood at the front window of her new home in Brooklyn, hugging her arms to herself as she waited for Evan.

They had been married close on five months now, but his daily homecoming was still an event. An hour before he was due, Nora would begin watching the window and listening for Evan's key in the door. They would embrace, share the news of the day, then collect the Fitzgerald children and take them for a walk in the park before dinner.

This evening, however, she was finding it difficult to summon any real excitement. Once again, her hopes had been dashed, leaving her spirit as barren and empty as she was beginning to fear her womb might be.

She had been so sure this time, almost convinced, she was finally with child. But, just as before, she had been wrong.

At least she hadn't told Evan. Had he known, he would, of course, conceal his own disappointment. Never did the man so much as hint that their life together was anything less than ideal. Their marriage was still new, he would say when he caught her fretting; they had plenty of time, after all. Besides, he would remind her, he neither wanted nor needed anything more than what he had.

But Nora *did*. From the beginning of their marriage, she had prayed for, longed for, a child. Her deepest wish was to give Evan a son. The only child of elderly parents, it was up to him to carry on the family name. A son would be her gift to him—the finest gift she could possibly give to this man who had given her so very much.

Lately, though, she was becoming increasingly anxious, even fearful, that she would never again experience the miracle of birth. They were not young, she and Evan. He was nearly thirty-seven, she thirty-four. Her child-bearing years would soon be over.

At times like these, when disappointment washed over her like a bitter wave, Nora had all she could do not to give in to the dread that she might be barren. It was her greatest fear, and one she could not bring herself to voice to anyone—not to Evan, not even to Sara Farmington, her dearest friend.

Before leaving Ireland at the height of the famine, she—like thousands of others—had lived for months at the very edge of starvation, warding off disease as her flesh wasted away, until she was only a shadow of herself. Then, the past winter, the scarlet fever had felled her, leaving her deathly ill for weeks. She could not help but wonder if that prolonged period of hunger and illness might not have caused some terrible, irreversible harm to her body.

The thought that she could not bear Evan's child was enough to tarnish her newly found happiness. Like a shadow on her heart, it threatened to stain the perfection of their union, dull the luster of her joy.

Tears stung her eyes, and she clenched her hands at her sides. She must stop this. She *must*! They had time—plenty of time. They had been married only a few months, after all. Their love was still new, and she was not yet an old drab. She need not, *would* not, give up her hope.

Pulling the drapery to one side, Nora managed to smile a little at the sight of wee Tom and Johanna playing in the leaves. She loved the view from the small house. By now the sun had fallen almost entirely out of sight, rouging the sky with peach and crimson. The spacious front yard was dense with trees, maples and oaks still lush with the honey gold and warm scarlet of October. A light evening wind had blown up, whipping the leaves about like swirling banners.

Autumn had ever been a bittersweet time for Nora, with its beauty teetering on the edge of a final farewell before the bleak hand of winter seized the land. She could never quite rejoice in the season's glory without a shadow of foreboding hovering near.

The specter of approaching winter.

Winter in famine-ravaged Ireland had meant only more suffering. For those evicted from their homes, the snow and cold promised certain death. Even for those with a roof above their heads, the lack of food and fuel meant unthinkable hardship.

Nora brought her hand to her throat, remembering the last winter in Ireland. Many had been the night her heart had keened with the wailing wind off the Atlantic. Throughout those months of sorrow and deprivation, her spirit had seemed to turn as cold as the dark, sullen waters of Killala Bay.

A shudder rippled through her, and she shook her head slightly as if to throw off her melancholy. Just then she caught sight of Evan turning the corner and starting for the house. For the first time since morning, she felt the weight of disappointment and dread lift from her heart.

Evan saw her at the window and waved. Nora watched him closely as he neared the cottage. This was his afternoon in Five Points with the new singing group, and she was learning to associate certain telltale signs of discouragement with Thursday afternoons.

But not today. Her own mood brightened still more when she saw that he wore a smile. Indeed, he was taking the walk with the eager, carefree steps of a boy!

Curious as to what might account for his obvious high spirits, Nora hurried to the door and flung it open. Eagerly, she slipped into her husband's embrace, feeling the last shadow of her earlier gloom disappear.

———

After dinner and the children's prayers, Evan and Nora sat on the sofa, reading. As was their habit each evening—and at Nora's insistence—Evan read aloud.

For several days now, they had been enjoying *Oliver Twist*—a novel by the English author, Charles Dickens. An indictment of the London society that so callously and routinely abused the poor, the book created a world of such realistic, distinctive char-

acters that both Evan and Nora found it difficult to put down
when day was done.

Although he was a highly successful author, Dickens was yet
regarded with suspicion and even disdain in some quarters. Fa-
mous while still in his early twenties, the prolific writer apparently possessed unlimited mental and physical energy. Yet the
sheer volume of his writings and their unanticipated success
seemed to contribute to the criticism leveled against him: that he
was entirely too commercial, too sentimental and unsophisti-
cated. He was nothing more than an entertainer, critics charged.

Even in America, where Dickens had toured early in the decade, the popular author was accused of lacking artistic taste and
relying much too heavily on cheap dramatic effects.

With a mixture of annoyance and amusement, Evan wondered
if the criticism would have been nearly as heated had Dickens not
so successfully and brilliantly exposed the corruption of an entire
political and social system. He personally found the man's work
nothing short of genius. Both the *Papers of the Pickwick Club*,
which he had read while still in England, and this new work,
Oliver Twist, were surely the products of an inventive mind, a
deeply sensitive and acute observer of the human condition. He
suspected the widely read, popular—and *entertaining*—author's
works would long outlast many of the more "literary" and "artistic" efforts of others.

Evan was somewhat surprised to realize that Nora had fallen
asleep, her head resting on his shoulders. Usually she protested
when he put the book away for the evening. A prickle of concern
intruded on his thoughts, and he turned slightly to study her face.

Still troubled, he noted the shadows under her eyes, the slight
frown even in repose. Being careful not to waken her, he settled
her more closely against his side and sat watching the fire.

Outside, the wind moaned. Despite the room's snug warmth,
Evan shivered. Staring into the fire, he let his thoughts roam. As
always, they went to his wife.

Nora thought him unaware of her sadness, her apprehension.
But he had known as soon as he saw her framed in the doorway
earlier in the evening that she had been weeping. Later, while
playing with Johanna and Tom outside, he had caught her staring
into the distance, an unmistakable glaze of sorrow in her eyes.

As always, she had evaded his questions, making an obvious

effort to be more cheerful. But by now Evan recognized the slight darkening of those magnificent gray eyes, the faint tightening of the skin around her mouth.

She was determined to give him a child. A son. And it seemed no amount of reassurance on his part would ease her anxiety.

Evan knew beyond all doubt that her desire for a child was more for him than for her. She seemed not to hear him when he insisted that he could not possibly want anything more than what he already had. He loved her, and he adored Daniel and the Fitzgerald children as if they were his own. He needed nothing more than his dear Nora and their ready-made family.

The truth was—and this he would *not* tell her—that the very idea of Nora's bearing a child frightened him. He deliberately kept his fear to himself, thinking it best that she not know of his uneasiness should the time come when she *did* conceive.

He would love the child, of course. He would be proud and happy and grateful, would feel all the things he imagined any normal man must feel upon becoming a father. But there was no denying the fact that his fear for Nora's safety far outweighed any desire on his part for a child.

Childbirth was a mystery that frankly terrified him. His father, a rural clergyman, had buried many a woman who had died either during her confinement or during the delivery itself. While Nora seemed to have regained most of her health, Evan still sensed she was not overly strong. How could she be, after months of starvation and a bout with scarlet fever that had almost claimed her life?

What if she *should* conceive? What would it do to her to carry a child, to give birth?

What if he were to lose her?

The wind rattled the window. Instinctively, he pulled Nora more closely against him. Squeezing his eyes shut, he cherished the soft warmth of her body next to his, the gentle fragrance of her hair against his cheek.

As was so often the case, her closeness made his heart swell with thanksgiving. He had waited all these years to love a woman and to be loved. Yet none of his dreams had ever come close to the reality of the bliss he had found with Nora. There was nothing in the world worth the risk of losing her. Nothing. Not even a child of his own.

Perhaps he was being selfish and small-minded. If a child meant all that much to her, shouldn't he at least try to share her longing, encourage her dream?

She sighed in her sleep, and he touched his lips to her hair. His entire world was right here, beside him. He wasn't sure he could pretend to want more. Yet, for Nora's sake, he knew that he would try.

3

A Radical Nun at Nelson Hall

What is there in man, frail clay and dust,
That will rise and die for a cause,
Yet cower and cringe like a motherless cur
When a Good Woman unmasks his flaws?

MORGAN FITZGERALD (1848)

Dublin, Ireland

It was just past dawn, but Morgan Fitzgerald had been at his desk in the library for nearly an hour.

The shooting incident of a year past that had left his legs paralyzed had also served to make him a light sleeper. Most days he rose before daybreak and, with Sandemon's help, was dressed and at his writing or other tasks by the time the sun rose.

It seemed an ordinary morning. A pot of Sandemon's robust, scalding coffee waited on the sideboard near the desk, and the most recent installment from Joseph Mahon's journal was spread out in front of him.

He took a deep sip of coffee, raising one eyebrow at the strength of the stuff. He drank tea less frequently since Sandemon's arrival at Nelson Hall. But, then, he reflected dryly, the West Indies Wonder had been successful in modifying a number of his former habits—not the least of which was his affinity for the whiskey.

With his pen still in hand, he turned back to the journal. For

34

some months now, he had been editing the Mayo priest's account of the famine. As yet he had not divulged his intentions to Joseph, but Morgan was convinced this painstakingly detailed, agonizing record of one parish's suffering must be published. Moreover, he was determined to see it printed across the sea as well as in Ireland.

The papers before him contained the reality of Ireland's tragedy, captured in this account of one small community in the remote west. Here, then, was the stark, bitter truth, a truth to counter England's denial and professed innocence in the evil that had been wreaked upon an entire nation.

Because of his rapidly failing health and utter exhaustion, the priest's entries were often little more than a hasty scrawl—a few terse words scratched out in the throw of fatigue or desperation. Yet the depths of the man's soul pulsed through his words.

In the pages of the journal, Morgan had discovered a side to the gentle priest he had not known. Joseph had made no attempt to hide his own anguish, his horror, his grief—even the occasional faltering of his faith. At times Morgan could almost hear his old friend's spirit straining, his heart breaking, one fragile piece at a time.

Removing his new reading glasses—a rueful concession to the encroachment of middle age—Morgan rubbed the bridge of his nose, then drained the last of the coffee from the cup. As he stacked the entries he'd just completed, it occurred to him there had been no new pages from Joseph for a number of weeks now. Knowing the burden of work under which the priest labored, the impossible hours he kept, Morgan supposed he shouldn't be unduly alarmed. Yet a nagging shadow crossed his mind as he sat staring at the stack of pages in front of him.

After another moment, he opened the right-hand drawer of his desk, pulled out a fresh sheet of paper, and reached for his pen. He would get a note off to Joseph yet this morning, before early classes or interviews.

He managed to pen only a few words before Sandemon entered the room. "She has arrived, *Seanchai*."

Morgan looked up. His black West Indies companion stood at ease, powerful arms at his sides, the sleeves of his favorite purple shirt flowing free. As always, the broad brow was smooth, the eyes dark pools of untroubled waters. In contrast, the gold-toothed smile hinted of some vague, anticipated pleasure.

"By *she*, I expect you mean the NUN," Morgan said grimly, replacing his pen on its brass stand.

Sandemon gave a nod, and the smile widened. "Sister Louisa, yes. She is waiting in the entryway."

Morgan gave a deep sigh. "We might just as well have done with it, then." Convinced now that the black man was indeed prepared to enjoy himself, Morgan glared at him. "I still think it's a mistake, hiring a NUN."

Sandemon inclined his head. "But you agreed to the wisdom of employing a woman, that her influence could be invaluable, both for the child and for the Academy."

"Aye, and I still agree that a woman on the premises might be a fine thing for Annie and for the school. That in no way means I think it wise to hire a NUN."

Sandemon shook his head. "It seems an ideal solution to me. Sister Louisa comes with classroom experience and the calling to a holy life. Surely both will serve as a positive influence for the child."

Morgan straightened slightly in the wheelchair. "*Sister Louisa*," he contradicted sullenly, "also comes highly suspect. I can't quite help wondering why the order would be so eager to send her off to a stranger's house outside the city."

Sandemon pretended not to notice Morgan's testiness. "The sister requested permission to interview, as you know." He paused. "She indicated God's guidance in the matter, I believe."

Morgan's only reply was another sour frown. He had nothing against nuns in general. He admired their self-sacrifice, appreciated their life of service, and acknowledged their usefulness to the church. Sandemon need not know the truth: that he tended to stand somewhat in awe of the sisters, indeed could be all too easily cowed by the smallest slip of a woman in a black habit. Nuns were saintly beings, lived holy lives—in general, bore no likeness to most of the women in his past.

In any event, it would not do for Sandemon to suspect that his employer could be terrorized by a nun. He would, no doubt, take great delight in such a discovery.

At the other's not-too-discreet throat-clearing, Morgan straightened. "Show her in," he said, replacing his spectacles. "Let us see why the sisters were so willing to part company with her."

While Sandemon went to fetch the applicant, Morgan wheeled the chair to the window. It was a soft morning, veiled with rain and light fog rising from the stream that ran along the west side of the grounds. Leaning forward a little, he stared out the window, mulling over his resolve to hire a woman for Nelson Hall.

Obviously, she would have to be a woman of impeccable reputation and unquestionable morals. No doubt a nun, as Sandemon suggested, might prove an ideal solution. And not simply for Annie, but for their new young friend, Finola, as well.

The thought of the golden-haired beauty brought a smile, then a frown. He was resolved to see Finola out of the brothel where she was living. He would bring her here, to Nelson Hall, where she would be safe, where he could see to her well-being. Perhaps, should she so desire, he could even arrange for her to study within the Academy. She had indicated more than once a desire to advance her education.

Certainly, the girl's muteness was no mark of a dull intellect. To the contrary, her mind seemed a place of shooting stars and bubbling springs, where light was ever stirring and ideas flying.

In the months since he and his household had befriended the mysterious young woman, Morgan had become more than a little fond of her. She was a frequent guest at Nelson Hall, and with each visit he desired to know her better. She was a continual delight to them all, a gift. Indeed, Finola's presence in the sprawling, gloomy halls of the estate was like a spray of sunshine, captured and poured out indoors.

Morgan was intent on finding the key that would eventually unlock the secret of Finola's silence. He had become increasingly convinced that she had once possessed a voice. His experience with his niece, Johanna, who was both deaf and mute, had given him some understanding of the affliction. He was absolutely certain that Finola held the memory of spoken words, as well as the instincts of one who had not always been mute. The ease with which she formed words on her lips as she signed on her hands, the way the muscles in her throat worked as if instinctively— Morgan knew with near certainty that Finola had once spoken.

He knew little else about her. Beyond her name and where she lived, she had revealed virtually nothing about herself, not even her age. That she was Irish went without saying. She knew the old language, readily understood Morgan when he spoke it. She seemed a devout Catholic, comfortable in her relationship with her God. But on those rare occasions when he inquired about her past, she simply gave a helpless shrug, turning on him a look of such bewildered dejection that he felt almost shamed for having troubled her with his questions.

Yet an urgency drove him to see her removed from Healy's Inn. He feared for her safety, living as she did in a known house of prostitution, in the heart of one of Dublin's most disgraceful slums.

The women who had taken her in years ago apparently treated her well, much as a pampered little sister. They dressed her in their own gowns, gave her light household chores to do around the establishment and, in their own careless way, looked after her needs.

But they also taught her to paint her face like theirs and frequently sent her off in the carriage dressed in one of their nearly indecent gowns. The sight of the girl's innocent loveliness marred by the garish cosmetics and gaudy apparel invariably set Morgan's blood to boiling like a fury. It was bad enough, he would rail at Sandemon, that her youthful beauty should be tarnished so cheaply. But couldn't the fools see the jeopardy in which they were placing the girl? A lovely woman, painted and packaged as if she were one of them, living in their midst—it was dangerous beyond imagining!

They professed, of course, to closet Finola from the "clients" who came and went. But there was no way they could protect her entirely, Morgan knew. She was at a continual risk, never completely out of harm's way.

The decision to employ a woman as a classroom instructor and a part-time companion for Annie had been, in truth, only one part of a larger plan. Eventually, Morgan wanted to move Finola here, to Nelson Hall. Certainly, a nun would provide such an arrangement the required respectability. Indeed, the more Morgan considered the idea, the more feasible it seemed.

At the sound of a commotion in the hallway, he wheeled around to look.

Just inside the doorway, dwarfed by Sandemon's presence, stood a diminutive woman in a nun's habit. Her carriage was rigid, her chin thrust forward as she came the rest of the way into the room.

Surprised, Morgan saw that the nun had firmly in hand two red-faced, spluttering boys, one on either side. The O'Higgins twins, Barnaby and Barry. Identical in appearance—roaring red hair, like caps of fire, and blue eyes—the two were equally matched in mischief. The school's first two scholars, these. And after only a few weeks of probationary enrollment, they had become the bane of Morgan's existence. When he had envisioned his Academy, they were *not* what he'd had in mind.

Only days after their arrival, the *gorsoons* had managed to fill his inkwell with tea and coat the chalkboards with soap. In short time, Morgan had realized that the father of the two, an acquaintance and fellow Young Irelander, apparently viewed the new Academy as a detention hall, where the boys might do penance for their sins while being disciplined.

Morgan had already written to Jerome O'Higgins in Cavan, by way of informing him he was not running an establishment for potential young felons, and that he could collect the two wee heathen forthwith. As yet he had received no reply, which didn't surprise him in the least: were such savages his own, he too would delay in having them home.

"*Seanchai*, I am pleased to present Sister Louisa," said Sandemon, breaking into the twins' grumbling with a look of dry amusement.

Sandwiched between the O'Higgins twins, the sister was small, even petite, with the ageless smooth skin that seemed endemic to nuns alone. Morgan knew from her records, however, that she was close on fifty.

At first glance she almost appeared to be held captive by the little pagans. Closer observation revealed, however, that it was the rowdy O'Higgins lads who had been apprehended, not the sister. Indeed, the nun had a firm grasp on the tender upper arms of both her charges; and though their flushed faces were wild with anger, they clearly knew they were trapped.

Taken aback by this remarkable scene, Morgan eyed the nun with a combination of awe and trepidation. Her eyes were too large for her face and too dark to reflect the soul behind them. A small, perfectly aligned nose turned up with a certain arrogance, while the woman's chin remained as fixed as a stone.

Morgan met her gaze, squirming under its intensity. For an instant, he felt as trapped as the unfortunate O'Higgins lads. He attempted a smile, felt it crumble under her fierce stare.

After a moment, Sandemon stepped in to redeem the situation. "Allow me to take these two off your hands, Sister. And, please, do forgive such a rude reception."

"You'll take them nowhere at all until they apologize for their behavior." Her voice was low, the tone unexpectedly smooth and composed, but her grip on the two troublemakers remained firm.

Morgan spoke for the first time. "Indeed," he rumbled, fixing his fiercest glare on the two miscreants. "Apologize to the sister. At once!"

Barnaby, whom Morgan distinguished by the wider mask of freckles that banded his nose, pursed his mouth to a pout, saying nothing. His twin, Barry, met Morgan's glare with a fierce scowl of his own.

Sandemon moved to transfer the two to his keeping. The nun bristled. "I *said*, they will apologize before leaving the room." Again, that peculiar voice—a velvet sheath, ribbed with steel beams.

"You heard the sister, you little monkeys!" Morgan snarled. He would not have his authority undermined by this wisp of a nun. "Say your piece, and say it at once!"

The apologies were muttered, the words indistinct.

"I'm afraid I cannot hear you," admonished the nun.

After identical scowls, the twins raised their voices and recited their regrets with more clarity, if not with any real enthusiasm.

"It's not for me to decide," said the nun, looking from Morgan to Sandemon, "but were they my responsibility, I would suggest mucking the stables on a daily basis. It seems a waste not to apply such energy to constructive use. Of course," she added thoughtfully, "they're quite old enough to help out in the kitchen as well."

"The KITCHEN?" shrilled the twins with identical outrage.

The nun's dark eyes seemed never to blink. "Indeed," she said in an entirely level voice. "The kitchen. Perhaps next time you will stop and think before throwing a dead wren into the path of a nun."

"A DEAD WREN!" Morgan exploded, half rising from his wheelchair by the force of his arms.

The nun lifted one dark brow as if to rebuke him for shouting. "I'm sure they'll not be so wicked again, Master Fitzgerald." After a moment she added, her tone still quiet and altogether controlled, "You'll be wanting my references, I expect. May I sit down, please?"

Sinking back in the wheelchair, Morgan stared at her, then managed a stiff nod.

He waited for Sandemon to haul the O'Higgins terrors, now noticeably subdued, from the library before commencing the interview. During the lull, he had the oddest sensation that he'd somehow skipped a moment in time—that Sister Louisa had been hired, had taken charge, and the rest of them were now in her employ.

———

The interview was nearing its end, and Morgan knew little more about the nun than he had at the beginning, at least in the way of any personal information.

Her references, on the surface, appeared exemplary. She had instructed in the classroom for nearly two decades, had even developed a specialized course of study for those children whose learning capacities were impaired. Her education was extraordinary, her achievements many and varied. She also, according to her records, excelled in the arts; in particular, she was an accomplished portrait and landscape artist.

Moreover, her deeds among Dublin's impoverished seemed too great to number. Obviously, she was an indefatigable worker, a selfless Christian servant.

Yet Morgan could not shake the suspicion that the order was altogether too willing to ship her off.

He leaned back in the chair, pushing himself slightly away from the desk. "I can scarcely think why you'd be agreeable to a position here. Your credentials are impressive. You are accustomed to fine educational facilities and established methods. This Academy is experimental, as you no doubt know."

By now he had come to anticipate not even a hint as to what the nun might be thinking. Those unblinking dark eyes seemed closed doors on her soul.

In reply, Sister Louisa merely lifted her eyebrows.

Trying another approach, Morgan said, "Even more surprising is the idea that the order would consider letting you go. I should think your experience would be invaluable, both in the classroom and in your work with Dublin's poor."

41

The nun leveled a look on Morgan that clearly said she recognized his dissembling.

"You may be direct with me, sir. If you are wondering what undisclosed stain on my record has brought me to this place, you have only to ask."

Morgan flinched at the nun's perception, but made no protest. Instead, he occupied himself by straightening the pages of her file on the desk in front of him.

"You are no doubt wondering if I am under discipline, and, in a manner of speaking, I am. You have every right to know that I am considered entirely too radical in matters of religious education. I have been severely reprimanded for my teaching methods in that regard."

Morgan shot her a startled look. *A radical nun?* Unthinkable!

As if reading his thoughts, Sister Louisa nodded.

"I am accused of departing from certain teachings of the church as pertain to the reading of Holy Scripture and the Mass."

Morgan managed, with difficulty, not to gape.

In the same controlled, direct voice, the nun went on. "According to Mother Superior, I have failed in my duty to give proper instruction concerning the Mass. I stress a personal relationship with Christ, you see, and I feel that certain parts of the Mass provide a perfect means for illuminating the various stages of this relationship." She paused, but only for a moment. "There is some thought that my approach tended to undermine the importance of the confessional."

Morgan's jaw dropped. "You took issue with a *sacrament*?"

The nun narrowed those dark, unreadable eyes. "According to the interpretation of some."

Morgan leaned forward, altogether fascinated. "And your own interpretation?"

A glint of something—was it amusement?—suddenly flickered across her features.

"I suggested to the young women—they were not children, by the way—that as we mature in the faith, we come to recognize our Lord's desire for us to have close fellowship with Him, to come directly to Him with our needs." The stubborn chin lifted a fraction. "Not only for confession, but for communion and worship as well. You might just as well know that I advocate a personal study of the Holy Scriptures. Some of my superiors believe me to be in rebellion."

She sat unmoving, perched forward on the straight-backed chair, her small hands folded neatly in her lap. For one deranged moment, Morgan was struck with a vision of the decorous, self-contained sister waving a banner of rebellion above her head and marching off to battle amid the rattle of drums and the thunder of smoking cannon.

Immediately he gave himself a mental shake in rebuke for such sacrilege.

"I have often observed," he said carefully, "that it is the rebels among us who ultimately make the difference, who get things done."

The nun's face brightened, and she seemed about to speak, but Morgan went on. "One might even refer to our Lord as a Rebel— of a kind. Unfortunately," he went on with a grim smile, "rebels are more often than not crucified or persecuted or imprisoned. I have a friend who even now reaps the consequences of his rebellious ways."

"Smith O'Brien," said the nun.

Morgan looked at her. "Aye. You know of him?"

The sister nodded. "And who in Ireland does not? The fallen hero of the Widow McCormack's cabbage patch."

Bitterness welled up in Morgan's throat. Smith O'Brien now languished in gaol, judged guilty of high treason and sentenced to be hanged, drawn, and quartered. Morgan and a number of the patriot's followers were even now exhausting all measures to have his life spared.

In the meantime, the English press had orchestrated a deliberate, ruthless campaign to make a mockery of O'Brien and the failed rising of 1848 by attempting to reduce the man and the final battle to a farce. Unable to raise a lasting army from Ireland's starving, defeated people, O'Brien had nevertheless played the revolt to its weak, whimpering end. In a last pathetic skirmish in late July, O'Brien and a half-armed mob of disorganized peasants had attacked a body of panicked police who broke ranks, barricading themselves in a widow's house on Boulah Common, near Ballingarry.

After a scuffle in the garden, the entire clash had ended in the humiliation of O'Brien and his insurgent "army." Within days the leader was arrested and jailed. The insurrection proved a total, debasing defeat, and the English newspapers had been having the time of it ever since, demeaning O'Brien as some sort of half-cracked clown and his "soldiers" as deranged peasants with pikes.

Turning his attention back to Sister Louisa, Morgan could not resist defending his old friend. "Perhaps he *was* mistaken in listening to his advisors, but it is a cruel end to an otherwise splendid career devoted entirely to Ireland."

To his surprise, the sister quickly agreed. "O'Brien is a good and noble man, but a man misled by his own sincere convictions and impetuous advisors. Pray God his life will be spared."

Morgan silently amended his earlier assessment of Sister Louisa: she was not only a radical, rebellious nun, but a *political* nun as well. No man but a fool would knowingly employ such a powder keg.

————

Later that morning, Sandemon was called to the library, where he found the young master behind his massive desk. With a number of lulls in the conversation, during which the *Seanchai* uttered a grim chuckle of something akin to admiration, he told Sandemon of the incredible interview with Sister Louisa.

When he had finished, Sandemon shook his head with a sigh. "Too bad, I think. We could have used someone of her presence and credentials with the young scholars."

The *Seanchai* raised his great head and smiled. "That was my feeling. She will serve us well, I expect."

Sandemon stared at him. "You hired her, then, *Seanchai*? In spite of her—questionable beliefs and rebellious tendencies?"

The smile widened as the young master leaned back in his wheelchair. "Certainly not," he said matter-of-factly. "I hired her *because* of them."

4

Fergus

Beast of the field, newly tamed, nobly named,
Freed from the wild by the love of a child.

ANONYMOUS

On Saturday morning, two weeks after Sister Louisa's arrival, Annie Delaney made her way to the stables of Nelson Hall, carrying an apple in one hand and a lump of sugar in the other.

Usually Annie looked forward to her daily visit with the *Seanchai*'s great stallion, Pilgrim. After all, Pilgrim was her personal responsibility. Nobody except Annie or Sandemon was supposed to groom him or walk him without special permission.

Taking care of the fine horse was one of the few duties—if not the only one—at which Annie had managed to prove herself adequate. At most other tasks, she came up alarmingly awkward and amazingly incompetent. But she and Pilgrim had hit it off right from the beginning, affording her a measure of respect on the part of the other groomsmen, who found the stallion cantankerous and even a bit frightening.

Today, however, Annie's delight in visiting Pilgrim was somewhat diminished by her concern over a pressing problem—what to do about that TROUBLESOME NUN the *Seanchai* had hired as a teacher for the Academy.

After two weeks of Sister Louisa's relentless discipline and endless rules, Annie was growing desperate to find some way—*any* way—to rid Nelson Hall of her unwelcome presence.

45

At first she had thought the terrible O'Higgins twins might just do the trick. Surely Beastly and Barbaric, as she secretly called them, could make short work of a small, frail-looking holy woman. But to Annie's dismay, Sister already had the twins behaving themselves—if not exactly like gentlemen, at least more or less like human beings.

There had to be another way. A prayer formed in Annie's mind—a reckless request to the Almighty to take action on her behalf. But as quickly as she thought it, she took it back again. It was highly doubtful that the good Lord would go helping the likes of her to purge the *Seanchai*'s Academy of one of His own saints.

"Well, then," she muttered to herself as she laid her hand on the latch of the stable door, "I'll just have to be finding my own way, I suppose."

The instant she stepped into the stable, Annie sensed something amiss. The horses were stirring restlessly, some snorting and pawing the ground. In his stall, Pilgrim was shaking his mane and digging with his front hooves as if in a temper.

Suddenly, from around the end of the stable, a great gray thundercloud came charging toward her. The next thing Annie knew she was smack on her backside, looking up into the scruffy face of the largest wolfhound she had ever seen! He gulped down Pilgrim's apple in a shake, then eyed the sugar lump that Annie still held in her hand.

Her momentary panic gave way to indignation. Scrambling up from the stable floor, Annie dusted off her backside, then turned to scold the canine thief. "You horrible beast! That was *Pilgrim's* apple, it was! And just what might you be doing in our stables, I'd like to know? We don't allow strays at Nelson Hall!"

The wolfhound swallowed the last of the apple—core and all— and wagged his huge tail, banging it loudly against the side of the stall. Clearly, he was not in the least intimidated by her fierce scolding!

Then, as if invited, he reared up on his hind legs, firmly planting both immense paws on Annie's shoulders. Her mouth dropped open, but when she would have shrieked at the animal's impertinence, he grinned broadly and began washing her face with his enormous tongue.

"*Ughh!* Get off me, you filthy beast!" Annie shoved the dog down, fixing him with a withering glare as she wiped her face with one sleeve.

The creature simply went on grinning, his idiot face rapt with delight.

Annie stared him down, taking a moment to study his condition. His wiry coat was rough and tangled, matted with burrs, and altogether filthy. She thought his color was brindled, but with all the dirt it was difficult to tell. His leering face was scratched, with a dried cut over one eye. His nose appeared to have been scraped by a quarrelsome tomcat.

In spite of his slovenly manners, however, she felt a sharp pang of sympathy for the beast. Where would anything so ugly or rude ever find a home? No doubt he was lost, thrown out on his keeping—just as *she* had been!

Obviously, he was hungry—he'd made short work of that apple, hadn't he? And, just as obviously, he was eager for company and a bit of affection.

As Annie stood there appraising the wolfhound, a thought struck her. Could this wretched beast just possibly be the answer to the TROUBLESOME NUN? Could he be the Lord's response to her unspoken prayer?

The wolfhound grinned, and Annie grinned back as she thought about a possible encounter between the beast and Sister Louisa. Sure, and wouldn't the ungainly brute quickly take the starch out of the nun's habit?

Of course, the *Seanchai* would at first resist the very thought of harboring such a huge, untidy creature. Yet, Annie knew his great heart to be tender for strays. He had taken her in, after all! Remembering her own state the day she'd arrived at Nelson Hall—her soiled clothing and raggedy hair and smelly shoes—she decided that there was indeed hope for the wolfhound.

Besides, she thought she knew how to assure the beast a home at Nelson Hall. It was all in how he was presented, that was the thing.

Growing more confident by the moment, she decided to give the wolfhound a name right away. A worthy name by which to introduce him to the *Seanchai*.

Searching her mind, she dismissed a number of possibilities as too grand or not quite grand enough. Finally, it came to her. She would call him by the noble name of *Fergus*! Fergus, son of Roy, hero of Ulster!

"Aye, that is it, then! You shall be called Fergus! The *Seanchai*

47

will respect you for your name until he learns to appreciate you for yourself!"

————

Fergus's introduction to the *Seanchai* did not go quite as Annie had planned. With the intention of making the dog more presentable for his first meeting with the *Seanchai*, she set about giving him a quick bath and a much-needed grooming. She soon discovered that the wolfhound was not of a mind to cooperate.

After heating the water so the beast would not freeze, she set to work in earnest on his disreputable appearance. A clash of wills developed over the washtub, and an hour later, Annie was near despair, having demanded and cajoled, threatened and shoved— all to no avail.

When she finally managed to coerce the dog into the tub, he refused to stand and let her scrub him. Instead, he turned playful, the result being that Annie was quickly drenched, wetter by far than the wolfhound.

"You are an ugly, cantankerous BEAST!" she bellowed at the dog, shivering from the water that by now had soaked through her own coat. "An EEJIT and a DISGRACE! Sure, no one will be of a mind to take you in and give you a home unless you have a proper bath! Now, then—if you don't obey me this instant, I shall cast you out of the stables and you can starve in the streets, for all I care!"

Still grappling with the animal, Annie let fly with a string of choice, forbidden curse words, relics from her former life in the Belfast slums. The dog perked up his ears and gave her his undivided attention, as if to indicate that here was a language he understood.

Just as Annie had hopes of getting him under control, she heard a voice from the doorway: "WHAT WICKED, WICKED CHILD IS IN THIS STABLE?"

With one foot in the washtub and the other braced upon the wolfhound's back, Annie shot a startled look toward the stable door. There, hands splayed on his hips, stood an angry Sandemon, nostrils flaring, wide mouth thinned to a displeased line.

All Annie's confidence fled, and she cringed at the thought of the words she had just uttered. She was a Christian now, after all, and she had promised her Lord Jesus—and her friend Sandemon—to be done with the language of the streets.

Worst of all, at Sandemon's side, in the wheelchair, sat the *Seanchai*. A narrow-eyed, tight-jawed, white-knuckled *Seanchai*!

Clearly, they were both outraged and furious with her. Annie wondered, fleetingly, which sin would draw the worst of their wrath: the ugly, forbidden dog—or the ugly, forbidden curse words.

Either way, she acknowledged with a sigh, it would seem she was in trouble. Again.

————

As Annie stood groping for a word of defense, Fergus preened, grinning at the sight of new faces. With a mighty leap, he cleared the tub and took off at a gallop.

He stopped only when he reached Sandemon and the *Seanchai*, giving a vigorous shake to dislodge the soapy water from his coat.

The *Seanchai*'s face turned as fiery as his hair, and Sandemon's nostrils flared like wings.

Suppressing a moan, Annie turned a bright, hopeful smile on them both.

"He is for you, *Seanchai*!" Annie exclaimed. "A gift!"

The *Seanchai* peered over the wolfhound's lathered shoulder as Fergus stood on his hind legs and embraced him.

Annie had all she could do not to wilt under the fire blazing out from those green eyes. Fergus's great head only partially muffled the unintelligible roar.

Annie pulled herself up with feigned confidence. "*Fergus!* Bad dog! Down!"

To her great amazement, the wolfhound dropped his huge paws from the *Seanchai*'s shoulders. Cocking his head to the right, he regarded the man in the wheelchair with solemn interest, then turned his dark eyes on Sandemon.

Annie blinked, her hopes rising a notch. "Good, Fergus," she managed. Daring a smile, she said, "Isn't he grand? He's very well trained, as you can see!"

Sandemon shot her a formidable glare, then took a step toward the dog. Instinctively, Annie moved toward Fergus at the same time. As if sensing an invitation, the wolfhound began to circle them both with frenzied swoops. Cutting in and out between their feet, he forced Sandemon to perform a light-footed dance to avoid losing his balance. When he righted himself, the normally unflappable black man loomed over Annie with a terrible scowl.

She again managed to calm the dog with a sharp command, but Sandemon seemed altogether unimpressed. Jabbing a warning finger at Annie, he demanded, "Where did this—*animal*— come from?"

"And what," broke in the *Seanchai*, taking up where Sandemon left off, "did you mean about his being a 'gift'?"

Taking heed of Sandemon's stone visage and the *Seanchai's* strangled tone of voice, Annie knew she had only seconds to redeem the situation—and save the wolfhound.

Lowering her head and folding her hands in front of her, she said in a very small voice, "He was meant as a gift to you, *Seanchai*. I thought you would be pleased."

"And what is the occasion for this . . . *gift*, might I ask?" he rasped in a scathing whisper. "Is it Christmas? My birthday? Have I missed an event of some importance?"

Relieved, Annie heard the faint shift in his tone from anger to acid. With deliberate hesitation, she raised her gaze to his, then lifted a hand to brush away an offending strand of hair. "Sure, and there is no special event, *Seanchai*. Didn't I think a fine animal such as this would be a help and a comfort to you? Why, he can fetch and guard the stables and hunt a bit." She paused to catch a breath, then hurriedly added, "And he's quite fierce enough to frighten off any intruders!"

"We do not *have* intruders," snapped the *Seanchai*.

"So far as we *know*," Annie pointed out.

Sandemon rolled his eyes toward the heavens, and Fergus whined.

"Where did he *come* from?" asked the *Seanchai*.

Annie shook her head. "Sure, and didn't he simply . . . *appear*, from out of the forest? 'Twas almost as if he came looking for us, as if he knew our need for a strong, noble watchdog such as himself."

Scrupulously averting her gaze, Annie pretended not to hear Sandemon's low sound of disgust.

"I'm truly sorry, *Seanchai*," she went on in a thin little voice. "I thought you would be pleased. Why, haven't I worked most of the morning, grooming him so you would be able to see his fine appearance? Having read about the bond between gentlemen and their hounds, I had thought to make you a gift you'd treasure entirely!"

Finally, she dared a glance in his direction. Her hopes soared as she saw him regarding Fergus with a critical but not unkind eye. "He's large for a wolfhound," he said doubtfully.

"No doubt he's of fine, sturdy stock," offered Annie.

"And no doubt he will eat as much as a pony," Sandemon said mildly.

"Perhaps," Annie admitted, dropping to her knees and wrapping her arms about the wolfhound's great neck. "But he will more than earn his keep, hunting game and standing guard."

After a calculated pause, Annie got to her feet. She beamed a radiant smile at both men in preparation for her final thrust. "I should think," she pointed out piously, "that with a child and a helpless nun to consider, you would want some means of protection on the premises."

Still smiling, Annie waited. The *Seanchai* turned slightly in the wheelchair to look up at Sandemon. The black man again lifted his eyes heavenward.

Holding her breath, Annie watched as Fergus padded with dignity to the wheelchair. He hesitated only an instant before laying his scruffy head in the *Seanchai*'s lap, nuzzling as close to him as he could possibly manage.

Annie silently applauded the wolfhound's instincts.

After a moment, one large hand began to scratch the dog's soggy ears.

Looking on with a beatific smile, Annie gleefully envisioned the first meeting between Fergus and Sister Louisa.

5

The Dark Side of the Soul

The dooms of men
Are in God's hidden place.

W. B. YEATS (1865–1939)

New York City
Early November

Tierney Burke knew the docks of New York Harbor nearly as well as he knew his own neighborhood. Nevertheless, he did not relish creeping about them at night. Especially on a *Saturday* night, when he could just as easily have been spending time with Connie Hawkes.

Patrick Walsh had acted as if tonight's job were some sort of a great favor, as if Tierney should be flattered at having been singled out in such a manner.

For his part, Tierney considered the assignment little more than snooping. Spying on two of Walsh's unscrupulous runners seemed a meaningless pursuit, not to mention a risky one at that.

He suspected his employer was testing him—and not for the first time. Pushing him to see just how far he would go.

Walsh's continual baiting was beginning to anger Tierney. He was not one to shirk an assignment, and the man knew it. The element of risk was no deterrent—it merely added a bit more spice to the stew. Nor was he particularly put off by the illegal nature of his employer's varied "enterprises." While he suspected that much of Walsh's vast wealth had been accumulated on the wrong side of the law, his own part in things was that of a mere messenger boy or a go-between. He was a paid employee—nothing more.

Besides, as he saw things, Patrick Walsh was no more a criminal than a number of politicians and policemen on the city's payroll—only a bit more clever and a good deal more successful. One thing was irrefutable: Walsh paid his employees well. Tierney earned more money in a month working for Walsh than he could have made in an entire year in any of the other mean, paltry jobs available to an Irish boy in New York.

He had his limits, however. It was no secret among Walsh's other boys that Tierney Burke would have nothing to do with any shady dealings involving the city's immigrants—in part, because his own da had come across years ago. He was the son of an immigrant, and he thought of the thousands of Irish now flooding the streets of New York as his own people. He would do nothing to add to their already considerable wretchedness.

Tonight's work, however, came uncomfortably close to violating that resolve. Tierney was repulsed by the despicable runners who infested the harbor-like rats. To him they represented the lowest sort of humanity, predators who fed themselves on the misery of others, many of whom were their own countrymen.

He knew how they worked well enough. The contemptible swindlers would ingratiate themselves with the immigrants before they ever got off the ship. A recent law requiring the scoundrels to be licensed had merely given them "credentials" to flash around the docks, affording them a kind of respectability.

By appealing to the foreigners' natural confusion and fear, the runners easily took charge, offering the frightened newcomers the benefit of their experience, as well as their "protection," as they herded their victims down the gangplank. Within hours, they usually managed to bilk their prey of what money and meager worldly goods they had brought with them.

Runners were known to have no scruples, no sense whatever of morality or decency. They would even go so far as to board ships in quarantine, mindless of the danger of typhus and other diseases. It wasn't unusual for them to have some hired thugs close-by to guarantee their own protection, as well as to make sure none of their victims escaped on the way out of the harbor.

Patrick Walsh and others of his ilk had refined this corrupt practice to a new level of efficiency. Using a middleman as a broker, Walsh would purchase complete lists of steerage passengers, usually from mercenary captains who sold out to the highest bribe. Upon arrival, entire groups of frightened, bewildered immigrants were herded off the ships, then led to boardinghouses owned by Walsh. Outlandish rents were demanded, and those who might dare to raise questions were threatened with the LAW.

To the already oppressed Irish, the LAW was synonymous with unfairness and brutality. Tierney's father, a policeman himself, maintained that the Irish immigrant's fear and hatred of the law was to be expected. Their experience with the police was limited to the toadying constables back in Ireland who, carrying out the demands of English landlords, tumbled the cottages of the poor and drove them out, half naked and starving, onto the road, where they would die of the hunger and the cold.

In Ireland, the LAW meant harsh judgment, swift punishment, and no mercy. Only God knew what the LAW might do to them in this strange new land!

The two runners Tierney was tailing tonight were little more than professional pirates who had been particularly successful during their short time in Patrick Walsh's employ. Too successful, perhaps. Apparently, Walsh was convinced that Monk Ferguson and Sweet Bailey were up to a bit of other business on the side.

The ship Tierney had been watching for the past half hour was a big one, an English coffin that had put in at South Street just this evening, after clearing the quarantine station at Staten Island. Steerage passengers were milling about on deck, the fretful cries of children and worried murmurs of their parents adding to the clamor on the docks.

Nighttime made little difference in the harbor. Even now, going on eleven, sailors and runners pressed through the noisy crush of disembarking immigrants. Cursing and shouting rose above the babel of foreign tongues. What laughter could be heard sounded shrill and uncertain. Women keened and strong men wept, and Tierney suddenly felt himself engulfed by a thousand dreams and as many sorrows.

How many of those dreams will be washed out to sea before this night ends? he wondered bitterly. *How many new sorrows will rise with the dawn of their first day in New York City?*

A foghorn bleated in the distance. Shivering, Tierney pulled the collar of his seaman's jacket snug about his throat. The night wind blowing in off the water stung his face, and he ducked his head against the cold.

Next time, he vowed sourly, he would not be so quick to rise to Walsh's challenge.

———

In the candlelit dining room of the mansion on Fifth Avenue, Sara Farmington and her father lingered over dessert.

"I can scarcely believe I have you all to myself this evening," Sara said, toying with her spoon. "That's rather a rare occurrence these days."

Lewis Farmington lifted one dark eyebrow. "Have I neglected you, dear? I'm sorry; I'm afraid it's been a somewhat hectic week for me."

"So it would seem," Sara agreed. "You've dined out, what, three times, with Winifred this week?"

If she'd expected to fluster him, she should have known better. Scooping up a spoonful of lemon pudding, he merely beamed a cheerful smile, saying, "Why, yes, I believe I have. I've been trying to help her make some order of her financial affairs."

At Sara's questioning look, he nodded. "Winifred hasn't much head for business, I'm afraid. Obviously, it's going to take a great deal of work to get her straightened around. But it seems the Christian thing to do, don't you agree?"

Sara kept her expression carefully bland. "Of course. And I'm sure Winifred is most appreciative."

His reply was another bright smile and a quick nod as he pushed his empty bowl aside.

"I must admit, I was rather surprised when Winifred decided to stay on after Evan's father went back to England," Sara said, returning her spoon to its place. "Naturally, we're all pleased. She's a delightful woman."

Lewis Farmington gave his mouth a hasty swipe with his napkin. "Yes," he said, "she is, isn't she?"

"Still, I should think the hotel would be awfully confining. Has she given any thought to more permanent lodgings?"

Her father leaned back in his chair. "As a matter of fact," he replied, "I believe I've found just the place for her. Pleasant little apartment over on West Thirty-fourth. One of Tomlinson's brownstones."

Sara lifted her gaze to his. "My, you *are* looking after her, aren't you?"

Her father narrowed his eyes. "I haven't done all that much, really. She *is* a woman alone, and in a strange city at that."

Amused, Sara thought Winifred had scarcely been alone since she arrived from England. Obviously, her father was quite taken with the attractive widow. And understandably so. Winifred Whittaker Coates was youthful, enviably pretty, clever—and great fun to be with. It would take an utterly dull man to resist her charm.

The truth was, Sara found herself pleased by her father's developing interest in Evan's aunt. Despite his furiously busy schedule, she knew him to be lonely, at least on occasion. Sara's mother had been dead for more than twenty years now, but he made no secret of the fact that he still missed her.

Certainly, he need not have lacked for female attention. Women—even much younger women—had been flirting openly with him ever since Sara could remember. While his wealth might have been the attraction for some, there was no denying the fact that Lewis Farmington was still a compelling, interesting man. Nearing sixty, his silver hair was thick and full-bodied, his skin bronzed from all the time spent outdoors at the shipyards. He carried himself with the bounce and vigor of a much younger man. Moreover, he was also a wonderful human being, a prince of a man and an extraordinary father to both her and her brother, Gordie.

Winifred Coates was the first woman, at least the first in Sara's memory, in whom her father had shown even a passing interest in all these years. While cheering him on, Sara could not help but be secretly amused by the idea that Winifred had "no head for business." Her own observation of the attractive widow led her to suspect that somewhere behind all that beguiling femininity and somewhat flighty demeanor lay a lively intelligence and an indomitable will.

Her father's voice roused Sara from her thoughts, and she turned her attention back to him.

"My schedule hasn't been entirely taken up with Winnie— Winifred—this week," he said. "I've also spent some time with the mayor. I've agreed to chair the new subcommission. Since it was my idea to begin with, I felt obligated to accept the appointment."

"Oh, Father, I'm so glad! You're perfect for the position. You said yourself it will require someone who really cares about the immigrants."

Sara knew all about the new subcommission. For weeks, her father had been urging its formation as a means of investigating the city's escalating crime wave and its effect on the immigrants, now arriving by the thousands.

Crime was out of control in New York, and the largest group of victims seemed to be the immigrant population. Before they ever left the ships in the harbor, they were caught up in the vicious trafficking of the runners who haunted the docks in search of new victims. Once settled in the slum districts, they then found themselves the victims of unscrupulous landlords and street gangs.

It seemed there was no escaping those who preyed on the less fortunate; in the New World, as in the Old, violence and injustice shadowed the poor.

It incensed Sara that New York's immigrants, the majority of whom had already endured shameful oppression in their native countries, found still more of the same upon reaching America. Arriving with dreams of liberty and opportunity, too often they were greeted by only more misery.

The various immigrant associations were only now beginning to be effective. While helpful in a number of areas, they still functioned primarily as mutual aid and fraternal societies, with no real voice or power in government.

Recently, though, a new body, the Commissioners of Emigration, had been appointed by the state. In addition to the mayors of New York and Brooklyn—as well as agents of the Irish and German societies—private citizens like Lewis Farmington had been appointed to serve as commissioners and committee heads.

"Dillon and Verplanck have both agreed that a variety of occupations should be represented," her father was saying. "Jess Dalton has agreed to serve, as have two of the Catholic priests. We've appointed an attorney, and hope to have two or three policemen as well. Which reminds me," he said, after taking a sip of water, "we've approached Michael about serving."

Sara's cheeks grew warm under his scrutiny. Annoyed with

herself, she forced a casual tone. "Michael? Well . . . certainly, he should be . . . an ideal choice."

"I thought so, too," he replied, smiling. Obviously, he enjoyed flustering her. And just as obviously, he knew the mention of Michael never failed to do so.

"What with Michael's being an immigrant himself," he went on, "and a policeman—he'll prove invaluable to us, I'm sure. Will he accept, do you think?"

"Why . . . yes . . . at least, I should hope he would. But, of course," Sara added quickly, "I can't speak for Michael."

One eyebrow lifted in a look of wry amusement. "You will, soon enough," he said. "Wives seem to take on this uncanny ability to predict their husbands' reactions, I've noticed."

"I can't imagine anybody predicting Michael. Or *you*," Sara shot back.

"Mmm. Perhaps." He dabbed at a spot of pudding on the lapel of his coat. "Michael's stopping by later, did I tell you?" he asked casually. "To discuss the subcommission."

"*Tonight?*" Sara jackknifed to her feet, banging the leg of her chair against the table.

Eyes glinting, her father nodded. "Why, yes," he said, getting to his feet, "he should be here within the hour. We'll take care of business first, and then you can have him all to yourself."

"I must change!" Sara nearly pulled one end of the dinner cloth off the table as she whirled around to leave.

Laughing, her father offered his arm and escorted her from the dining room. They stopped at the bottom of the stairs. "I don't suppose you two have set the date yet?" he asked casually.

Instinctively, Sara glanced down at the ring on her left hand, a small diamond chip Michael had paid for by working weeks as a night security guard at the pipe factory. Sara thought it quite the most beautiful ring she had ever seen.

Looking back at her father, she saw that he was waiting for an answer.

"No, we haven't," she said, her voice low. "Not yet."

Half-irritated with his good-natured probing, Sara nevertheless understood. She and Michael had been engaged for two months now, with still no word of a wedding date.

"We'd thought to give Tierney time," she answered unhappily. "He still . . . resents me, I'm afraid."

Her father's dark eyes searched hers. "Sara," he said, shaking his head, "that boy is almost a man. Indeed, for all practical purposes, he *is* a man. Don't get your hopes up for any real changes there. You and Michael need to plan a life *without* him, not *around* him, it seems to me."

Sara looked away, troubled as always by the thought of Michael's rebellious son. "I know you're right, Father. But it's difficult. Michael had so hoped we could all be a family. I hate what Tierney's disapproval is doing to him. Yet, I think I almost understand why the boy resents me. I represent everything that Tierney dislikes and distrusts, just by the fact of who I am."

Again her father shook his head. "The boy's disapproval of you is only a part of the trouble between him and his father. There were problems there long before Michael asked you to marry him. He told me as much."

Again Sara nodded. "That's true, but—"

"Some things don't change, daughter," he said softly, taking her hand. He seemed hesitant, as if he weren't quite certain he should go on. "So the delay is your doing, then?" he asked gently. "I thought as much."

Sara avoided his gaze. "I don't want to make things worse between Michael and his son. I couldn't live with that. Tierney is his only child—"

"Tierney Burke is no child!" Her father's hand tightened on hers. "Listen to me, Sara. Allow me, just for a moment, to be an interfering father."

Surprised, Sara turned back to him. Over the years, her father had made it a point to reserve his advice for only those matters of great importance. A man who had an opinion on almost everything, more often than not he kept his feelings about Sara's personal life entirely to himself.

"Courting you can't have been easy for Michael," he said in his characteristically direct manner. "The man is no fool. He knows there's every likelihood he'll be marked as just another fortune hunter—"

Sara bit her lip, stung by his words.

"Now don't take on," he said quickly, clasping her shoulders. "Anyone with half their wits can see the man is in love with you! Still, I'm sure it's no easy thing for him to deal with the assumption and speculation. There's no ignoring the truth, after all: Michael is an immigrant policeman who presumed to ask a millionaire's daughter to change her entire life for him. The fact that he believes you love him enough to do so—and the fact that he believes in you enough to think you can manage it all—is a real tribute to you. But don't think for a moment it's easy for him."

He silenced Sara's renewed protest with a wave of his hand, then went on. "It seems to me the man has quite enough to handle without worrying that you might be having regrets. Your reluctance to set a date is bound to trouble him."

Smarting from the undercurrent of criticism she sensed in her father's words, Sara stood looking down at the floor, not trusting herself to answer. At the back of her mind lurked the discomforting awareness that he was right. He usually was.

His words followed her all the way upstairs into the bedroom. As soon as she entered the room, she sank down onto the vanity stool. With unsteady hands, she loosened the thick twist of hair at the nape of her neck, smoothing it and repinning it in place.

Michael was fond of teasing her about what he called the "proper little knot on her neck." Once they were married, he said, he was going to insist that she let her hair down. "We'll create a scandal," he would say. "The proper Miss Sara Farmington lets her hair down at last. Ah, the shame of the woman!"

In truth, he had tried more than once to coax her into doing just that—letting her waist-length hair down for him. Invariably, he found Sara's flustered refusals a matter of great amusement. "I believe the woman is deceiving me," he would say, his eyes dancing with fun. "The proper little knot is nailed to her neck and will not budge."

But then, as was so often the way with him, his mischievous mood would suddenly turn. His eyes would darken, his mouth soften, and the teasing note in his voice would disappear. "Sara *a gra*," he would say softly against her cheek, "promise me this, that once we are man and wife before God, you will allow me to take the pins from your hair and let it fall free, in all its glory. Promise me that you will take your hair down for my eyes alone when you are my wife."

The instant the predictable blush spread over Sara's face at this promised intimacy, he would smile into her eyes, then gently kiss her.

Sara closed her eyes, hugging her arms to herself at the memory.

Was she making a mistake in delaying the wedding? Just last week, while discussing the date yet again, Michael had become almost cross with her, had even hinted that her reluctance might not be entirely due to Tierney.

She could still see the uneasy question in his eyes as he searched her face. "You are sure it's Tierney, Sara? You'd not be having second thoughts about marrying me?"

Dismayed that he would even think such a thing, Sara had made every protest she could think of. Still, when they parted soon after, she wasn't at all sure she had managed to convince him.

Laying her brush on the vanity, she stared into the mirror. There was nothing she had ever wanted more than to be Michael's wife. Nothing! The very thought of being married to him made her heart leap like a spring.

That she could be so foolish over a man still amazed her. She stammered like a schoolgirl every time Michael walked into a room. And when he gave her that special, caressing look she knew to be just for her, the world around them simply faded away.

Even now, months after he'd made his feelings known, she found it nearly impossible to take in the fact that he loved her— really loved her—that he had actually asked her to be his wife. Her, with her too-wide mouth and her turned-up nose with its unladylike freckles, and her hateful lame leg.

She knew her father was right. There were those who would undoubtedly accuse Michael of being a fortune hunter. Why else would such a handsome, vital man give her a second look, they would say? Just as certainly, there were others who would think her mad for marrying a man like Michael. *Common*, they would call him.

They would not believe what she had found with him, the wonder, the splendor, the pure exultation of their love. Why, if it had not been for Tierney, she would never have *thought* of delaying the wedding! She smiled briefly at her reflection in the mirror. On the contrary, she would more than likely have set the date indecently soon!

The smile faded as the thought of Tierney came to mind. Michael had been at his wits' end about his son even before their engagement, openly admitting he did not understand him, could not fathom what drove the boy.

"I never know what to expect from him," he had told her one night, long before asking her to be his wife. "One minute he's a shooting star, bright, happy—lighthearted, even. The next he's a dark stone, hard and cold—a mystery."

That same night he had confessed his fear for Tierney. Even now, the memory of the terrible pain in Michael's eyes sent a shudder of dread pitching over Sara. "It's almost as if the boy has some sort of wildness whipping him on, driving him away from me and all I've ever held holy. Sometimes, Sara, I have a fierce terror for my son: that the part of him I know to be good will eventually be overcome by this other thing . . . this dark side of his soul. Sometimes I feel he's being driven straight down the road of destruction."

Remembering Michael's taut face, his tortured words, a cold shadow passed over Sara's own spirit. The truth was that, even in her few brief encounters with Michael's son, she had sensed the same darkness, the same portent of some awful destiny.

It was more than an awareness of Tierney's resentment of her, although he made no attempt whatsoever to hide his animosity. What she felt in him was a kind of compressed heat, a strain of savageness that, even controlled, burned through him, searing everything he did—everything he was—with the same wildness that gave a panther its fury and made it deadly.

Sitting there, staring into the mirror without really seeing herself, Sara was suddenly gripped by the conviction that her father was right: She should marry Michael as soon as he would have her, not put things off in hopes Tierney would change.

Michael needed her now . . . would need her later . . . as his wife, as his friend. He needed her by his side—in case Tierney *didn't* change.

———

It was another half hour before Tierney spied Ferguson and Bailey. They were nearly impossible to miss. Sweet Bailey's youthful, choirboy face would have charmed a nun, while Ferguson's ugly mug looked like a doughy, half-baked loaf of bread. They were a fine pair, those two.

Leaning against the wall of an abandoned warehouse, Tierney watched the two runners lead a dozen or more immigrant families off the ship. He knew right away something was amiss, for had they been doing their job for Walsh, they'd be herding a far greater number down the gangplank.

Pushing himself away from the wall, Tierney started off behind them, being careful to keep his distance so he wouldn't be seen. Two or three rods back of the runners and their entourage, he slotted himself in with some rowdy dock workers. Following at this distance, he was able to catch bits of the runners' conversation.

"Sure, and don't we do what we do as a service for Irish families?" Sweet Bailey was saying as he shepherded his charges away from the docks. "Us being Irish ourselves, we take it as a serious matter entirely, finding respectable lodgings for fine families from the ould sod."

"Now that is the truth," offered Ferguson. " 'Tis lucky we thought to check the manifest of your ship as we did. There are some, don't you know," he went on with an exaggerated shudder, "what would take advantage of good, trusting people like yourselves. Swindlers and thieves, the lot of them!"

Tierney ground his teeth together, wanting nothing more than to throw a punch at the swine's lumpy face.

Most of the dock workers had broken up by now, starting for Front Street. The runners and their victims were almost in the clear on Maiden Lane, and Tierney had to fall back, slowing his pace so he wouldn't be noticed.

"Sure, and you'll be liking the Porter's Inn just fine," Bailey was saying. " 'Tis a decent dwelling, with water-closet facilities and lockers where you can store your belongings. We'll be there in a shake, it's that close by."

Tierney's eyes narrowed. Porter's Inn wasn't one of Patrick Walsh's boardinghouses. It was owned by Chance Porter, a minor thug who ran several rackets on the docks.

So Walsh's suspicions about the two runners had been sound. More than likely they were plying their trade with both Walsh and Porter, reasoning that they could easily cut a few families from Walsh's list without him ever being the wiser. All prearranged with Porter, of course.

An anxious father must have inquired about expenses, for Bailey was quick to reassure him. "Oh, you'll be treated more than fairly, don't you worry a'tall, a'tall! Doesn't Mister Porter allow special rates for immigrants, himself having come across? He's an honest man, as you'll find. Everything honest and above board at Porter's!"

Tierney nearly gagged at the scoundrel's lies! Porter's place was even worse than some of the dumps owned by Patrick Walsh. As many as five or six families were squeezed into a tiny cell of a room, practically imprisoned as their money and their belongings were taken from them. They lived in filth and abject fear, held hostage to a heartless innkeeper or landlord, too intimidated even to explore a means of escape.

The group turned on Water Street, then veered almost immediately into a narrow, unnamed alley. Except for an occasional drunk or solitary prostitute, it was deserted.

Tierney edged close to the decaying brick walls that lined the right side of the alley, staying completely in the shadows as he followed on. He had already heard enough to give Walsh his report, but he decided to wait until he actually saw them enter the inn, just ahead.

He stopped when they did, pressing himself against the cold brick wall that joined the darkened Akrom's Shoemakers with Porter's place. Both runners were counting the heads of their victims before starting down the steps to Porter's below-ground entrance.

Intent on the scene just ahead, he heard the step behind him an instant too late. There was a sudden rush of air at the back of his neck. An iron pipe of an arm crushed his windpipe!

Tierney's breath exploded in a gasp. He tried to break free, but the muscular arm turned him and shoved him against the wall, cracking the back of his head against the bricks.

In the darkness, his attacker's hard eyes—Oriental eyes— bored into Tierney's. The man's face was round, the lips drawn back in an ugly sneer.

Panicked, Tierney now saw that there were two of them! The silent one hovering behind the Oriental was big and heavy-shouldered. "You got business with the shoemaker, boy?" the Oriental growled. "You can't see the shop is closed?"

One arm pinned Tierney in place by the throat, while the other hand jerked his chin up with a snap. "Only business for a boy on his own down here is *bad* business!"

The man slammed Tierney's head against the wall a second time, hard enough to rattle his teeth. Pain blazed from his ears down his throat.

"Why you following the foreigners, boy? Maybe you one of them, huh? You lost, is that it?"

Tierney tried to shake his head, but couldn't move.

"Captain Rynders got no use for snoops like you, boy! Only thing he got for troublemakers is *trouble!*"

Rynders! Gasping, Tierney tried to twist free. He couldn't budge. His mind spun. He should have known the two runners were from Rynders' bunch. Otherwise, they would never have had the nerve to double-cross Patrick Walsh. Only Rynders generated more fear than Walsh among the gangs.

"Who you working for, boy?" Again the Oriental snapped Tierney's head against the wall. "Walsh, maybe? You tracking his men, huh? Checking up on his runners?"

Tierney managed to twist his head sideways. "No! I was . . . I was just looking for a woman, don't you see . . . I got lost. . . ."

The Oriental grinned. "Irish boy, huh? What a dumb Irish boy like you want with a woman?" His arms tightened against Tierney's windpipe. "You lying, Irish boy! We been behind you all the way from the docks! You lying!"

Suddenly his arm left Tierney's throat. Wheezing, Tierney fought for a breath. The Oriental yanked him up by the collar of his jacket, pressing his face close enough that Tierney could smell his putrid breath. He stank of rotten teeth and something sickly sweet.

"You looking for information for your boss, boy? Okay, we give you a message to take back!"

The other figure stepped out of the shadows. Tierney spied the glint of the knife in his hand only an instant before the Oriental knocked him to his knees and began to kick him.

The last thing he saw before he blacked out was the tip of the knife snaking down toward his face.

————

Blaize cleaned his knife with care, then slid it back down into the side of his boot. "What now, then?"

He watched with no real interest as the Chinaman prodded the boy with the toe of his shoe, finally kicking him over onto his stomach.

Again the Chinaman kicked the boy. "Now we see to it he gets delivered to his boss. Captain Rynders says, anytime we catch

Walsh's boys where they don't belong, we fix them good and make sure Walsh knows who's responsible."

Blaize nodded, then wiped the back of his hand over his nose. "Then let's have done with it. I'm froze clear through."

"Tack a message to his coat," said the Chinaman, "and we'll stick him on the ferry. Rue can deliver him to Walsh first thing in the morning."

Blaize wiped his nose again, then felt in the boy's pockets until he located a pencil and a small pad of paper. He held the pad up to the dim light and began to laugh. "Hah!—what d'ya make of that!" he said, indicating the paper with the name of Patrick Walsh's hotel printed across the top. "We'll send Walsh a message from himself!"

Still laughing, Blaize watched the Chinaman again prod the unconscious boy as if he were a dead dog. At last he shook his head and began to write.

6

Dark Thoughts and Bright Dreams

Oh Gather the thoughts of your early years,
Gather them as they flow,
For all unmarked in those thoughts appears
The path where you soon must go.
Full many a dream will wither away,
And Springtide hues are brief,
But the lines are there of the autumn day,
Like the skeleton in the leaf.

WILLIAM EDWARD HARTPOLE LECKY (1838–1903)

For the first time in weeks, Patrick Walsh had spent the night in his wife's bedroom.

When the hammering began early the next morning, he first thought the noise was coming from downstairs. Only when he heard the shrill voice of Nancy, the maid, did he realize she was right outside the bedroom door, pounding with a vengeance.

"MRS. WALSH! MR. WALSH? PLEASE, COULD YOU COME? 'TIS A TERRIBLE THING!"

Walsh sat up, now fully alert. Beside him, Alice clutched his arm. "Patrick?" Her eyes were still glazed with sleep. "What is it?"

Tossing the bed covers aside, Walsh fumbled for his dressing gown. "You'd best stay here," he said, getting up. "I'll go and see."

By the time he opened the bedroom door, the maid was gone. He found her downstairs in the entryway, staring with horror-filled eyes at the front door, which stood ajar.

"Out there, sir!" she shrilled. "On the porch!"

The damp cold of early morning flooded the hall from the partly opened door. Disgruntled by his abrupt awakening and annoyed by the maid's threatened hysteria, Walsh let go an oath as he flung the door the rest of the way open.

It took him a moment to identify the motionless heap on the porch as Tierney Burke. Even when recognition dawned, he stood unmoving, staring down at the body.

Finally, belting his dressing gown more tightly around him, he knelt down beside the limp body. The side of Tierney's face was bruised and stained with dried blood. Walsh turned him over on his back. His eyes narrowed when he saw the note buttoned onto the boy's blood-stained jacket. Removing it with trembling hands, he let out yet another curse as he read.

"COMPLIMENTS OF CAPTAIN RYNDERS."

Walsh crumpled the note in his hand. Anger and disbelief mixed inside him as he surveyed the still form.

Suddenly, the eyelids fluttered, and a soft moan escaped the swollen lips. Walsh's first response was relief. A corpse on his front porch would be hard to explain—especially the corpse of a policeman's son. Still, there was no mistaking the fact that the boy was critically injured, perhaps even dying. What was he to do with him?

Glancing back over his shoulder, he saw the maid still standing in the doorway. "Send Sparky for the doctor!" he snapped. "Right away! And bring a blanket!"

Getting to his feet, Walsh turned to find his wife stepping onto the porch, her childish blue eyes round with astonishment. Her fair hair, unpinned, fell in disarray, and her pink satin dressing gown was pulled carelessly around her plump figure. The sight of her squat, buxom form in the light set Patrick's teeth on edge with annoyance.

Controlling his distaste, he went to the door and led her back inside. "I'll handle this, Alice. You go and get dressed before you catch cold."

"But—it's *Tierney*, isn't it, Patrick? Tierney Burke? Whatever has happened to him?"

Ignoring her questions, Walsh moved her toward the staircase. "I've sent for the doctor. We'll take care of things. Just go along now and get dressed."

"I'll get Lemuel to bring him inside," she said, resisting his attempt to send her back upstairs.

"Inside?" Walsh stared at her.

"Of course, inside, Patrick!" she said, pushing by him and starting for the kitchen. "We can't just leave the boy lying out there in the cold! I'll have Nancy open one of the bedrooms at the end of the hall for him."

Halfway to the kitchen, she called back, "We'll have to notify his father right away! The poor man may be searching for the boy this very minute!"

"Alice, I hardly think—"

She waved off his attempt to protest and hurried on. Walsh stood staring after her, clenching his fists in controlled fury. He wanted to shake her! Alice the Earth-Mother. She'd take in anything that strayed near the house, anything hungry or hurt. He should have curbed her do-gooder instincts long ago.

She was right about notifying Michael Burke, of course. There was no way to avoid it, with the boy on his doorstep, unconscious. And if he delayed too long, he'd arouse Alice's suspicions. But what possible explanation could he give for the boy ending up *here*?

The beginning throb of a headache knocked at the back of his skull. He frowned, trying to think, and the pain sharpened. Swearing under his breath, he started upstairs to get dressed.

Even as he took the stairs two at a time, he began concocting a tale for the boy's police-captain father.

———

Michael Burke woke up just after dawn. The morning light was dim, the bedroom cold, but he didn't mind. Nor did he care that it was his day off, and he'd awakened long before he needed to get up.

The truth was, he savored such a rare moment of leisure. He lay there, with the soft silence of daybreak wrapped around him and a heart brimming with pleasant thoughts to consider. Yawning, he gave one huge stretch before the cold drove him back under the bed covers. He would give himself another few minutes, he decided, a few stolen moments in which to be an idle man.

Burying his face in his pillow, he smiled, remembering the night before—and Sara. She had amazed him entirely by declaring that she thought they should set the date for their wedding. Curiously, she seemed uncertain, almost shy, as if she'd half expected him to announce that he had changed his mind and didn't wish to marry her after all.

That unexpected lack of confidence was Sara's way, he knew, and just one of the things that endeared her to him. In the beginning, the slight unhinging of her composure in his presence had confused him, even tested his own assurance. He'd thought perhaps he made her uncomfortable by who he was, that he somehow offended her sensibilities. A lady of her quality wasn't likely to be keen on having an Irish cop hanging around, after all.

But later, as he came to know her . . . and to love her . . . it secretly delighted him that he could fluster the unflappable Sara Farmington. Sure, the woman had no lack of backbone. She could be a terror about her causes and her principles. There was no arguing with Sara when her mind was set, and that was the truth.

Yet, with him, her self-assurance seemed to tilt in the most delightful manner. She would turn crimson, even stammer, without the slightest provocation, and in his arms . . . ah, in his arms, she was all shy, glistening eyes and sweet, sweet loveliness.

At those times, he felt himself to be a man blessed. He thought he could survive for the rest of his life on the look in Sara's eyes when he held her close.

He would marry her tomorrow if she'd but say the word!

His smile broke even wider as he recalled how she'd scolded him just last night about his impatience. His immediate suggestion, when she agreed to set the date, had been a Christmas wedding.

"It wouldn't be *decent*, Michael! Why, we've only been engaged two months!"

"And who decides what is decent?" he countered.

"Well . . . custom. Tradition."

"So, then, we'll establish a new tradition—a more sensible one!" he'd replied, attempting to kiss her into submission.

"Not before April," she'd insisted between kisses.

"April? I'll be mad by April, Sara!"

"Michael, really!"

"I'm in love with you, woman! I want to be with you. I *need* to be with you! You'd make me wait until *April?*"

"March, then," she'd said with a bit less starch.

"March is cold and ugly, Sara. You'd not want such a dismal wedding, sure."

"February?"

"*Christmas Eve.*"

Hadn't she smiled at him then, a baffling smile that set him to wondering if she hadn't wanted Christmas all along, but simply meant to be quite sure he was sincere.

Turning onto his back, Michael mulled over the rest of their conversation. He was still troubled about her insistence on a small, private ceremony. He'd been so sure she'd want a large wedding at the Fifth Avenue Church, as befitting her family's position in New York. For his part, he found the idea of an elaborate ceremony repugnant, but he had convinced himself to endure it, for Sara's sake.

But Sara had other ideas. "Actually, that's not what I want at all. I'd much rather be married at home, in the chapel, if that suits you."

He had made an effort to reassure her that he'd suffer the whole show if she would prefer a big wedding. But she was adamant in her refusal to even consider it.

"I don't want a large wedding, Michael! Truly, I don't. Besides," she added quietly, "I think with Tierney feeling . . . as he does about our marriage, it's best that we keep things simple."

Again, Michael shifted restlessly on the bed, jamming his fist into the pillow to plump it. He should be relieved. Hadn't he dreaded the thought of an extravagant society affair all along?

If only he could feel more confident about her reasons.

So far as Tierney was concerned, there was no pleasing him anyway. Keeping things simple wouldn't change the boy's attitude about the marriage. The fact was, he disliked Sara, resented her for her wealth, her family, her social position—thought her a "society spinster" who had taken advantage of his father simply to "get a man."

It made Michael furious every time he thought of the terrible accusations his son had leveled. No, catering to Tierney would do

71

nothing to soften the boy's opposition to the marriage.

Besides, the discomforting truth was that he couldn't help but wonder if Sara was being altogether honest about her reasons for wanting a small ceremony. Mightn't it be that, as time went on, she was beginning to question her decision? Surely by now she realized how altogether peculiar her choice of a husband was going to seem to her society friends and acquaintances.

And could he blame her? Admittedly, it would be no easy thing for Sara Farmington to present to her peers an Irish immigrant cop as her bridegroom.

Even if that weren't the case, even if—*please, God*—he were wrong about Sara having second thoughts, how was her father going to take to the idea? Lewis Farmington might be an extraordinary man, even a bit of a maverick in the eyes of his contemporaries—but he was still one of the wealthiest, most powerful men in the state of New York—and Sara was his only daughter. Surely he would want to give her away in style.

"Father will want what I want," Sara had replied without the slightest hesitation when Michael had posed the question to her.

Perhaps. Michael wasn't so sure. Yawning, he rubbed a hand over the heavy stubble of his beard, still reluctant to get out of bed. This morning he would face Tierney with the fact that he and Sara planned to wed on Christmas Eve. He dreaded the encounter, certain to be an unpleasant one.

Tierney never missed an opportunity to throw out one of his snide remarks. There was no explaining his antagonism for Sara; Michael had given up trying. The announcement of their engagement had sent the boy into a sulk for days. Finding out the wedding date had finally been set was sure to set him off once again.

With a sigh, he pushed himself up. He might just as well get it over with, he decided, refusing to let the thought of yet another confrontation spoil his mood.

————

In the bedroom he shared with Tierney, Daniel stood staring out the window. It was well past daylight, and Tierney still hadn't come home.

It wasn't the first time, of course. Tierney seemed to get away with his escapades with incredible ease. Uncle Mike slept like the dead, and more than once Tierney had sneaked up onto the roof and through the window just past dawn, with his da never knowing the difference.

But not *this* late, and never on Uncle Mike's day off, when he was sure to be hanging about the flat all morning. This time he was going to get into trouble for sure.

A sudden pounding made Daniel jump.

Who would be knocking at the kitchen door so early? Certainly not Tierney! He'd not come to the front door for anything, sneaking in past dawn!

He heard Uncle Mike's voice, then another, this one unfamiliar. Still in his nightshirt, he opened the bedroom door just enough to peep out.

Uncle Mike was dressed, in his shirtsleeves, talking to a black man at the door. Daniel heard Tierney's name, and cracked the door a bit farther.

"Yessir, that's what Mr. Walsh said. That you shouldn't worry 'bout your boy, that he'll see to it he gets the best of care. Thing is, he can't be moved to bring him home just now."

Puzzled, Daniel stood listening as Uncle Mike fired off an entire round of sharp questions. The black man just kept repeating himself, saying he "shouldn't worry," and was welcome to come and see his son "as soon as he liked."

Finally, Daniel moved, entering the kitchen just as Uncle Mike shut the door. "What is it?" he asked, shivering at the cold of the room against his bare legs. "What's happened to Tierney?"

Uncle Mike turned around. His face was pale, his dark eyes frightened and confused.

"He's been—hurt. Beaten up," he added in a terrible voice. "He's at Walsh's house, on Staten Island."

Bewildered, Daniel stared at him. "Beaten up?" he repeated blankly. "Wh-what do you mean?"

Uncle Mike's Adam's apple worked hard, up and down. "I don't know," he said, his face grim as he hiked his suspenders over his shoulders. "I don't know. But I'll be finding out. Of that you can be sure."

7

In the House of the Enemy

There is something here I do not get,
Some menace I do not comprehend.

VALENTIN IREMONGER (1918–)

The Walsh estate on Staten Island was much as Michael would have expected: grand in size and ostentatious in appearance. Sara might have referred to it as *vulgar*.

White stone, trimmed with rose-colored shutters, it sprawled beyond a winding gravel driveway, complete with a glass conservatory and a stable. No gardens gentled the grounds. No random shrubbery broke the precise landscape design. The few trees on the property stood thin and new.

To Michael, the place looked as artificial as he suspected its owner to be. As his gaze took in Walsh's estate, it occurred to him that one reason he found the man so loathsome was his deceit. Walsh presented the face of a successful businessman, but Michael could see the skull and crossbones lurking in the shadows behind him. Patrick Walsh was a pirate, but a pirate without the courage to raise his own treacherous flag. Instead, he cloaked his true intentions under a banner of respectability.

Chilled from the ferry ride, Michael accelerated his pace, hurrying up the flagstone walkway. As he approached the ornamental front door, he knew a moment's surge of dread. Until now, he had thought of little else except the condition in which he might find Tierney. Yet, the question as to how and why his injured son had ended up at Walsh's estate had been there, cowering in the shadows of his mind like a hidden attacker, waiting only for the chance to strike.

Michael knew he would eventually have to confront the question, and the answer would more than likely bring him grief. His already fractured relationship with his son could all too easily be further shattered.

But for now he could not think beyond the massive oak door in front of him. Beyond that door dwelt the man who headed his personal list of corrupt, self-serving vipers—a man targeted by the new subcommission as one of the key crime bosses, albeit the least visible, in the city.

This was a hard thing, a bitter thing indeed, to learn that a man he so thoroughly detested had given his injured son shelter and succor. He had long held Patrick Walsh as an enemy—an enemy of the law and an enemy of his own people, the Irish. Indeed, his primary reason for agreeing to serve on the subcommission was the opportunity he sensed to bring down Walsh.

He was resolved to ruin the man. Ruin him and destroy his corrupt, ill-gained empire. But now—now, he would face him in his home, with his own son in Walsh's bed.

Michael bit down on his humiliation and squared his shoulders. Drawing in a long breath, he raised his fist and, ignoring the ornate brass knocker, pounded on the door.

Upstairs in the lavish guest room, Patrick Walsh was in the midst of prompting the barely conscious Tierney Burke one more time. When the maid peeked in to announce the arrival of Captain Burke, he didn't even turn around, but snapped, "Have him wait. Tell him I'll be right down."

Studying the boy's battered face, Walsh straightened. "It's entirely your choice, of course. I have no problem with telling your father the truth, that you were scouting some double-crossing runners on my behalf."

The boy's left eye and cheekbone were bandaged. The other eye glared out at Walsh with a mixture of pain and anger. Moistening his cut, swollen lip, he finally managed to reply. "No. We'll do it your way," he rasped.

"I think that's best," Walsh said agreeably.

He paused. "He won't expect you to remember details. You were badly beaten and unconscious for several hours, after all."

The boy nodded weakly, then turned his face toward the wall.

Finally satisfied, Walsh said, "I'll go and get your father. I'm sure he's anxious to see how you are."

———

It took Michael less than ten minutes to realize that both Tierney and Walsh were lying.

Walsh did all the talking.

"The lad was mugged as he returned to the hotel, after making a delivery to Sheff's Warehouse in the harbor," he explained. "When he fought back, his assailants beat him up and left him on the docks. Two of my other delivery boys recognized him and, not knowing what else to do, put him on the ferry and brought him here."

The man was smooth, clever and hard to read; but, practiced as his delivery may have been, his story held far too many loose ends and discrepancies. Besides, Michael knew his own son well enough to recognize the boy's evasive glance for what it was: deceit.

Walsh seemed intent on lingering in the room, even after he'd supplied a number of details for the second time. Tierney offered nothing at all, but merely lay, dull-eyed and silent, except for an occasional nod.

Obviously, the boy was too weak to carry on a conversation. Yet, it wasn't so much his silence that nagged at Michael—it was more the look that passed between his son and Walsh, a look that somehow served to shut Michael out. It was the look of a conspiracy in the making.

Finally, Walsh left them alone. Ignoring the chair beside the bed, Michael stood, staring down at his son. The boy had to be in great pain. His good-looking face was now a patchwork of bruises and cuts, his mouth gashed and swollen, his left eye bandaged. The knife had sliced dangerously close, but, thank the good Lord, the eye itself had been spared.

Walsh had spoken at least one truth: It could have been much, much worse.

"Now perhaps you can understand why I didn't want you working for a man like Patrick Walsh," Michael said to his son. "You could have been killed. From the looks of you, you very nearly were!"

As soon as the words escaped his lips, he regretted them. This was not the time to rail at the boy or make accusations.

When Tierney's face darkened with anger, Michael swallowed down his own. "Ah, son, I'm sorry! It's just that you gave me such a fright, don't you see? All the way over on the ferry, I worried that I might find you dead once I got here!"

"I'll be all right, Da," the boy muttered. "I just want to go home."

Michael studied him. "According to Walsh, the doctor says you can't be moved for several days yet."

Tierney moaned. He tried to shift positions, gasping aloud at the effort.

Michael bent over him. He hesitated for a moment, then grasped the lad's hand. "It hurts pretty bad, I expect."

For once, Tierney made no attempt to play the big man. Nodding weakly, he clung to Michael's hand. "Please, Da, can't you just take me home? I don't want to stay here!"

Nor did Michael want him to stay. The idea of being obligated to Patrick Walsh was more than he could stomach.

"I'll do what I can, son. Perhaps I can manage a word with the doctor," Michael said, still holding Tierney's hand in his.

The boy looked up at him.

"Is it true, then, what Walsh is saying—about the way it happened?" Micheal held his heath as he waited for his son's reply.

An expression flickered across Tierney's face, so fleeting that Michael almost missed it. Was it remorse? He held the boy's gaze with his own, desperately willing the return of the son who seemed to be slipping away from him more and more all the time.

Then, just as quickly, the expression disappeared. Tierney tore his eyes from his father's face, and when he looked back again, the shadowed, haunted, closed look had once more replaced the momentary glimmer of sorrow and repentance.

"You heard what he said."

"Aye, I heard," said Michael, his voice betraying his bitter disappointment.

Silence hung between them. Michael wanted to say more, to ask questions, to probe for the truth. But there was no denying the lad's weakness and the seriousness of his condition. It was not the time. His questions would have to wait.

"All right, then," he said quietly. "I'll leave you to rest for now."

When he would have straightened and released Tierney's hand, the boy held on to him. "You'll not forget to see the doctor?"

Michael frowned. "Why are you so determined to go home? Isn't Walsh treating you well, then?"

Tierney attempted a shrug, but it seemed more a shudder of pain. "Oh, sure, it's nothing like that. And Mrs. Walsh couldn't be nicer. I'm just not comfortable, that's all. I don't want people I scarcely know taking care of me."

Michael nodded, understanding. "Aye, I'd be the same. I promise you, I'll do what I can. In the meantime, you get some sleep. I'll come back soon." He stopped. "If you want me to, that is."

Again something opened in Tierney's eyes, some faint light of youthful affection that Michael had not seen for a long time. For a moment, he was reminded of the little boy his son had been, once, long ago. An urge to gather the boy into his arms and hold him next to his heart seized Michael, shaking him with a sense of love and loss.

And then the moment was gone. He had waited too long. "Sure, when you can," Tierney replied dully, his voice low. "Come back when you've time. But I'll be fine. You needn't worry."

After a moment, the boy seemed to drift off to sleep. Still, Michael delayed leaving. Going to the tall, narrow window across the room, he stared out on the dismal, barren grounds for a long time. Deeply troubled by the undeniable seriousness of Tierney's injuries, he was even more dismayed by the certainty that his son had lied to him.

A part of him backed away from knowing why. He wasn't at all sure he wanted the truth. But another side of him, and this one much stronger, resolved to know what had brought Tierney to such a state—and why he was so determined to keep it secret.

He stood in silence for another few moments. When he came back to the bed, Tierney was still sleeping.

Bending over his son, Michael did something he had not done

78

for years. With a light hand, he brushed a shock of hair away from Tierney's face, then touched his lips ever so gently to the boy's forehead.

He could not swallow down the knot in his throat, could not stop the mist that glazed his eyes when he straightened. Looking down on the swollen, cut face of his son, a face taut and anxious even in sleep, Michael almost choked on the memory of a dark-haired little boy—a happy little boy who, a very long time ago, had always fallen asleep with a smile on his face.

———

Downstairs in the entryway, Michael was stopped by a short, plump woman with fair hair and a round, pleasant face. Her eyes appeared kind, her smile somewhat timid.

"Captain Burke? I'm Alice Walsh. I wanted to tell you . . . how sorry I am about your son. But the doctor is sure he'll be just fine."

Mrs. Walsh was not at all what Michael would have expected. She was anything but the flamboyant, blowzy sort he might have imagined for a rogue like Patrick Walsh. Her looks were plain, her manner unassuming, and her concern for Tierney appeared entirely genuine.

"Thank you," Michael said, feeling awkward. "I apologize for the imposition. I plan to see about getting the boy moved just as soon as possible."

"Oh—please, no!" she exclaimed, one hand going to her throat. "Why, having Tierney here is no trouble! No trouble at all! We're just horrified that a thing like this had to happen! He's such a fine young man. My husband sets great store by him, you know. He feels responsible."

Studying her good-natured face, Michael wondered why such a seemingly decent woman would take up with a blackguard like Walsh.

"Responsible?" he repeated.

"Why, yes. After all, Tierney was making a delivery for Mr. Walsh when it happened. You mustn't for a moment think you're imposing, Captain. We're only too glad to help."

"It's very kind of you to say so, Mrs. Walsh, and I thank you."

After insisting that he wait to see her husband, Alice Walsh swung about, skirts swaying, and hurried off down the hall. Michael watched her go, again musing over the contrast between husband and wife.

In a moment Patrick Walsh appeared from the library across the hall, carrying what looked to be Tierney's billfold and keys. "I thought you might want to take these with you, Captain," he said.

Michael noted Walsh's finely manicured, slender hands as he reached for Tierney's things. "Odd," he said quietly, thumbing through the money in the billfold, "that the thugs didn't think to rob him as well."

Walsh's pale, hazel stare never wavered. "Yes, I wondered about that myself. Perhaps they were frightened off before they could finish their mischief."

Michael studied the other man, masking his disdain with great effort. Walsh exuded prosperity and soft living. Tall and slim, he was perfectly tailored, clean-shaven, and fastidiously neat. His cravat was expertly folded, his linen snowy white. Although up close, silver could be detected in his sand-colored hair, his overall appearance was youthful and stopped just short of genuine elegance. Michael felt rough, even oafish, in his presence.

Nothing in the man's sleek sophistication betrayed a hint of his Irish roots. Just as nothing, Michael thought sourly, gave away the scoundrel's true character. Unless, of course, one considered his eyes.

Small and pale, they seemed almost fixed in place, like cold, pale marbles. Neither blinking nor squinting, they were merciless eyes—empty and unfeeling.

Like the eyes of a snake. . . .

Without warning, a shudder seized Michael, leaving him chilled. Once more, he confronted that reptilian stare. He felt something—a shot of malice, an arrow of enmity—arc between them.

Without the slightest shifting of expressions, Walsh said, "You have a fine son, Captain. He's one of my most dependable boys."

Michael acknowledged the man's words with only a short nod.

"I know you're distraught over what's happened," Walsh went on, ignoring Michael's silence. "You can be sure I'll do all I can to find out who was behind this. Those responsible will pay."

The man was a consummate liar. An actor and a fraud.

A swell of aversion rose up in Michael. He deliberately avoided clenching his fists, for fear he would strike Walsh in his lying face.

Rigid with anger, he met the other's impassive gaze. "Aye," he said tersely, "they will indeed. They will pay."

Then he turned away, anxious beyond reason to make his escape from Walsh and his cold, graceless house.

8

The Dreams of a Child

My Life is like a dream,
I do not know
How it began, nor yet
How it will go.

MONK GIBBON (1896–)

Dublin

Clad in her shift, Finola stood, brushing her hair and smiling to herself. Small One, the black and white cat that had come to her as a stray, sat on the bed, watching her every move with solemn green eyes.

Eyes as green as the Seanchai's . . .

Finola's hand stayed the brush in midair at the thought of the great poet who had become her friend. Her heart skipped in anticipation of the hours ahead. Sandemon would be coming for her soon to take her to Nelson Hall for the evening. Would the *Seanchai* accompany him today? Of late, he was often in the carriage when it arrived for her, despite the effort required for him to get in and out of the wheelchair.

It pleased Finola no end that he would trouble himself so in her behalf. But, then, it did seem the man's kindnesses knew no limit. Always, he went to great effort to prepare a surprise for her visits; sometimes a small but special gift awaited her, occasionally, a significant event—but, always, something meant to delight.

82

Once there had been a mime, hired to entertain. Another time, a sisters' duo who sang most sweetly in different languages! But the most recent surprise had been the best of all. The *Seanchai* himself had written a poem about the princess Finola, daughter of the mythical King Lir, set it to music—and he sang it for her!

The memory of his rich, lulling voice, his large hands on the ancient harp, the soft smile in his eyes as he had sung to her made Finola squeeze her eyes shut and hug her arms to herself just to keep the joy from overflowing. He had been kindness itself to her, this big, gruff man with the tender heart. Befriending her over the months since she had first brought Annie Delaney to his door, Morgan Fitzgerald had made her a welcome guest in his grand home. He deferred to her as if she were a noble lady instead of a homeless mute with no memory—and no name.

Replacing the brush on the vanity, Finola went to don the new blue gown that Lucy had bought for her. Small One mewed, and Finola went to sit beside her on the bed. Immediately, the cat settled herself into Finola's lap with an expectant rumble of a purr.

Finola finished buttoning the bodice of her gown, then began to stroke Small One's velvet fur. Soon her thoughts drifted off to the ways her life had changed since her first meeting with Annie Delaney. She could not have known then that a frightened child's cry in the street would eventually open to her a new world!

God had been so good, leading her to Nelson Hall, to these generous new friends who had taken such an interest in her. At times Finola could almost pretend that at last she had a family— a family of her own!

Gemma and the other women had certainly been kind to her over the years. They had taken her in when she was lost and ill, nursed her back to health, given her clothing and a room of her own—sure, they had indulged her and pampered her as if she were a younger sister, rather than the stranger she was.

Yet, with the *Seanchai* and his household, Finola felt a different kind of belonging. A unity, as if they were each a part of something larger. The *Seanchai* himself, Annie, Sandemon—and now Sister Louisa, the vinegary nun for whom Finola had quickly come to feel affection and great respect—each was a part of God's family. They loved Him and endeavored to serve Him—and that, according to the *Seanchai*, made them family in the truest sense of the word.

One day early in their friendship, Finola had attempted to refuse yet another invitation, feeling shy and uncertain—afraid she might impose. The *Seanchai* had touched her hand in the brief, hesitant way he had, saying, "Finola, you do not presume. You are one of us, not a guest. A member of our family. God has made us one," he'd gone on to explain, including Annie and the sister and the smiling Sandemon with a sweeping gesture of his hand. "We are His children. United, with God . . . and, so, with you."

Still stroking the little cat, Finola closed her eyes and gave a sigh. Of late, she found herself wishing more and more that she had an identity to bring to her new family. A name, a past—at least a remnant of memory of who she was and where she had come from.

As long as she was . . . incomplete . . . she was different from the others. No matter what the *Seanchai* said, she could not be like them. Even Annie, rejected and unwanted, had a name, remembered her beginnings, her yesterdays. Would an unhappy past not be better than no past at all? Yet, no matter how hard she tried to remember, the DARK TIME remained closed to her. A black, empty cavern, barred and unsearchable.

A torrent of emotions warred within her as she sat there thinking. At times like these, when she tried to remember, a strong pall of dread would invariably sweep over her, warning her off, holding her back.

Yet in spite of the sense of foreboding, an urgency was growing deep within Finola—a need to *know*. She yearned to have a name like others, a full, complete name that would identify her as a *person*. And she yearned for a past, not only a present.

She spent most of her days feeling somewhat bewildered, as if she lived suspended between the real world as she knew it and a dream she could not recall. She longed to be whole, not only for herself, but for the others. For her new family. Especially for the *Seanchai*.

She was coming to know him, the great and small things, the subtle and distinct things, that made him so completely, uniquely himself. He seemed to want to know *her* as well, and Finola *wanted* him to know her, wanted it with a desperation she did not understand.

But how *could* he come to know her when she did not know *herself*?

Small One's wee, rough tongue lapped at Finola's wrist once, then again. She glanced down at her little friend. The cat was almost asleep, curled into a warm, trusting ball of contentment. Finola went on stroking her, half envying such innocent peace and tranquility.

Was this what it was like, then, to be a child? To be held close, in a mother's lap, warm and wanted, protected and cherished?

She thought of Annie—wonderful Annie, with her huge zest for life and her bursting love for the *Seanchai*. Annie had been rejected, the *Seanchai* said, mistreated and cast out. An unwanted thing. A stray.

Ah, but no longer. For the *Seanchai* had taken her in, given her a fine home—indeed, he was now working to make Annie his own child, to give her his name and the legal right of inheritance. Annie was a fortunate child indeed!

A thought of the *Seanchai*'s face came unexpectedly, his strong, craggy features and wounded eyes. As she had in the past, Finola wondered why such a generous, kindhearted man had no wife, no children.

His injury was recent, according to Sandemon. But what about *before* the injury? Finola wondered. Had there never been a special woman who shared his life? The wheelchair would surely make no difference to a woman who knew his great heart! Such a man should have a wife—and children, to warm his world, to fill the spacious empty rooms of Nelson Hall with happy laughter and contentment.

Children. A great, aching sorrow swept over Finola. She wished she had the memory of being a child, the recollection of having a father and a mother. Her childhood—however happy or miserable it might have been—seemed forever lost to her. She did not know what it was like to be a child. She could not remember . . . and she feared she never would.

———

That evening, in the marble-tiled entryway of Nelson Hall, Annie Delaney confronted Sandemon with her most recent complaint.

"Is the sister to be taking all her meals with us, then? I thought she was to be an EM-PLOY-EE, not a member of the family."

"The sister," replied Sandemon, "will dine with the scholars more often than not, just as soon as we have others besides the O'Higgins twins. For now, however, she will dine with us."

He ignored her mutter of annoyance, studying her. The child wore a presentable dark wool and an even darker frown. Her unruly black hair had grown long and was forced into thick braids in an attempt to make it appear less unkempt. Despite all efforts, however, a number of stubborn, wiry strands invariably managed to escape their confines and stick out at ridiculous angles about her face. Somehow, it did seem that every endeavor to turn this one into a young lady met with failure.

By now he had grown accustomed to the child's sly digs at Sister Louisa. She seldom missed an opportunity to make known her antagonism to the nun, even to cast some veiled, incredible allusion on the sister's character. The truth was, of course, that the child did not so much dislike Sister Louisa as she resented the discipline that the nun had readily enforced upon Nelson Hall and its inhabitants.

The sister had made quick work of establishing herself as headmistress, if not of the entire estate, certainly of the Academy itself. Even Sandemon found the woman's relentless standards somewhat tiring on occasion. Yet, her unyielding insistence on adherence to the rules would doubtless prove good for the scholars—certainly for young Annie.

Admittedly, he and the *Seanchai* might have been somewhat lax in matters of discipline, perhaps had indulged the child to a fault. She had quickly become precious to them, this fey Belfast street urchin. Abused by her stepfather and rejected by her mother, she had made her way to Dublin in search of Ireland's rebel poet and her childhood hero—Morgan Fitzgerald.

In short order, Annie Delaney had stolen the great man's heart—and Sandemon's as well. So taken with the girl was the *Seanchai* that even now he was preparing to battle the courts for the right to adopt her as his daughter. For his part, Sandemon did try to keep a firm hand, but it took little more than a trembling lip or a gap-toothed smile to melt his heart. Small wonder the child had soon come to recognize her power over them both!

But the precocious mannerisms both he and the *Seanchai* found so endearing did not affect Sister Louisa in the least. The nun had made it clear from the beginning that there would be no exceptions made for Annie Delaney, no matter how much the

Seanchai might dote on her. The child had reacted with predictable rancor, and by now the relationship between the two had become an ongoing conflict of uncommonly clever wits and tenacious wills.

Now, as his gaze scanned the sharp-featured, puckish face, Sandemon managed to suppress a smile. "You should be pleased to know that the *Seanchai* is a most progressive, liberal employer. He encourages his employees—like Sister Louisa and me—to dine at the table with the family."

"Why, it's perfectly fine for *you*, Sand-Man!" the child declared. "You're not simply an employee, after all—you're more like family! Like me. But Sister is only a TEACHER! Isn't that so?"

Still controlling his amusement, Sandemon inclined his head. "Thank you, child, for including me as family," he said dryly. "But we both know the gentry would be horrified to find me eating at your table. Surely Sister Louisa is more deserving of such a liberty than I. Besides, the *Seanchai* finds her interesting and—"

"—*intellectually stimulating*," finished the child with a terrible scowl. "Though I can't think why. They argue a great deal, it seems to me!"

"They do not argue," corrected Sandemon. "They *discuss*."

Annie sniffed. "Well, she assumes too much, I'm thinking. It is obvious to me that the *Seanchai* would much rather talk with *Finola* than a sour old nun, and just see how she monop—monop—"

"Monopolizes," Sandemon offered helpfully.

"Aye, *monopolizes* his time. No doubt that's why he whisked Finola off to the library after dinner, so Sister couldn't interfere." She stopped, pulling her mouth into a pout. "And I don't think *that's* a bit fair either, his taking Finola off alone, so. She came to visit *me* as well as himself!"

Sandemon lifted his eyebrows in rebuke. "That is a spoiled and altogether childish thing to say. The *Seanchai* told me he had something of importance to discuss with Miss Finola, that they would require privacy."

As he might have expected, his words triggered an immediate interest in the child. The petulance in the dark eyes gave way to eager curiosity. "What do you suppose they're talking about, Sand-Man?" She raised herself up and down on the balls of her feet as if unable to contain her energy. "Do you know?"

"No, I do *not* know," he said firmly. "And even if I did, I would not confide it to a curious child."

The scowl returned. "How many times must I remind you that I am *not* a child?"

"Endless times, it would seem, so long as you insist on *behaving* like a child," he replied mildly. "Now, then, *Young Miss,* we will see to the horses while the *Seanchai* and Miss Finola have their talk. Come along."

The black-marble eyes danced with mischief. "Perhaps the *Seanchai* wanted Finola's advice on how to get rid of Sister Louisa," she suggested saucily, breaking into a grin.

"You are a most impudent child," Sandemon said, taking her by the hand as they started for the front door. "I shall applaud the sister's every effort to tame you."

"You'd encourage the nun to break my spirit?" retorted the child with a toss of her braids.

Sandemon lifted both brows in warning. "I would encourage the sister," he said as sternly as he could manage in the face of her gleeful grin, "to break your bad habits. And as quickly as possible, for the sake of us all."

———

Annie knew Sandemon was only pretending to be annoyed with her. The black man was seldom vexed, unless, of course, she'd done something really *sinful.*

While he feigned impatience with her ill feelings for the nun, Annie suspected Sandemon himself found Sister Louisa a bit exasperating at times.

And who would not? Unbelievably, the nun had even managed to terrorize Fergus. She had turned her hand of discipline to the enormous wolfhound, and, to Annie's dismay, the animal seemed to be responding to her. Why, the big, fierce-looking beast turned into a slavering pup each time the nun came within view!

But perhaps it wasn't too late. Fergus still had enough bad habits that he might yet be the nun's undoing. And perhaps Annie could just give the beast a bit of encouragement in the wrong direction. . . .

Annie wondered where the wolfhound had taken himself to. Most often, on those rare times when the *Seanchai* ordered him out of the library, he came round to Annie, bullying her into play-ing toss. This evening, however, he had disappeared shortly after dinner, and Annie had not seen him since.

No doubt he was pouting upstairs in their bedroom, disap-pointed that the *Seanchai* and Finola had not invited him to share their company. Feeling a pang of understanding sympathy for the wolfhound—it seemed nobody wanted *her* company this evening, either—Annie stamped upstairs to join him.

If she had thought to find him in her bedroom, she was mis-taken. Disappointed, she left the room and started down the hall.

A low voice sounded from the nun's room. The door stood slightly ajar, and Annie stopped, curious.

She retreated a bit and hugged the wall with her back, glanc-ing furtively up and down the hall. No one seemed to be about, so she quietly—very quietly—took a step or two toward the door.

A low growl reached her ears—the unmistakable voice of the wolfhound. But what could he be doing in Sister Louisa's room?

Annie's curiosity got the best of her, and she craned her neck to peer in through the crack.

Fergus lay near the hearth, his forepaws down and his tail up in an attitude of play. In his enormous mouth he held something bright red. Was it . . . could it be. . . ?

Annie focused hard on the object of the dog's attention. Yes—it was a stocking.

A red stocking. Sister *Louisa's* stocking? But nuns—even nuns like Sister—did *not* wear red stockings! *Did they?*

Fergus, the noble beast, whipped the thing from side to side in a vicious manner as if determined to kill it once and for all.

Annie's heart raced with a wicked delight. *Good boy, Fergus!* she cheered silently. It was perfect, absolutely perfect. The wolf-hound, her gift to the *Seanchai*, had invaded the private territory of the terrible, TROUBLESOME NUN, and now proceeded to destroy Sister's property. This just might be the final blow that would send the nun packing.

Annie watched for a moment longer, congratulating herself for her ingenuity and the beast for his inventiveness. At last she turned to go, intending to leave Fergus to his destructive duties, when another sound stopped her in her tracks.

It was a laugh—a low, musical, breathless laugh. And it came from behind the half-closed door!

Forgetting that she was spying, Annie edged herself into the doorway. Her gaze whirled from Fergus on the hearth to another figure on the rug a few feet away from him.

There, on the carpet in front of the fire, knelt Sister Louisa—not praying or meditating, but instead hunched nose to nose with the wolfhound, tugging at the other end of the bright red stocking.

The dog was grinning like an eejit. The nun's wimple was askew, and she was laughing like a tinker woman. Dog and nun were hilariously engaged in a game of tug-o-war, the object of which was the long red stocking—the very stocking Annie hoped would be the killing blow to the sister's patience.

As Annie watched, Fergus let go of his end, and Sister Louisa fell backward in a heap. Two feet flew out from under her black habit—one, an actual human foot with five toes attached, the other sheathed with a red stocking identical to the one Fergus had set out to destroy.

Annie stood dumbstruck. She hardly knew which shocked her more—the sight of an actual nun's *foot*, or the forbidden red stocking.

As she watched, the wolfhound bounded over to Sister Louisa and began to lick her face. The nun, laughing helplessly, lay back on the floor and embraced his great gray head.

Still unseen, Annie backed quietly out the doorway and made her way down the hall toward her own room. It would seem that the TROUBLESOME NUN was destined to be at Nelson Hall for a long, long time.

9

Finola's Lament

And the swan, Fianoula, wails o'er the waters of Inisfail,
Chanting her song of destiny.

JOHN TODHUNTER (1839–1916)

In the dim, spacious chapel of Nelson Hall, Morgan sat in his
wheelchair in the aisle, sharing the surprise he had arranged. At
his side sat Finola, then Annie.

Mindful of Finola's impassioned love of music, he had convinced the highly accomplished organist from St. Patrick's Cathedral, along with a renowned Dublin contralto, to offer a private concert at the estate.

The organ in the chapel was reputed to be one of the finest in
Dublin. Installed in the late sixteen hundreds when Nelson Hall
was already half a century old, it had been conscientiously maintained by each generation. Only the oldest cathedrals of Dublin
boasted more elaborate pipes.

The chapel itself was impressive. Built to accommodate at
least one hundred, it was a hushed sanctuary of hand-carved oak,
stone, and marble. Other than adding a tabernacle for the Eu-
charist and a simple wooden crucifix behind the altar, Morgan
had left it exactly as it was. He was determined that it should
serve as an inviting place of worship for scholars of all faiths.

Seeing the dark-haired contralto turn to the small gathering
in the pews, Morgan smiled in anticipation. As he had requested,
the singer now commenced her honeyed-voice rendering of the

91

song he had written some weeks past for Finola.

Finola turned to him, her face radiant with surprise and delight. Morgan gave her hand a gentle squeeze, his heart warming at her obvious pleasure.

Trying to be discreet, he watched her response to the music. He had based the lyrics, loosely, on an ancient Milesian myth— "The Children of Lir," one of the *Three Sorrowful Stories of Erin.*

The sons of King Lir and his only daughter, Finola, were all victims of their jealous stepmother. Convinced that her husband prized his children more than her, Eva, the stepmother, ordered the four youths to Lake Derravaragh, in the middle of Ireland, where she struck them, one by one, with a druid's wand. Immediately, they were changed into beautiful snow-white swans. The full term of their enchantment equalled nine hundred years, to be divided between Lake Derravaragh, the Sea of Moyle, and Inish Glora.

Too late appalled at the horror she had wrought, the stepmother attempted to ease their suffering by leaving them with the power of human speech and the gift of making sweet, plaintive music that would soothe the mind and hearts of all who heard it. According to the myth, the lovely swan, Finola, and her brothers sang their sorrowful laments over the centuries, until Kemoc, a follower of St. Patrick, built a church on Inish Glora. Hearing the sound of Christian bells for the first time, the enchanted swans turned their singing to a hymn of gladness. Kemoc took them under his protection, teaching them about the one true God and His Son, and guiding them to heavenly peace.

Aware of Finola's rapt attention, Morgan continued to hold her hand as they listened. As was always the case, she seemed lost in the music, utterly absorbed and removed from her surroundings. Her wide blue eyes glistened with something akin to ecstasy, and the muscles along the long, slender column of her throat pulsed almost in unison with the singer, as if Finola were trying to sing in her silent voice.

There was much in the girl's delicate beauty and graceful demeanor to hint of the enchanted swan, Morgan thought. Like the lovely creature of the myth, Finola had been robbed of her identity. Her memories, her home—all that once must have been cherished and familiar to her—were now gone. Bereft of family, deprived even of name, she had been cast out, cruelly banished to an existence where strangers made up her only existence.

Sorrow clutched Morgan's heart as he studied the girl beside him. At least the mythical swan had been left with a voice, a voice that could speak and sing and pray. But the lovely Finola's only voice was the silent song that smiled out from the depths of those morning-sky eyes.

———

Later, in the library, Morgan and Finola sat near the hearth, across from each other. The heavy rose-colored drapes had been drawn against the night. A fire snapped and hissed in the vast stone fireplace that covered almost one entire wall of the room. Squat candles burned low, dappling the room and its inhabitants with gold and copper hues.

Morgan was finding it unexpectedly difficult to broach the question he had intended to ask. The girl's beauty was enough to numb even a songbird's tongue. Clad in a simple blue gown that he had not seen before this night, Finola sat staring into the fire as if entranced. Her magnificent hair, falling free almost to her waist, had caught the glow from the fire and now shimmered with the radiance of silvered gold.

As if sensing his gaze, Finola suddenly turned, capturing him with a questioning smile. Not for the first time, Morgan knew a sharp stab of regret and futile longing. While he had faced the truth that he could never be more than a friend or a brother to her, the lovely Finola aroused in him an affection, a yearning he had known for no other woman save Nora Kavanagh.

He had become fiercely protective of the voiceless young beauty, almost obsessed for her safety and well-being. Yet there were times when he had all he could do not to fantasize about losing himself in the incredible blue of those eyes or wonder what it might be like to bury his face in that glorious golden hair.

Shamed by what he sensed to be a forbidden—and futile—desire, he felt his face burn, and he quickly turned away.

The differences between them were simply too great to allow for anything other than friendship, no matter how much he might secretly desire more. For one thing, he was obviously years older than Finola, and although that in itself might not ordinarily be a hindrance, their situation was anything but ordinary.

That she trusted him he did not doubt. Indeed, he suspected

that she bore him at least some small affection. At times, the girl seemed *too* trusting, too vulnerable—almost childlike in her eagerness to please and her ready acceptance of him, and of others as well.

Not surprising, perhaps, given her life. A life with no memory of the past, an existence closely sheltered and protected by the women who had taken her in. Like a delicate flower whose bloom had been forced and nourished in the hotbed, she had known no other environment apart from warmth and tranquility and tender care.

All the more reason to be careful of her feelings, gentle in the handling of their friendship. At another time, in another place—as a whole man—he might have dared to love her, might have even hoped his love would be returned. But now...

Morgan's mouth tightened as he glanced down over his useless legs beneath the lap robe. There would be no other time, no other place. He was bound to this infernal wheelchair, a cripple, with nothing to offer but his friendship and a kind of security, if she would have it. That he was still a man with a man's desire, a man's normal passions, must not be allowed to make a difference.

Their eyes met, and, disconcerted by the warmth and expectancy in her gaze, Morgan looked away. There was no denying that Finola's presence in his life made him despise the cursed wheelchair even more.

———

Finola had sensed the *Seanchai*'s eyes on her. Just as quickly, she sensed his discomfort when she turned to him. In the instant before he looked away, she had encountered something in the deep green of his gaze that caused her heart to swell with a fierce desire to comfort him. She had seen something—some private torment, some secret wound—that sent a wave of dismay shuddering through her.

Shaken, Finola studied the big man in repose. Throughout most of the evening, he had worn the face of youth, the rare, boyish expression that was at once both exuberant and uncertain—and only one of the myriad colors of the man. The sadness so briefly reflected in his gaze was seldom seen and, when caught unawares, quickly concealed.

In the months since the poet had befriended her, Finola had

94

come to realize that he was a man of many facets, none of them simple. He could be both stern and indulgent, somber or buoyant. She had seen the tenderness of his great heart in his treatment of young Annie, had felt the heat of his rage when he thundered at the injustice inflicted upon his friend, Smith O'Brien. Other times, he would bait the good-natured Sandemon with merciless humor; yet for Artegal, the secretive footman, he seemed to bear only a cynic's scorn.

Morgan Fitzgerald was a man with shadows in his heart and sunlight in his soul, and Finola had come to realize that the very essence of the man—what made him real, what made him great—was far too complex for her ever to comprehend completely.

His was the soul of the wounded warrior, the stricken chieftain at odds with his world. Yet he could quickly turn and be caught up in the throes of an ecstasy with life itself.

The hero was fallen, his armor chinked, even rusty in places, yet he wore his mantle of nobility with ease and grace. His eyes might be pained and battle-weary, but there still burned a radiance of spirit, a hard-won faith that shed its glow on everyone about him.

To Finola he had become friend and benefactor, sage and brother. Instinctively, she knew she could trust what he was and accept what he offered without ever once questioning his intent.

He turned back to her now, and Finola smiled at him with fondness. He smiled a little in return, his expression brightening.

"There's something I would ask you, Finola," he said, leaning slightly forward in the wheelchair. Despite the fact that she could hear his voice and understand, he had taken to making signs with his hands even as he spoke. His way of sharing her own means of communication had put Finola at ease early in their friendship; now it endeared him to her still more.

"Don't feel that you need answer me right away," he added. "I know you will need to give it much thought, for it would mean an important change for you."

Puzzled by his apparent uncertainty, Finola continued to smile in encouragement.

Still the *Seanchai* hesitated, his gaze moving to the fire. "I would hope that you might consider . . . moving here, to Nelson Hall," he finally said. "We will be needing trustworthy persons to help with the scholars, and I know I can depend on you. But I would ask you to keep company with Annie as well. She admires you greatly." He turned back to her with a rueful smile. "I had hoped that she and Sister Louisa would become close, but the child insists on antagonizing the nun at every turn. I find myself wondering if they will ever do more than vex each other."

Finola sat staring at him, thinking she must have misunderstood his words.

"I would arrange wages for you, of course," he went on, confusing her still more. "You could choose those responsibilities you most enjoy."

"*I don't . . . understand,*" Finola finally managed to sign, at the same time mouthing the words. *"You're asking me to come and stay here . . . at Nelson Hall?"*

Inexplicably, the *Seanchai* flushed. "Forgive me!" he said, leaning forward still more. "I should have explained! It would be entirely proper and respectable, I assure you. You could have rooms next to Annie's, if you like; and, of course, there will be other women on the premises as well—Sister Louisa, Mrs. Ryan, the day maids."

Still bewildered, Finola frowned. Staring into those brilliant green eyes, she found it difficult to comprehend his meaning.

He reached out as if to touch her hand, then stopped. "I assure you, Finola, I intend only friendship, nothing else. I enjoy your company, of course," he added quickly, "but more than that, I'm concerned—for your safety, your protection. I am thinking such a move might be beneficial to both of us."

When Finola made no reply—for, indeed, her head was spinning at his astounding suggestion—he added, "I don't mean to offend, lass, but the place in which you're living . . . it might not be altogether safe."

At last Finola understood. And, of course, he was right. Hadn't Lucy and the others warned her often enough about the mean streets below, that she must avoid them at all costs?

Rough, brawling men shouted and fought one another in the darkness. Scarcely a night passed that the sounds of scuffling and breaking bottles did not awaken Finola at least once. Sometimes the angry shouts and menacing voices kept her awake long into the night.

She no longer left her rooms after dark, certainly never alone. This had not always been the case. Until some weeks past, she had thought little of coming and going as she pleased. But these days, because of Lucy's incessant warnings and the *Seanchai's* obvious concern, she seldom ventured from the inn, even in daylight.

Wanting to ease his mind, she signed this to him, adding, *"You need not worry. God's angels are always near to protect me."*

His eyes searched hers, and Finola's heart leaped as the tenderness in his gaze reached out and drew her in.

"And no doubt," he said softly, "you are very dear to God and His angels. Yet I ask you to consider my suggestion, all the same. As a favor to me. Will you? Please, Finola?"

Impulsively, Finola reached to squeeze his hand, nodding her assent without really understanding why it should be so important to him.

———

Late that night, a raw wind blew up, sweeping through the Dublin streets like a wintry gale. The two sailors across the street from Healy's Inn were hunched down deep in their coats, standing under the eaves of the tinsmith's shop as they argued.

Mooney, the larger of the two, had no mind to return to the ship before morning. Rice, ever the sorehead when drunk, insisted loudly they should go back. He had the devil of a fire in his gut, he said, and would be ill, right here in the street, if they didn't get away.

They stopped their squawking at the sound of approaching hoofbeats and carriage wheels. As Mooney watched the fancy gilded carriage pull up in front of the inn, he was overcome by a sense of anticipation.

He knew who was inside the coach.

The street was dark and thickly shadowed, but the coachman held a lantern for the occupants of the carriage. Staring hard, Mooney recognized the big black man with the seaman's cap who leaped from the carriage and helped the beauty down.

The drunken Rice muttered and lurched forward. Mooney flung out an arm to force him back into the shadows of the doorway.

No one was paying them any heed, nor likely would. A huddle of lads playing pitch-and-toss, and the few passersby in the street appeared to be either drunk or indifferent to their surroundings.

Rice swore at being manhandled, and Mooney warned him in a hoarse whisper, "Shut up! 'Tis *her*—the beauty they keep shut away upstairs! Keep quiet!"

Pressed tightly against the door of the tin shop, the two watched the black man lead the woman, almost completely concealed by her hooded cloak, around the corner of the house toward the back stairs. As they climbed, the wind renewed its force with a mighty blast, and the hood of the girl's cloak dropped away. For an instant, the golden veil of her hair fell free. Quickly, she reached to tug the hood back over her head.

Mooney swallowed as a blaze of heat roared up inside him. He had seen her come and go more than once from the streets, but she was always well hidden in that cloak.

Ah, but he had seen her *without* the cloak, and she was a beauty! No doubt he was one of the few to have managed more than a stolen look at the one they called the Innocent.

He had seen her close up, he had. Just once. He had seen her face—like that of an angel—and that bedazzling mane of golden hair. And he had seen the fine, delicate, womanly shape of her.

He had been upstairs at Gemma's, just leaving the room of the girl called Poppy, when one of the older, used-up women opened the Innocent's door at the same time. They had slammed it shut at once, but not before Mooney had seen the "beautiful dummy," the subject of so much speculative talk on the docks.

She was naught but a simple child, they said, a child in a woman's body. Could not speak a lick, according to those who had caught forbidden glimpses of her. Talked on her hands.

An Innocent, they would say, tapping the head with a knowing smile. Simpleminded.

But a beauty, all the same.

Aye, and she was that! Mooney had made himself a regular at Gemma's since that night. He would slink about near the outside stairway, or lurk in the upstairs hall. At times, he stood in the shadows across the street, staring at the door, waiting to see the glimmer of lamplight behind the curtain.

He had seen her only twice since. Once, just as tonight, she'd been escorted upstairs by the big, thick-chested black. The other time she'd appeared for a fleeting moment in the open doorway at the top of the stairs, waiting for the cat to come back inside. And both times, Mooney had been there waiting . . . waiting. . . .

His mouth went dry as he watched her hurry inside the room at the top of the steps. Outside, the black man waited, looked around, then went back downstairs.

Mooney dragged his gaze away from the beauty's door just long enough to see the black man climbing into the carriage. The coach pulled away, and he stepped out of the shadows, staring once more at the darkened doorway.

This was his best chance. If he went now, she would likely think he was the black man returning. If she was slow, as was claimed, he'd be in the door before she could stop him. But if he waited too long, he'd miss his chance entirely.

She would never make a sound . . . he could do whatever he wanted to her, and no one would know. . . .

The fire inside him blazed higher. Rice sprawled drunkenly against the wall; he would be out for hours.

Mooney's eyes returned to the door—*her* door. His dark gaze bored into the wood as he imagined the beauty who stood behind it. Then, his heart pounding against his chest, he started across the street.

When the soft rapping on the door came, Finola was just slipping out of her hooded cloak. Small One had wrapped herself around her legs, mewing and begging for attention.

Looking toward the door, Finola wondered what Sandemon had forgotten. With her cloak still loosely draped about her shoulders, she reached down and gently lifted Small One into her arms. Then she crossed the room and turned the key.

Smiling, she opened the door with her free hand. Her mind formed Sandemon's name, then froze. For a moment she could do nothing but stand and stare at the rough-looking man in the doorway. Then terror seized her, and her heart began to hammer wildly with exploding dread.

She felt the frenzied beat of Small One's heart against her own at the sight of the stranger.

Not Sandemon . . . a stranger . . . Instinctively she knew that this stranger was different—sinister, somehow . . . evil.

Too late Finola realized her foolish mistake. She moved to slam the door, but the man wedged one leg in the opening. Shoving Finola hard enough to throw her off-balance, he charged the rest of the way into the room.

The cat in her arms screeched in panic, digging its claws into Finola's shoulder. Ignoring the pain, Finola clung to Small One, holding her close.

The man threw the lock on the door, then turned back. His face wore a hungry, wolfish look, like a wild beast cornering its prey.

Finola opened her mouth to scream. Nothing but a ragged, painful rush of breath came out.

The man's eyes narrowed. "So it's true, then, what they say! You can't talk, not at all!"

His mouth was misshapen, looked to have been sliced from his upper lip to the lower in one corner. The split lip gave his speech a heavy lisp, a whistling quality.

Finola looked wildly around the room for some means of escape. But there was nothing, not even a weapon. She was trapped!

The big man came at her slowly, as if he had all the time in the world. Finola's mouth filled with the hot, vile taste of fear. She knew she was teetering on the edge of total panic. She shrank backward, and he snaked out an arm and jerked her back. Small One yowled, and the man flung the cat away from Finola with one hand, hurling her across the room. The cat landed on her feet and bolted under the bed, howling.

A silent scream tore through Finola. She lunged toward the cat, but the man yanked her arm, holding her. Pain seared through her, choking off her breath, bringing hot tears to her eyes.

He caught both her wrists behind her back, trapping her with one hand as he jerked her around to face him.

In the throes of terror, Finola's mind spun, desperate for a way to escape him. But he held her fast. With his free hand, he tore her cloak from her body and flung it to the floor.

The mutilated mouth twisted in a leer as his eyes raked over her. "Small wonder they keep you locked up!" he said thickly, ogling her like a pirate examining his treasure.

His unnatural, hissing voice sent a chill of revulsion coursing through Finola.

"Aye, you're a looker, no lie! Even better up close, like this. Much better. They keep you reserved special, for the gentry, is that it, then?" he sneered. "Like His Honor what owns the carriage?"

Still holding her hands trapped behind her, he raked the calloused fingers of his free hand over Finola's throat.

"A beauty, and that's the truth." His eyes held a feverish glint of obscene fascination. "But not so innocent after all, I'll warrant. No doubt your rich gentleman has taken care of that long before now."

He gave an ugly laugh. "Or has he? Like as not, you've no inkling of what a real man is like!" He licked his lips. "Aye, I'll bet that's the truth, now, isn't it, lassie?"

At the mention of the *Seanchai*, Finola's fear gave way to total repugnance, and she turned her face away. He jerked her closer, peering at her with narrowed eyes.

"So that's it, is it?" he spat. "Such a fine lady you are, you can't even look at the likes of me?" His fingers dug into her tender wrists, and she gasped in pain. "I've seen that look before, I have. Think you're too good for me—well, I'll teach you a thing or two about who's good enough—"

Her heart slamming like a fury against her chest, Finola lowered her head and pitched forward, trying to wrench free. He yanked her head up with such force her neck snapped. He struck her across the face with the back of his hand, and Finola gagged as a blast of pain exploded in her head.

"Don't you *fight* me, girl!" he hissed. "You'll give me what I want, or I'll beat it out of you!"

A terrible darkness rose up in Finola. A part of her was dimly aware of Small One's cries from beneath the bed. The floor swayed under her, and the room went spinning.

The man pressed his face close to hers. Revulsion washed over her like a wave as she felt the heat of his body, smelled the scent of the sea and unwashed flesh.

And whiskey . . . the sweet, cloying smell of whiskey. . . .

Suddenly, her assailant's face gave way to a different one. As if a mask had dropped over the face of the man holding her captive, Finola now stared into the eyes of another.

Feverish eyes that seared her skin, burned her soul . . . This was a face she knew, a face that was sickeningly, wrenchingly familiar. . . .

Finola squeezed her eyes shut, as if by refusing to look, she could banish from her mind this new face, once so gentle and aglow with affection, suddenly turned vicious and cruel with lust. . . .

Without warning, he had turned on her, shattering her trust, crushing her devotion like filthy rags. He had hurt her, done terrible things to her. . . .

Savage hands tore at her clothing, mauled and bruised her without mercy. Words pummeled her, knifed through her, slashed at her. Words steeped in filth and degradation, they flew through the darkness like vindictive ravens bent on tearing her to pieces.

She was being attacked by two men, one a stranger, one—

Her mind swirled, threatened to shatter. She tried to cry out for the angels.

No angels here . . . nothing but darkness . . . evil darkness. . . .

The brutal hands of her betrayer went on tearing at her flesh, pounding her body. Far away, like the pitiful echo of a grieving child, Small One wailed on.

Finola knew one last moment of raw, annihilating terror. Then the soft shroud of darkness slipped over her, and she fell, tumbling slowly into an empty silence.

————

Her ears laid back and her body flattened against the floor, Finola's cat watched from beneath the bed as the man rose, straightened his clothing, and made for the door. She growled— the low, deep, threatening sound of her ancestors—and with a mighty leap, attached herself to the departing leg, sinking teeth and claws into fabric and flesh.

With a roar and a curse, the man shook her off and made his getaway, slamming the door behind him.

The cat turned from the attack and moved cautiously toward the still form on the floor. She nudged and pawed at the unconscious body; then, getting no response, she sat down forlornly and set up a howling, keening lament for her fallen mistress. . . .

10
Weep for the Innocent

Begging for my living, yet wishing I were dead—
Lonely and bitter are the tears I shed.

LADY WILDE ("Speranza") (1824–1896)

When Lucy first heard the plaintive wailing, she thought it was one of the stray toms in the alley below. She considered getting up and shouting out the window to silence him, but after a moment the cries subsided.

Yawning, she dug at her pillow with a fist, knowing from experience she would not quickly fall back to sleep. Yet she was exhausted. Too many late nights. Too many rough men. She was tired, depleted, and sick at heart.

Sick of herself.

Sometimes, as now, in the hushed hours before daybreak, she would lie awake in the cold darkness of her room, weary to the point of exhaustion, yet sleepless. Sleepless and frightened. Frightened of the future, of what might lie ahead.

Even more frightening was the possibility that *nothing* awaited her, at least nothing she could bear to think about.

Lucy Hoy was close on thirty-five. For a prostitute in Dublin City, thirty-five was old. Old, and worn out. Used up.

Used. More and more, Lucy cringed at the word. For years, she had allowed herself to be used. Like an object. A *thing.* Something worthless and easily discarded. At best, she was an obscene joke, a leer, an object of the sailors' coarse laughter on the docks.

At worst, she was a shame. A disgrace.

She had been little more than a child when she came to her present life. A thousand nights she had wondered what she might have been, what she might have done, had she been born to a decent, God-fearing family who knew how to treat a daughter proper-like. Instead, she'd grown up under the bruising hand of a shiftless, whining father and a drunken mother, neither of whom had possessed the slightest bit of affection for their children.

The parents had begun hiring Lucy and her sisters out to the lechers in Cross-stick Alley before any one of them was twelve. When Lucy was thirteen, they sold her, as if she were naught but a cabbage, to a sulfur-breathed old coffin-maker no decent woman with good eyes would have had.

The old devil had quickly reached his wits' end with Lucy's resentment and resistance. When his every attempt to beat her into submission failed, he tossed her out into the streets. It was mid-winter, and she hadn't a farthing to her name, nor a shawl for her back.

Gemma Malone had taken her in, given her a room and a fancy dress, and made her one of her "girls."

"Things'll be better for you here, lass," Gemma had promised. "Oh, you might have to fend off a frisky sailor in his cups now and then, but Healy and myself will always be near to give you a hand, should one of the lads get too rough. You're a fine, buxom lass—just the sort the sailors are looking for when they make port. Give 'em a smile and don't let on they need a wash, and you'll turn a fair profit for us both, just see if you don't."

Sighing restlessly, Lucy rolled onto her back, deliberately not counting up all the years that had passed since that day. There was no avoiding the truth: Gemma's clients asked for her less and less these days, and Healy was beginning to make noises about her working in the kitchen, where she might at least pay her way.

She wouldn't make spit in wages, of course. But at times, Lucy thought she would welcome the kitchen. Perhaps in time, with enough soap and hot water, she'd be able to wash away at least a bit of her corruption.

She would have drifted off to sleep again had the cat not begun its screeching anew, this time in earnest. Lucy pushed herself up on one arm, listening. The wailing sounded louder now, more insistent, even demanding.

Then it dawned on her with chilling certainty that it wasn't a stray she was hearing at all. It was Small One, Finola's cat.

Odd. The cat never cried, at least not in the middle of the night. The only time it cried was when Finola was gone.

Finola. . . .

For a moment, Lucy lay rigid, unmoving. "Finola?"

Fear made her voice sound tight and strangled in the hush of the bedroom.

There was no answer except for the pleading cry of the cat.

"Finola!" Even as the name exploded from her, Lucy swung herself out of bed and flew from the room.

Her shouts and furious pounding on Finola's door quickly roused Poppy and Sile in the neighboring rooms. Soon they, and others, were milling about in the hallway, crowding around Lucy as, one by one, they also began to call Finola's name.

Silence was the only reply. Struggling not to give in to the tide of terror rising within her, Lucy hurried back to her room and grabbed up the key to Finola's door.

Returning, she fought to get her breath as she turned the key with a trembling hand. She pushed the door open slowly, cautiously, just wide enough to enter.

The only sound in the room was the shallow, ragged breathing of the women who followed her inside . . . and the pathetic cries of the small cat pacing up and down next to Finola's lifeless body.

Poppy reached down and scooped the cat out of the way as Lucy dropped down beside Finola.

She was vaguely aware of small, whimpering sounds close-by, then realized they were coming from her. Pain knifed through her—savage, hacking pain—as she took Finola's limp hand. Only sheer force of will kept her from being sick as her stomach went into spasms.

Her first thought was that Finola was dead. The clear blue eyes were closed, and she was as still as a stone. The glorious fair hair was a limp, tangled mass. And her face . . . *oh, the dear Lord, her face* . . . that lovely, lovely face was a grotesque, swollen mask of angry cuts and bruises. A dried ribbon of blood trailed from one corner of her mouth down the side of her neck. Just below her left cheekbone, an ugly gash trickled fresh blood.

With hands that shook like a palsied old woman's, Lucy pulled Finola's skirts down about her ankles, then reached to straighten the torn bodice of her dress. She steeled herself not to scream when she saw the ugly bruises on the girl's white shoulders and bosom.

Somebody seemed to have remembered from long ago a prayer for the dying and was chanting it in a soft, tear-choked voice. Lucy's throat threatened to burst from a knot of grief, and she wept like a child as she gently put her head to Finola's heart . . . *and heard it beating!*

"She's alive! *Finola's alive!*" The words ripped from Lucy's throat, rousing the other women from grief to action. They moved, circling and murmuring in futile attempts to help.

"Finola . . ." Lucy whispered. "Finola, wake up, love . . . can you hear me? Oh, Finola, what *happened?* Who did this to you?"

But Finola lay unmoving—so still she seemed not to breathe at all.

Lucy couldn't think. Her mind froze on the tragedy before her.

The innocent, golden-haired beauty had been the one pure, untarnished facet of Lucy's life. Like a shining gift, Finola was the one person Lucy had ever dared to love, unreservedly—and the one person who had loved Lucy back, unconditionally.

To see her lying so, beaten and bloodied, as still as death, filled Lucy with a horror, a savage rage that shook her to the very depths of her soul.

Somehow she forced herself not to focus on Finola's pain, not to speculate on what had been done to her. Besides, didn't she know all too well what had been done to their golden girl? Oh, she knew, she did. And God—if He existed—He knew. And He knew what filthy animal had done it! It was God who would have to deal with the beast that had hurt Finola!

What mattered now—*all* that mattered now—was saving Finola. Saving her life.

"Lucy? Shall we go for Doctor Lammercy?"

"No!" The word snapped out with bitter force. Lammercy was half-cracked with one foot in the grave himself. She'd not let him touch their Finola!

"No," she repeated, her gaze not leaving Finola. "Send for the black man. Send for the man from Nelson Hall."

———

"Ye can't be sure the girl was raped!" argued Healy. Visibly shaken as they stood outside Finola's room, awaiting the carriage from Nelson Hall, the innkeeper vented his outrage and fury on Lucy. "Ye'll not be tellin' such a tale!"

Lucy turned on him. She felt an insane urge to ram her fist into his spluttering face; instead, she clenched her hands at her sides. "She was *raped*, I tell you! And beaten near to death as well! We might just as well tell them right off—the surgeon will know as soon as he has a look at her!"

Healy screwed up his mouth in a scowl. Lucy was furious with the man for taking on so. Only the knowledge that he, too, prized Finola enabled her to hold her tongue.

"There's no hiding it, don't you see? We *have* to tell them. It will only go worse for us if we don't."

Healy's expression went from anger to fear. "They say the Fitzgerald treats her like a treasure—like a daughter, even. He'll send the black to kill us all when he finds out what's been done to her! He'll blame *us*, just wait and see!"

Disgusted that the man could fear for his own hide at such a time, Lucy fought to keep from screaming. Yet, the truth was Healy might be right. From all indications, the copper-haired giant in the wheelchair did dote on Finola. And the black man— well, Finola might call him *gentle-hearted*, but from the looks of him, he'd be fierce if provoked.

Still, it was *Finola* who mattered now, and nothing else.

"I won't lie for you, Healy!" Lucy grated out. "They should know the truth right off, to help Finola! Besides," she added dully, "you know as well as I that we should have made her leave here long ago. We could have found her a proper home—a decent place, where this horror would never have happened."

Healy looked at her, then lowered his gaze to the floor. "We did our best for the girl, now didn't we?" he muttered. "We took her in when she had nowhere else to go. We looked after her. We did our best."

Lucy nodded slowly, admitting the sad truth of his words. *Aye, we did that. We took her in. We looked after her. Some of us even loved her. And because we loved her, we kept her here, with us, instead of doing more—instead of doing what might have been best for Finola.*

And for that, perhaps we all deserve to burn. . . .

———

When the black man came downstairs, Lucy was standing at the door holding Small One against her shoulder. He carried Finola in his sturdy arms as easily as if she were a child. Wrapped in a heavy brown blanket, she looked even more ashen and helpless than before.

He stopped when Lucy spoke. "We sent for you," she said tremulously, "because we thought you'd know what to do. We thought it's what Finola would want."

After an instant, he nodded, his eyes searching hers. Where Lucy would have expected condemnation, she encountered only a terrible depth of sadness, a raw grief, obviously controlled at great effort.

Lucy shrank within herself. Somehow she thought it might have been easier had he exploded in rage and damned them all.

"You did well to send word," he said, his voice low. He paused, his eyes going to the limp Finola in his arms. "You are certain no one saw . . . who did this thing?"

Again Lucy sensed his rigid control. Swallowing hard, she forced herself to look him in the eye. "Believe me, man," she choked out, "if I knew, I would kill him myself!" Her voice shook, and her eyes burned with tears.

The black man regarded her with a measuring look. His gaze went to the cat in her arms. "That is Small One?" he asked softly. "The little cat she is so fond of?"

Lucy glanced at the cat, then nodded.

The black man's expression gentled still more. For a moment he stood, studying Lucy as if trying to make a decision. His voice was low, even kind, when he spoke again. "Perhaps you would like to come with us?"

Lucy stared at him. "You'd let me?"

He nodded. "When she wakes, it might be well if you were nearby." He paused. "And the cat . . . bring the cat as well."

Lucy nearly strangled on a sob of gratitude. Unable to answer him, she cuddled Small One close to her heart and ducked her head. The tears spilled over from her eyes as she silently followed them outside to the waiting carriage.

In the library of Nelson Hall, Morgan waited. He sat, rigid and unmoving in the wheelchair, engulfed in agony and a deadly rage. Staring out the window, he was only dimly aware as the dull light of a rainy dawn struggled to rise past the horizon. And for the first time in months, he wished—almost desperately—for a drink. He allowed none of the whiskey at Nelson Hall, and now he knew why. If a bottle had been within his reach, he surely would have used it to dull the searing knife-edge of his pain.

When the word came that Finola had been injured, he had almost lost his grip from shock and fear. Now, waiting for Sandemon to return with her—at the same time waiting for the surgeon to arrive—he grappled with an entire storm of emotions, ranging from an almost debilitating fury to a numbing despair.

And helplessness.

Now, more than ever, he cursed his dead legs. He could not even go with Sandemon to get her, lest his slowness in getting dressed, the time-consuming procedure of getting himself in and out of the carriage, prove too much a delay for Finola.

Instead, he could only sit here, in the infernal chair, a great, useless lump, waiting. Waiting and worrying.

He tried to pray, but his heart was numb, his mind frozen. All he could manage was a whispering chant, a drone for mercy.

God help her . . . God keep her . . . God save her. . . .

He had never—never, in all the agonizing months since the shooting that had paralyzed his legs—felt more useless . . . or less a man . . . than he did at this moment.

He did not know yet what had happened—not exactly. Only that Finola had been hurt, and that it was bad. Why else would they have sent to Nelson Hall for help?

He felt as if he were trapped in a nightmare. He blamed himself, cursed himself, for not acting sooner to get her away from that place. If only he had acted last week . . . yesterday. . . .

Why did I wait? Oh, God . . . why did I wait?

Blind rage and guilt roared through him. A violent trembling seized his entire body. He gripped the arms of the chair until pain shot through his hands and the thunder in his head subsided somewhat.

But his terror for Finola, his guilt and anguish for his own fault, went on raging in his heart like a storm at sea.

11

The Silent Scream

I think the most dread sound,
The most terrible cry to the human ear,
Is not the common lament for the end of life,
But one heart's keen
For the death of Innocence

From the Journal of JOSEPH MAHON, County Mayo (1848)

Throughout the long morning, Nelson Hall lay still as a tomb. Outside, the soft dawn rain had increased to a frigid downpour, weeping through leaden skies that blotted the day's light and drummed away all other sounds.

Within, no voices were raised; indeed, no conversation was made that was not absolutely necessary, and then words were limited to furtive whispers. The maids went about their work in doleful silence. The classrooms were empty; the four scholars who now lived on the premises had been excused to their rooms in the absence of Sister Louisa and the *Seanchai*. Even the great wolf-hound lay silent and mournful outside the chapel doors, as if standing guard over a holy place.

It seemed for all the world as if there had been a death during the night.

And so there had. Under cover of darkness, in the concealing shadows of Evil, Innocence had suffered yet another blow.

———

In her twenty-five years as a nun, Louisa Moore had seen much pain, much ugliness, inflicted by one human being upon another.

She had worked among Dublin's destitute, nursed in hospitals, ministered to the homeless and the dying. During the past months, she had labored to the point of exhaustion among the famine immigrants who flooded the streets and alleys of Dublin with their misery.

Through it all, she had determined not to let the suffering and the tragedy of her fellowman destroy her. Most of the time she managed a precarious balance, keeping a safe step's distance away from the dividing line that separated ministry from madness.

But as she stood by the bed of the young woman called Finola, she knew herself to be in danger of crossing the line. Nothing in her memory had shaken her quite so violently as this.

Louisa believed with all her heart that God's Word was true, and that, just as He promised, He would work good from all things entrusted to Him. Indeed, she had seen that promise fulfilled more times than she could remember.

But standing here as witness to this young girl's tragedy, she could not for the very life of her imagine how even the Lord could turn this kind of disaster to good.

The girl had as yet showed no sign of rallying, although she was anything but lifeless. Every touch of the physician's hand seemed to bring pain; every labored breath was accompanied by a choked sigh or an anguished moan.

Perhaps the Lord in His wisdom had hidden the girl, for now, in a shelter known only to Him. Louisa had seen this before in many victims. They lived, but in another place. A place unknown and unapproachable by those outside the pale.

In God's presence—in His arms, close to His heart—the victim waited until the Lord moved to give safe passage to whichever side of heaven He chose.

It was difficult to imagine how beauty could possibly shine through such stark evidence of evil. Yet, shine it did. Finola's carefully formed, delicate loveliness made the ugly manifestation of man's depravity all the more visible, all the more terrible.

Louisa bent to sponge the girl's forehead with a cool cloth while the surgeon bound her midsection. "The animal spared her nothing!" muttered the physician, more to himself than to Louisa.

"She is broken . . . a broken doll. Broken bones and fractures, her kidneys bruised—" he stopped, overcome, his hands trembling as much as his voice.

He met Louisa's gaze over the girl's still form. She would not have expected to see such agony, such rage, in a man who surely must encounter the very depths of tragedy in his profession. He was still a young man, but Louisa suspected that after this day he would feel much older.

"Will she live?" Louisa asked quietly.

The surgeon looked from her to Finola's bruised face, now swabbed with ointment. "Yes," he said in a voice hoarse with emotion. "I would say that she will live." He looked up. "But tell me this, Sister: Do you think that she will *want* to live?"

Louisa could not drag her eyes away from the girl's poor broken body, her bruised loveliness. "As God enables us," she said softly, "we will do everything we can to be sure she does."

———

Less than an hour later Finola began to fight her way back to consciousness. Watching her struggle, Louisa anguished for the pain the child was obviously enduring. Her own body winced with each difficult breath, every flail of the hand and tortured gasp uttered. The slightest movement seemed torment.

But the most terrible thing of all, indeed the one evidence of Finola's suffering that Louisa found most painful to witness, was the voiceless cry, the futile, tortured rasp of a whisper that the girl gave over and over again throughout her agony.

As she twisted and cringed, her face drawn in a taut rictus of horror, her hands knotted and raised as if in self-defense, Finola repeatedly opened her mouth in a futile attempt to cry out.

Shuddering with the girl's every effort, Louisa thought that silent scream must be the most heartbreaking sound she had ever heard.

———

The ship had put out just past dawn. By now Dublin City was only a stretch of coast, great rocks, and a number of lighthouses.

Mooney took a moment to give it a last look. The wind was numbing, the spray off the ocean laced with ice. He hunched deep inside his jacket and stood, watching.

It would be months before he saw the harbor again. Months of rough seas, hot-tempered sailors, and squalid living. Months of hard work and cold nights. Months of boredom.

He would look her up when he came back. He wouldn't forget her, that was certain. Not for long.

His lips cracked in the semblance of a smile. She'd not be forgetting him either, he would warrant. Not for a minute.

12

Doing Battle With the Enemy

A starless landscape came
'Twixt that scene and my aching sight,
And anon two spires of flame
Arose on my left and right;
And a warrior throng
Were marching along,
Timing their tramp to a battle song,
And I felt my heart from their zeal take fire,
But, ah! my dream fled as that host grew nigher!

THOMAS D'ARCY MCGEE (1825–1868)

Only the nun was allowed to remain in the bedroom where
Finola had been taken. She had been summoned to help Lucy put
Finola to bed, and, no doubt because she was a woman and a nun,
the surgeon had requested that she stay.

Just as quickly, he had ordered Lucy to leave. More than likely
her kind of woman was offensive to the nun—perhaps to the surgeon himself.

Lucy would not have expected anything else. Still, she begged
to stay with Finola, insisting she might be of some help. The
physician, however, remained adamant: only the nun would remain; Lucy would wait outside. With the big black man watching
her and the stricken-faced Fitzgerald looking as if he might spring

from his wheelchair in a raving fury at any moment, Lucy knew it would be foolish to press. It was enough that she had been allowed to come, more than she could have hoped for.

Upon arrival, as she hovered near the bedroom door, she had been surprised when the black man—they called him *Sandemon*—brought a straight chair, indicating it was for her. Bracing the chair with his hands, he said kindly, "You can wait here. No doubt you will want to stay close-by, for you may be needed soon."

Now, nearly two hours later, Lucy sat, still cradling Finola's wee cat in her lap, her eyes filling with tears as she remembered what the black man had said to her. There had been a time when such words might have thrilled her heart. To be *needed*, to be of some value—to *someone*—she could not imagine such a thing. She might have lived long and content on the knowledge that, at least once, she had been important to someone, that her life had counted for more than a few years of emptiness.

But now . . . now, she could only mourn the waste her life had been. Her lack of worth, her uselessness, somehow seemed to make what had happened to Finola just that much more tragic and unthinkable.

What cruel fate had dictated that she, an aging prostitute whose very existence had been squandered on sin, should be spared the pain and degradation of violence—so often the lot of Dublin's whores—while Finola . . . innocent angel . . . endured such a vile, merciless attack?

If the God Finola had so often referred to did in fact exist, where had He been last night? Couldn't He see what had been done to this innocent one who trusted Him . . . loved Him? Didn't He care?

Lucy remembered a street preacher who had once appeared, night after night, on the corner near Healy's place to speak of God. She had stood with Finola at the top of the stairs and listened to the old man talk of God and His Son—called *Jesus*—who was sent to show His father's love to the world.

The preacher said that God was aware of every child in the world, called them by name, knew the hairs on their heads—indeed, had them numbered. He knew the needs of every soul, claimed the preacher: heard the pleas of all the helpless, felt the pain of those who suffered, wept with every broken heart throughout the ages.

Finola had clung to the man's words, believed them, fed on them—claimed them for her memory. And she had tried, with her hand signs and pen and paper, to explain it all to Lucy.

But Lucy had known, although she smiled and pretended to agree, that the preacher's God—*Finola's* God—wasn't accessible to the likes of Lucy Hoy.

Not wanting to disappoint Finola, she had kept her feelings to herself. Obviously, the lass set great store by this God of Love.

But nobody loved the Lucy Hoys of the world, and that was the truth. A thing had to be worth the loving, now, didn't it? Even for Finola's God—the God of Love—a woman like herself would not be worth the effort.

Of course, such a God could easily love Finola. She was goodness itself, pure and gentle—and innocent. Everyone loved Finola. *But where . . . where had Finola's God of Love been last night?*

———

In his room, Sandemon was on his knees, waiting for the Light. It had been a long time—a very long time—since he had met in direct encounter so bold an evil, so deep a darkness.

In his own strength, he might have chosen to ignore the old enemy's presence. He might have cowered, all too aware of his own sin and weakness in the face of the dark one, the one who hated all innocence, all things pure and holy—who hated anything touched by the Light. But, although he felt alone, he had the promise that he was not alone, and so he braced himself to persevere.

Besides, his efforts were not on his own behalf, but for the poor girl downstairs whose life hung suspended by a fragile thread. It was for Finola that he must overcome.

The times were rare when his own dealings with the darkness would surface, dredging up from the deep those hideous memories that could, even after so long a time, still shake his peace and haunt his spirit. More often than not, the door remained firmly closed on that time in his life, before the island priests had done battle for his soul . . . and won.

But now, despite the wall of heavenly fire, the promised hedge of divine protection, he was once more assailed by a savage onslaught of images from the past. Memories, ugly memories, of what he had been, the dark things in which he had played a part, dived at him, attacking him like crazed vultures. He was caught up in a maelstrom of memories—memories of his own wickedness, his corruption, and the tragedy he had inflicted on the lives of others before his deliverance.

He covered his head with one arm as if a veritable host of evil predators would swoop down from the air and fall upon him. Forcing a fist against his mouth, he muffled his cries. As he struggled against what he knew to be an already vanquished foe, he cried out with such vehemence that he drew blood from his hand.

Finally . . . finally . . . he felt the darkness begin to fade, until at last, it was replaced by the Light. The blessed Light now banished the fear, gave route to the enemy, then breathed, like fresh air from heaven, the cleansing reminder of love and new life into Sandemon's spirit.

His body and soul wrung dry, drained from the exertion of this unheralded attack, he lifted his head, and then his hands. Enfolded by the Light, he sent up to the throne not a plea for protection, but a power-filled psalm of high praise.

———

Morgan thought he had known the full force of rage before this day, had been caught up countless times in the whirlwind of anger, to be tossed and battered by storms of blind fury.

But those times had been different, had stopped just short of madness—for then, he had not been helpless, had not been trapped in the cursed wheelchair. Then he had possessed the means to make a difference, to turn his rage outward, into action, instead of inward, on himself—on his weakness, his helplessness, his guilt.

Now, as he sat staring with dull fixation into the fire, it occurred to him that even if he could have freed himself from the wheelchair, there would still be no way to damp the fire that blazed inside him.

He felt as if he might die from the sheer agony of remembering how Finola had looked when Sandemon first carried her inside. So still, so pale and lifeless . . . so broken.

Until today he had not admitted that he loved her. He had called his affection for the girl by many names, rationalized his feelings by labeling them "brotherly" or "protective."

He had used every conceivable excuse—all of them justified—

for *not* admitting his true feelings: first and most obvious, his being a cripple. The vast age difference between them—clearly, more than a decade. The mystery of her past, who she was, where she had come from—he had even tried to reason that she might belong to another man, although her youth and the years spent in isolation at the inn made it highly unlikely.

It was a bitter thing, that it had taken a night of terror, an unthinkable vicious attack to make him face the truth . . . that he loved her. *He loved Finola.*

Unhappily, his newly recognized love served only to add yet another dimension to the helpless rage in which he was already trapped. He did not know which knife now pierced more deeply into his soul: the imagined horror of the attack, the anguish of knowing how she must have suffered, or the guilt born of thinking he might have prevented her agony, might have spared her this grief, if only he had been a whole man.

The man he used to be might have overcome the obstacles— what was age, after all, or a missing past?—and gone in pursuit of her love, ignoring the consequences. The man he used to be might have claimed her affection, secured her promise, made her his bride.

But the man he was now, at this moment, could not even offer her a measure of comfort if . . . *please, God* . . . she managed to survive this nightmare. What possible comfort could he be, what haven could he offer?

What difference could he make?

You could be her friend. . . .

The thought came unbidden, like a whisper from the very recesses of his aching heart.

Aye . . . that much, at least, he could do. He could be Finola's friend.

And how she would need one! What anguish, what horror, lay ahead if she survived?

At the very least, he could give her shelter, the protection of his household. A home. A family.

A faint, slowly dawning glimmer of hope began to rise in him. Hadn't he told her, and not so long ago, that they were all family, united in God? Finola and himself. Annie. Sandemon. Sister Louisa.

If Finola would allow it, they would be her family from this day on.

As for himself . . . he would be anything . . . everything . . . she needed him to be.

He blinked, straightening in the chair. He felt a sudden and urgent need to be with the family. *His* family.

He rang for Artegal. As soon as the pale footman appeared in the doorway, Morgan demanded the whereabouts of Annie and Sandemon.

"The girl—Miss Annie—is in the chapel, I believe, sir. As for *him*"—the footman's mouth thinned in distaste— "he said something about going to his room to . . . to do *battle*."

Morgan managed a ghost of a smile. He might have known that's where Sandemon would be. On his knees.

"Go up and tell him to come to the chapel, please, Artegal. Tell him to come at once if he can."

The footman gave a disapproving sniff and a reluctant nod. "Very well, sir."

"Tell him," Morgan added, ignoring the footman's pinched expression, "that the family will do battle together."

———

Annie Delaney had heard nothing from the Lord. She had prayed and begged, stayed on her knees for more than an hour now—the longest she had ever prayed in her entire life!

But no answer came. Not even a whisper. Not a single word of explanation or assurance.

Annie felt both anger and fear: anger at God's silence and fear that she would dare to be angry with Him. She supposed it was wicked to feel anger toward God, wicked to let go of such thoughts, for they might fly straight to heaven.

But she had kept them to herself as long as she could. She simply could not understand why God had helped her, a child unwanted, even by her own mother, to escape drunken old Tully and fly free to Dublin City, unharmed. Yet Finola, so good and gentle—a true child of God, loved by *everybody*—had been left on her own, unprotected, to be . . . savaged in such a terrible way.

Why? Why had the Lord not rescued *Finola*? Why had He allowed her to be hurt? She might even die. . . .

Annie began to cry harder. She would not think so! She would *not*! Finola would not die . . . *could* not die!

"Please, Lord . . . please, Sir," she managed between sobs, "if someone has to die today—and I confess I don't understand why that should be the case—but if it is, Lord, couldn't you just take somebody bad, somebody wicked—instead of Finola? I know you'd probably like to have her company, her being so pretty and as nice and kind as any angel must be! But we need her down here, don't you see? I'm not asking just for myself, Lord—the *Seanchai* does dote on her so. And he's near out of his wits, he's that frightened!"

The thought of the *Seanchai*, the brokenhearted look on his face when he had explained about Finola, brought on still another fit of weeping. Annie swiped at her eyes with her sleeve, blotting tears that simply would not stop falling.

———

Morgan stopped outside the chapel doors to give the wolf-hound a reassuring pat on the head, then wheeled himself inside.

He stopped when he saw Annie. She was on her knees at the altar. As always, her thick black braids were askew, unable to contain the heavy, stubborn hair that Mrs. Ryan daily attempted to force into place.

Her back was turned to Morgan, but he saw the heaving of her narrow shoulders and knew that she was crying.

His own eyes stung at the sight of her grief, but he remained where he was for the moment. It was a rare thing indeed to see Annie weep. She might pout, often scowled, and could wither a strong man with her smile. But seldom . . . seldom, did Annie weep.

She prided herself on being nearly grown, and on being strong. She hated it when she was caught unawares, being a child.

But now Annie was crying, sobbing at the altar, weeping like a stricken child whose heart was broken. And yet, Morgan saw that, between sobs, the lass was praying.

Praying, no doubt, to her newly found Savior for the life of her newly found friend.

Annie, wee fey Annie of the sturdy heart and stubborn will, did love Finola, and now was grieving—and pleading—at the altar of the Lord.

She did not seem to hear his approach. She made no move to resist as Morgan wheeled himself down the aisle and reached for her. She looked up, scrambling to her feet and into his arms. He settled her securely on his lap and cuddled her head against his shoulder.

He thought his own heart would break as she shuddered in his arms.

"Seanchai . . . oh, Seanchai . . . I don't understand!" was all she could manage between wracking sobs.

Squeezing his eyes shut, Morgan held her small, thin frame close. Murmuring softly in the Irish, he tried to console her. Even as he comforted, he drew a kind of strength from the child, this child he loved as his own.

Annie had suffered the torment of violence, too. She knew all too well the terror, the pain, of being beaten and abused. Perhaps she, better than any one of them, could understand and share the horror of Finola's nightmare.

As her sobs gradually subsided, Annie rubbed at her eyes with the palm of her hand. "Why didn't God rescue Finola, *Seanchai*?" she asked, her voice choked with unshed tears. "Why didn't He help her?"

Like a bitter echo of his own challenge to the Lord, Annie's question hovered between them. "Some things we are not meant to understand, child," Morgan choked out. He went on rocking her in his arms as if she were naught but a babe.

Another tremor seized the narrow shoulders. After a moment, she pulled back just enough to look at him. "I don't understand why I got away, but Finola didn't," she said, her dark eyes searing his skin.

Morgan realized then that she was remembering her drunken stepfather's last assault on her, the attack that had sent her fleeing her home, seeking shelter in the narrow streets of Belfast.

"Why," she said again, "didn't God help Finola escape, instead of allowing her to be so badly hurt?"

Morgan drew a long, shuddering breath. "Ah, Annie, *alannah*, I do not know. I do not know. Your questions are my own, and I have no answers. For some questions, I'm afraid, there simply are no answers."

Behind them, soft footsteps drew near. Two large hands—dark hands and strong—clasped Morgan's shoulder, then the child's.

Sandemon stood behind the wheelchair, touching them, drawing them into a circle of three. "You speak the truth, *Seanchai*," the black man said quietly. His own voice seemed choked with emotion as he went on. "For some questions, there may not always be an answer. But, always . . . always, there is Jesus."

————

Louisa found the three in the chapel. The child was in the *Seanchai*'s lap, the black man at their side, when she entered.

As one, they turned to watch her approach.

"What word?" the *Seanchai* blurted out.

"The surgeon is about to leave. He wants to speak with you."

The big man in the wheelchair made no reply. He seemed to be holding his breath, reluctant to learn whatever the physician might have to tell him.

Finally, he managed a word. "Finola?"

Louisa had not understood before that moment. Morgan Fitzgerald was a man of impressive self-control. Even stricken with grief or dread, he kept his own counsel. His eyes revealed no secrets, though at this instant a glimpse could be gained of a mighty heart under siege. Yet the way he said the girl's name, breathed it, like a prayer, his intent green gaze pleading, told Louisa what she had not recognized before. He loved the broken girl with the silent scream.

She must not let him wait a moment longer. "Finola will live."

He sagged with relief in front of them all. He simply went limp, with the child in his arms. Ducking his great head like a penitent restored, he moved his lips in what was obviously a prayer.

The child's thin little arms went around his neck, and when she murmured something in Irish to him, he nodded.

Sandemon's eyes locked with Louisa's in a question.

She shook her head as if to say she had no answers. They would wait on God.

The *Seanchai* lifted his head. "May I go to her now?"

Instinctively, Louisa again looked to Sandemon before turning back to her employer. "I think not," she said carefully. "Not just yet."

His gaze never left her face. "Why?"

Louisa hesitated. There was nothing, of course, but to tell him the truth. Still, she did her best to soften it. "The girl is just beginning to rouse. She's confused, naturally—disoriented. Her mind is wandering." She paused, drew a steadying breath. "She is still very agitated—very disturbed. Even the sight of the surgeon seems to panic her."

The entire time Louisa was explaining, she could almost feel the sinking of the big man's heart. But she must finish. He must know. "The surgeon isn't quite easy about her mind. He—"

"What *about* her mind?" Her employer's hands gripped the arms of the wheelchair as he sat forward. "What about her mind?" he repeated, his voice deadly quiet.

Louisa cringed inwardly, but she met the pain in his eyes straight on. "No one escapes violence unscathed, Master Fitzgerald. But it has been my experience that the innocent—those who seem to have an essential goodness, a purity to their spirit—most times suffer the most severely."

His gaze never wavered as Louisa went on. "Finola is the victim of a particularly vicious, savage attack. And Finola," she said, her voice faltering for an instant, "is a very gentle, sweet, trusting young woman. She has been plunged into a nightmare, and, as yet, is quite . . . unable to deal with it. At present, she is in a state of hysteria—she is not herself. Dr. Fielding strongly recommends that as long as this is the case, it would be better if you don't try to see her. She won't even allow *him* near her. Obviously, the girl is terrified."

The man looked so stricken that Louisa longed to find some word of comfort to offer. "It may not last very long at all," she added. "I'm sure that the moment she starts feeling . . . better . . . she'll want to see you. It's just that, for now . . ."

She let her words drift off, unfinished. It was obvious the *Seanchai* was no longer listening.

13

The Folly of Delay

Too long a sacrifice
Can make a stone of the heart.

W. B. YEATS (1865–1939)

New York City
Mid-November

When Sara realized that the incident with Tierney was not
going to change Michael's mind about a Christmas wedding, she
hardly knew whether to feel disturbed or relieved.

She didn't *want* to delay the wedding. The very thought cast
a pall of gloom over her days, made her heartsick. Yet given the
seriousness of Tierney's injuries—and his unrelenting opposition
to the marriage—she could only believe that to push ahead with
their plans might serve to increase the boy's antagonism.

Even now, a week after Tierney's beating, she continued to
argue that perhaps they should postpone their plans. Yet every
time she broached the subject, Michael remained adamant in his
refusal even to consider a delay.

This evening he had stopped by after dinner with the news
that he'd be taking Tierney home on Friday. As they stood talking
in front of the low-burning fire in the parlor, he pulled Sara to
him, smiling a little. "The doctor says Tierney should be entirely
recovered before the holidays. So you see, there's no need for any
further talk of delaying the wedding."

Sara allowed herself to be held for a moment. "You're sure

he's strong enough to handle the ferry ride? It's been only a few days, after all."

Michael nodded distractedly. "He's on the mend, right enough. He's been wanting to get out of Walsh's house since the first day, of course, but the doctor wouldn't give his approval until now."

Neither the note of cheerfulness in his tone nor the reassurance of his strong embrace helped to ease Sara's nagging doubts. She was convinced that Tierney would resent her all the more for intruding upon his relationship with his father at such a crucial time.

She confided these concerns to Michael, adding, "I can't help but wonder if we wouldn't be wise to wait."

Michael clasped her firmly by the forearms and pulled away just enough so that he could study her face. "Sara," he said, his impatience not quite concealed, "you *know* that my relationship with Tierney is already strained to the breaking point! More and more we are like two strangers."

The pain in his eyes belied the hard edge to his tone. Sara tried to interrupt, but he shook his head and went on. "The boy has virtually shut me out of his life. He makes no secret of the fact that he resents me, wants no part of what he calls 'my kind of life.' So tell me, then, Sara, what, exactly, do you think we could accomplish by delaying our marriage?"

Sara drew in a long, shaky breath. "I just don't want to make things any worse than they already are," she said softly. "Tierney is your *son*, Michael!"

His expression of pain gave way to a smoldering anger. "And you will be my *wife*! Even my son will not rob me of that!"

His hands tightened with such force that Sara winced. Immediately, he gentled his touch. "I'm sorry, Sara! I'm sorry," he said again, his features softening to a look of remorse. "But don't you see, *asthore*, there is nothing you can do—nothing *we* can do! If Tierney is bent on turning away from me, and from everything that matters to me, there will be no stopping him."

The hurt in his eyes made Sara want to weep. "Oh, Michael, I'm *sorry*! I hate it that Tierney dislikes me so much, but I could bear *that*! What I *can't* bear is the thought that I might come between you and your son."

Again his hands tightened on her. "Sara, listen to me: God knows I'd do almost anything to change things between me and

Tierney. But one thing I will *not* do: I will not give you up for his foolishness! I will not lose you—not even for my son!"

The intensity of his love hit Sara like a blow. If she had ever before this moment doubted the depth of Michael's feeling for her, she knew she never would again.

He gathered her into his arms, holding her so tightly she could scarcely breathe. Sara felt as if she would melt into his strength, be absorbed by the exquisite tenderness in his eyes as he lifted her face to his and kissed her.

"Christmas," he whispered. "You will be mine at Christmas. You promised me."

Unable to do more than nod her agreement, Sara wrapped her arms tightly around him, pressing her face against his shoulder. Clinging to him, she silently prayed . . . again . . . that they were doing the right thing.

———

The next day, a midmorning summons to her grandmother's house caused Sara to turn her attention, at least temporarily, from the difficulties between Michael and his son to her own family.

Robert, the elderly driver who had been in Grandy Clare's employ ever since Sara could remember, came for her just before eleven. Since it was only a short walk to the rambling Gothic mansion on Thirty-fourth Street, Sara was somewhat alarmed to see the carriage pull up.

Her grandmother's recovery from a light stroke the past summer had been slow and not altogether complete. The fact that she still insisted on living alone, with only the aging Robert and a small staff of servants—most of whom were as old as Grandy—was a constant source of concern for the entire family.

Robert, however, relieved Sara's mind by assuring her that her grandmother was not ill. "Nothing like that, Miss Sara. She said I should tell you right away that she's not feeling poorly, just lonesome for your company. It looks like rain, she said, and I should bring the carriage for you."

As Robert helped her from the carriage, Sara was glad for her grandmother's thoughtfulness. The air had turned bitterly cold overnight, and the first drops of a frigid rain were, indeed, beginning to fall.

Her grandmother was waiting in the tearoom upstairs, Sara's favorite room of the house. The lace curtains had been pulled back to allow entrance to as much light as possible. Grandy Clare, small and erect, sat by the window at a lacquered desk.

As soon as she saw Sara, she replaced her pen and extended her hands. "Ah! You're just what's needed to brighten this dismal morning! Come in, dear—come in! Come, sit close to me."

Sara bent to kiss her grandmother's scented cheek and squeezed her hands—thin hands, dry and not as strong as they had once been. Sara noted a slight trembling as she clasped them.

Pulling up a rose brocade chair next to the desk, Sara smiled at her. "You're certainly about your correspondence early this morning, Grandy. You're not writing another letter to the *Tribune*, are you?"

With an indignant sniff, her grandmother reared back in her chair. "I'd not waste the ink!"

"Why, Grandy! I thought you *liked* Mr. Greeley."

"Oh, Horace is all right, I suppose." Her grandmother gave a small shrug of her shoulders. "If you don't mind the fact that he's pompous, dogmatic, and altogether too emotional. Horace hasn't yet learned to line up his ducks before he starts shooting."

"But he *does* take a stand," Sara reminded her, laughing. "He's sympathetic to the Irish, remember." The colorful editor of the *Tribune* had made a personal contribution to assist Ireland and also printed an appeal for public donations. "And he's virulently opposed to slavery."

"And women's suffrage," Grandy Clare pointed out dryly. "If Horace would simply learn to control his temper, he'd sound a great deal more like a crusader and less a fool. At any rate, I'll not bother to write him again. Even though we're friends, he quite obviously thinks me brainless because I'm female. No, what I'm doing this morning is writing out some instructions for Robert and the other servants, just to keep on hand. Things were a shambles when I came home from the hospital; I mean to make certain it doesn't happen again."

Alarmed, Sara leaned forward to clasp her grandmother's frail wrist. "Grandy! Robert said you were well, but you're *not*, are you?"

"I'm *quite* well," her grandmother countered, her eyes snapping. The small, oval chin—the same chin as Sara's—shot up. "I am, however, eighty-three years old. I have had one stroke and two rather serious bouts with pneumonia. It seems only good sense to take precautions. Good heavens," she went on briskly, "the last time I had to lie in, nobody could seem to find *anything.* Why, the servants didn't even get their wages on time!"

Sara couldn't suppress a smile. Her grandmother's ruthless household organization was a family joke. "We've told you for years you shouldn't be so efficient, Grandy. Now you see what happens when you're indisposed."

"Indeed I do, and that's why I don't intend to let it happen again. Such an uproar!" Pushing back from the desk, she turned around to face Sara.

Again, Sara felt a stab of concern at her grandmother's appearance. The silver hair, still remarkably thick, was neatly tucked into its customary knot at the nape of her neck. A hint of pink dusted the frail cheeks, but even the rouge and soft rose of her gown couldn't quite disguise the ashen pallor of her skin. The truth was that this particular morning, Grandy Clare looked every day of her eighty-three years.

Sara loved her small, frail grandmother deeply. When Sara's mother died, Grandy Clare had come to stay with them for several months. During that time of loss and bewilderment, the frightened five-year-old Sara had forged a bond of love with her grandmother, a bond that had only grown stronger through the years. They were more than family; they were friends. To Sara, life without Grandy Clare was inconceivable.

"I don't want to talk about me," her grandmother said firmly. "I want to talk about *you.* And your young man. How *is* Michael, by the way?"

The faint twinkle that usually danced in her eyes returned and Sara responded with a smile of her own. "He's just fine, Grandy. Father *did* tell you about Michael's appointment to the new subcommission?"

Her grandmother nodded, smiling. "You must be very pleased. And I'm sure Michael will be a real asset. Perhaps he'll light a fire under some of those stuffed-shirt do-gooders." She paused. "I don't mean your father, of course. Lewis is a fine man, if a bit hardheaded at times."

She studied Sara for a moment. "You're still planning a Christmas wedding, I take it? A private ceremony?"

Sara nodded, but even her slight hesitation seemed to trigger Grandy Clare's suspicions. "Sara? There's nothing wrong between you and Michael, surely?"

"No—oh no! Of course not!"

"Good! You know, for a time, I was afraid the two of you might allow the boy's injuries to change your plans. I'm glad to see you haven't."

Sara looked at her. "Then you don't think we're wrong to go ahead with the marriage?"

"Wrong?" Grandy Clare lifted an eyebrow. "Certainly not! Your handsome Irishman is quite wonderful! I say, marry him, and Godspeed!" She stopped, her sharp gaze probing Sara's. After a moment she frowned and leaned forward on the chair. "You *are* thinking of delaying the wedding, aren't you? Why, Sara? Because of the boy?"

She shook her head. "No," she said uncertainly. "I mean, I *was* . . . but not now. Michael is so determined . . . he won't hear of our postponing things—"

"Good for him! It would be altogether foolish to delay! I'm glad Michael is a strong man. Decisive. That's what you need, you know. Your father and I saw that years ago. Only a man as strong-willed as Michael could live with you."

Sara managed only the feeblest of smiles. Still, her grandmother's confidence gave her a boost. Grandy Clare didn't lend her approval lightly. If she saw no harm in going on with the wedding, then surely it was the right thing to do.

Her grandmother moved to press her fingers over Sara's hand. "It will all work out, Sara. You'll see. God has a way of *making* things work when you follow His leading. Sometimes you can only do what you think is right, what your heart tells you is best. Michael is God's choice for you. You just concentrate on being a good wife to him—God will take care of the rest, in His own way."

She straightened in her chair and released Sara's hand. "As a matter of fact, that's one reason I sent for you, to discuss your wedding plans. Or, more to the point, your plans for *after* the wedding." She paused, lifting a hand to the ivory brooch at her throat. "Where have you decided to live after the wedding?"

With her grandmother's question came the reminder of still another problem. "Actually," Sara said, giving a long sigh, "we haven't quite worked that out yet."

Again her grandmother lifted an inquiring eyebrow.

A familiar knot of tension rose in Sara's throat. She and Michael had been over this same question countless times. "There's Michael's flat, of course," she said weakly.

"But with those two boys underfoot—you said the apartment is small," her grandmother pointed out.

Sara nodded. "It is. But Daniel will be moving in with Nora and Evan soon. Nora's eager to have him at home again, and he's agreed."

"Still . . . there's Michael's son."

"I could manage. It's *Michael* who's being difficult about where we live," Sara said, frowning. "He has this foolish notion that the flat isn't . . . good enough for me, that I wouldn't be happy there after—"

"After growing up on Fifth Avenue?" her grandmother prompted gently.

Sara got to her feet. "But he's wrong, Grandy! He *is*! I could be happy *anywhere*, so long as Michael is there! But I can't convince *him* of that!"

"It would be awkward, Sara," her grandmother said, reaching for Sara's hand. "With the boy being nearly a man, and this the second marriage for his father—"

"Marriage to a woman Tierney detests," Sara finished miserably, feeling once again a painful clenching of her heart at the thought of the boy's resentment.

Her grandmother squeezed her hand.

"Father offered us rooms at home, of course."

"But Michael wouldn't hear of it."

Sara shook her head. "No. Michael's very proud, you know. There are the brownstones on Forty-ninth Street—one is empty, and Father says we could move right in. But Michael isn't keen on that either. What he's thinking of is renting a small house for a time if we can find one we can afford on his salary."

"Will the boy live with you at all, do you think?" her grandmother asked.

Again Sara shook her head miserably. "Tierney insists he won't live with us for a day! Oh, Grandy—I don't know what we're going to do, I really don't!"

Only with her grandmother did Sara feel free enough to let out her pent-up frustration. "It's all so difficult! Michael refuses to accept help from Father, yet I don't see how we'll manage anything but the flat otherwise. Policemen are paid such pathetically low wages—even captains."

Grandy Clare motioned for Sara to sit down. Neither spoke for a long time, and when her grandmother finally broke the silence, she seemed to choose her words with great care. "How do you think Michael would feel," she asked slowly, "about living here?"

"*Here?*" Sara repeated, sinking down onto the chair. "You mean here, with you?"

Her grandmother folded her hands in her lap and sighed. "This house is ridiculously large, Sara. Quite too large and too drafty for an old lady alone. Why, I seldom venture any farther than the dining room or the parlor these days. It's all a foolish waste, so much house for just me. Besides . . ." Her voice faltered, but only for an instant. Straightening her shoulders and lifting her chin, she went on. "Besides, lately I find myself feeling . . . dissatisfied with living alone. Quite frankly, I'd like nothing better than to have some *people* in my house again! Some noise and bother! It's so insufferably—*quiet!*"

Astonished, Sara sat staring at the older woman. Was her grandmother *lonely*? She had never given the possibility a thought. "Why, Grandy, it never occurred to me—"

"Now don't misunderstand what I'm saying!" The firm little chin lifted still more. "I still like my solitude—a measure of it. And I'm certainly not helpless. Not yet. But this house needs some *life*!" She gave a sly smile. "Perhaps the noise of children again. And," she hurried to add before Sara could interrupt, "it also needs far more care and supervision than I can manage these days. I wouldn't be doing you any favors, you know. It would mean a great deal of work on your part. But I'd see that you and Michael have all the privacy you need. We'd only keep company when you want. I wouldn't interfere."

"Oh, Grandy! You could never interfere!" It struck Sara for the first time how very difficult this must be for her grandmother. She was asking for help, admitting her need, her loneliness—she, who had been the rock of the family for all these years. Even Father stood in awe of Grandy Clare's strength.

Sara reached to grip both her grandmother's hands. "I'd love being here with you, really I would."

"Yes, but it wouldn't be just *you*," her grandmother cautioned. "I wouldn't for a moment try to convince Michael of something against his will."

She was right, of course. Still, it occurred to Sara that if Michael understood Grandy's need, he might not be entirely resistant to the idea. It was accepting something for nothing that seemed so repugnant to him.

For the first time in weeks Sara began to think there might be an answer to at least *one* of their problems. No matter how often she reassured Michael, she found it almost impossible to conceive of living in the small, cramped flat with the belligerent Tierney so near at hand. Privacy would be impossible, and there would be no getting away from Tierney's hostility. Yet she had grave doubts they'd be able to afford anything better.

Whether Grandy Clare realized it or not, she would be giving more, much more, to such an arrangement than she would receive. Overwhelmed with gratitude and excitement, Sara gave her grandmother a quick smile. "You needn't worry about convincing Michael to do something against his will. I doubt *anyone* could manage that."

But if anyone can win him over, Sara thought, *it's Grandy Clare.* The two of them had hit it off splendidly right from the start. Michael made no secret of the fact that he thought Sara's grandmother "a grand lady—a delight." If he were ever going to compromise his pride for anyone, he might just do it for Grandy Clare.

"Michael's son would, of course, be welcome here," her grandmother went on. "But if he refuses to come with you, perhaps Michael could afford to keep the flat, at least for a time, and let the boy stay there on his own." She gave a thoughtful nod, then went on in her brisk, no-nonsense manner. "Let's do this: you and Michael come to dinner one evening this week. We'll talk about things together, openly. Perhaps if Michael understands that I'm not attempting to *give* you something, but instead asking *you* to help *me,* he'll take more kindly to the idea."

Sara nodded eagerly. She couldn't for the life of her imagine anyone—even Michael—successfully resisting Grandy Clare. Even Father, who could be every bit as difficult and stubborn as Michael in his own way, invariably capitulated to Grandmother Platt's considerable charm.

Hope rose slowly in her like a distant beacon. Perhaps things *would* be all right, after all. Sara got up and wrapped her grand-mother in a hug.

"You always could make things right with my world, Grandy! Somehow, I think you just did it again!"

Her grandmother patted her hand, then clung to it. "I'm afraid there's one thing I *can't* do for you, my dear. It's something only you can do—something you *must* do."

Still smiling, Sara gave her an inquisitive look. "What, Grandy?"

"I believe you should pay Michael's son a visit, either now or when he comes home. The two of you need to face each other alone."

Sara's immediate response was denial. "I *couldn't*! He's still in bed, he was badly hurt—"

"I understood that he was doing very well, that he's recovering nicely."

"Yes, but he's still—oh, Grandy, I don't think that's a good idea at all! Tierney is so . . . hostile toward me! And besides, I'm not at all sure how Michael would feel about it."

Her grandmother caught her hand, and Sara was surprised by the strength of the thin fingers. "Have you and Michael's son ever actually *talked* to each other? Alone?"

"No, but—"

"I've always found it best to confront what's unpleasant, not avoid it. Even if the boy won't budge, you need to make the effort, don't you think? It seems to me that you've both danced around your differences quite long enough. Evasion is not the answer, Sara. Avoiding the issue won't make it go away."

Apprehension swelled to a strangling knot inside Sara's throat. Still clinging to her grandmother's hand, she sat, thinking. Grandy Clare's wisdom had never failed her. She had always known the right thing to do, and had never been slow to make her opinion known. She had taught Sara not to avoid the difficult, the unpleasant, in life, but to meet it head on. Indeed, even Father often attributed what he called Sara's "boldness" to her grand-mother's influence.

But this? Could she go through with it? What could she possibly say to Tierney that wouldn't make things worse? Would he even *see* her? And Michael—how would he feel about it?

As she stood there, unable to meet her grandmother's piercing gaze, Sara's mind played through any number of reasons why *this* time she could not heed Grandy Clare's advice. Yet even as she resisted, something deep inside her seemed to turn and acknowledge the fact that her grandmother was right.

And she knew then that, no matter how difficult she found the idea, she would go. God help her, she would go and confront Michael's son.

14

Caught in the Net of Love

You gave me the key of your heart, my love;
Then why do you make me knock?

JOHN BOYLE O'REILLY (1844–1890)

Sara had no idea what to expect upon reaching the Walsh estate. She had met Alice Walsh once, more than a year ago, at a city-wide mission bazaar, but in truth she scarcely remembered her, beyond a dim, elusive image of a plain woman with a shy smile.

She was uncommonly nervous about being here, and it wasn't only apprehension about how she might be received. She was, in fact, about to enter the home of a man reputed to be one of the most ruthless, unscrupulous criminals in the city—a man Michael had resolved to ruin. That realization alone made her feel as if she were somehow trapped in a dream episode. Nothing seemed quite real; yet in some vague, inexplicable way, she felt threatened.

She put her hand to the brass knocker of the front door and hesitated, her heart pounding. Surely she had been altogether foolish in coming here. Why on earth had she ever let Grandy Clare convince her it was the right thing to do?

Even as she was ushered inside by a pinch-faced maid, Sara was seized by an irrational urgency to turn and run. More than likely, Tierney would not even see her. And even if he *did*, why would she expect anything but more of the same cold contempt he habitually turned on her?

When Alice Walsh bustled into the spacious entryway from an adjoining room, Sara's first thought was that she'd been mistaken in her memory of the woman. She wasn't really plain at all. Short and plump, she was actually rather sweet-faced with a pleasant smile and wide, shining blue eyes that held a look of timid uncertainty.

"Miss Farmington? How nice of you to come and visit Tierney! He'll be so pleased."

He'll be livid, Sara thought with a tight smile, but said nothing.

"Would you like tea before you go up? It will only take a moment."

Alice Walsh seemed so eager to accommodate that Sara felt almost guilty for refusing. "That's very kind of you, but I'm afraid I can't stay. I just wanted to say hello to Tierney and talk with him briefly."

The woman actually looked disappointed. As she followed her up the sprawling stairway, Sara found herself wondering about Alice Walsh's life. Somehow she sensed the woman was lonely. If she was as decent as she seemed—and she remembered that Michael, too, had been puzzled by the contrast between Walsh and his wife—how could she bear being married to a man like Patrick Walsh?

But, then, many would question her own wisdom in marrying Michael, she was sure, although for entirely different reasons. It wasn't for her to approve or disapprove of the choice Alice Walsh had made.

Still, she could not help but wonder how a woman could love a man if he truly possessed, as Michael claimed, *"no more conscience than a snake."* Worse yet was the possibility that Walsh had deluded his wife, that perhaps Alice Walsh was indeed a good, decent woman who simply lived with a man she did not know.

At the top of the stairs, Sara paused, shivering. When she had first entered the house, she thought the temperature unduly warm. Now, she felt chilled, as though she had walked inside a dank underground cellar untouched by the light or warmth of the sun.

———

After checking to make sure Tierney was awake, Alice Walsh left him and Sara alone, stopping only long enough to remind

Sara again that, should she change her mind, there would be tea downstairs in the parlor.

Sara could hardly believe that the young man lying in Patrick Walsh's guest-room bed was the same handsome, slightly arrogant Tierney Burke who had so vehemently opposed her marriage to his father. His skin was an ashen gray, his left cheek still swollen, the bruises turned to an ugly purplish-green. The cut in his lip, half-healed, contorted his mouth into a perpetual sneer.

But the worst by far was his eye. From the center of his left eyebrow, at an angle sloping toward the outer corner of his eye, ran a deep, angry gash held together by a dozen stitches. It was a miracle, Sara realized, that Tierney hadn't lost the eye altogether. Another half inch, and . . .

Sara forced herself not to consider the possibilities of what might have happened. He was alive; he *hadn't* lost the eye, and although he would undoubtedly have a noticeable scar as a permanent reminder of the attack, it could have been worse—much worse.

Tierney's surprise at seeing her was obvious. He sat up in bed, arranging the pillows to support his back. For a moment—only a moment—the boy's usual air of defiant scorn seemed to slip. By the time Sara approached the bed, however, the cloak of cold, hard cynicism in which he normally wrapped himself was securely back in place.

Bracing herself against his antagonism, Sara managed to force some warmth into her smile and her voice. "Hello, Tierney. I thought you might like some company by now."

It was like watching a fort under siege. Gates slammed shut, bolts thudded into place, and weapons were raised to the ready. He made no reply, simply gave her a flinty, waiting look from those piercing blue eyes. The swollen gash on his lip enhanced the menacing expression.

Determined to ignore his rudeness, Sara stepped slightly closer to the bed. "I've brought you the *Tribune*," she said, handing him the newspaper. "Your father said you enjoy the papers."

His gaze flicked from her face to the newspaper, and Sara thought for a moment he was actually going to refuse it. Finally, though, he reached for the paper, muttering a grudging, "Thank you."

He's only a boy, Sara reminded herself, determined he would not get the best of her. *He's Michael's son.*

Once he had been a boy, a little boy who lost his mother. *Had he been frightened?* she wondered. *Had Tierney ever been a frightened little boy instead of the erratic, complicated youth of today?*

Trying for a cheerful tone of voice, Sara said, "Your father told me you'll be going home on Friday. I'm sure you're looking forward to it."

He nodded. A curt nod, followed by a low rumble of acknowledgment.

"Yes, of course," Sara said lamely. "You're feeling much stronger, he tells me."

The fortress held. "Aye."

She would not be cowed by a boy. She would *not*. "Tierney—" She tried to swallow, found her throat dry and tight. "Tierney, I had hoped we could talk."

His gaze never wavered. "Why did you come here?" he asked, his words glazed with ice.

His bluntness unnerved Sara. She deliberately delayed her reply, studying him, the straight dark hair, the terrible scar over his eye, the blade-sharp cheekbones, a beard already as heavy and dark as his father's. She sensed his anger, smarted from his undisguised contempt.

Suddenly she realized something else, something both she and Michael had missed: Tierney was no longer a boy. He was a man. A young man, perhaps too soon grown—but a man, all the same. Because Michael still thought of him as a boy, still referred to him as a boy, Sara, too, had fallen into the same error.

But this lean-faced, angry young man had left the innocence of childhood far behind. It was an unsettling realization, for Sara had presumed all along that, in time, she could win over a *boy*. With enough affection, enough attention and care, she had told herself, he would come around. He would accept her, and thereby, accept her marriage to his father. They would eventually be a family.

It wasn't going to be that easy. . . .

Something in the disturbing blue eyes, the hard mouth, the tight set of his jaw served notice that she was up against more than what might have been an understandable antagonism and resentment of her intrusion. She suddenly knew herself to be pitted against an adult intelligence—a *formidable* intelligence, she

139

suspected—and the highly volatile temperament of a troubled, complex young man.

Shaken, Sara clenched her hands at her sides, struggling all the while to keep her smile in place. "Tierney, I really want us to be friends. I thought it might help if we could somehow . . . clear the air between us. Perhaps get to know each other a little better."

Every angle of his face was taut, his eyes guarded, openly hostile. He reminded Sara of a drawn bowstring with an arrow ready to fire. "I think I know you well enough," he said, his voice dripping with scorn.

Anger flared in Sara. She had all she could do not to rail back at him, to go on the offensive. Instead, she met his contempt with a level look and said evenly, "I know that's what you *think*. But, in fact, you don't know me at all. I'm suggesting that, for your father's sake, you at least be fair enough to give me a chance."

His unpleasant, freezing gaze raked her face. "What do you care," he said slowly, "whether I *know* you or not? You've got what you set your cap for. I understand the wedding is to be a Christmas event."

Sara gave a stiff nod. "Your father told you. Did he explain that it will be just family and friends—a small service at home?"

His mouth twitched, then cracked to a nasty smile. "At *home*? That would be the mansion on Fifth Avenue, I expect?"

Clinging to a remnant of her self-control, Sara said, "In the chapel, yes. You . . . you *will* be there, for your father?"

Something flickered in his eyes, then ebbed. "Not bloody likely," he said in a low, hard voice.

"Tierney!" Shocked by the profanity, Sara fought against the hot tears flooding her eyes. That he would dare to wound Michael by deliberately staying away from the wedding was inconceivable!

"You wouldn't do that to your father," she said, blinking furiously to blot the tears before he saw them. "Surely you wouldn't hurt him that way. Don't you know how much you mean to him?"

He glared at her in insolent silence. For a long time they remained that way, as if engaged in a duel of wills. Frozen between indignation and disbelief that he would actually behave in such a crude, hateful manner, Sara felt a wild urge to lash out at him, to loose an entire stream of invective just to see if she could pierce his control.

Just as quickly, she remembered that she had come to make things better, not worse. "Why..." Her voice faltered, and she hesitated, then went on. "Why, exactly, do you dislike me so much? If you question my feelings toward your father—"

He laughed, an ugly, harsh sound. "Oh, I don't question your *feelings*, Miss Sara," he shot back in a mocking tone of voice. "Not for a minute."

She stiffened. "And what, exactly, is that supposed to mean?"

He shrugged, a gesture of indifference.

Sara knew she was rushing headlong into treacherous water, that she was dangerously close to losing what was left of her composure. But something urged her on, forced her to ignore any sense of caution. "You don't understand why your father wants to marry me—is that it?"

Tierney shrugged again, a gesture of indifference. When he lifted his eyes to hers, they held a look of such transparent scorn that Sara felt as if he had struck her.

"No, that's *not* it!" he drawled with an ugly sneer. "Only a fool could fail to see why he's marrying you."

His scathing look held a world of innuendo. Rage warred with despair in Sara. For a moment she thought she would strangle on the torrent of fury and pain washing over her. "How *dare* you!" she burst out, her voice trembling as violently as the rest of her body. "How dare you insult your father in such a way! You *know* he would never play false with a woman, not for all the money in the world!"

Sara stepped closer to the bed, her pain and anger out of control. "You know the kind of man your father is! How can you possibly lie there and pretend you don't?"

He reared toward her, his mouth open to counter her blast of anger. Sara flinched, but refused to back down. The blood roared in her ears, her voice shook, but she went on. "I came here because I'd hoped to convince you that I can make your father happy. I thought if we could talk, alone, you might see that you have no reason at all to resent me."

Resolved not to flinch under the look of pure enmity he now fastened on her, Sara strained to keep her voice from breaking. "The truth is," she choked out, "you don't care at all about your father's happiness. If you did, you wouldn't be lying here, the victim of your own foolhardiness. You wouldn't have gone to work for a criminal like Patrick Walsh in the first place, and this never would have happened to you! You're altogether too selfish to concern yourself with your father's happiness, or anyone else's, for that matter! You don't care about anything or anybody except *yourself*, and—"

A light rap on the door brought Sara's tirade to a halt. She whirled around, momentarily at a loss at the unexpected interruption.

The door opened, and a tall, slender man in an elegantly tailored suit stepped into the room. Sara knew immediately who he was: Patrick Walsh. She was struck by an unsettling sense of cold as he entered. Nothing in his appearance—the immaculate grooming, the impeccable attire, the veneer of good looks—gave the slightest hint that he was anything but the well-to-do, successful businessman he purported to be. Yet for all his outward charm, a faint aura of corruption hovered about him like a vile stench in the air.

Admittedly, she knew too much about the man, mostly from Michael's merciless indictments, to be in the least objective about him. Yet she instinctively knew that the uneasiness he touched off in her had little to do with Michael's accusations. There was something wrong with Patrick Walsh ... something *missing* in him, something vital.

Unable to help herself, Sara met his eyes. She gave an involuntary shudder at the pale emptiness she encountered.

———

Patrick Walsh found himself sharply irritated by the Farmington woman.

Alice had gone back inside the house, but he still stood on the front porch, watching the hired hack drive away with Sara Farmington. He wasn't quite certain what it was, exactly, about the woman that grated on him so.

She was a proud one, that was evident. The look she'd given him upstairs had held a mixture of aversion and censure. Not what he was used to from women. Even the hoity-toity society toads uptown usually found him hard to resist, if he chose to lay on the charm.

But Sara Farmington had eyed him as if he were a snake. Her

haste to leave would have been amusing had her revulsion not been quite so obvious.

As the hack disappeared down the lane, it occurred to Walsh that what he found more galling than the woman's arrogance was the fact that she was soon to become the wife of that stiff-necked police captain, Burke. The Farmington fortune would eventually fall into the lap of that crusty, crusading cop.

Turning to go back inside, he uttered a low grunt of disgust. Obviously, the high and mighty Miss Farmington must be stupid beyond belief.

But, then, he reminded himself, most women were.

———

That night, when Michael showed up at the mansion well past eight, Sara knew he had been to see Tierney. His expression was positively thunderous.

She went to the door herself, half expecting him. He wedged past her, stopping just inside as she closed the door.

"I've just come from Walsh's," he clipped without preamble.

He made no move to touch her. His face was flushed, more than likely from anger rather than the long walk from the ferry. His hair was dripping wet from the rain, as was his coat. He was, quite obviously, about to explode.

"Let me take your coat—"

"*Bother the coat!*" he burst out, glaring at her. "I'm far more interested in finding out what you were doing on Staten Island today! Whatever possessed you to do such a daft thing?" The brogue in his speech had thickened noticeably, as was usually the case when he was angry or tired. Sara had learned to trust it as a surprisingly accurate barometer of his moods.

Forcing down a stab of irritation that he would speak to her so harshly, Sara said, "Michael, you're quite drenched! Please, give me your coat and we'll talk."

Before he could say another word, she moved to help him shrug out of his coat, draping it over the coat-tree near the door. "There's a fire in the parlor," she said. "Let's go in there."

With his mouth set in a grudging line, he followed her. In the parlor, he stood, hands knotted behind his back, looking for all the world like a smoldering pyre about to erupt in flames.

He started in at once. "I'm waiting, Sara. I'd like to know what you hoped to accomplish. What were you *thinking* to do such a thing?"

Still struggling not to lose her own temper, Sara turned to face him. "I was thinking," she said with carefully controlled calm, "of you. And your son. I had hoped that if Tierney and I could have a chance to talk alone, I might somehow convince him to let go of his resentment toward me. That's why I went, Michael; and quite frankly, I don't think it's cause for you to bully me."

His jaw tightened still more. "I'm not *bullying* you! And for your information, the only thing you accomplished was to make Tierney more spiteful than ever!"

"I scarcely think that's possible," Sara said sharply. "Nor do I think you have the right to scold me as if I were a child."

"I am simply trying to figure why you didn't at least tell me you planned to go."

"Because you would have asked me *not* to go," Sara said reasonably. "Or, rather, you would have *ordered* me not to go."

She saw his shoulders stiffen.

"It *seemed* like a sensible idea," Sara went on. "Grandy Clare thought it was the thing to do, and—"

"Grandy Clare?" he bit out. "Your grandmother put you up to it, then?"

"No, my grandmother did *not* put me up to it. She simply suggested—"

"Why does it seem that she's suggesting quite a number of things for us lately? First, she would have us living with her, and now she's sending you off to Staten Island to the house of a known crime boss—" He broke off, scowling murderously. "Perhaps your grandmother might try stirring her own broth a bit more instead of ours!"

"Michael!"

Another blast of anger flashed from his eyes. "You truly don't see it, do you, Sara? You don't have an inkling of the danger you let yourself in for today—going to that viper's house alone?"

Sara stood staring at him in hopeless silence. Only now did it begin to dawn on her that he wasn't angry because she had gone to see Tierney. Rather, he was angry . . . because she had *frightened* him.

She didn't know whether she should feel pleased that he cared so much, or enraged that he thought her such a fool she couldn't

144

take care of herself around a disgusting man like Patrick Walsh.

Once her mind had registered the reason for his anger, she stood searching his relentless features, undecided as to how to respond. "I wasn't in any real danger, Michael," she began carefully. "Mrs. Walsh was there—and the servants. What do you think might have happened to me in a house full of people?"

Something flickered in his eyes, and Sara thought that at last the full heat of his anger was beginning to abate. Speaking more quickly now, she went on. "As for Grandy Clare—when I told you last night about her suggestion that we live with her, you didn't seem to feel she was interfering. You said it was worth thinking about. I don't understand why, now—"

As she watched, his shoulders sagged just a fraction and the fire in his eyes began to go out. "I don't mean to say she's interfering," he said, his voice strained. "But I'll not pretend I like her prompting you to go off to Walsh's house."

Sara shook her head. "You're making far too much of this." Meeting his eyes, Sara asked him directly, "Did I frighten you? Is that it?"

He unlocked his hands from behind his back, passing one across his chest in a distracted gesture. The look he gave her was still guarded, defensive—but no longer angry. "And why *wouldn't* I be frightened for you? You know well enough what Walsh is. I've spared few details in telling you about the man. If you felt you had to go, I should have gone with you!"

She groped for patience. "If you had gone with me, it would have defeated my reason for going. I told you, I wanted to talk with Tierney alone."

"Yes ... well, I can't very well look after you if I don't know what you're about half the time. It seems to me you might have told me what you intended."

And therein, Sara realized, lay at least a part of the problem. She had ventured out of the range of his protection without letting him know what she intended—and without asking him his opinion.

Or his permission?

The hateful thought was quickly gone, but left Sara troubled. She was being unfair, of course. Michael's over-developed sense of responsibility, his desire to protect her, was unquestionably motivated by love. Yet she could not quite shake off the disqui-

eting image of a grim-faced Michael attempting to confine her—
and everyone else he cared for—inside a clinging net woven from
his love. A net that would give them protection but precious little
freedom.

Trembling, she lifted her hand in a tenuous appeal, then let it
fall when he remained motionless. "Will you *listen* to yourself?"
she said, her voice thick with emotion. "Michael, for goodness'
sake, I'm not a child! I don't need you to—to 'look after me'! I'm
quite capable of taking care of myself. I've been managing for
several years now."

He stood staring at her in silence for a long time. Finally, he
sighed, saying, "Aye, you have. But you can't expect me to love
you as I do, Sara, and not want to protect you."

"Michael, please understand something about my feelings,"
Sara said, choosing her words with great care. "Of course, I'd be
hurt if you weren't concerned for my safety. But I have no intention of becoming your . . . your ward, once we're married. I want
you to be my *husband*—not my *guardian*."

A deep flush spread over his face, and for a moment Sara
thought he was going to explode in a temper. But he merely swallowed, then drew in a long, ragged breath. "It's just that I know
the kind of evil Walsh and his kind are capable of. It's been hard
enough as it is, having Tierney under his roof—in his bed." He
paused and raked a hand down the side of his face. "When I
learned you'd been there, alone—" Again he flushed and scowled.
"The swine had the nerve to compliment me on my 'taste in
women.' "

He looked so distraught that Sara could no longer keep her
distance. "Oh, Michael, I *am* sorry!" she cried, closing the space
between them and putting an uncertain hand to his arm. "Perhaps I *should* have told you I was going."

He glanced at her hand. "I won't deny that I wish you had."

Moving still closer to him, Sara said softly, "But you *would*
have asked me not to go. You know you would have."

He searched her eyes, then after a moment gave a nod. "Aye,"
he said somewhat grudgingly, covering her hand with his own.
"That's the truth." He sighed deeply. "Sara, please—let's not argue. The thing is done. I'm sorry for storming in here as I did,
sorry if I hurt your feelings. I wouldn't want to hurt you, *asthore.*
Not ever."

He pulled her against his chest and held her, saying nothing for a long time. Gently, then, he tipped her face to his. "I can be a great fool at times, Sara *a gra*. But I do love you. Never forget that I do love you."

Then he kissed her, and, at least for the moment, Sara forgot the unsettling image of being caught in a net, a net made of Michael's love.

15

Finbar

So in peace our tasks we ply,
Pangur Ban, my cat, and I;
In our arts we find our bliss,
I have mine and he has his.

ANONYMOUS (Eighth or Early Ninth Century)

Now that the weather had turned colder, the new choral group had been granted permission to use one of the two rented mission rooms above the tavern for their weekly rehearsals.

Today, Evan Whittaker climbed the steps to the rehearsal room with unusual reluctance. Ordinarily, he would be eager to get started. The boys in the group were showing an increasing enthusiasm for the music and a growing unity of spirit—at least, most of the time. If he did say so himself, they were beginning to sound quite good.

Today, however, in spite of the hours of preparation he had put into the new music for rehearsal, he found himself too distracted to be genuinely enthusiastic. He could think of nothing but Nora as his mind searched for something—something special—that might serve to lift her spirits, to perk her up a bit, as Mr. Farmington would say.

It had been days since he'd seen a smile on her face—a *real* smile, that is, not the faint, uncertain curving of her lips she routinely managed just to reassure him. Evan knew that despite her efforts to be cheerful, the longing for a baby had never quite left her. Each day when he returned home from the shipyards, Nora was waiting in a fresh dress, her hair neatly done up and fragrant, the small, sad smile bravely in place. Later in the evening, if she happened to glance up from her sewing to see him studying her with concern, she would immediately urge the smile back into place.

Giving a deep sigh, he now entered the mission room. The boys were already seated, waiting for him, and at last his heart lifted a little. He stood at the front of the room, scanning the group for a moment. They actually appeared eager to begin.

There were at least fifteen boys in attendance, a mix of Irish and black youths. Today he noted two new faces among the regulars, one white and one black. Here, at least, the ongoing enmity between the races seemed to take a backseat to the combined efforts of the group.

Straightening his shoulders, Evan gave them a smile. If the Five Points Celebration Singers never accomplished anything else but to help break down the wall between races, it would make all their hard work worthwhile.

––––––––

This was Billy Hogan's first time to attend a rehearsal of the Five Points singing group.

Twice before, when the boys were practicing in the Big Tent, he had stood outside, listening, yearning to be a part of it all, yet reluctant to take the first step inside.

Until today. His friend, Tom Breen, had finally coaxed him into coming along. And so he was here, his face scrubbed, his shirt clean and pressed, his hair slicked down. Mr. Whittaker insisted on cleanliness, said Tom. Cleanliness and obedience. He would stand for no shenanigans from his singers. He was strict, but a fair man, all the same.

Something in the Englishman's soft eyes and kind smile assured Billy that Tom was right. Still, he was as jumpy as a toad on hot bricks, and would be until the hour was safely over.

He wasn't worried about the singing. He had a voice, after all. Didn't Mum say he had a voice that could dig down low and scoop up the bottom notes of a tune—or fly high as a sparrow and sail right over the top of a building?

Sometimes the voice did things that surprised Billy. The truth was, it wasn't entirely predictable.

Billy liked to sing. He would choose a song over a pastry—not that he often had a choice, for pastries were dear in Five Points.

But it wasn't until Tom had mentioned that the new singing group sang what they *heard*, rather than what they *read*, that Billy had agreed to come to rehearsal. If he didn't have to read the music, why, then, he could sing just as good as the rest of them, he would warrant.

He was not eager for the other lads to know he couldn't read. He wasn't the only one, of course. In Five Points, there were more who could *not* read than those who could.

But they were not Hogans. They were not sons of educated men, like his da, taught by Grandfar Liam himself, who had once kept a hedge school in Sligo. Had the fever not claimed them both before Billy was old enough to learn his letters, no doubt they would have taught him as well.

Now there was nothing for him but to work; there was no time to go to school. He had his papers to sell, and coal to shovel onto the wagons, and on weekends he still went looking for additional odd jobs.

It was a matter of pride to Billy that this inability to read be kept secret. He would remedy it when he could. For today, he would not fret about the reading. He would do what he had been longing to do for weeks now: he would join this fine group of singers and lift his voice with the rest of them.

If only Finbar did not spoil it all.

Please, Lord Jesus, there was nothing else I could do but to bring him . . . please, please, let Finbar be good!

————

Halfway through rehearsal, as they stampeded toward the first chorus of "Yankee Doodle," Evan's attention was caught by an unfamiliar sound. High-pitched and excruciatingly sharp, it was gone too soon to identify.

He continued on as if he had heard nothing. Although his ear seldom failed him, it was possible he had only imagined the dissonance. The acoustics in the drafty, high-ceilinged room were deplorable, after all, and—

Ah—there it was again! So, he had *not* imagined it! He rapped his baton, stopping the song on "Dan-dy." Eyes narrowed, he scanned every face in the group, resting on each for an exaggerated length of time.

Unwilling to embarrass any one of the boys by singling him out, Evan decided to try once more. Most likely, one of the lads was simply indulging in a bit of mischief. Still, even the most incorrigible among them seldom misbehaved during one of their favorite numbers. And "Yankee Doodle" was indeed a favorite.

Evan had done a special arrangement of the tune, complete with endless verses. The boys had enjoyed a good laugh at his expense when he explained that the song, originally sung in derision by the English about the Colonists, had ended up being turned against them when the Minute Men of Concord adopted it as their own. Indeed, when Cornwallis surrendered at Yorktown, it was to the tune of "Yankee Doodle."

He sighed, thinking it altogether possible he had a boy with a pitch problem. A troubling thought, since he wasn't quite certain how he would handle things if one of the lads turned out to be sharp.

Bracing himself, Evan gave the upbeat and they started in again. All went well until the third verse when Captain Washington's Slapping Stallion turned into a Screeching Shrew.

Evan stiffened, stopping the music with a sharp rap of the baton and a resounding "ENOUGH!"

Laying his baton on the music stand, he straightened his shoulders and stretched to his full height. With a frown that he hoped would prove daunting, he silently and thoroughly studied each face now turned on him with guarded attention.

He thought one of the new boys—the small one with wheat-colored hair that stood askew and more freckles than Evan had ever seen on one small face—looked suspiciously ill at ease. Perhaps even frightened.

Evan found it difficult to imagine that one so young would prove troublesome his first time out. Yet, the freckled face now turned crimson under Evan's scrutiny, and the boy appeared unduly fidgety. As a matter of fact, the lad was practically writhing where he stood.

Evan knew he had his culprit when he closed the remaining distance between himself and the boy and the same high-pitched shriek erupted. The sound seemed to be coming from the youth's jacket, a loose brown garment that hung on the narrow shoulders like a sack.

Stopping directly in front of the boy, Evan gave a curt nod. "I d-don't believe we've met, young man. Your name?"

The boy's eyes bugged, and he opened his mouth. But before he could speak, something moved beneath his jacket.

Evan stared, first at the squirming jacket, then at the boy's wide-eyed expression of dismay.

As Evan watched, one side of the jacket opened and a small, furry face pushed out. Astonished, Evan stared at the creature in disbelief.

The kitten was an odd mottled color, gray and black with random spots of tan. It was obviously quite young—and hopelessly cross-eyed.

The kitten cocked its head and perked its ears, appraising Evan with some interest. At last it blinked, then gave a small mew.

Evan dragged his gaze away from the cross-eyed kitten to hush the snickering onlookers with a withering glare. Then he turned back to the boy.

Before he could say anything more, the red-faced offender burst out, "I'm sorry, sir—Mister Whittaker! He almost never makes a sound at home, and that's the truth!"

The boy's Irish brogue was thick. He was fairly new to the city, Evan was sure. The little fellow looked about to strangle.

"I, ah, I'm afraid we d-don't allow animals at rehearsal, Mr.—"

"Billy Hogan, sir! And, sure, I know it was wicked to sneak him upstairs! But I found a home for all the others—there's only wee Finbar left, you see . . . and—"

"Finbar?"

"Aye, that's his name—for Saint Finbar, you know." The boy went on, his words spilling out like pebbles tossed over a waterfall. "Finbar is the one I hoped to keep, but Uncle Sorley says we can't be feeding another cat, in addition to Sally—that's Finbar's mother—for food is dear enough as it is for the five of us."

"The five of you?" Evan repeated, bemused.

"Aye, we're five—there's Mum, Uncle Sorley, myself, and me two little brothers, Liam and Patrick. Uncle Sorley said I must find a home for the litter or else he'd *drowned* them. I found a place for the other three at some pubs what wanted mousers. But nothing yet for Finbar. And I was afraid to leave him for fear Uncle Sorley would be cross and drowned him anyway. I thought I'd just keep him with myself another hour or so, then speak to the owner downstairs. He's usually so quiet, Finbar is—I never thought he'd be a bother."

As the boy finally came up for air, Evan puzzled as to how to handle the situation. The poor lad looked perfectly miserable, whether from apprehension of punishment or the certain loss of his kitten.

Evan glanced at the kitten, which seemed altogether content and even somewhat bored. The crossed eyes met his, and again came the inquisitive mew. The small head stretched cautiously up as if to sniff the air.

Evan eyed the small intruder for another moment. A faint smile rose inside him, finally spreading to his lips. "I say, Mr. Hogan, is it? Perhaps I can b-be of some help to you and, ah, Finbar."

———

"Evan!" Nora flew at him as soon as he was inside the door. "What on earth kept you? I was that worried—you're always home long before dark! Is something wrong?"

Evan kissed her and apologized profusely. "N-nothing is wrong! Nothing at all. And you m-mustn't fuss over me so." He smiled at his own duplicity. He would be altogether *devastated* if she *didn't* fuss over him.

"But—"

He shushed her with another kiss, then stepped back. "Where are the children?"

"Johanna is helping Little Tom get ready for bed; then they'll be down," she said distractedly. "I promised they could stay up for prayers with you. But you'll have your supper first."

She moved toward him. "Here, let me take your coat—"

"No!" Evan jumped back as if he had been struck. "I . . . I c-can manage."

"Evan, whatever is the matter? Sure, and you're acting strange tonight," Nora said, giving him a puzzled look. "Did something go wrong at rehearsal?"

Evan suppressed a smile, keeping his empty sleeve turned away. "Wrong? N-no, of course not. What c-could possibly go wrong at rehearsal?"

Nora narrowed her eyes at him, her frown deepening. "Evan? Are you quite certain you're well? You seem—peculiar."

"Peculiar?" he repeated evasively. "No, I'm fine, just—OW!" He grabbed at his empty sleeve.

"Evan? What is it?"

Nora ran to him, taking him by the shoulders. When Evan averted his eyes, she insisted, "There *is* something wrong! I knew it, you—" she broke off, looking down at Evan's empty sleeve as it began to move.

The sleeve jerked hard, then again. From within the folds came a high-pitched, indignant screech. Grimacing, Evan yanked at the pin holding the material in place. At last the sleeve came loose, and the small, bewildered-looking kitten emerged.

For a moment it simply dangled at Evan's side, its tiny, needle-like claws embedded in the fabric of his sleeve. Suddenly, it let go, racing down his leg and tearing about his feet in a frenzy. Spying Nora, it stopped. In one furious sweep, it climbed her dress, attaching itself to her and burrowing its small head close to her heart.

"N-Nora," Evan said with a shaky smile as he rubbed his throbbing shoulder, "I'd like you to m-meet Finbar."

———

That night, after Evan had fallen asleep, Nora lay studying his shadowed profile in the weak ribbon of light drifting in from the hallway.

Without his glasses, he looked younger. Younger and sweet and so very, very vulnerable.

As always when she looked at him, her heart swelled with love for this gentle, unassuming man who daily poured himself out for her happiness. He was a slender man, her Evan, not large or especially muscular. Yet his body housed a heart big beyond all measuring.

She smiled as she remembered his expression when the kitten had tumbled out from his empty sleeve. So pleased, so eager. Eager to make her happy, to see her smile.

She understood what he was about, of course. He was far too sensitive, too attuned to her moods, not to sense that she had been less than happy lately. Guilt ate at her for worrying him so, for the shadow she knew she had cast on his own happiness by her incessant brooding about a baby.

Somehow she must stop. It was unfair, so unfair, to wound

him like this. He deserved more, much more. He deserved only joy.

She touched his bearded cheek with her fingertips. He sighed in his sleep, and she smiled. How precious she counted these quiet times, these warm, tender times of closeness when something as simple as a sigh, as gentle as a touch, could affirm the bond of their love.

And she *did* love Evan. She loved him for his gentleness, his quiet kindness, his goodness, his godliness. She loved him for his shy, unassuming manner, for the way he never took anything for granted, but was always grateful for even the smallest deed done for him.

And she loved him for loving *her*. For loving her enough that he would take in a stranger's children and make them his own—and tuck a wee cross-eyed kitten into his sleeve because he had known it would make her smile.

In the darkness, her smile widened. Finbar had been almost immediately taken over by the children—indeed, now lay sleeping on Tom's bed. But not before he had entertained them all with a variety of shenanigans.

She had been aware of Evan's watching her, his delighted smile when she responded to the kitten.

I must stop brooding, she told herself again. *I must bring no more gloom into his life. Whatever God gives . . . even if it's only a stray kitten . . . I will take it and rejoice in it and cherish it. For Evan. For our love.*

"*I love you, Evan . . . I do love you so. . . .*"

She didn't realize she had spoken aloud until he reached for her. His eyes fluttered, unfocused, heavy with sleep. Then, as if the very intensity of her love had wrapped itself around him and awakened him, he smiled and gathered her closer.

16

Dublin Vigil

And oft her wasted fingers
Beating time upon the bed:
O'er some old tune she lingers,
And she bows her golden head. . . .

RICHARD D'ALTON WILLIAMS (1822–1862)

Dublin
December

In the weeks since the attack, Nelson Hall had come to be an
unnaturally silent, somber place. Christmas was coming, and yet
it approached almost unacknowledged, as if the entire season
itself was overshadowed by a dreadful foreboding.

Everyone who walked the vast, dim hallways seemed keenly
aware that quiet was imperative. It was, thought Sandemon, as
if all who dwelled within feared that even the everyday, common-
place sounds of the household might somehow snap the fragile
thread of the *Seanchai's* control.

A routine had been established almost immediately after the
tragedy. The servants glided in and out of the rooms as quietly as
cats in the night, whispering or murmuring only when required.
Even in the classrooms, there was total discipline, with instruction given in quiet tones and voices held low during recitations.

The entire household seemed poised upon a precipice, hushed
and uncertain and apprehensive. The domestic routine went on,

but now there seemed little difference in day from night. Days were for working and waiting. Nights were for *praying* and waiting.

Sandemon had begun his morning as always, on his knees beside the bed, with a hymn of praise—a quiet, restrained hymn, for he sensed that even the Lord God desired stillness in these days. For a long time, his spirit bowed before the Glory in adoration. Today, more than ever, he felt a desperate need for closeness, for refreshing from the Spirit. For light.

Finally, he began to lift before the throne those who had become dear to him, those for whom the Lord would have him intercede, with love. . . .

The child, young Annie, whose adoption proceedings had become snagged in the unlikely hands of the mother who had rejected her and the stepfather who had abused her. Two of the finest attorneys in all Ireland—and who, according to the *Seanchai*, were also among the most ruthless—had been employed to pursue matters in Belfast. As yet the child did not know of the delay. The attorneys were convinced that enough money would bring results, and the *Seanchai* had authorized them to offer whatever it took.

Sandemon gave a deep sigh, pausing in his prayer to think on the situation. Sadly, he wondered if young Annie might not be surprised to learn how vigorously the *Seanchai* was pursuing the adoption. The child was obviously feeling somewhat adrift, perhaps even a bit neglected. The *Seanchai*, indeed the entire household, had been so distracted by the attack on Miss Finola that there was little time or energy for one precocious child.

Finola. . . .

Even as Sandemon held the name of the stricken young woman on his lips, the thought of her anguish wrenched his heart. It had been weeks since the Almighty had returned her from the chasm that lay between Today and God's Forever. Yet she continued to show no real awareness of her surroundings. She scarcely responded to whatever distress she might be feeling, although surely her pain must be excruciating.

Sandemon saw her only from a distance, of course; the surgeon was still insisting that all male members of the household avoid close contact. But even a glimpse of her brought a terrible sorrow to his spirit. She lay limp and unmoving in the tall, spacious bed, her eyes fixed in an unfocused, unseeing stare. Her friend, Lucy, said she responded to touch, but only when it seemed to evoke pain—and, even then, she merely sobbed or gave a muffled sound of distress. She ate negligible portions of food, and only when assisted, with much coaxing.

She could not speak, of course, but now, in addition to the muteness, there was a kind of silence in her eyes. It was as Lucy said: a light had gone out somewhere inside Finola.

The same could be said of the unhappy *Seanchai*, Sandemon thought, frowning as he mused over the young master's heartache. Every day the sad-eyed poet would bring his wheelchair to a stop just outside the sickroom, where he would sit, staring with eyes that willed the young woman within to revive, to be herself once again.

Gone was the anger—at least all outward evidence of it— which had threatened to explode during those first dark days after the savage attack. Gone, too, was the restlessness, the abundance of energy that had once made the *Seanchai's* confinement to the wheelchair such a rigorous trial. Now there was a stillness in the young giant, a sense of quiet restraint that did not seem so much born of despondency or despair, but of waiting. Waiting, and standing guard.

He spent his days, those times when he did not wait outside her door, at his desk in the library among his many books and correspondence. Sandemon had posted numerous letters for him: to the adoption attorneys, to his friend, Mr. Smith O'Brien in gaol, to his friends in America—and to a man who was unknown to all but the *Seanchai* himself, and to Sandemon.

Concerned that Miss Finola might have family who were, even now, attempting to locate her, the *Seanchai* had retained a person to investigate her past. To Sandemon, he had confided his fears about such a search. He was aware, he admitted, that danger might lie in discovery. Yet he felt convicted to try.

"If there's a chance at all that someone out there might be able to help Finola through this time, we have to find him," he had said to Sandemon only days ago. "The man I've retained is entirely reliable—I trust him as I trust few men. He'll use discretion. Should he learn anything that could prove harmful for Finola, it will remain a secret."

Finally rising from his knees, Sandemon felt the same prickling of dread he had experienced when he'd first learned of the investigation. He trusted the *Seanchai's* judgment in such matters, understood his desperation to help the stricken young woman. Yet it was a chilling thought, that whatever, or *whoever,* had been responsible for Miss Finola's lonely silence—a silence devoid of memories and even her own identity—might at last become known. And with what consequence?

Perhaps the *Seanchai* would not agree, but Sandemon could not help but wonder if there might not be some things best left untouched and unknown. Could not too much probing of the past rouse old demons, once imprisoned, perhaps even set them loose on the present?

Or did he only fear such a possibility because of his own dark yesterdays?

———

Later that morning, Morgan Fitzgerald sat hunched over his desk in the library, working through the considerable volume of correspondence that required his attention.

These days he had to force himself to give any real thought to matters that weren't of the utmost importance. Anything pertaining to Annie's adoption received highest priority, of course, but to date there had been no new developments. An excessive amount of money—and a not-so-veiled threat—had been hung out to the child's mother. He believed—and the attorneys concurred—that if the threat of legal charges to the woman and her drunken, abusive husband did not bring the desired response, the exorbitant amount of money *would.*

Not for the first time, Morgan wished he might have the use of his legs again—if only for the time required for a trip to Belfast. He was sure if he could get his hands on that soak of a stepfather— Tully—he could successfully convince both him and the mother to relinquish all claim on Annie.

Sighing, he turned his attention to a more cheerful task, that of replying to Evan Whittaker's most recent letter. Picking up his pen, he sat thinking about the Englishman who continued to amaze him. Somehow, Whittaker had landed himself what, to most, would seem the unenviable task of directing a singing group composed of both Irish and black youths—and this in the midst of a New York slum.

As if that weren't challenge enough, he had also involved himself in arranging music for them. His recent letter was by way of enlisting Morgan's help in acquiring some Irish songs—simple melodies, he stressed—which could be incorporated into his American arrangements. These, as well as some of the music of the Negro slaves, would constitute Whittaker's first attempts to create what he referred to as "ethnic-American" songs.

Daniel John, Whittaker remarked, was helping him as best he could, but hadn't enough musical notation to supply detailed scores.

I am teaching him the basics, however, and daily thank God for the surprisingly thorough musical education I received at university some years ago. Daniel quite enjoys the irony in an Englishman teaching him the rudiments of harmony, so that he can arrange his Irish melodies.

Morgan smiled a little at that, and read on. Whittaker hoped to eventually integrate a variety of music of other races and nationalities into his own arrangements. The man seemed convinced that a new kind of American song was beginning to emerge, one containing a mixture of ethnic melody and American form. Ultimately, he believed it would represent the true spirit of America, the "land of a thousand dreams," as he called his newly adopted country.

I hope to encourage this new music among the youth in the slums. In some small way, I believe it can help to bridge at least a part of the divisions that now exist.

An ambitious undertaking. Morgan shook his head at the idealism of the man, but he had to admire him. Removing his reading glasses, he propped his elbows on the desk, resting his chin on his folded hands.

What a marvel the Englishman had turned out to be. A memory of the slight, almost timid Whittaker, with his poor eyesight and fierce stammer, brought a wry smile. This same timid, stammering Britisher had gone and married Morgan's own childhood sweetheart, winning her away from both himself and Michael Burke—and then proceeded to take in Morgan's niece and nephew to raise as his own. At the same time, he'd managed to make a place for himself in the employ of one of the wealthiest men in America.

Timid, indeed!

Morgan could only cheer him on. Many men strived for nobility of soul, but Evan Whittaker was one of the few he had
known who seemed to have attained it.

The thought of his niece and nephew made Morgan again pon-
der the question of whether or not he should bring Tom and Johanna back to Ireland. He was providing for them financially, of
course, had settled a generous sum of money on them under the
supervision of Evan Whittaker. He wrote to them, and, with Nora
and Evan's help, they sent him messages in response.

But was it enough? They were his brother's children, after all;
he had always been more than fond of them. Yet he could not see
uprooting them again, at least not at the present.

He could offer them a fine home, see to their education, provide security. But with Ireland in such dire straits, he was convinced that America could offer them far more.

He wished only to do what was best for them. Whittaker had
assured him time and again that he and Nora loved both the
children as their own and wanted them in their home, and Morgan did not doubt their sincerity. Still, at some point in time, the
question would more than likely have to be posed to the children
themselves.

With a heavy sigh, he deliberately set the problem aside for
the time being. He was too preoccupied to make an objective
decision about even the most inconsequential things these days,
much less something as important as the future of his brother's
children.

Putting on his glasses again, he laid Whittaker's letter aside;
he would collect the melodies he'd requested, perhaps even provide some original songs of his own. But for now, he should answer Michael's letter.

This missive, too, was, for the most part, filled with good news.
News of the coming wedding between Michael and his Sara, his
promotion to police captain, his appointment to a special subcommission on crime.

At least two of their circle of three had found happiness....

The thought was without envy, though not without a certain
regret for the course his own life had taken. He had given little
heed to the idea of home and family when he'd still been a young
man . . . and whole. For most of his life, Ireland had been his love,

his consuming passion. Any notion of becoming a husband and father had been, at best, only a vague, distant possibility.

Nora's eventual marriage to Owen Kavanagh had jolted him to the realization that the one woman who might have loved him enough to forgive him his faults, even share his divided devotion, was lost to him. The door to love had been closed with a resounding finality. From that time on, Morgan never seriously considered taking a wife.

And now . . . now, he was no longer young. No longer whole. Certainly, no longer of any interest to women. Yet only now did he think that he might finally have matured enough to be an adequate husband. Now . . . when the very possibility seemed the remotest star in the heavens. . . .

Raking a hand through the hair at the back of his neck, he forced himself to pen a letter of congratulations and good wishes to Michael. He found himself somewhat amused at the thought of Michael's taking on a society wife—a wife who apparently had a mind of her own. A *fine* mind—and a decidedly strong will, according to her husband-to-be.

Fair enough. Perhaps she'd prove a match for her strong-hearted and often hardheaded husband, he thought with a wry smile.

Evidently, the disapproval of Michael's son lent the one gloomy note to the romance. It would seem that the boy was being deliberately difficult.

He stopped writing for a moment and sat tapping the end of his pen on the desk. The more Michael told him of his boy, the more Morgan found himself drawn to young Tierney. His affinity for the lad might be nothing more than the fact that he was the son of his best friend. On the other hand, he conceded with the ghost of a smile, it might just be that he recognized a great deal of himself in Tierney Burke's feckless, rebellious nature.

Poor Michael. Practical, sensible, straight-ahead Michael. No doubt he would find such a son a great challenge.

The thought of his friend's difficulties with his son made Morgan stop and realize again just how much he appreciated Annie. The child might not be of his own blood, but she was unquestionably of his heart—her quicksilver mind, her insatiable curiosity and love of the books, her generosity of affection.

Her penchant for mischief and mixups . . .

Ah, but she was a gift, for all her scalawag ways. A gift for which he was daily grateful. He did cherish the lass, surely more than she could know.

Putting down his pen, Morgan flexed his fingers, then leaned back a bit from the desk, giving a deep sigh. The child might not feel all that cherished of late, he worried. He had tried not to let his distress for Finola interfere in his relationship with Annie, but of course it did.

Annie's energy exhausted him, and her transparent attempts to brighten his spirits fell flat. Somehow, when this was over, he must make it up to her. He would reassure her that she was as dear to him as if she had been his own. Whatever it took, Annie must never, never feel unwanted again.

In the meantime, he wished the child and Sister Louisa could make it up. The sister was more than willing, of course, but Annie had at some point decided "the Nun" had it in for her.

The situation sorely grieved Morgan, for he had hoped Sister Louisa would be good for the child. He had noted her attempts at friendship, but Annie obviously had other ideas. And Annie, he knew, did not easily change her ideas.

He simply could not deal with any of it at present. He had neither the heart nor the strength. Perhaps that's why he spent so much of his time writing letters. It required little concentration and a minimum of energy. With a pen in his hand, his mind remained free to dwell on Finola.

It was still a source of great pain, the surgeon's admonition to keep his distance. It pierced his heart every time he stopped at the door of her room. To see her lying there, eyes open without really seeing, occasionally moaning or sobbing in pain—and not go to her—took every shred of self-control he could summon.

He *ached* to gather her in his arms, to hold her . . . gently, carefully . . . close to him. Involuntarily, he winced at the thought. It was scarcely conceivable that Finola would allow herself to be held by a man—*any* man—ever again.

But it would be enough for him to sit beside the bed, just to look at her, talk with her. *Be* with her.

At times, he secretly questioned the surgeon's instructions. But just as quickly, he dismissed his doubts as nothing more than his own selfish need to be close to her. He must do what was best for Finola, and if staying away from her was what it took—then that is what he would do, and without complaint.

———

Lacking human companionship, Annie went looking for Fergus. What a fix to be in, to have no one with whom she could share her deepest feelings, except for a scruffy old dog!

She stopped where she was, hunching her shoulders and squeezing her eyes shut. "Sorry, Lord . . . again. Sure, and I know I can always share my deepest, *deepest* feelings with you. It's just that there are times of late when I might get to feeling a bit lonely, don't you see, and even though Fergus isn't human—he only *thinks* he is—there's no one else, besides yourself, of course, with the time to listen to the likes of me!"

These days, Annie frequently found herself turning to the wolfhound for companionship. The *Seanchai* was naturally distracted by his worry for Finola. And Sandemon—well, he was busier than ever.

"You understand, don't you, Lord? I mean, the two people I count on most simply can't be bothered with me right now. I'm not complaining, mind," she quickly added, starting on down the hallway in search of Fergus. "I'm not blaming the *Seanchai* at all for being worried to distraction for Finola. We all are, and that's the truth! And Sand-Man is that busy, what with his own responsibilities and some of the tasks the *Seanchai* tends to neglect lately."

She had promised herself she would not be a nuisance, would not aggravate the grown-ups. Sandemon and the *Seanchai* needed her to be a help during this time, not a bother. She did her utmost to be quiet about the house and lend a hand wherever she could.

But sometimes she got to feeling terribly alone, perhaps even a bit fearful. Lately, she couldn't help wondering if the *Seanchai* would actually go ahead with the adoption. She wouldn't ask, of course. More than likely, he hadn't given it a thought since the terrible business with Finola, and that being the case, she didn't think she'd want to hear him *say* it. It was painful and frightening enough just to *think* it.

"Please, Lord, Sir, if that's the situation, could you perhaps just prod the *Seanchai's* memory a bit, once Finola starts to feel better? Not now, of course—he's too worried and distracted at present, I know. But later, perhaps you could just make sure he doesn't forget it entirely."

Reaching her room, Annie went in. She was pleased to find Fergus asleep on the floor at the foot of the bed, but she couldn't resist scolding him a bit. "Napping, are you, lazy beast? What's the matter, then, did the TROUBLESOME NUN tire of your company?"

For the life of her, Annie could not understand the bond between Fergus and the nun. Starched and stern with *her*, the nun played the great fool over the wolfhound—when she thought nobody was looking, that is.

And, great eejit that he was, Fergus reveled in the attention. At times he seemed inclined to be almost as much a friend to the nun as he was to Annie!

"I'm that put out with you, you know," she grumbled, dropping down on the floor beside him. "I'm tired of having to coax you away from that TROUBLESOME NUN when I want you! You're *my* dog, after all. 'Twas me who took you in and convinced the *Seanchai* and Sand-Man to let you stay, you might be remembering! You're ungrateful entirely, I'm thinking, and if you don't change your ways, you might just find yourself sleeping in the stable!"

The dimwitted dog simply grinned at her and threw a large, ungainly paw in her lap.

"Don't try your tricks on me, you ungrateful beast," Annie muttered, nevertheless taking the big paw into her hand and holding on to it.

After a moment, though, she forgot her irritation. "Have you been to visit Finola yet today?" she asked him, giving a deep sigh. "I stopped in, just a bit ago. There's no change. She just lies there, staring at people as if she doesn't see them at all. She doesn't even seem to recognize me, and we were getting to be great friends."

Annie paused, again unsettled by the worrisome thought that Finola might *never* be any different, that she might simply stay as she was . . . forever.

"Oh, Fergus! It's such a sad thing, her being as she is! She's so lovely and sweet and good! I *hate* that awful person who did this to her! I hope God strikes him—"

Annie clamped a hand over her mouth, staring in horror at

the wolfhound as she realized what she'd been about to say. "Oh, I'm sorry, Lord! I am! I know I'm not supposed to wish bad things on anyone—not even a creature like the one who hurt Finola! But it's simply not fair! It's not fair at all! He ought to be punished, and punished severely, it seems to me."

She paused, thinking. "Sand-Man says that you're in charge of—of *vengeance*, that you'll see him pay, whoever he is. I hope so, Lord! I can't think of anything bad enough to pay him back for what he did to Finola, but perhaps you can."

The dog whimpered as if commiserating with her, then lay his great head in her lap. Rubbing his ears, Annie went on, her voice lower now so as not to invite heavenly repercussions for her previous outburst.

"I get so angry sometimes, Fergus! So angry I could pop! Sand-Man says that kind of anger is wrong, but I can tell *he* gets angry, too, whenever somebody brings up poor Finola. He doesn't say a word, but I can tell he's angry, all the same. I see it in his eyes."

Stroking the wolfhound's back, she gave another huge sigh. "I wonder how Finola feels inside," she said. "I wonder if she isn't in a fierce rage, even if we can't see it." A small, hard knot of unhappiness swelled in Annie's throat. "It must be a terrible thing, to be hurt and angry and not be able to tell anyone about it."

The wolfhound moaned his understanding, and Annie went on. "One thing I believe, Fergus, and I wouldn't say it to anyone else but you—not that anyone would pay heed to me even if I *did*—but I think that surgeon is *wrong* entirely, not to let the *Seanchai* near Finola!"

The dog raised his big head, studying her face, and Annie nodded. "Aye, I'm convinced of it! Finola does dote on the *Seanchai*, I *know* she does! Why, the way she looks at him—at least the way she *did* look at him before this terrible thing happened— it seemed the morning sun rose in her eyes! And the *Seanchai* adores her. I saw it in his face! If the surgeon would only allow him to sit beside her and talk to her . . . perhaps even sing his songs to her . . . she loved it when he sang. I could tell she did . . . why, I wouldn't be at all surprised if she didn't get better right away! I just *feel* it, Fergus! Truly, I do!"

"I'm not so sure but what I agree with you, Annie Delaney."

At the sound of the quiet voice behind her, Annie whipped

around hard enough to dislodge Fergus from her lap.

"I believe you may be absolutely right," Sister Louisa repeated. "Perhaps the two of us should say as much to the *Seanchai*."

Annie gaped at her, speechless. The nun stood close enough to touch her, and for once she looked less the policeman and more a warm-blooded human being. Then she did a most amazing thing: she actually put her hand to Annie's shoulder—and *squeezed* it!

"It occurs to me," Sister Louisa said reasonably, "that the two of us might just go and talk with him right now."

Faith, and didn't she sound almost *kind*? Why, even her eyes— eyes that ordinarily would slice marble—were kind!

Annie stared. "The two of us? Talk to the *Seanchai*?"

The nun gave a nod and then—and then, the most incredible thing happened: she smiled. *The TROUBLESOME NUN smiled!*

Annie scrambled to her feet. "D'you mean it, Sister? You'll go with me?"

Again, Sister Louisa nodded. "Indeed, I will," she said firmly. "I've thought as much for quite some time now, but was reluctant to suggest it, for fear I would offend. But you know the two of them far better than I. I trust your judgment."

Annie swallowed hard. Her mouth had gone dry as straw. "You—you trust my judgment?"

Sister nodded. "The surgeon's way isn't working at all, that much is evident. If there was indeed a bond of trust and affection between Finola and the *Seanchai* before the attack, it's quite possible that this business of keeping them apart may only be making things worse for her."

Taking Annie by the hand, she said, "Come along." The wolfhound barked, and she added, "Yes, you, too, old boy. You can come with us."

Fergus fell in between them, and again the nun smiled. Suddenly, an astonishing thing struck Annie: Sister Louisa seemed to have lost her vinegary look! Where had the stern and stuffy face gone?

Uncomfortably, she shifted from one foot to the other. The truth was, she had seen the nun smile before today. The *entire* truth was, the nun had smiled at *her*, and on more than one occasion. She had simply ignored it, until now.

But now she noticed. Annie stared at the smile, transfixed to see that the nun was not so unattractive, after all. She was old, of course—she must be well past forty if a day—but in spite of that, she had a rather nice face when she smiled. Why, it might even be considered a somewhat . . . pretty face.

Immediately, she squeezed her eyes shut and shuddered. No doubt it was a wicked and blasphemous thought, to think of one of God's nuns as—*pretty!*

When Annie finally opened her eyes, Sister was watching her with a very strange look. But, wonder of wonders, the TROUBLESOME NUN was still smiling!

17

The Singer and the Swan

Long the swans have wandered over lake and river.
Gone is all the glory of the race of Lir,
Gone and long forgotten like a dream of fever;
But the swans remember the sweet days that were.

KATHARINE TYNAN HINKSON (1861–1931)

On the third consecutive day of disobeying the surgeon's instructions, Morgan took his harp along when he went to Finola's room.

The first day, he had scarcely drawn breath as he sat beside the silent, slender form on the bed. He simply sat watching her, praying for her, willing her to acknowledge him.

It was an unnerving thing, seeing those glorious blue eyes opened wide, even turned in his direction, yet seemingly unaware of his presence. It made him feel invisible—and altogether helpless.

There had been no change on the second day, although he'd ventured to speak a few soft words. The words had gone unanswered, and his fear for her had only increased.

At last he had decided to heed Annie's suggestion. She had reminded him, this fey, capricious child, of Finola's great love for the music, of the depth of emotion it seemed to call forth from her in the days before the attack. Although he could not bring himself to hope too much, Morgan allowed that the lass's idea was at least worth a try.

And so today, when he wheeled himself into the bedroom, the harp was in his arms. He stopped halfway through the doorway, waiting. Although Finola seemed to pay no heed whatsoever to his being there, there was always the danger she would stir and panic at his presence, just as the surgeon had warned. He would not risk it.

After a moment, he wheeled himself up to the bed where Lucy was seated on the opposite side. At Morgan's approach, she moved to go, but he gestured that she should stay.

Small One, Finola's cat, lay dozing near the foot of the bed. This was Lucy's idea, her attempt to keep things, as much as possible, the way Finola was used to them.

The cat stirred, raised her head just enough to eye Morgan, then settled back to her nap.

"No change?" Morgan questioned Lucy in a hushed voice.

The woman shook her head, her gaze intent on Finola's face. She had proved a most excellent nurse, this strange friend to Finola. A small cot had been moved next to the bed for her, and for weeks now, she had lived in this room, refusing to leave for more than a few moments at a time. She kept Finola impeccably groomed, her flaxen hair clean and shining, her bed immaculate.

"Pardon me, sir," she said now, rising, "but if you'll be staying with her a bit, I'll just go down and prepare the medicine tray."

Morgan watched her hurry from the room, then turned his attention back to Finola. He noted with satisfaction that her face, although still somewhat bruised, seemed to be healing nicely. Scrubbed of the excessive paint the women at Gemma's had taught her to use, she looked younger than before . . . and lovelier still. Her hands were folded atop the bed linen, her hair fanned out on the pillows. She appeared peaceful, and, although too thin by far, more fit than Morgan had seen her for weeks. Had it not been for the vacant stare and a certain slackness to her facial muscles, she would have looked to be enjoying a perfectly normal rest.

He had to knot his hands into fists to keep from reaching out to her, to smooth back the golden strand of hair that had fallen across her forehead. Instead, he sat, unmoving, speaking to her in soft, lulling tones. He spoke of the crisp, bright December day. He told her of Annie's having at last mastered a complete lesson in Latin. He promised they would attend a concert as soon as she was stronger. He told her that Small One was growing quite fat and lazy.

As he spoke, he lightly plucked the harp. When he could no longer think of anything to say, he went on playing. Slow, quiet ballads at first, then a happier, carefree children's tune. Finally, he began to sing, at first so softly the words played over the bed like water lapping across small stones in a riverbed.

He sang his own music, childish airs to which he had set a number of the folk tales, then melancholy songs of country and home. At last he turned his voice to the song he had written for her—"Finola's Song." The song of the beautiful, enchanted swan whose sorrowful lament was eventually transformed to a hymn of glory.

———

When Annie heard the *Seanchai* singing inside Finola's room, she plopped down on the floor in the hallway to listen, cautioning Fergus to be very quiet.

She didn't think the *Seanchai* would mind. She loved to hear him make the music, would have sat listening to him play and sing for hours at any opportunity.

He was a true artist of the ancient instrument. Under his hands, every melody became a quiet stream of liquid gold. And his voice—ah, he could do things with his voice like no other man, and that was the truth! He could rumble deep and thunderous—why, he could shake the foundations of Nelson Hall, should he choose to do so! But when he sang, as he did now, that rich, gentle voice did flow so sweetly, the very birds in the trees would soon be weeping!

"He does have a gift for the music, the *Seanchai*."

Sister Louisa had a way of coming upon a person without a bit of warning. Did she really have feet at all, Annie wondered, or did she have herself a wee magic carpet underneath all those skirts that allowed her to glide up and down the hallways like some silent specter?

Annie shot her a guilty look from her perch on the floor.

"I wasn't eavesdropping, Sister! Truly, I wasn't! I only wanted to listen to the *Seanchai* sing!"

"Of course, you weren't eavesdropping," Sister Louisa replied matter-of-factly. "That would be childish. Besides, I'm sure the

Seanchai wouldn't mind your listening. So long as you sit quietly and don't intrude. I was wondering, however, if perhaps you would like to join me and Sandemon for vespers this evening?"

Annie's head shot up, and she gaped. "Vespers? *Me?*"

Sister nodded. "And Fergus, of course," she said, her mouth twitching slightly. "Sandemon suggested we—'join forces,' I believe he calls it. 'Join forces to do battle.' For the *Seanchai* and Finola."

Annie ran her tongue over her lower lip. "And—and you want me and Fergus to—to join forces with you?"

"Of course, we do. You're the *Seanchai*'s daughter, child!"

Annie looked away. "Not yet, I'm not."

Surprised, she felt Sister's hand on her shoulder. "Look at me, Annie Delaney."

Annie looked up, saw the kindness in the nun's eyes. She blinked, waiting.

"You *are* the *Seanchai*'s daughter," Sister Louisa repeated quietly. "A man is not a father because of a legal document or even because of the bloodtie. A man is a father by a choice of the will and a commitment of the heart. The *Seanchai* thinks of you as his daughter, and certainly loves you as his own." Without giving Annie time to respond, she straightened, saying, "Now, come along, you and Fergus. While the *Seanchai* does what *he* can for Finola, we will do what *we* can for them both."

Finola moved among a tapestry of dreamscapes. She had rejected the real world. It was *too* real, too harsh, too painful.

At times the world of her mind, the new world that she was even now still creating, was also frightening and painful. Yet even the darkest of its ominous shadows were less forbidding than the pitiless reality of the other world . . . the real world. . . .

She was walking beside a lake, watching the swans, listening to birdsong. In one hand she held a tin whistle. From time to time she stopped to imitate a bird's call, then went on.

The sun was going down, but there was still light for walking and gazing into the lake. Suddenly a shadow, wide and deep, fell across her path, and Finola started, whirling to look around her.

A huge black bird—no, not quite a bird, but a bird-like creature—sat beneath a large beech tree, watching her. Without knowing how she knew, Finola was suddenly aware that the bird had been following her all along. Without casting a shadow, without making a sound, the ugly black thing had hovered over her from the sky, dogging her steps, never letting her out of its sight. She knew this, and it chilled the blood within her.

The creature was nearly as tall as a man, and, perched as it was with its long, webbed wings folded at its sides, it took on the appearance of one of the hideous other-world beasts of the ancient legends. The small eyes locked on Finola were the color of slate and altogether lacking in expression.

Frozen by fear, Finola saw the sinister creature take a step with one large, clawed foot. Slowly, with a rush of air, it spread its wings and stood, poised, not to fly, she sensed, but to spring at her in attack.

Suddenly, as if the sun itself had recoiled in horror and fled the sky, the last light of evening trembled, then went out. Now there were no stars, no moon, no light at all except for the dim glow that seemed to rise like a vapor off the lake.

Panicked, Finola tried to scream, but no sound came. She looked around in desperation for help, but there was no one. She was alone.

Unable to take her eyes off the creature's looming presence, she began to back away, darting a glance over her shoulder to judge her distance from the water. As she watched, the bird's beak opened, and the thing seemed to smile—a terrible, menacing rictus of evil.

A shudder of cold terror seized Finola. At that moment she realized that this loathsome creature, obviously bent on her destruction, somehow embodied the whole of her worst fears. Whatever evil she might have imagined, whatever danger she had ever sensed lurking in the night—every horror that had ever struck her with dread—faced her now, in the form of this dark abomination.

She whipped around to run, but there was nowhere to go. She was surrounded by dark forest and lake water. Even if a path of rescue existed, she would never find it. The forest was entirely unknown to her. In the forest, she would meet with death.

Or something worse.

Her only hope was the lake. Somehow she knew the vile bird-creature could not touch her in the lake. She would go to the lake with the swans. She would become one of them.

Finola, the enchanted swan . . .

She tossed the tin whistle onto the ground, then slowly walked into the lake, where the swans were waiting. In the pale glow of the water, she saw the vast, dark shadow above her, circling, heard the grinding of wings, the angry screeching. . . .

She followed the swans into the middle of the lake, and felt herself changing, diminishing in size, becoming more graceful and fleet. Drifting now, gliding over the lake, a peace began to settle over her.

Overhead, the huge wings beat the wind . . . swooping . . . hovering . . . watching. Finally the shadow lifted, then disappeared altogether.

She was safe. For a time, Finola glided with the swans, serene, comforted by the cool, placid water all around her, the stillness and peace of the lake.

But now the swans broke away, began to move swiftly toward the shore, as if in answer to a call. Finola tried to call them back, but they could not hear her silent voice.

Alone in the middle of the lake, wondering, curious, but not yet frightened, she waited and listened.

The sound at first seemed to come from the forest. Softly, so softly she thought she might be imagining it . . . but, no, it was closer now, clearer.

A voice. The sound of singing . . .

At last Finola followed after the swans, gliding across the quiet, glowing lake in search of the Singer. Growing stronger, the voice nevertheless retained its infinite gentleness, its low, sweet tones of grace and beauty.

As she approached, the other swans parted, allowing her to move among them, then past, toward the shore.

The voice was near now . . . so near . . . yet still soft and ever so gentle . . . and familiar. . . .

As she approached the shore, Finola became aware that the voice of the Singer was calling to her . . . only to her . . . calling her to leave the lake . . . to come to him. . . .

Suddenly, Finola looked up, above the forest, and saw the dark shadow looming over the trees. The demon bird was still there, waiting . . . waiting for her.

Terrified, she started to turn back, then stopped. The Singer was still calling to her, and, unable now to turn away, Finola began to drift toward the voice . . . toward the song . . . toward the Singer. . . .

The shadow dipped lower, the whirring of wings grew louder. If she left the lake, the creature would be waiting for her, lurking in the forest.

If she stayed on the lake, she would be safe. But she would never reach the Singer, never hear his song again.

Leave the lake! whispered her heart. *Leave the lake . . . go to the Singer. . . .*

Go to the Singer. . . .

———

When Morgan first saw the hand flutter, he thought he had imagined it. He went on playing, singing, scarcely aware of the words, lost in the tide of his thoughts as he sang.

"Morgan?"

Morgan's fingers stiffened on the harp strings, and his throat went instantly dry. Had someone called his name?

He jerked his head toward the door, expecting to see Sister Louisa or Sandemon. But no, the door was shut tight, just as Lucy had left it.

"Morgan?" the whisper came again—very faint, far away.

Morgan wheeled his chair around and stared hard at the still figure on the bed. Finola lay motionless. Small One had moved to the head of the bed and was pawing at the pillow, mewing piteously.

Morgan shook his head as if to clear the cobwebs from his brain. He must be imagining things. Who would be calling to him? There was no one here—no one but himself, and Finola, and the cat. And, in truth, no one in this house ever called him by his Christian name. He couldn't remember the last time anyone had called him *Morgan*; it was always *Seanchai*.

Only in sleep did he hear his true name spoken, in dreams where he stood upright like a man, and the woman he treasured called his name with love and laughter on her tongue. He had yearned for it, prayed for it, wondered a thousand times what it would be like to hear Finola whisper his name, she who had never uttered a sound in his presence.

He shut his eyes and heaved a ragged sigh, then put his fingers once more to the strings of the harp.

"Morgan!"

Morgan's eyes snapped open, and then he saw it—her right hand moved! She reached out, slowly, and touched Small One's soft fur. The cat pressed her head into Finola's outstretched palm and began to purr.

Carefully, his hands trembling, Morgan braced the harp between the bed and the night table. Holding his breath, he wheeled closer, looking first at her face, then at her hand.

Finola's right hand went on stroking the cat gently. Ever so slowly, she extended her left, reaching—reaching for him.

Morgan inched his hand toward hers and touched her gently. Her fingers closed over his, and held.

Then her lips moved. *"MORGAN!"* she cried, her fingers gripping his hand like a vise.

It was no dream! Finola had spoken, had called his name—*his name!*

Tears lodged in Morgan's throat, and he had difficulty answering her at first. "Aye," he managed at last, his breath coming in short gasps. "I'm here, lass."

The wide blue eyes locked on his face, and she whispered, " 'Twas you . . . you were the Singer?"

"Aye," he choked out, his heart rising up on a thundering wave of love and incredible relief. "You heard me, then? You heard me singing to you, Finola?"

She strained toward him. "I was afraid," she whispered. "I was afraid to leave the lake. . . ."

He stared at her, not understanding, aching to gather her into his arms, to hold her close, to reassure her . . . knowing it could not be. "Don't be afraid, lass," he said softly. "You will stay here, with me. This will be your home. You need not be afraid any longer. Not now. Not ever."

She nodded, gripping his hand even more tightly. Her eyes closed, fluttered open, then closed again. "Don't . . . stop singing, Morgan."

Then, as if exhausted and utterly spent, she drifted off to sleep, his name still on her lips, her hand still clinging to his.

Somewhere inside him, in a safe, hidden place untouched by the world's tragedy and pain, "Finola's Song" swelled to a kind of anthem, rising to fill the emptiness of Morgan's heart.

18

Confrontation

So here is my desert and here am I
In the midst of it alone,
Silent and free as a hawk in the sky,
Unnoticed and unknown.

THOMAS MACDONAGH (1878–1916)

New York City
Christmas Eve

Daniel went on ahead of his mother and Evan. He was to be at the Farmington's early, with his harp, to provide the wedding music. But first he intended to stop and have one last talk with Tierney.

One last *argument* with Tierney, he corrected himself, for more than likely that's what it would be.

Despite the festive cheer of Christmas that hung over the city of New York, despite his happiness for Uncle Mike and Miss Sara, Daniel brooded during most of the ferry ride over. These last weeks had been hectic with change: moving in with Evan and Mother; the resulting separation from Tierney; Uncle Mike's marriage; Morgan's news about his attempt to adopt an orphan girl, the starting up of his school in Dublin, the black West Indies man he had hired—Sandemon—and his mysterious new friend, Finola.

And throughout the United States, change was occurring almost as quickly. America had elected a new president—one Zachary Taylor. "Old Rough and Ready," he was called. A peculiar man for the head of an entire country, Daniel thought, if the newspaper accounts could be believed. As a general in the Mexican War, the President-elect had worn old farm clothes, even a straw hat, into battle, and his legs were said to be so short he had to be given a leg-up by his orderly whenever he mounted a horse! But stranger still was the fact that this man, who was to head the entire government of the United States of America, had never even voted!

Far away, in a place called "California," gold had been discovered, while here in the state of New York, women were holding conventions about an issue called "suffrage." At the same time, antislavery organizations were holding conventions of their own, determined to free the black slaves in the South.

While all these events were no doubt of great importance to the country, Daniel's thoughts kept returning to the changes in his life, and in Tierney's—and, especially, in their friendship.

He hoped to find him at the flat. He would be alone, if he was there at all. Uncle Mike had already moved most of his things to the home of Miss Sara's grandmother, where they were going to be living after the wedding.

Daniel had moved *his* belongings to Brooklyn just a week ago. It had been difficult, making the break from Tierney and Uncle Mike. His stomach had been in knots for days before he moved out, and the final day of his move, he had all he could do to keep from blubbering like a babe.

He knew he would miss Uncle Mike something fierce, but he would miss Tierney even more. He already did.

He hated to think of Tierney living by himself in the flat. There would be no one to talk to—no one to *argue* with, Tierney would say. Daniel didn't think *he* could bear to be alone like that, not for days at a time. Tierney, however, vowed it would suit him just fine. He even boasted that he was looking forward to having no one about to nag him or give him grief about his comings and goings.

"You can't be serious," he'd joked when Daniel voiced his concern. "It'll be grand! Don't take offense, Danny-Boy, but I doubt that I'll miss Da's grumbling or your snoring for very long at all!"

Patrick Walsh had offered him a coachman's cottage on his

Staten Island estate, but Tierney had only made light of it to Daniel. "He may be my boss, but he'll not be my keeper as well! Blazes, I can't imagine having to endure that awful Isabel all the time!"

More than likely, Tierney meant every word he said. That being the case, Daniel supposed he should cease worrying about him.

For his own part, although the break was painful, it was something he felt he had to do. Mother wanted him with her. She and Evan had been after him for weeks to move to Brooklyn, and the truth was, now that he had made the break, he was glad. He and Evan got along just grand, his mother was obviously happy to have him about the house again—and it was fine being back with Little Tom and Johanna.

Still, he could not quite forget about Tierney, alone in the flat.

———

When Tierney opened the door, wearing only an undershirt and a pair of faded trousers, Daniel's heart sank. Obviously, he had no intention of going to the wedding.

"Well, look at the boyo, would you!" Tierney cracked in an exaggerated brogue. He made no move to step aside so Daniel could enter. "You're on the wrong side of town, dressed in your finery, I'm thinking. We don't often see the likes of you down here."

Ignoring his sarcasm, Daniel pressed through the door. The apartment was dark, with only one small candle flickering on the kitchen table. A single empty glass sat on the table next to the candle, and the room was filled with a faintly pungent smell. A fleeting picture of his friend sitting alone in the dark room unnerved him. He couldn't help but question the wisdom of Uncle Mike's decision, to allow Tierney the use of the flat. Yet, what else was he to do? Tierney had been enraged by even the suggestion that he live with Uncle Mike and his new wife.

"I'd hoped we could talk."

"I think not." Tierney heaved the door shut, then turned to face Daniel. "I expect I know what you want to talk about, and we've already had that conversation, remember?"

"Tierney—"

"Save it, Danny! If you came here to rag me about the wedding, you're wasting your breath and my time."

"Don't you *care* how you're hurting Uncle Mike? Doesn't it bother you at all, then?" Daniel hadn't intended things to heat up so quickly. He'd thought to talk with him in a reasonable way, try once more to make him see just how selfish he was being. Instead, Tierney was already in a temper, and Daniel feared he was close to losing his own.

"I'm the last thing the old man is thinking about tonight," Tierney jeered, his face hard. "He won't even know I'm not there."

"What's your point, Tierney?"

"What do you mean?" The ice-blue eyes narrowed, the mouth turned down.

"What do you think to prove by not going to your own father's wedding?" Daniel felt the blood rush to his head, but he had gone too far to stop now. Somehow he had to make Tierney *think* about what he was doing.

"You're wanting everyone to know you don't *approve*, is that it? But we already know! Or is it more that you're not willing to back down, even if you're *wrong*?"

Tierney's chin shot up, and the eyes narrowed still more. "That'll do, Danny-Boy," he said quietly. "That'll do."

Daniel studied him for a moment. "Do you know," he answered quietly, "that you sounded very much like Uncle Mike just now?"

Tierney made no reply; he just stood, arms crossed over his chest. Again Daniel thought of Uncle Mike. They were so much alike, Tierney and his da. So much alike . . . yet a world apart.

He softened. What was there about his mercurial friend, he wondered, that made it impossible to stay angry with him for more than a few moments at a time? "I didn't come to fight."

"Then why *did* you come?"

"I had something to say. I'd hoped you'd listen."

Tierney regarded him with a measuring look. "Have your say, then. I'm listening." His voice was quiet, but his eyes remained unyielding.

Daniel swallowed, dug one hand in his pocket and looked at Tierney straight on. "Uncle Mike has already had his share of pain, it seems to me. It must have been a terrible time for him when your mother died."

When Tierney's expression didn't change, Daniel faltered a little. Drawing a deep breath, he forced himself to go on. "But he did his best to be a good father to you. To give you a proper home and more than your share of affection. That couldn't have been easy. He must have been lonely many a time, but he did right by you, Tierney. You told me so yourself. He *always* did right by you."

Tierney turned and walked to the window, looking out on the street below as if Daniel were no longer in the room.

"What I'm trying to say is . . . I don't think it should make a difference to you tonight, whether or not you like Sara Farmington or approve of the marriage. I just don't think any of that should matter. Not tonight."

Tierney half turned to look at him. His eyes were still hard, but he didn't look quite so angry now.

"I think the only thing that should matter to you tonight is that Uncle Mike is your father, and you're his son. You may not always agree with his ways, and you may not approve of his choice in a wife. But he's still your *father*, Tierney, and he's done his best to be a *good* father. He's spent his life on you!"

Daniel stopped, clenching his fists at his sides. "I just think," he choked out, "that you owe him one hour of respect for that. One hour, Tierney. That's all."

Without waiting for a reply—without even looking at Tierney—Daniel lunged toward the door and bolted out.

He ran all the way downstairs, tears scalding his eyes. His legs felt as heavy as lead weights. His heart felt even heavier.

19

Love, the Greatest Gift

With trembling hands, I hold your dreams,
With trembling heart, I give you mine. . . .

ANONYMOUS

Sitting on the side of the bed, Jess Dalton smiled down at the top of his wife's copper curls. She had already adjusted his tie, and was now buttoning his cuffs.

"I imagine you're feeling rather smug this evening," he said, smiling.

With the tip of her tongue pressed against the corner of her mouth, Kerry frowned intently over her labors. "And why should I be feeling smug?" She didn't look up.

"You more or less predicted this marriage, I seem to recall."

Kerry smiled a little, finishing off one sleeve, then turning to the other. "I did, didn't I?"

"You still approve of the match, I trust?"

"Indeed! I think they'll be splendid together, don't you?"

Jess didn't have to consider his reply. "I'd say so, yes."

"This will certainly be one of the smaller ceremonies we've attended recently," she remarked. "Odd, isn't it? One would expect Sara Farmington to have a royal affair, complete with all the trappings."

"This was her choice," Jess pointed out, "although Michael made no secret that he was greatly relieved."

Smoothing his cuff, Kerry lifted her face for a kiss. "You look extraordinarily handsome this evening, Mr. Dalton," she said after a moment, appraising him with a critical eye. "I expect I'm a lucky woman indeed."

"You're a woman with the gift of the blarney, is what you are," he said, planting a kiss on her cheek. He stood, pulling her to her feet as he did. "And I love it."

She held his suit coat for him while he slipped into it. "Do you think Michael's son will come to the wedding, Jess?"

He sighed, turning back to her. "Michael doesn't think so. But let's hope he's wrong. He's already been greatly hurt by the boy's opposition to the marriage, that much is obvious."

Kerry stood on tiptoe, adjusting his tie for him one last time. "I think," she said archly, "Tierney Burke is an entirely selfish young man."

Jess shook his head. "Perhaps. On the other hand, he may simply be a very *troubled* young man. Troubled and confused."

"Sara says he's angry. She makes all sorts of allowances for him."

"Sara has a very generous nature."

"Aye, she does," Kerry replied, extinguishing the oil lamp before starting for the door. "And something tells me that sooner or later, her new stepson will test that generous nature to the very limits."

———

Instructing Little Tom not to pick up the kitten now that he was dressed in his wedding clothes, Evan went to see what was keeping Nora. If they didn't leave soon for the ferry, they'd never make the wedding in time.

"Nora?" He peered into the bedroom. "Are you ready, d-dear? We really should be going."

Seeing no sign of her, he walked the rest of the way into the room. "Nora?"

She appeared in the doorway of the small, adjoining dressing room. "I'm here, Evan. And I'm ready. Or at least I shall be in a moment."

She was dressed in a lovely suit the color of lilacs, a suit Evan insisted she have made for today, despite her protests that it was much too extravagant. At first glance, she looked splendid. A closer look, however, made Evan frown in concern. Her skin was absolutely ashen, and her eyes appeared sunken and smudged with shadows.

Alarmed, he crossed the room and took her hand. "Nora? What is it, dear? Are y-you all right?"

"Of course, I'm all right." Although her smile was somewhat shaky, her voice was firm. "Perhaps I rushed too much, that's all. And this suit is very warm."

"You look won-wonderful." Holding her hand, Evan stood back just enough to enjoy the picture she made. "But you *are* pale, dear. Why d-don't you sit down for a moment before we leave?"

She shook her head, still smiling. "No, I'm fine now, truly I am."

"*Now?* So you haven't been feeling well?"

She smiled at him as if she were about to say something, then changed her mind.

A thought struck Evan, one he was half-afraid to voice. "Is . . . is it the wedding, Nora? Are you b-bothered by this marriage?" He hesitated, then finished his thought. "Because of M-Michael?"

With a look of utter dismay, she pressed a finger to his lips to hush him. "*Evan!* You foolish, foolish man! How can you *possibly* think such a thing? Can you really be so uncertain of my love, even now?"

Instantly contrite that he had doubted her, Evan quickly pulled her to him. "I'm sorry, Nora! I *am*. It's just that . . . sometimes I still find m-myself amazed that you chose *me*. . . ."

"That's exactly right, Evan Whittaker!" she said, searching his eyes. "I . . . chose . . . *you*. And not for a moment have I ever regretted that choice! Now, then," she said firmly, taking his arm, "let's be going to the ferry! We have a wedding to attend, and then, later—gifts to exchange!"

"Why, that's right," Evan said. "In all the excitement about the wedding, I'd al-almost forgotten: it's Christmas Eve!"

She put her hands to his shoulders, smiling into his eyes. "It is, indeed. And I just might have a very special gift for you."

He opened his mouth to quiz her, but she shushed him, laughing. "Later," she said, her eyes twinkling. "Not until later."

Sara had determined she would not cry at her own wedding. She cried at *other* people's weddings—invariably—caught up in the emotion and the romance and the almost magical atmosphere. But she would *not* make a fool of herself on her own special day!

Her resolve lasted all the way through Daniel's beautiful harp serenade. She was even able to smile at her father—who was, himself, somewhat misty-eyed, as was Winifred, beside him, though she was beaming through her tears.

Sara managed to remain dry-eyed, with Jess Dalton about to begin the nuptial reading, and with Michael—splendidly handsome and surprisingly nervous—at her side. Indeed, she might have made it all the way through the ceremony without disgracing herself had she not looked up toward the doors of the chapel just as the last sweet, sparkling notes of Daniel's music died away—to see Tierney walk in.

He stopped for a moment, looked from Sara to his father, who visibly started and drew in a sharp breath. Then he slipped quietly into the back row, unsmiling, but apparently resigned. At least for tonight.

It was enough. For now, Sara told herself, it was enough.

Her breath caught on a sob, and her hands began to tremble. She gripped her bridal bouquet more firmly. Her tears, contained with such effort, spilled over and trailed down her cheeks. Michael took her hand and gave it a gentle squeeze, and Sara turned to look at him.

There were tears in his eyes, too! The sight of her square-jawed, straight-backed Michael, resplendent in his stiff white collar and black suit, about to weep, was almost Sara's undoing.

But at that moment, Jess Dalton, as if sensing the impending crisis, lifted his rich, vibrant voice and filled the chapel with a joyous proclamation: "THIS IS THE DAY WHICH THE LORD HAS MADE! WE WILL REJOICE AND BE GLAD IN IT!"

―――――――

Daniel almost tripped getting into his seat beside Evan, so surprised—and pleased—was he to see Tierney walk into the chapel.

As soon as he sat down, he glanced up at Uncle Mike. The expression on his face brought an ache to Daniel's heart and a lump to his throat.

Oh, Tierney . . . Tierney . . . look at your father . . . just look at

*him and see how much your being here means to him . . . how much
you mean to him. . . .*

———

Nora's eyes burned with unshed tears as Michael and Sara
exchanged their vows.

She clung to Evan's hand, knowing that he, like she, was more
than likely remembering their own wedding, right here, in this
same chapel. Wave after wave of emotion flooded through her.
Love for her husband rose up inside her, a love so sweet, yet so
overwhelming, she could have cried aloud for the sheer wonder
of it. Happiness for Michael and Sara made her smile through
the glaze of tears, and as Pastor Dalton pronounced them husband and wife, she knew a sense of completeness as if something
very precious had at last been sealed.

But even as her heart hummed with the joy of the hour, a
shadow fell over her thoughts. For one still, bittersweet moment,
she remembered three children in an Irish village . . . three
friends, joined by bonds of loneliness and love and need.

She looked at Michael, saw his happiness, looked at her own
hand clasped securely in Evan's, then looked at the harp her son
had propped at the end of the altar. And she remembered . . .
remembered the one whose dreams had always been bigger and
grander and nobler than hers and Michael's added together. The
one whose spirit had always seemed to soar, to fly, beyond the
village, beyond what *was*, to reach for what *could* be.

The one who had risked his life to make all this possible for
her. The one who had stayed behind . . . but urged her to go.

She tried not to think of the wheelchair, tried not to wonder
what it must be like for him. Instead, she closed her eyes just for
a moment . . . and prayed for him—prayed for a special gift of
love and happiness for Morgan . . . and thanked God for the special gift of love He had given her and Evan.

———

Later that night—much later—Evan and Nora sat, side by
side, contentedly watching the fire.

Daniel John and the children, after opening one small gift
each, declared they would save the "large gifts" for Christmas

morning. Exhausted from the long day, they had gone on to bed without complaining.

"This is so fine, isn't it, Evan?" Nora didn't take her eyes away from the fire. "Sitting here, by the fire, knowing the children are safe and healthy—knowing that Michael and Sara are as happy as we are, if that's at all possible. This is truly a gift in itself, isn't it?"

His arm around her shoulder, Evan pulled her close. "A v-very precious gift. No m-man could ask for more, not at Christmas or ever."

Nora turned to look at him. "Truly, Evan? There is nothing else you would ask for, nothing more than what we have?"

Her gaze went over his face. As always, Evan felt himself loved. And counted himself blessed. "Nothing," he choked out, touching his lips to hers. "I have everything a m-man could possibly want— and more."

After they kissed, Nora smiled. A peculiar smile, Evan thought. Almost secretive.

"Ah, that's too bad, then," she said, her expression strangely cryptic, but tender. "Because I have another gift for you, you see— a very special gift indeed—but if you'd rather not know about it—"

"B-but I thought we agreed to wait until morning and open our gifts with the children."

"We did, yes, but . . . I don't believe I can wait that long. Besides, I'd like us to be alone . . . just for this one gift." She went on smiling, more mysterious now than ever. "We can share it with the children in the morning."

Evan forced a stern frown. "Are you g-going to tell me what this secret is all about, Mrs. Whittaker?"

The woman looked as if she simply couldn't stop smiling. "Here is my gift to you, Evan," she said. Taking his hand, she placed it gently over her abdomen.

Evan stared at her hand, then slowly raised his head to study her face. "Nora?"

She increased the pressure on his hand, just slightly. "I am with child, Evan," she said, her voice soft. "Before *next* Christmas comes, I will give you the gift of a child . . . a child of our own."

Stunned, Evan could only sit, gaping at her still slim waist, his trembling hand, her shining eyes.

"A . . . child?" he echoed shakily, trying to put down the panic he felt and show the pleasure she obviously expected from him. "A ch-child of our own?"

Nora now took his hand, brought it to her lips. "Happy Christmas, beloved," she murmured, her eyes never leaving his. "Oh, Evan—happy, happy Christmas!"

———

"Happy Christmas, Mrs. Burke."

In the dimly lighted cottage at the rear of the Farmington mansion, Michael Burke smiled and watched his bride open the small package he had just presented her.

"Michael! Oh—how very lovely!" As she lifted the blue satin ribbon from the tissue, Sara's face glowed more brightly than the candles that had been placed all about the room.

"It's for your hair," Michael said softly. He couldn't take his eyes from her, this woman who had tonight become his wife. This woman who counted herself plain, yet had a beauty that glowed from within, a beauty that could light an entire room. Certainly, she lighted his entire world.

"You are lovely, Sara *a gra*," he said thickly, meaning it. "I think you are quite the loveliest thing I have ever seen."

She blushed furiously beneath his scrutiny, just as she always did. She stood there before him, obviously ill at ease in her bridal nightdress, looking as if she could not quite decide whether to fall into his arms—or bolt from the room.

"Lovely," he repeated, holding out his arms.

She took a step—a small, uncertain step—toward him. "Am I? Am I *really*, Michael?"

She held the blue satin ribbon from trembling fingers. Michael caught one end of it, pulling her a little closer. "You are," he said, his voice low and somewhat unsteady, "the most beautiful thing in my world. And I am a fortunate man, indeed, to have you as my wife."

With one hand, he tugged a pin from her hair, then another. Smiling, he held up the blue satin ribbon, dangling it in front of her. "Tonight," he said gently, pulling yet another pin free, "I will take the pins from your hair . . . just as I told you I would. Tonight,

Sara *a gra*, we will take down your hair, and you will wear a blue satin ribbon in it . . . just for me, for your husband."

With the next pin, Sara's hair tumbled free, falling almost to her waist as she took the last remaining step into his arms.

PART TWO

DREAMS ABANDONED

—

Night Shadows

Let him who walks in the dark,
who has no light,
trust in the name of the Lord
and rely on his God.

ISAIAH 50:10

20

The Start of a Quiet Rebellion

*The best lack all conviction, while the worst
Are full of passionate intensity.*

W. B. YEATS (1865–1939)

*Staten Island, New York
February 1849*

Seated at the piano at ten o'clock in the morning, Alice Walsh willfully ignored the stab of guilt that almost always accompanied these early-morning music sessions.

Just the thought of her mother was usually enough to make her get up and leave the room. Mama would be absolutely aghast if she could see her daughter perched on a piano stool this time of day. A good German housewife had countless other things—*important* things—to occupy her mornings.

Today, however, Alice did not get up. When the blade of guilt began to twist a little deeper, she simply began to play a little louder. And much faster.

Equally adept at Mozart or Bach, Alice nursed a secret penchant for the "new" American music, music which, according to Mama, was "frivolous," "inferior," and, in some cases, even "pagan."

Alice harbored her own private collection of it in the very back of the music cabinet. Her most recent favorite, and the one now open in front of her, was an admittedly frivolous little number entitled "Oh! Susanna." Mr. E. P. Christy of the Christy Minstrel shows credited himself as composer of the piece, which by now had become wildly popular among the gold miners out West. Rumors continued to circulate, however, that the song had actually been penned by a young, heretofore unknown composer named Stephen Foster. Mr. Foster, it was whispered, *drank*.

Alice knew nothing about the rightful composer, but at times like this, when the house was empty of everyone but the servants, she did love to gallop though the spirited little song. At present, she was on her third frenzied run through the number, as if to give vent to the nagging unrest that seemed to plague her more and more often of late.

Up until recently, Alice had known nothing about *restlessness*, indeed scarcely knew what it meant. The product of staunch, practical German upbringing, she lived a life in keeping with the standards of her parents, the tenets of her church, and the demands of her husband and children.

She had always considered her life full and immensely satisfying. Although she had married late and, according to some, beneath her station—Patrick was Irish and five years younger—she adored her husband. He was handsome, intelligent, and enterprising, and a devoted, if often distracted, husband. If he wasn't the most attentive or thoughtful of men, he still treated her with respect and sometimes even waxed romantic, occasionally bringing her flowers, and, more rarely, spending the night in her bedroom.

Alice had fallen in love with Patrick Walsh the first time he sat across from her at the dinner table in her parents' home. After fifteen years of marriage, she only loved him more. Their two children were clever and healthy, if somewhat indulged; their home was lavish and comfortable. All in all, Alice considered herself a thoroughly happy, remarkably fortunate woman.

If her days were somewhat predicable, what of it? *Excitement* was a distasteful word, almost an obscenity to people like her parents, and *variety* applied only to the dinner menu. No, Alice preferred the orderly progression of her life and had never felt a desire or a need for anything other than what she already had.

Until recently. Of late, mostly in the mornings, after Patrick had gone off to his work and the children had left for school, she had begun to find herself feeling . . . restless. Restless and somewhat at loose ends.

She had little to do around the house; the servants took care of everything, with only minimal supervision. Mrs. Cooper, the cook, viewed the kitchen as her own private domain and managed to make Alice feel like a virtual intruder whenever she dared to enter. She did her own mending, but was always caught up. She detested knitting and tatting, and disliked flower arranging even more.

Her one indulgence was her music. Even so, she deliberately limited the time spent at the piano or organ, feeling too many hours squandered in self-entertainment must surely be hedonistic, and therefore wicked.

Over the past few weeks, however, she had found herself giving in more and more to the enjoyment of the keyboard. The excellent upright piano in the parlor was the same one she had grown up with. The ornate, hand-carved organ across the room had been a surprise birthday present from Patrick some years ago. She had an extensive collection of music, and her tastes were varied enough to keep her interested.

Lately, though, she seemed to have trouble concentrating, even on the music. At the oddest moments, she caught herself feeling idle and useless. These feelings of worthlessness only served to strengthen a growing burden of guilt and stir all sorts of alien, disturbing emotions in her.

It would have made all the difference, she thought as the last notes of "Oh! Susanna" died away, if someone *needed* her. These days, Patrick was seldom at home for more than an hour or two in the evening, was often gone for days on end, attending to "business." Since he had made it a policy never to discuss "business" at home, Alice hadn't the faintest idea what, exactly, he did. She knew only that he owned some hotels and boardinghouses and invested in other properties throughout the city. Obviously, he was successful.

Even the children had reached an age where they were rapidly growing more resourceful and independent of her. At thirteen, Isabel was quite the little woman; indeed, she had a way of treating *Alice* like a child. And Henry, already nine, disappeared most evenings after dinner to his room, where he presumedly studied and looked out the window through his telescope. Henry, Alice thought with no lack of affection for her youngest, might be just a bit odd.

The past weeks of restlessness had spurred her to do some serious self-examination and thinking about her life. In the process, she had discovered two significant facts about herself that were not altogether comfortable.

Alice had come to realize that she was almost entirely motivated by the needs of others. She *had* to be needed—indeed, she *existed* to be needed.

Yet her importance to her family was definitely on the decline. That was a situation not likely to change. As Patrick became more and more involved in his business interests, and the children grew older, they would need her less and less.

The other discovery Alice had made was that she had been *given* a great deal, and, up until now, had taken much of it for granted in the most shameful way. The only child of prosperous, middle-aged parents, she had lacked for nothing. She had known only comfort for all of her thirty-nine years, had been somewhat pampered, if carefully disciplined, by her parents, and had then gone on to wed a man who denied her nothing, indeed almost *encouraged* her to be extravagant.

Lately, these discoveries had begun to provoke her into serious questions. What, exactly, did she intend to do as her children grew older—and even more independent of her nurturing—and as Patrick grew more involved than ever with his business concerns? And how might she give back at least a portion of what she had been given?

She thought perhaps the time had come to involve herself in the church's charity outreach. As one of the member churches in a city-wide organization, Alice's church was perpetually in need of volunteers to aid in the extensive mission program.

Because her time had been so taken up with her family, up until now Alice had paid little attention to how the organization functioned. She had simply given money when a need was expressed. Recently, however, she had decided to learn more about this particular venture. And next week would provide the ideal opportunity.

Sara Farmington Burke was serving as hostess at an ambitious bazaar being held to bring together volunteers from all the member congregations throughout the city. The event would take place at the Farmington mansion on Fifth Avenue. The Reverend Jess Dalton, a vital force behind the mission effort, and one of its primary organizers, was to speak; and during the afternoon there would be an opportunity for new volunteers to become acquainted with the various slum mission programs.

Alice intended to go. She had sensed a kindness, a genuine warmth in Miss Farmington—*Mrs. Burke*, she corrected herself—when the young socialite had come to visit the injured Tierney Burke some months past. Although she'd seemed ill at ease, she had been cordial. She hadn't affected to patronize Alice or, even worse, ignore her—as did many among Alice's church acquaintances.

Alice had tried not to mind the social rejection she faced after her marriage. Patrick had risen above his Irish roots long ago, and there were as many who seemed to respect him for it as those who did not. At the same time, there were others who deliberately ostracized them. Such treatment both wounded and puzzled Alice. Occasionally, she even felt persecuted, as if she were the victim of something far more vicious than ethnic prejudice. At times, it was as if they were outcasts—despised outcasts, almost like criminals, though she supposed she might be exaggerating the situation.

At least, she reminded herself hopefully as she rose from the piano stool, she would not receive such shabby treatment from Sara Farmington Burke. The Farmington heiress had, like Alice, married "beneath her station."

Somehow, Alice found great comfort in that fact. If a woman of Sara Burke's standing could face the often cruel and painful consequences of following her heart, it made Alice feel somewhat proud that she had done likewise.

———

Patrick Walsh was beginning to sense the screws tightening against him, thanks to that sanctimonious, self-serving police captain—Burke.

He stood, one hand in his pocket, the other knotted at his side, looking out the window of his Pearl Street office. A light snow had been falling since early morning and was now being whipped about the streets by a bitter February wind. Pedestrians hurried along, hats pulled down, mufflers slung over their faces, in their haste to take refuge indoors.

Angry, Walsh frowned as the thought of the new *Subcommis-*

sion on Immigrant Crime—and Michael Burke—again intruded on his peace of mind. There were a number of politicos and do-gooders on the subcommission, but from what he was hearing, it was Burke and his father-in-law, Lewis Farmington, who were stirring up most of the trouble. No doubt Farmington, as the chairman, had given his obnoxious son-in-law a free hand.

Apparently, that included a personal strike at *him*. According to one of Patrick's men on the force, Burke was out for his hide. To Patrick, that meant the policeman must have sniffed out his involvement with the runners. No doubt some misplaced sense of loyalty to the Irish—Burke was an immigrant himself—lay behind his tactics.

Had it been another cop besides Burke on the prowl, Patrick would have simply paid him off. But the word on the hard-nosed captain was that he couldn't be bought, and Patrick was inclined to agree. He'd seen enough of the man to suspect that money wasn't his weakness.

It *was* a fact that some men—though they were few—could not be bought with *money*. But it was also a fact, Walsh was convinced, that *every* man had a price of some kind.

Somehow, he was determined to make it his business to find out what the honorable Captain Burke's price happened to be.

21

Pharisees and Sinners

The lawyers have sat in council,
The men with the keen, long faces,
And said, "This man is a fool. . . ."

PADRAIC PEARSE (1879–1916)

"Michael, you *are* going to be at the bazaar next week, aren't you?"

It was early Sunday morning. Sara sat across from her husband at breakfast, who, for the most part, seemed to have forgotten she was in the room.

"Michael?"

Finally, his dark eyes met hers across the top of the newspaper. "You're joking, of course."

"I'm not. But I *am* counting on your help."

"*My* help?" The paper slipped another notch, down to his nose. "What sort of help would that be?"

"I had hoped you might speak about Five Points—from a policeman's perspective." Ignoring the strangled sound that bounced off the paper, Sara went on. "You can explain better than anyone else about the illegal boardinghouses—and what happens to the immigrants who end up in them."

The newspaper came down, although he clung to it like a shield. "Sara," he said reasonably, "I'm a policeman, remember? I arrest robbers and help elderly ladies across the street. Some-

199

times I crack heads, and I often chase pigs. But I never, *never* address mission bazaars. Never."

When he would have hidden once more behind the paper, Sara reached across the table and stayed his hand. "It's important, Michael. These women need to know the hard truth, even if it makes them uncomfortable."

"What will make them uncomfortable, Sara *a gra*, is the visible proof that their genteel lady chairman has gone half-cracked and not only married a crude Irish cop, but is actually parading him about at her teas."

Sara glared at him. "You are not at all crude—except when you choose to be, as you are doing right now. More than likely," she added with a smug smile, "I'll be the envy of every woman there for having the courage to marry such a dangerously handsome man."

He grinned at her. "No doubt. But I'm still not giving a speech to your church ladies," he said with annoying finality. "Your grandmother is late this morning, isn't she? Have you checked on her?"

"She's getting dressed. I expect she'll be down any time now. Don't change the subject, Michael. There's another reason I'd like you to be at the bazaar, although I really *do* hope you'll consider speaking. I think Jess Dalton is going to need all the support he can get; having you there will guarantee him at least one ally."

Michael sighed, folding his papers with great precision as if to make a point. "Why is that?"

"The news is out about their plans to keep Arthur Jackson in their home indefinitely."

Michael groaned his understanding, and Sara went on. "The Pulpit Committee has already called a special meeting."

Michael straightened his chair, frowning. "You don't think they'd ask him to leave?"

Sara looked down at her plate. "Quite frankly, I don't know what to expect. I wouldn't be so concerned if Father were on the committee, but he isn't." She sighed. "There are some truly good people in our congregation who won't be bothered in the least by the Daltons taking in a Negro boy. But there are others . . ." She let her words drift off, unfinished.

"There are others who will make things miserable for them," Michael finished for her, scowling. He shook his head. "It's too bad. He and Mrs. Dalton genuinely care for the lad, that's obvious."

Sara nodded, then brightened somewhat. "Well, one thing is certain: Jess Dalton isn't a man to back down in the face of opposition. If he's decided to give Arthur Jackson a home, he'll do just that."

"Aye, he will," Michael said, still frowning. "But let us hope he doesn't lose his pulpit in the process."

Just then Sara's grandmother appeared in the doorway of the dining room. "It's outrageous," she said, walking the rest of the way into the room. "Heaven help the Daltons—and the boy—if the wrong people happen to discover he's a runaway slave. Someone will turn him in to those awful slave catchers."

Michael rose and helped her into her chair. "Fortunately, those who know Arthur's background are very few," he pointed out, bracing her cane against the table. "And there's no one among them who would deliberately hurt the lad."

"Still," said Grandy Clare, "there will be trouble. You wait and see if there's not."

"Speaking of trouble," Michael said, shooting Sara a look over her grandmother's head, "is Whittaker still bringing his singers to your bazaar?"

Sara smiled and nodded. "He is indeed. The Five Points Celebration Singers will provide the entertainment for the afternoon."

Still standing, Michael drained the last of his coffee from his own private mug. From the very outset of their marriage, he had flatly refused to drink from Grandy Clare's delicate china teacups. "Not one of your more clever ideas, Sara," he remarked dryly.

"I'm sure they'll do just fine," Sara said defensively.

"Oh, I'm not doubting that for a minute. They do a grand job, there's no denying it. It's just that it might be a bit much for the refined sensibilities of your church ladies, that's the thing." He winked at Grandy Clare. "All those black and Irish faces in the same room at one time, you know."

Not to be baited, Sara shrugged. "Perhaps it will distract them from Jess Dalton's . . . 'radical behavior.' At any rate, my main purpose in asking Evan to bring the boys wasn't necessarily for entertainment. I'm hoping to impress some of the mission sponsors, show them what can be done in a place like Five Points with just one godly man who is willing to make an effort. I think Evan has accomplished wonders with those boys."

Michael nodded. "He has, indeed. Now—if you ladies will excuse me, I'll go and bring the buggy around."

"I will remind you again," said Grandy Clare, "that Robert would be more than happy to drive us to services. That," she added dryly, "is one of the reasons I pay him."

Michael grinned at her. "And I will remind you, my lady, that I am perfectly capable of driving a buggy now and then. Besides," he added, "I happen to enjoy it."

Sara followed him to the back door, where she held on to his hand for a moment. "You still haven't answered my question," she reminded him. "About whether you'd speak at the bazaar."

"And I thought you followed me out here for a private kiss," he said, pulling her into his arms. "Besides, I did answer you."

"*Really*, Michael!"

"Ah, Sara . . . Sara, you are going to be my undoing, and that's the truth."

Out of her grandmother's view now, Sara gave him an ardent kiss and embrace. "You'll at least think about it, won't you, Michael? Promise me you will."

He smiled, a smile Sara took to be the beginning of defeat. "Perhaps," he said, making no move to release her. "Then, again, it's possible that I might require a bit more coaxing."

Kerry Dalton sneaked a look at her husband, standing beside her as they greeted the departing worshipers from the morning service.

Jess looked tired, she realized with concern. Tired and somewhat disillusioned. Of course, no one would even suspect the disillusionment unless they knew him well. His kind and cheerful countenance successfully masked the turmoil Kerry knew to be going on inside him.

She had to fight to keep her own anger and disappointment from showing. Although reactions had been mixed, she was convinced that even the most supportive members of the congregation were not altogether untouched by some of the wilder rumors that had been circulating.

The decision to take Arthur Jackson in, to give him a home as long as he wanted to stay with them—and to actually *encourage* him to stay—had, just as Jess predicted, brought on an entire hailstorm of exaggerated stories. The most farfetched one to date, and the one that most infuriated Kerry, was the perfectly ridiculous tale that the pastor's interest in Arthur was motivated by the fact that the young black boy had taken a bullet actually meant for *Jess*!

No one seemed to pay any heed to the fact that Arthur had suffered a lengthy, difficult recovery from his injury, that he was virtually destitute, and that they were merely trying to provide him with shelter and a measure of protection.

The truth was, she and Jess had grown more than a little fond of Arthur Jackson—as had their son, Casey-Fitz. While it was true that Arthur had a father somewhere in Mississippi, the poor man was a slave and could offer nothing in the way of assistance or protection to his son. She and Jess *could*, and were determined to do so.

Jess's warning that Arthur's background remain a secret caused Kerry to study the faces of the departing worshipers even more closely as they passed through the line. The contrast in expressions made it painfully clear that those who took issue with the Daltons' decision far outnumbered those who did not.

The Kenneth Maltbys, for example, made a point of breaking out of the line just before reaching Jess and Kerry. Some, like the elderly, sharp-tongued Horace Pollard, were more inclined to direct confrontation.

The stooped, fiery-eyed importer brought the entire procession to a halt when he stopped, leaned on his cane, and squinted up at Jess. "Pastor," he said sharply, "I've supported you in just about everything you've done since you came here. Some were worried that we were getting ourselves one of those abolitionist preachers who thought black folks were just as important to the good Lord as us white folks."

He paused, and Kerry felt Jess stiffen, as if bracing himself for what might come next.

"I'm happy to see that they were right," Horace went on. "This town has more than enough preachers who call themselves 'abolitionists' when they're propped up behind a pulpit—but who wouldn't be caught dead shaking a black man's hand! I for one am proud to know a man of the cloth who isn't all talk. But you watch your back, Preacher. Good men make good targets, if you take my meaning."

After pumping Jess's hand and winking at Kerry, he went on out the door. Kerry felt somewhat reassured to know there were men like Horace Pollard among the congregation, even if they were few in number.

As the line continued to move forward, her suspicions were confirmed that many of those who seemed most opposed to the idea of a black boy in their midst—and in the home of their pastor—were the same ones who found it . . . *difficult* . . . to be civil to *her*.

Apparently, an Irish immigrant wife was equally as undesirable as a homeless black boy.

———

Evan Whittaker found himself unable to concentrate during the morning worship hour. Nora, again feeling poorly, had insisted that he come and bring the children, but he was finding it difficult, if not impossible, to pay attention.

It did not help that the congregation still occupied temporary quarters, the church building having been destroyed in a January fire. Then, too, Mr. Beecher was again absent from the pulpit. Of late, there had been frequent bouts of illness, and it was rumored that he might be gone for several weeks.

Although Evan had mixed emotions about the highly popular—and often controversial—pastor, there was no denying the fact that his presence was greatly missed. His impassioned messages about the evils of slavery, his insistence on vigorous congregational singing, and his flamboyant charm, both in and out of the pulpit, made his absence keenly felt.

Yet, Evan doubted that it would have made much difference at all this morning had Beecher been present. He would still have been distracted.

He was absolutely sick with worry about Nora. She was having an extremely difficult time with her condition. Lately, he delayed leaving the house in the mornings because it meant leaving her alone, ashen with nausea, with only Little Tom to see to her. When he returned home at evening, more often than not she was still pale and unsteady, though she would insist that she was "feeling much better." She would sit through supper with him and the children, but Evan was all too aware that she took only a few bites of food, and then with visible effort.

Unbeknownst to Nora, he'd conferred with Nicholas Grafton, but the kindly physician had been able to offer little advice, and even less encouragement. "I'm keeping close check on her, you can be sure, Evan. Still, there's very little we can do except to make certain she gets proper rest and a good diet."

When Evan explained that he felt she was getting neither, the doctor had frowned, but said only, "Yes . . . well, watch her closely and be sure she doesn't overdo. If she doesn't perk up soon, she may have to lie in for most of her term. I do wish she'd been stronger at the outset."

At times Evan had all he could do to keep from actively wishing that Nora had never conceived this child. Knowing it would break her heart if she should learn his true feelings, he continued to pretend he was wildly happy about the baby, forcing a smile for her sake, when what he really felt was stark terror.

A nudge from Johanna, then a tug at his hand from Tom, made Evan start and glance about him. The congregation had risen and the interim pastor was midway through the benediction.

His face flaming, Evan scrambled to his feet. He had worried through most of the service.

Lewis Farmington was helping Winifred into the carriage after the morning worship hour when Chester Pauling walked up.

"Lewis, I wonder if I might have a word with you?"

Lewis speculated on how the hawk-faced Pauling would react if he refused, as would be his preference. Instead, he grunted an assent, indicating to Winifred that he'd be only a moment.

Turning around, Lewis found himself eye level with Pauling's thin gray mustache. Chester was a tall, cadaverous man with a perpetually morose frown. Lewis suspected that Chester Pauling had been born frowning.

"Lewis, there's a meeting tomorrow night at my house that I thought you'd want to attend."

Quite certain he *wouldn't* want to attend, Lewis merely gave a forced smile and said, "What sort of meeting, Chester?"

Pauling's heavy eyebrows drew tighter, forming a bridge over his beak of a nose. He cleared his throat. "Some of us are getting together to, ah, discuss this thing with the pastor."

Irritated, Lewis raised his chin. "What *thing* might that be, Chester?"

Pauling again cleared his throat. "Ah . . . this abolitionist business . . . and the Negro boy he's taken in. You know."

"The pastor will be at the meeting, I take it?"

"Well . . . no. No, we simply want to, ah, examine the situation."

"It seems to me," Lewis said sharply, "that any kind of meeting about the pastor should include *him*."

To his credit, Pauling looked uncomfortable. "It's not quite that simple, Lewis. We have to take a close look at how Dalton's actions may affect the entire congregation. Before we actually confront the pastor, we want to be sure we're in agreement."

You back-stabbing Pharisee, Lewis thought. *You've already decided to try to force a resignation.*

Drawing himself up to his full height—which was still considerably less than Pauling's—Lewis summoned all the self-control he could muster. "I don't want any part of your meeting, Chester. I don't want anything to do with this whole business. Mostly," he said, scowling, "because I happen to believe it is *none of our business*. Quite frankly, Chester, I think you should be ashamed of yourself."

When the other man tried to stammer out a protest, Lewis ignored him. "I can almost guess who *will* be at your meeting, though. Ashton and Maltby and Felix Willard—oh, yes, and I'm sure Charles Street as well." He stopped, drew in a long breath. "Thank you for asking, Chester, but I believe I have a prior engagement tomorrow evening."

Without giving the red-faced Pauling an opportunity to reply, Lewis turned and got into the carriage.

Winifred was all concern. "Lewis? Is something wrong? You're *quite* flushed!"

He patted her hand and managed a smile, although he wanted nothing more than to drive his fist through the roof of the carriage. "Everything is just fine, my dear. Don't worry your pretty head. I just had to present my apologies that I couldn't attend a meeting tomorrow night, that's all.

"Oh, I'm sorry, Lewis. Are you disappointed?"

Lewis looked at her. "Actually, Winnie, I am," he said quietly. "I'm *very* disappointed."

As they drove off, he silently reminded himself that Jesus had also preferred the company of sinners to that of the Pharisees.

22

Hope for the Hopeless

And love can reach
From heaven to earth, and nobler lessons teach
Than those by mortals read.

JOHN BOYLE O'REILLY (1844–1890)

When Mr. Whittaker asked to talk with him just before rehearsal on Thursday, Billy Hogan immediately started worrying
that he'd done something wrong.

Ever since he'd been caught sneaking Finbar into the practice
room, he'd taken extra care to be on his best behavior. Of course,
the business with Finbar had worked out all right, after all. Mr.
Whittaker had taken the mischievous kitten home to his wife and
family, and they liked him just fine.

As he gauged the director's expression just now, he saw that
he didn't look a bit cross; indeed, he seemed to be smiling. Still,
Billy's mouth felt dry as dust, and his belly burned with anxiety
as he faced the Englishman at the door. Trouble always meant
the chance that Uncle Sorley would find out.

Billy would do just about anything to avoid another of his
uncle's fierce thrashings.

––––––––

Evan quickly went out of his way to reassure the freckle-faced
youth, for he looked about to bolt at any moment. "How old are
you, B-Billy?"

"Sir? Oh—nine . . . close on nine, sir."

Evan nodded, thinking the little fellow looked even younger. "Then I should imagine you're old enough to accept the additional responsibility I have in m-mind for you."

The boy simply stared. Evan was struck by the dismaying realization that the lad seemed to be afraid of him. He could not think why; moreover, he found the idea highly unsettling. To his knowledge, he had never intimidated a single soul in his life. Certainly, he had no wish to frighten a child.

Gentling his voice even more, he went on. "Of course, you remember that next week is the m-mission bazaar at the Farmingtons', and that we will be singing."

"Yes, sir."

"Yes . . . well, I have something rather special I'd like you to do that d-day, if you will. You know that we've b-been rehearsing the 'Star-Spangled B-Banner'—"

At the boy's nod, Evan went on to explain. "I'd like you to t-take a solo p-part in the song, Billy—I'll show you where today as we rehearse. Also, there's a short reading I thought you might render just b-before we sing."

Evan had expected the youth to be pleased. Instead, young Billy simply gaped at him, obviously appalled. "A—a reading, is it, sir?"

"Why . . . yes." Puzzled by the boy's behavior, Evan added, "Just a b-brief recitation about why and when the song was written. A paragraph or so, no m-more."

The boy squirmed and looked away. "I'd—I'd rather not, sir, if you don't mind."

Evan frowned. The boy's face was absolutely white. "But why *not*, son? You have a s-splendid voice—for reading, I expect, as well as for singing. And this is a m-most important song."

Still avoiding Evan's eyes, Billy mumbled, "I'll do the singing part, right enough, Mr. Whittaker. I know all the words. It's just that I'd rather not do the reading, don't you see?"

Something in the tremulous tone of voice and averted gaze told Evan he mustn't press. "Very well, B-Billy," he said reluctantly. "That's fair enough. You will sing the solo, and I'll assign the recitation to one of the other b-boys."

The lad nodded, keeping his gaze lowered.

An uneasy suspicion stirred in Evan; it continued to nag at

him throughout rehearsal. Trying not to be obvious, he watched the Hogan boy more closely than usual. After a time, he began to study some of the other youths as well. By the end of the hour, he thought he understood.

With a heavy heart, he wondered why he hadn't seen it before today. He already knew that none of the boys could read the music itself. Most of them, though, used the scores he passed among them to learn the words.

But not Billy Hogan. Billy, and at least four other boys, were, he was convinced, learning by rote: memorizing what they heard as they went along.

It was, Evan strongly suspected, the only way they *could* learn. Unless he was mistaken, and he rather thought he was not, the boys could not read.

————

Throughout the entire ferry ride home, Evan fretted about his discovery. He could not imagine what it would be like being unable to read. For most of his life, reading had been both a passion and a comfort to him. He had explored the world through books, and in the process gained a certain solace in his childhood loneliness, found a kind of escape from his miserable shyness and the hateful stutter of his speech. Books had enlarged his schoolroom, expanded his vision, encouraged his dreams. He simply could not conceive of a life without reading.

His mind went to the wretched souls in Five Points, that abysmal slum so infested by evil and hopelessness. For some, decimated by their poverty and in despair of a mean survival eked out in filthy cellars and garrets, reading might well represent the only chance of escape. At least for a few moments, they could be transported to another place, another time. They might even catch a glimpse of a dream of their own, or find a glimmer of hope in the words of another.

Yet, here were at least five boys—five that he knew of—within his singing group that could not, he feared, so much as read the Scriptures for themselves!

It wouldn't do. It simply would not do!

As he stepped off the ferry onto the dock, Evan paused, shivering in the cold. It was almost dusk; the spray off the river was icy, the wind rising. Yet, he stood, thinking, unable to shake off his troubled thoughts.

The Hogan lad had obviously been embarrassed that he'd had to refuse Evan's request. No doubt the other boys, if confronted, would have felt just as awkward.

No one, Evan thought sadly, young or old, should have to be shamed by illiteracy. Yet, more than likely it was a common problem throughout most of the slum settlements, especially among the immigrant population.

Something needed to be done. Obviously, only those more fortunate—those who could read—were in a position to help.

I'm one of those, he reminded himself. *At least, I know enough to help my boys.*

Tugging the collar of his coat more snugly about his neck, Evan started to walk. He smiled at his own thought . . . *my boys* . . . then realized that in a very special way, that was exactly what they had become: his boys.

Well, *his boys* would not be cheated of this immeasurably precious gift. *His boys* would have the opportunity to learn to read. He would see to it!

It was a promise to himself . . . and a promise to God as well.

———

Arthur Jackson hunkered down inside the buggy that Mr. Jess had sent to fetch him and Casey-Fitz home.

It was almost dark. Casey-Fitz had fallen asleep on the seat across from Arthur. A cold rain pattered against the roof of the buggy. Somehow, rain after dark always made Arthur feel cold. Cold and kind of lonely-hearted and sad.

Would he ever get used to the cold weather in the North? Seemed as if he hadn't seen the sun for months. Mr. Whittaker claimed the sun shone more in New York than it did in England, but that seemed near about impossible to Arthur. For sure, he wouldn't like a place like England. Uh-uh, not a bit!

He thought Mr. Whittaker had acted a little strange today. More than once Arthur had caught him staring at him and Billy Hogan and some of the other boys, too, during rehearsal.

Had he done something wrong? He didn't think so. Unless maybe Mr. Whittaker had caught him not paying much attention to the songs.

That was possible. Truth was, he was having a time of it, trying to keep his mind on singing—or on much of anything else, for that matter. He couldn't stop thinking about the trouble the Daltons had gone and gotten themselves into, all on his account.

Miss Kerry, she went around looking so worried most of the time—and when she wasn't looking worried, she looked *angry*. And Mr. Jess—he kept up a good face, but he didn't laugh near as much as usual.

Just last Sunday, Casey-Fitz had finally told him a little about what was going on, had explained that his folks weren't saying much about things, so as not to worry Arthur. Casey hadn't wanted to tell, but Arthur just about made him.

That boy just couldn't lie, nossir! Casey-Fitz's face would give him away every time. He couldn't even pull a joke, that boy couldn't! So, once Arthur started in on him serious-like, Casey had talked. Told him how some of the people at the big church were kicking up a fuss because of the Daltons wanting to give Arthur a home.

When Arthur got all upset and vowed to leave so as not to cause any trouble, Casey-Fitz liked to have had a fit! He said Arthur couldn't do that or he'd break "Little Mother's" heart.

Little Mother. That's what Casey called Miss Kerry because of her being such a small lady, and also because he had called his real mama, who had died in a factory fire, "Mum."

"She's become attached to you, don't you see? It would hurt Little Mother something fierce if she knew you were even *thinking* of going away!"

Arthur *didn't* see. There were a lot of things about these people he didn't see. Like, why such a nice white woman like Miss Kerry could give a hoot about a runaway slave boy. Or why an important preacher-man like Mr. Jess would knowingly take on trouble on his account.

Back home, he remembered most people doing just about anything at all to *avoid* trouble. 'Course, trouble did seem to have a way of shadowing black folks, no matter how hard they tried to get around it. But for a white man to invite it into his house for the sake of a Negro boy?

Arthur shook his head. There was no figuring it. Anyhow, Casey-Fitz had made him promise to stay.

"Vow you won't leave," he'd insisted in that little-old-man way he had. "Give your word. All we can do is to pray. But God and Dad will take care of this. The two of them will handle everything, you'll see."

Arthur didn't know about God. He didn't know God very well, leastways not just yet, although Mr. Jess was doing his best to get them acquainted.

But when it came to Mr. Jess—well, he did believe that man could handle just about anything that came along! So, even though he felt ashamed that he'd brought trouble on the Daltons, he couldn't help but think that Mr. Jess would work it out.

If not . . . well, he guessed Casey-Fitz would just have to understand if the time came he needed to break his word.

Because one thing was certain: he wasn't going to be responsible for Mr. Jess or his family getting hurt. Nossir, not ever!

23

Help in Unexpected Places

For the poor body that I own
I could weep many a tear. . . .

PADRAIC COLUM (1881–1972)

Michael Burke had never doubted that his investigation of Patrick Walsh would take him to some strange places.

Still and all, he would not have expected to end up at one of the dime museums in the Bowery. He hated these pits of wretched humanity as much as he despised any of the myriad horrors the city had to offer. "Freak Shows," as they were called by most of the other policemen on the force, weren't entirely confined to the Bowery, of course, but they seemed to thrive best here.

The name "dime museum" had to do with the price of admissions; not by the remotest stretch of the imagination did the places bear a resemblance to any respectable institution.

As Michael approached the entrance doors, he saw that Roscoe Brewster, the establishment's owner, was at his usual place in front, hawking the "wonders" on display inside. A big, florid-faced con man who had invested his faro winnings in "business," Brewster sported a fierce mustache and fingers blazing with flashy diamond rings. At his side, dressed like a gambler's dandy, stood a bulldog-faced little man called Plug.

Slightly bigger than a dwarf, Plug at first glance appeared jovial and harmless. However, like most policemen familiar with the Bowery district, Michael knew the little man was never with-

214

out a knife and a specially crafted set of brass knuckles, honed with ridges sharp enough to slice a man's ear with one blow. Plug was Brewster's bodyguard—and he was anything but harmless.

Michael caught Brewster's eye, and the man gave a grudging nod that he should go on in. For a moment, he hesitated, reluctant to subject himself to the "museum." He knew what waited inside. In his years on the force, he had closed down two or three similar establishments, mostly for fleecing the customer with petty thievery right on the premises, or making outrageously bogus claims about the "wonders" within.

There were always the few authentic poor wretches whose deformities lived up to the garish billboards. As it happened, Brewster's place was known to have some of the "best" attractions.

Trying to ignore the gaudy paintings emblazoned across the outside, Michael pulled in a long breath and walked through the door.

Brewster ran his place like a theater: the attractions were paraded across a stage, with a "lecturer" explaining and elaborating on the qualities of each. Already on stage was the predictable Tattooed Man, a feature of every dime museum in the city. A tall fellow in a shabby suit—the lecturer—was at that moment introducing the "Smallest Living Man in the World."

And indeed, he would seem to be just that. The ridiculous little black hat on his head fell off as he bowed and greeted the audience in a sharp, thin voice. He claimed to weigh only twelve pounds, and Michael would not have questioned it.

Most of the other "attractions" on stage were the usual: two dwarfs, an albino, a bearded lady. Michael turned his gaze away from the stage to scan the crowd. Working people mostly. Day-laborers and factory girls, out for the evening to spend their hard-earned wages. A number of newsboys. An entire mix of reprobates: gamblers, pickpockets, and other petty crooks.

Not for the first time, he found himself angered by the perverse streak in the heart that provoked one human being to pay for a glimpse of the misery of another. Moreover, he wondered what kind of a man it took to earn a living—and a high one at that—by mongering such wretchedness to a hall filled with gawking eyes.

Steeling himself, he walked halfway down the aisle, then

crossed to the side door that led backstage. A grizzled custodian on a stool stopped his advance.

Michael showed him his star, saying, "Where would I find Bhima?"

The aging custodian curled his lip and revealed the dark cavern of a toothless mouth. "Bhima?"

"Aye, Bhima." Michael paused. "The one they call the 'Turtle Boy.' "

"Last door on the left," muttered the old man with a marked lack of interest.

Michael followed the dim, vile-smelling corridor almost to the rear of the building. Stopping at the last door on his left, he hesitated before knocking.

This part of the theater building was eerily quiet. Foul smells seemed to ooze from under the doors, smells too old and mixed to identify. It was almost as if the building itself were corrupt, a breathing, stinking entity of wickedness.

For a moment, Michael was tempted to turn and bolt from the building. He had seen the Turtle Boy on stage, chatted with him once about inconsequential things. He knew what lay within the room.

With a heavy sigh, he finally lifted a fist to knock on the paint-blistered door.

———

The room was pathetically stark, barren of any warmth or appeal, lighted only by one narrow, cracked window. The wallpaper was peeling in some places, completely missing in others; the wooden floors were marred and rough. In one corner leaned a slant-backed chair, in another a lumpy—but clean—bed.

Michael noted a neat stack of a dozen or so books and newspapers. For some reason, this surprised him. He would not have expected the Turtle Boy to be a reader. Still, the room's occupant *had* written his own message and signed his name.

The one who had summoned him waited against the wall, next to the books and newspapers beneath the window.

Michael managed not to stare. Even though he had seen the boy before, the sight of the poor, deformed body hit him like a blow.

The face was that of a youth little more than twenty years old, olive-skinned with large dark eyes and a rich head of black hair. The face was sensitive and mournful, of obvious Indo-European extraction.

Clad in a gray wool sweater and worn blue shirt, he appeared slender and well-set in the shoulders, altogether different than he looked in his "stage dress," a slick, tube-like affair that served to emphasize his deformity. Indeed, he appeared a normal youth. Until one looked below the waist. For the Turtle Boy had no legs, no legs at all—only flipper-like feet attached directly to his torso.

Presumedly, he was an accident of nature, more than likely born to one of the city's many prostitutes or poverty-stricken immigrant girls who rejected him at birth.

The Turtle Boy was one of the few who had found a permanent home with Roscoe Brewster's dime museum. He had been moved about from circus to circus until Brewster signed him on, giving him a room and his board in exchange for the boy becoming a "resident freak."

A few years back, a kind-natured Bowery stagehand had fashioned for the boy a type of four-wheeled cart, whereon he could hoist himself and ride about at will. Apparently Brewster had come to depend on his loyalty, for the Turtle Boy was free to come and go. He could be seen at all hours of the day rolling along on his cart, doing errands for his employer or just taking in the neighborhood.

At first, the boy did not look directly at Michael. He remained where he was, propped on his little cart beneath the window, his eyes cast slightly to one side.

"Bhima?"

Michael saw the eyes blink, a muscle twitch beside one corner of the mouth, as if the sound of his own name had caught him off guard.

"*Bhima* . . ." the boy finally echoed quietly. "Yes, I am Bhima. Forgive me . . . I so seldom hear the name."

The voice was soft, with an unexpected note of humor. Michael felt altogether awkward; he could not think of what to say to this most unusual boy. "Your message said you had information for me."

The boy nodded, still averting his eyes. "You have . . . an interest in a man named Walsh, I believe."

Michael tensed. "Perhaps. Among others."

Again Bhima nodded. The last of the day's light was fast disappearing, leaving one side of his face—the side turned toward Michael—in shadows. "Rumor has it you're seeking evidence you might use to curtail some of Walsh's . . . business activities."

Wary, Michael waited, saying nothing.

"There are few secrets in the Bowery, Captain." The boy's lips curved in a faint smile, as though he could sense Michael's skepticism. "Between the newsboys and the rag-pickers, there are few secrets indeed."

He paused, then asked, "Tell me, Captain, what would you do with such evidence if you should come by it?"

"Hang the devil if I could," Michael bit out. "If not, I'd do my best to see his miserable bones rot in jail."

The boy—Bhima—at last turned to look at him, and Michael caught his breath. In truth, the lad had a beautiful countenance—the face of a saint. Delicately formed, kindly features, and an unexpected warmth.

The dark eyes raked his face. Michael knew himself to be under a disturbingly shrewd scrutiny. He forced himself to meet the boy's gaze straight-on. "I'd do with it whatever I could," he said evenly. "It would count for something, you can be sure."

The boy smiled, suddenly looking much younger. "It is said in the Bowery that Captain Burke is a man of his word. A dangerously honest man, some say." He nodded slowly, still studying Michael. Then his expression sobered. "Across the street," he said, motioning up toward the window with his head, "there's a warehouse building. You know the place?"

Michael nodded. A dark, rambling structure that had once been a garment warehouse, the building had stood abandoned for over a year. "What of it?"

"It's not as empty as it might appear on first glance, Captain," Bhima replied. "In fact, there would seem to be a good, brisk business going on there some nights." He paused. "Do you know who owns the building?"

Michael shook his head.

"Walsh—Patrick Walsh. 'Snake Eyes,' he's called in the streets."

Michael felt the blood rush to his head. Could it finally be that, after all these months of futile searching and digging, he was about to get something concrete on Walsh? "You mentioned

218

'business.' What sort of business? One of his gambling dens, is it?"

The boy smiled, a bitter slash, quickly gone. "Oh no. Not gambling." He stopped, studying Michael's face as if gauging his level of interest. "More in the way of a slave market, I'd say."

Michael's head jerked up. Bhima nodded, and again came the bitter smile. "Not quite the kind of slave market we associate with the South, however. This one is more . . . specialized."

Michael tried not to let his impatience show. "In what way?"

"There's no auction involved. No bidding. They simply herd Negro children—boys and girls, most of them guttersnipes picked up off the streets—into the warehouse, where they're released into the hands of certain buyers. Apparently, the purchases are prearranged. All that's left is for the owners to pick up their property."

The dryness of Michael's mouth turned sour with the bile of revulsion. He had known this sort of thing went on, of course; black children in the slums disappeared by the dozens every week, with no explanation.

But this was the first time he might have the opportunity to identify a *place* where the ugly business was being transacted. And at least one of the individuals behind it all.

It was also his first hint that the filthy "enterprises" of Patrick Walsh might actually extend to this—what he personally considered to be one of the most inhuman, conscienceless acts one human being could wreak upon another.

"Captain? What happens to the children, do you know?" the question was guarded, almost as if the boy dreaded the answer.

"A number are sent South, more than likely," Michael answered. "I'll warrant that just as many end up in the brothels, right here in the city. The committee I'm working with has come up with information that indicates a good deal of trafficking among wealthy buyers who pay exorbitant sums for the youngest . . ." He scowled and looked away for a moment. "They buy them for their own personal—perversions."

A look of pain crossed the other's features. The dark eyes closed for an instant, as if to shut out the cruelty of Michael's words. When the boy opened his eyes, they were shadowed with a great sadness.

"These children . . . they have no choice in what becomes of them? No chance to escape, isn't that right?" he questioned softly, all hint of lightness now gone from his voice.

The thought struck Michael that Bhima might well have been describing himself. "That would seem to be the case," he said tightly. "How sure are you of this?"

The boy met his gaze. "I am absolutely certain, Captain." He glanced behind him, up toward the window. "I can't see out, of course—but I have friends who can. Besides, I've heard the goings on over there for myself. I'm easily overlooked, as you can imagine. I can squeeze into the smallest of hiding places. I promise you, I know what I'm talking about."

"You did a good thing in getting word to me," Michael said finally. "But why did you bother?"

"Because you're a man who can be trusted, I'm told. A decent man. A Christian." He paused. "And so am I. Does that surprise you?"

For some reason, it did.

"How can I love a God who made me this way—is that what you're wondering?" The boy smiled at Michael, a faint, sad smile. "Some would consider that a fair question. I don't mean you, Captain, but . . . some." He paused. "I think the real question is, 'How can I *not* love a God who gave up His only Son for me?' "

Something stirred deep inside Michael.

"These children, Captain," Bhima was saying, "these children who are being sold like cattle—they have no hope. It ought not to be that way. Some of us may seem to be . . . locked into our destiny, without hope of escape. But it shouldn't be that way for children, should it? Black or white, shouldn't children have at least some measure of hope?"

By now Michael was scarcely aware of Bhima's deformity, only of the compassion in his eyes. In this lad—this boy whose poor, distorted body would seem to mark him as hopeless—he saw what was perhaps the most vivid testament he had ever encountered of the wondrous difference God could make in a life.

"Why do you stay here?" he asked, his voice gruff with emotion.

Bhima gave a small shrug. "Even a freak needs a roof over his head, Captain. And food."

Michael found himself angry at the sound of the ugly word. It simply didn't fit—indeed, stood in stark opposition to the gentle eyes, the sensitive nature so evident in the boy.

"You don't have to stay here," he said abruptly. "I can try to get you a better place."

Bhima regarded him with a studying look. "Thank you, Captain. I believe you would. But for now, this is where I need to be. This is where I am *meant* to be, I think. There are people here who . . . depend on me, as difficult as that might be for you to understand. Although there is little I can give, I can at least share a touch of God's comfort, at times even His Word. For all I know, that might be more than they would have without me."

With full certainty Michael realized in that moment that there was no ugliness in this young man, no real deformity, other than what happened to exist in the eyes of the beholder. There was only nobility and the grace of God made evident.

"There is something you *could* do, though," Bhima went on. "As you might imagine, love—even God's love—is not easily experienced here . . . or anywhere else in the Bowery, for that matter. Perhaps, if you happen to know some good people brave enough to venture among us, you might make them aware of the . . . darkness in this place. The need for God's caring heart and a touch of human kindness exists, even here."

Michael nodded. Immediately, he thought of Jess Dalton. And Evan Whittaker.

And Sara. His wife, who, if she knew of the need, would no doubt come charging into the midst of this abyss, armed only with her faith and the determination to make a difference.

But, of course, he would not tell Sara.

24

Quest

Men are measured by what they seek—
A dream, a truth, a star.

Ireland

In Belfast, attorney John Guinness was making his third visit to speak with Annie Delaney's mother and stepfather.

The stench of the city's poverty districts hung heavily on the damp afternoon as he got out of the hired carriage. Telling the driver to wait, he turned, standing for a moment in the street.

A combination of smells assailed him in the time it took to dart inside the hovel where Annie Delaney's family lived. The entire neighborhood seemed to reek of dunghills and breweries, outdoor privies and sewers, and something else—some indefinable, vile odor that hinted of disease.

All around him, Guinness could feel the miasma of hopelessness. In this city where the looms were seldom silent, where the linen mills continued to spew out even greater wealth for the already wealthy owners, the plight of the poor seemed never to change. The stinking atmosphere of poverty and degradation hung over Belfast like a fixed cloud.

In the midst of it all one could sense the wall of hostility that had changed the complexion of the old city forever. In the confines of the "settlements" built up around their church, the unwanted Catholics remained the aliens, while the Protestant poor watched them with suspicion fueled by their own misery. The divisions had developed to the point over the years that, now, there was nothing between the two but rancor and mistrust and a fierce resolve to hold on to the little they had.

If there ever was a more hopeless city than Belfast, Guinness thought as he made his way up the sagging stairs, he hoped he never had to see it firsthand.

The woman let him in. To Guinness's relief, her husband was nowhere in sight. The attorney had deliberately waited until late afternoon, on the chance that Tully would be at one of the local pubs. His last time at the flat, he had sensed a faint change in the woman, a suggestion of willingness to accept Fitzgerald's offer after all, if Guinness were to press. Today, he intended to do just that.

Mrs. Tully appeared disheveled and downcast. Her gray hair was unkempt, her apron soiled, but she stopped just short of being slovenly. Her eyes were hard: suspicious and unforgiving. The woman wore the look of one who had resigned herself to the poorest of life's leavings long ago.

To Guinness's surprise, she let him in without protest; the last time he'd come, she'd gotten angry and warned him off. Of course, the last time, her husband had been there—drunk and agitated and abusive.

Anxious to be done with the affair entirely, Guinness got right to the point as soon as he entered the room. "Well, then—I said I'd be back, Mrs. Tully. I've brought the necessary papers for your signature."

"You heard my husband," she muttered sourly. "He said we'll not be signing your papers."

"Yes, he did say that, didn't he? Still, as I pointed out to you both, it's for *you* to decide the future of your child. As I understand things, your husband has never adopted Annie, never claimed legal custody of her."

Even as he spoke, Guinness noted a large, angry bruise on the woman's cheek—a bruise that had not, he was certain, been there at his last visit. Lest pity interfere with what he had to do, he reminded himself that this woman had rejected her own child.

She stood now, arms crossed over her thin bosom, glaring at him. "And what sort of mother would I be, then, signing me rights to me own child over to a stranger?"

Guinness fought for patience. He would do Fitzgerald's cause no good by losing control. "A mother who wants something better for her daughter, it seems to me," he said carefully. "One who recognizes a golden opportunity when it's placed in front of her."

The woman's eyes went to the sheaf of papers in Guinness's hand. "Frank is against it."

Again, Guinness controlled his temper with a good deal of effort. "I understand. But I must remind you again that the decision is not his to make. Besides, it may be that your husband doesn't fully appreciate his choices." He went on quickly before she could interrupt. "I've already explained that Mr. Fitzgerald intends to legally adopt your daughter, make her heir to his considerable fortune. She'll be educated, cared for—she will have every opportunity for a wonderful, prosperous life, I can promise you."

"But not a mother's love," the woman whined.

Guinness studied her, a hot surge of anger rising in his throat. "That's true," he bit out, unable to stop himself. "But then, I doubt that she was accustomed to all that much of it before."

"Now, see here—"

"No, *you* see here!" Guinness had had enough. He stepped closer to the woman, close enough to smell the faint bitterness of cheap gin on her. "You'd best mind my words, woman," he said, his voice low with a deliberate threat. "As Morgan Fitzgerald's attorney, I can tell you that the man is out of patience and about to reconsider his generosity. He has offered your daughter an unheard-of opportunity! But unless you act and act now, that offer will be withdrawn."

He paused. "You should know, too, that Fitzgerald can be a hard man entirely, if provoked. A *very* hard man, if you take my meaning."

Guinness stopped, just long enough to let his words sink in before going on. "After today, Mrs. Tully, I will not return. I have one final offer to make you, so you'd do well to listen closely."

Ignoring the woman's sullen stare, Guinness quoted her the figure Fitzgerald had authorized—a figure of such enormity it had even made Guinness catch his breath. Before she could speak, he added, "Perhaps I should define your choices in this matter in detail, so that you'll have a clearer understanding of what to expect.

"You sign these papers, and you accomplish two things," Guinness said, managing to restore a note of calm to his tone. "You will ensure a fine home and a promising future for your daughter. At the same time, *you*"—he paused for effect—"will become a woman of means. A woman who will no longer have to work in the mills to eke out a living. You will not need to depend on anyone—*anyone*—for your livelihood."

Guinness watched her closely. The woman's tongue darted across her lower lip, and her eyes took on a glint. He *had* her! He was sure of it.

"You will, of course, be relinquishing all rights to the child," he said quickly. "You will not, under any circumstances, have communication with her again or make any attempt to contact her or her new family. You also need to understand," he added with cutting emphasis, "that, should you refuse Mr. Fitzgerald's offer, he intends to have you and your husband prosecuted for criminal offenses."

Her eyes bugged and she stiffened. "What's this? What do ye mean, *criminal offenses*? We've done nothing wrong!"

"Oh, I think you know what I mean, Mrs. Tully," said Guinness quietly. "And I think you know that your husband deserves whatever mean hand he is dealt. You will simply be caught up in the wake of things, don't you see? Now, then, while we're still alone, I suggest that you—"

At that moment the door crashed open, and Tully came charging in, drunk completely and wild with rage.

"WHAT ARE YOU DOING HERE AGAIN?" he exploded, grabbing Guinness by the lapels of his coat and yanking him around. "I TOLD YOU TO STAY AWAY!"

The drunken man's face was mottled with an ugly crimson. His eyes, not quite focused, blazed with fury.

The woman screamed, but her husband ignored her.

Tully was a big-bellied, heavy-shouldered man, and drunk beyond all reason. Guinness felt an instant of sheer panic as he stared into the man's glazed eyes.

"Frank! No! Don't hurt him! He means to make us rich! He's talking a fortune!"

Still held captive in Tully's grip, Guinness began to talk, fast. "She's right—you'd do well to listen! You're set for life, if you use your head! Besides, what's the girl to you, anyway? Not your own blood, after all!"

Tully didn't drop Guinness all at once, but eased off slightly, looking bewildered. He shot a glance at his wife, who now stepped toward him.

"It's the truth!" she told him. "Wait till you hear!"

"The lass is not for sale!" Tully slurred righteously, with a misdirected wave of his hand. "Not for any price, d'you hear?"

Guinness managed to quote the price again in a more or less steady voice. To his vast relief, Tully dropped his hands away altogether.

"You don't mean it?" the man said thickly.

"I mean it," Guinness said quickly, sensing victory within reach. "Won't you let me explain what I've just told your wife?"

Tully looked at his wife, who nodded urgently. At last he gave a grunt of assent. Looking round the room, he spied a near-empty gin bottle on a table against the wall, and went for it.

"Perhaps we'll hear what you have to say, lawyer," he muttered, swaying as he lifted the gin bottle to his mouth. "Speak your piece, then, and be quick about it."

———

Frank Cassidy had thought the most logical place to carry out his assignment would be the streets of Dublin City.

Although Fitzgerald had stressed that the girl, Finola, was clearly not *of* the streets, but more than likely had gentry—or at least decent folk—behind her, she had nevertheless emerged from the Liberties, that infamous womb of Dublin's slums.

After five days searching, he had turned up not even a whisper of information. Those that recognized the lass's name appeared to be genuinely ignorant of any knowledge, not only of her past, but of her present whereabouts as well.

Finally, just this morning, a brief chat with a bird-market man on Bride Street had yielded the suggestion that he seek out a gleeman—a street minstrel—called "Christy Whistle."

"If anyone can put you on to something, it'll be Christy," his informant had promised. "He knows what's worth knowing, and a good deal that's not."

So this afternoon Cassidy had again tromped the cobbles to the Liberties, where Christy Whistle was supposed to have digs. He was on Thomas Street when he heard a tin whistle and spied a crowd. Stopping at the fringes of the bystanders, he took a long look at the musician in their midst.

The gleeman was unkempt, dressed in a worn frieze coat and cape, outrageously baggy trousers, and oversized brogues. Despite his looking the ragamuffin, however, he was a fine one with the tin whistle.

Cassidy saw that he also had himself a mouth harp hanging from one pocket and a squeeze box at his feet. Within a matter of minutes, the entertainer managed to play all three instruments and dance a bit of a jig. People threw money to him—a considerable collection, it appeared.

Obviously, the raggedy minstrel was another of the countless imitators of the legendary blind "Zozimus"—one Michael Moran, who, now passed on, had been acknowledged throughout the countryside as the grand patriarch of the ballad mongers. Such had been Moran's reputation that he'd spawned any number of mimics, who not only aped his bizarre apparel and eccentric lifestyle, but went to great lengths to match his musical ability.

This one was good. Cassidy turned to an old-timer standing next to him and asked, "Is he a Dublin lad, then, d'you know?"

The old man didn't bother to glance at Cassidy, but simply jabbed a finger in the minstrel's direction as he replied. "Indeed, Christy is one of our own, don't ye know? Raised in Faddle Alley, just like Zozimus. And as near like him in skill as any I've seen."

Pleased to have found his man so easily, Cassidy stood watching, enjoying the show. The itinerant gleemen had always fascinated him, what with their traveling lifestyle, their scorn for ownership and ties, their fierce independence. Except for the winters, which they usually waited out in the city, they spent most of their days on the road, making their way up and down the countryside, taking in the fairs and all the towns along the way.

Closely related to the Traveling People—the Tinkers—and the *Seanchais* from olden times, the gleemen were known not only to be the preservers of the old music and traditions, but bearers of news and gossip as well, relaying what they knew in each town they traveled.

Like the revered and esteemed storyteller—the *Seanchai*—who was welcomed with honor in any village he chose to visit, the itinerant musician could also count on a generous measure of hospitality during his wanderings. The people seemed drawn to these blithe spirits, with their outrageous and often capricious manners, honoring their talents and respecting their ways.

Cassidy had long thought Morgan Fitzgerald to be a fascinating combination of both the wandering troubadour and venerable _Seanchai_—the name by which he was often called about the country. At least he _had_ been, he reminded himself sourly, when he'd still had the use of his legs to carry him.

The thought of his friend's misfortune jarred Cassidy back to his surroundings and the reason he had come to Dublin in the first place. If there was information to be had about this girl Morgan was so taken with, he would find it. This, at least, was one thing he could do for the man who had befriended him when he needed a friend most.

Eyeing the street musician, who looked about to take a breather from his entertainment, Cassidy began to thread his way through the onlookers to speak with Christy Whistle.

25

The Dawn of Darkest Fears

Why is it effects are
Greater than their causes?
Why should causes often
Differ from effects?
Why should what is lovely
Fill the world with harness?
And the most deceived be
She who least suspects?

OLIVER ST. JOHN GOGARTY (1878–1957)

In the dark hour before daybreak, Finola awakened, violently ill again. Lucy held her head as she heaved, then sponged her face with a cool cloth. All the while she comforted her, she wrestled with the problem of whom to call.

They would have to send for the doctor, no matter the early hour. The queasiness had come upon the girl, off and on, for days now. She was growing too weak, too faint by far, and it must not, could not, go on.

Just when it seemed she might be gaining a bit of strength, walking about, sitting up for her meals, she had taken this unexpected turn for the worst.

In the beginning, Lucy had tried not to make too much of it. Even to herself, she insisted it might only be the result of a cold, or the increased variety in her diet.

The nun had noticed, of course; there was no hiding anything from that one. Up until the past two days, however, they had refrained from telling the Fitzgerald how often the sickness came upon the girl, and how severe it was when it came.

That had been Finola's doing. She had tried her utmost to convince them all that this was no more than an unsettled stomach, that it would soon pass. Lucy knew what she was about; no doubt the girl was feeling shamed by the trouble she had brought upon the Fitzgerald household and meant to avoid any further imposition. She was too much the innocent to recognize that the man was hopelessly besotted with her, that nothing she could do would ever prove an imposition.

In any event, there could be no more delay. They must send for the doctor, and the sooner the better.

Leading Finola to believe she was going for more towels, Lucy hurried from the room. But whom to awaken? The nun, she supposed, although she dreaded the thought. The religious treated her well enough, but Lucy was no fool. No doubt her very presence offended the sister. More than likely, the woman crossed herself at the very mention of Lucy's name.

No, she would rather deal with the black man. Although she had always been a bit afraid of the dark sailors from the foreign ships, this Sandemon did not strike her as someone to dread. Big as he was, he had a kindness, a gentleness, about him. He seemed a man to respect, but not to fear.

Besides, something in his eyes gave Lucy to know that he did not condemn her—indeed, did not condemn anyone. The black man just might be the one person in the household to whom she could turn—if it turned out she was right about Finola. . . .

But not now, at this early hour of the morning. He slept in a connecting room off his employer's bed chamber, so it was likely that to wake him would mean disturbing the Fitzgerald as well.

There was nothing for it but to wake the nun. With a reluctant sigh, Lucy turned and started down the dimly lighted hall.

———

Sandemon had been half-expecting a summons to send for the surgeon. Something had roused him awake nearly an hour ago. Now, as he lay listening, he identified sounds alien to the usual early morning rumblings of the household. After a moment, he surmised that Miss Finola must be ill again.

Quietly, he slipped from his bed. He dressed quickly, then entered the *Seanchai*'s quarters to check on him. Assured that his employer was still sleeping soundly, he tiptoed from the room.

He stood outside the door for a long moment, listening. The hall was cold and shadowed, lighted only by candles at each end and midway, but there was enough light that he saw Lucy Hoy headed toward Sister Louisa's bedroom.

Taking the hall with quick, light steps, he cleared his throat so as not to startle her. She stopped when she saw him, waiting for him to reach her.

"Miss Finola is ill?" he asked without preamble.

She nodded, and Sandemon saw that the normally suspicious eyes were dark with worry. The woman looked heartsick and worn with fatigue.

"Shall I go for the surgeon?"

Again she nodded. "She's growing worse, I fear. The sickness comes upon her much more frequently now. We'd best not delay."

The round face had been heavily painted when she first came to Nelson Hall. Now it was always scrubbed clean, and usually appeared years younger. This morning, however, it was lined with weariness and concern.

Sandemon's gaze locked with Lucy's. With a sinking heart, he saw his own fears reflected.

———

A few moments later, back in Finola's bedroom, Lucy jumped when the door creaked open.

The nun stood just inside the room for a moment, appearing much smaller than usual in the voluminous dressing gown. Lucy tried not to stare. Without the ever-present wimple, the nun's short dark hair was revealed, tossed with curls and lightly streaked with silver.

"I heard you and Sandemon in the hallway," she whispered. "You've sent for the surgeon, have you?"

Lucy nodded.

Sister Louisa approached the bed, then stood perfectly still, looking from Lucy to Finola, who now lay sleeping. For the first time, Lucy forgot to be ashamed or apprehensive in the nun's presence. So surprised was she by the depth of sadness she saw in the sister's eyes, she did not even think to leave the room in order to spare the nun offense.

———

Long past the breakfast hour, the household was astir with the sounds of morning. Pans clanged in the kitchen, and the day maids scurried back and forth from room to room. A number of tradesmen had already appeared at the back door.

Morgan sat in the library, a cup of Sandemon's strong hot coffee at his side. Only in the vaguest sense was he aware of the noise elsewhere in the house. Unable to take breakfast, unwilling to endure the mincing of Artegal in and out of the dining room, he had wheeled down the hall, into what had become his favorite room of the mansion. His retreat.

Now he sat waiting for the surgeon to come down. When Annie appeared in the doorway instead, he beckoned her inside.

"Sand-Man told me the doctor is here," she said, her black eyes solemn and watchful.

He nodded. "He's upstairs now. Finola took ill again this morning."

He sensed the child's uncertainty as she approached the desk. "I thought Finola was gaining." Still she watched him, as if she feared saying the wrong thing.

Morgan looked at her, then gestured that she should come closer. Her eyes brightened, and she hurried around the desk to stand beside him.

Taking her hand, he managed to smile at her. "You're fond of Finola, aren't you, lass?"

"Oh, of *course* I am!" she burst out. "I think she's grand!" With her customary bluntness, she added, "And I'm sure Finola likes me as well. Indeed, we were beginning to be good friends before—"

She broke off, looking at Morgan as if she weren't sure she should finish.

"Would you like to know what Finola thinks of you?" Morgan asked. "It's very complimentary."

The dark eyes grew wide, and she nodded eagerly.

He drew the child closer still. "I know for a fact that Finola thinks you have a beautiful soul, and that you will one day be an extraordinarily lovely young woman."

Annie gaped, her eyes glistening. "She *doesn't!*"

"Ah, but she does. And do you know what *I* think?"

Beaming, Annie shifted from one foot to the other, obviously impatient to hear.

"I think," Morgan said soberly, "that Finola is exactly right. I think I shall have to hide you in the cellar once you're past thirteen. Otherwise, I'll spend my days doing nothing but tossing out lovesick *gorsoons*! Perhaps—"

Out of the corner of his eye, Morgan saw the surgeon appear in the doorway, then Sister Louisa.

Still holding Annie's hand, he turned toward them, glancing from one to the other. He observed that the doctor would not quite meet his eyes. It was the nun who spoke first. "Master Fitzgerald—*Seanchai*—we would speak with you, please."

Morgan stared at her. This was the first time the sister had ever addressed him by the affectionate *Seanchai*. His throat tightened with apprehension as he gestured for them to enter.

Sister Louisa glanced at Annie. "Perhaps we should speak alone."

Morgan looked at the child. She was unable to conceal her disappointment, but at his nod, she slipped her hand from his and left the room without protest.

When neither the nun nor the doctor made a move to speak first, Morgan deliberately fastened his gaze on his hands, now knotted in fists atop the desk. "Well, then?"

Sister Louisa took a step closer, while the doctor remained a discreet distance from the desk. "*Seanchai*, this is a hard thing. But you must know. Finola . . ."

Her voice faltered, and Morgan looked up, shaken by the undisguised pain staring back at him.

"Finola is with child," she finally said in a strangled voice.

Morgan felt as if his heart had stopped . . . just for an instant. What he had feared in the long hours of the night, what he had suspected for days, but refused to face—had now become a bleak reality.

Framing his face with his hands, Morgan closed his eyes for a moment. When he opened them, Sister Louisa was watching him with knowing concern. Behind her, the surgeon waited with sad eyes.

Thrusting his arms straight out toward the desk, Morgan regarded the sister. "Well, then," he said in a voice less than steady, "we must take care of her, of course. We must take care of Finola . . . and her child."

26

The Vanishing Smoke of Dreams

We must pass like smoke or live within the spirit's fire;
For we can no more than smoke unto the flame return
If our thought has changed to dream, our will unto desire,
As smoke we vanish though the fire may burn.

GEORGE W. RUSSELL ["Æ"] (1867–1935)

By the next afternoon, it had been decided that Lucy should be the one to tell Miss Finola of her condition. Although Sandemon understood the decision, he was not entirely comfortable with it.

He questioned his own uneasiness as he walked along the stream at the west of the house. It was a soft day, as the Irish people called it—cool, but not bitter cold; wet, with a continuous, light rain from a pewter sky that promised still more to come. He was glad of his cape to keep out the wind, yet at the same time he savored the soothing feel of the rain on his face.

He thought of the woman, Lucy Hoy. It was not that he doubted her devotion to Miss Finola. To the contrary, he suspected she would lay her life down for her young friend without protest.

What troubled him more was a certain cynicism he had detected in her, the jaded air of one who has known only life's darkness—and neither believed in nor expected anything else. He would have understood bitterness and resentment from the woman, even anger. She doted on Miss Finola, after all; no doubt the news that there would be a child as a result of the attack was greatly troubling to her, as it was to the entire household. Yet, she went about in a silent, tight-lipped manner, while something in her eyes implied that she had anticipated the worst all along.

That she was world-weary and hard came as no surprise. The woman *was* a prostitute, after all, and no doubt had lived her demoralizing existence for some years. Yet, there were times when Sandemon caught a sense of softheartedness, a warmth that belied Lucy Hoy's brittle exterior.

He walked on, heading back toward the house now. He tried to persuade himself that he was overly concerned. Certainly, the physician would have cautioned Lucy Hoy to take great care in approaching Miss Finola with this latest shock.

Still, he could not help but wish the *Seanchai* had seen fit to ignore convention and speak with Miss Finola himself. Shaken as he was, the young master would nevertheless have found the strength and necessary wisdom to cast this latest dilemma in the best possible light, leaving the door open for God's grace to redeem the situation.

No doubt Lucy Hoy would do her best for Miss Finola. But unless he was mistaken, she was more likely to focus on the evil that had been done. Indeed, she seemed unable to see anything beyond the wickedness of the attacker and the tragedy of the attack itself.

That was understandable, of course. But at some point . . . soon, please, God . . . somebody needed to consider the unborn and, sadly, unwanted child.

———

She was being told now . . . at this moment . . . and Morgan felt as if he might as well have been an ocean apart from her.

Even during the long and terrible time of her silence, when she lay removed from them all in what had seemed an endless dream—even then, he had not felt so altogether *separated* from her.

In the solitude of the chapel, he tried to close out the sounds of the household, that he might be alone before God and with his own thoughts. He stayed in the back, in the shadows, staring at the simple wooden crucifix behind the altar.

For a long time, he simply sat in the wheelchair, his eyes locked upon the cross. His heart was too anxious, his thoughts too troubled and confused, to do anything more than simply . . . be still. Be still and wait, hoping that some glimmer of light, some faint wisdom or insight into the darkness of these days would come to him.

She is to have a child . . . the child of the animal who raped her and beat her. . . .

As always, the memory of what had happened to Finola slashed at his heart, made him moan aloud.

Wasn't it enough that she had been beaten and abused? Was she now to bear the irrefutable evidence of her horror, a daily reminder of the agony? Why this, now, when she had finally begun to heal?

"Why?"

The sound of his own voice raised in anger amid the hush of the chapel made him glance around guiltily. After a moment, he slumped a little in the chair, closing his eyes.

He was mortal-tired, so exhausted his bones ached. He had not slept throughout the long, dismal night, and all during the morning, his emotions had raged from one storm to another. At first seized with a white-hot anger—a righteous anger, he told himself—he had gone on to utter bewilderment, frustration, and finally raw grief.

Now, however, he was merely tired. Tired and heartsore. Yet he was determined to find a way to keep this thing from destroying Finola.

Morgan massaged his aching temples. *Oh, Lord . . . Lord, you know the innocent she is. You know what she has been through— the evil and pain inflicted upon her. You know the horror she has endured, only to be assaulted with still another burden.*

How is she to survive it all, then? It would be easy enough for her to lose her mind altogether, to simply drift back to wherever she was before. . . .

He opened his eyes. A cold hand of fear clutched the back of his neck. He could not, *would* not, let that happen. For this time, he knew with a chilling certainty, she would not return to him.

He gave a long, heaving sigh, once more turning his eyes on the crucifix at the front of the chapel.

Give me the wisdom to know what to do for her, how to help her. Please . . . You who are called Merciful . . . show our Finola your mercy. . . .

Finally, he again closed his eyes, his mind repeating the plea for mercy like a litany. He sat that way for a long time, slumped wearily in the wheelchair, allowing the cool, quiet peace of the chapel to enfold him.

———

"A *child*?" Finola pulled herself up in bed, gripping Lucy's hands as if to stop the violent trembling of her body.

"There now, *alannah*, hush . . . hush. You will hurt yourself! It will be all right . . . we will make things all right, you will see. . . ."

Finola scarcely heard Lucy's words of reassurance. She was only dimly aware of the room around her: the high, plump mattress that seemed to be swallowing her whole . . . the gray afternoon light fighting its way through the drapes . . . the mirror on the opposite wall . . . the massive chiffonnier. . . .

"A *child*?" she whispered, more to herself than to Lucy. "I am to have a child?" She fell back against the pillows, stunned to the point of numbness.

Once she had dreamed of having a child, of being a mother. She remembered . . . a long time ago, in another place, she had rocked a rag doll and sung childish little lullabies, pretending it was her very own babe. A boy babe, it had been. . . .

Lucy clasped her shoulder, rousing her from her thoughts with a gentle squeeze. "Finola, do you understand, love? Do you mind what I'm saying?"

Slowly, Finola nodded, looking about the room again to make sure this was no dream. There had been so many dreams of late. Sometimes it was nearly impossible to distinguish the real from the imagined.

This place—Nelson Hall—this was real, she knew, as were its people. The *Seanchai*—Morgan. Lucy. Annie and her big wolfhound. The kindly Sandemon. Sister Louisa. The gently sloping grounds outside, the trees and gardens she could see from her window—all this was real.

She had put away the ugliness and pain, relegated it to the dream world. She would not think of it again, that terrible dream. The man who hurt her . . .

Had there been only one? Sometimes she thought there were two . . . she would not remember him. He was not real. None of the evil was real, not any longer.

But a *child*? A child made it real! Now she could not be certain what was a dream . . . and what was not.

"So it was real, then?" she said aloud.

Still bending over her, Lucy held her hand, smoothed her hair. But she made no reply. Even when Finola tugged at her hand, drawing her closer, she remained silent.

"*His* child!" The words tore from Finola's throat like a cry of raw pain.

Not looking at her, Lucy gave a short nod. "Aye, *his*." She fairly hissed the words, her eyes burning with undisguised hatred. "Spawn of the devil!"

Finola went limp. She tugged her hand away from Lucy, hugging her arms to herself like a shield.

So it had been no dream, after all. The brutal man . . . the pain . . . the terror . . . the ugliness . . .

It had all been real. She would bear a child. A child who would make it impossible to forget.

"Finola . . . it will be all right . . . listen to me now . . . *listen to me!*" Lucy braced both hands on either side of Finola's shoulders, forcing her to meet her eyes. "You need not have this child! That much at least, we can spare you!"

Still hugging her arms to herself, Finola stared at her, unable to think of anything but the child.

"There are ways," Lucy went on. "The girls at Gemma's— many's the time they got rid of a sailor's unwanted seed. I did it myself, once. Do you understand, Finola? *You need not bear this child!*"

Understanding filtered through the maze of Finola's mind. She had heard whispers among the women, bitter, coarse words, angry murmurs . . . quickly silenced when they realized she was near.

She searched Lucy's eyes, listening in spite of herself.

"There are midwifes—wise women—in the Liberties. And surgeons, too. We'll get the black man to fetch one of them here. You need not trouble yourself, *alannah*. I will see to this for you."

Finola began to tremble again. Avoiding Lucy's eyes, she

looked desperately around the room, as if she could somehow escape the truth.

"Finola?"

Reluctantly, Finola turned her gaze back to Lucy.

"Don't think about it now, child. Just you rest for a bit. We'll fix you some warm milk and get you a sleeping draught. Later, after you're more yourself, we'll talk. Later."

———

Long after Lucy left the room, Finola continued to stare at the closed door. She felt as if a horse had kicked her in the heart. A hot flood of tears welled in her eyes, and, caught up in a sudden seizure of hopelessness, she wept uncontrollably for a time.

This was not the way a woman should have a child, this was not what she had dreamed of. A child should have a good mother who loved it, with all her heart. There should be a home, a husband—to be father to the child. Bright days. Music and laughter within the rooms. And love. Much love. Things should be . . . right! Exactly right.

It should not be like this. Without love, without family—a child born out of cruelty and terror, conceived in sin!

Spawn of the devil, Lucy had called it.

A choking sob ripped from her, a wail of hopelessness. Her dreams had turned to a hideous, ugly nightmare!

After a long time, she lay, depleted, weakly attempting to combat the violent swells of nausea rising up in her.

Somehow she found the strength to face the truth, that the ugliness she had thought a nightmare was all too real. All of it. The terror . . . the ugliness . . . the pain . . . the child—all real. There was no denying it. The vicious shards of reality stabbed at her mind and heart, tearing her to pieces.

God help her . . . it was too real . . . too unbearably, horribly real. . . .

But Lucy had said she need not bear the child. There were ways, she said . . . there were ways. . . .

Could she do that? Destroy a child? A child growing inside her?

A guilt so fierce it took her breath slammed against her heart, frightening her with the enormity of what she was considering.

What Lucy had suggested was surely the worst kind of sin!

Would it not be murder? The priests said life was sacred . . . God-given . . . *all* life, they said, was precious, even that of the unborn.

Could she actually do such a thing, such a wrong, sinful thing?

For an instant she attempted to pray, but allowed the words to fall from her lips, unfinished.

God would not hear such a prayer. She could not speak to Him of the nightmare, the evil things that had been done, her sinful thoughts about the child—she did not dare to bring such vile things before a holy God!

27

Acquainted With Evil

A vulture preys upon our heart,
Christ, have mercy!

RICHARD D'ALTON WILLIAMS (1822–1862)

Lucy stopped short just inside the enormous, drafty kitchen at the sight of the black man, Sandemon. He sat alone at one of the small worktables by the window, in the act of slicing a cheese. He looked up as she entered, and immediately got to his feet.

The man's fine manners never ceased to catch Lucy unawares. Who would expect such breeding from one of his kind? He was a puzzle, this one, a baffling combination—part mystic, part scholar, and part servant.

And there was something else . . . something that put Lucy in mind of a large, stealthy panther which, while not dangerous or threatening, nevertheless evoked an anxiety in her, a discomfort she could not quite identify. There was something in this man that hinted of both the holy and the chieftain, and Lucy neither understood it nor felt at ease with it.

Still, here was the opportunity to speak with him about Finola. He was alone, with most of the household at rest. More than likely, they would not be disturbed.

With his large hands braced upon the back of the chair, the black man inclined his head in greeting. "How is she?"

"She knows," Lucy replied, walking the rest of the way into the room. "I came for some warm milk and some of the sleeping potion the surgeon left."

"But . . . how *is* she?" he asked again.

Lucy gave him a look. "As well as could be expected, all things considered," she replied bitterly.

His expression was unreadable. After a moment, he gestured to the sideboard that ran half the length of the kitchen. "There was much food left at the evening meal. You must be hungry after this long day. I will leave you alone—"

"No! Wait . . . I would speak with you." In truth, Lucy *was* hungry; she had eaten nothing but a bite since dawn. But she was far more interested in recruiting the black man's help than in filling her stomach.

With a small gesture of the hand, he indicated that she should sit down.

Lucy crossed to the table, but remained standing. Pulling in a long, steadying breath, she studied the man's face as closely as she dared. Something in that dark, keen gaze invariably made it impossible to meet his eyes for more than a moment.

"I have talked with the girl," she said bluntly. "To make her understand that . . . she has a choice in whether or not she goes through with the birth."

Hearing his sharp intake of breath, Lucy deliberately fixed her eyes on the wall behind him.

"I see," was all he said.

"I . . . she might not understand just yet, not completely. Even after—after all that has happened, Finola is still the innocent."

"Yes," he replied, his voice soft. "She is very much the innocent, I think." He paused. "Why would you suggest such a thing to her?"

Discomfited, Lucy darted a look at him. "Why *indeed*? Sure, and you're not implying she should have the swine's ill-gotten child? You would see her suffer more than she already has?"

The man gave her a long, steady look. "As I understand such things," he said quietly, "what you are suggesting may also cause suffering. To Miss Finola . . . and to the infant as well."

" 'Tis not an infant!" Lucy shot back, clenching her fists at her sides. "Not yet! 'Tis nothing at all but another burden! Why, then, should she be forced to bear it? Anything born out of such a horror could only be wicked itself! Evil begets evil!"

A look akin to distress passed over the dark features. "Surely not. You speak of an unborn babe, an innocent creation of God—"

Gorge rose in Lucy's throat at his calm assurance. She fairly spat out her protest. "Don't speak to me of *innocence!* Finola was the *innocent,* I would remind you! There can be nothing innocent in something sired by the devil's own! There's nothing in this but still more pain and grief for Finola! Well, she's had enough of both, it seems to me!"

The black man remained silent for a long time. Lucy looked away, but she could feel his eyes on her, studying her. *Judging* her, no doubt.

Yet, when he spoke again, there was no hint of anger, no noticeable tone of reproach. "So, then—why are you telling me this?"

Lucy caught her breath. Perhaps she'd been wrong about him. He was taking it coolly enough. Perhaps he would be willing to help after all!

"It should be done quickly," she moved to explain. "There are midwifes in the Liberties—one in particular I know of, who is clean and reliable. The girl would be safe in her hands. But someone would have to fetch the woman here." She stopped. "And no doubt himself would have to be told. We would need his consent."

The black man regarded her with sad eyes. "The *Seanchai* would never consent to such a thing." Straightening slightly, he crossed his brawny arms over his chest. "Nor would I."

Lucy glared at him. "We don't need *your* consent! Only your help! But I can see you'll not be caring about what's best for the girl. Only the teachings of your precious church!"

"Not the church," he countered quietly. "The teachings of our Lord and Christ. We are commanded not to take a life. I could not be party to such a thing as you suggest, or I would be guilty of murder."

Lucy spat out an oath and whipped around to go.

"Wait."

The voice behind her was still and quiet, steady. Nevertheless, Lucy heard the command implicit in the word. In spite of her anger, she turned back.

"I wonder," he asked, watching her, "do you truly believe what you said—that evil begets only evil? Can you not allow that God can bring good out of all things—even that which may appear to hold only evil?"

Lucy glared at him. "When the sky falls! Ugly is ugly and bad is bad, and I have never seen it any other way! I may be corrupt in your eyes, man, but don't take me for the fool!"

He let his arms fall to his sides. "You are not . . . corrupt in my eyes. Not in the least. And certainly I do not find you foolish. But I must tell you that, in this, you are wrong. God can . . . and often does . . . take what men intend for evil and turn it to good. There is nothing in this world so wicked, so lost, that He cannot redeem it."

Something deep inside Lucy stirred at his words, attempted to rise up, but she quelled it. "What would *you* know about evil?" she grated. "You know *nothing*! Nothing at all!"

For a moment, the black man made no reply, but simply stood, staring down at the floor. When at last he looked up, Lucy was stung by the sorrow of his expression.

"If only it were so," he said softly. "But I fear I know a great deal more about evil than you could ever imagine. Far more than any man should ever know."

Confused, Lucy stared at him. Her mouth went dry, and she shivered at the terrible bleakness looking out at her. But when she would have turned to flee that dark, unnerving gaze, he stopped her once again.

"Wait—please." He took a step toward her, then stopped. "I would ask you to refrain from any further discussion with Miss Finola about this . . . choice you have proposed. She must still be very confused, very weak and heartsick. But she is a child of God, and when she is able to take it all in and make a decision, I know she will choose to do what is right, what God wills."

He paused, and the midnight eyes looked away. "What you are suggesting . . . it is not God's will. Please—you must allow her to make her own decision."

Without another word, Lucy whirled about and bolted from the room. The old feeling of shame, of rank corruption, once more seized her, flooding her with self-hatred. All the way down the hall, she had to struggle against an overwhelming urge to burst into tears.

———

Sandemon watched her rush from the room, his heart heavy with an old, wrenching sorrow.

Poor woman. Poor lost, wounded woman, with her frightened

eyes and shame-bound heart. He could almost hear the chains clanking as they tightened about her spirit, could hear the anguished outcry of her soul.

As he stood there in the silence of the dimly lighted kitchen, Sandemon felt an all too familiar heaviness settle over his own spirit. Some secret chamber of his heart began to bleed with a sorrow not his own. A violent shudder of dread gripped him, a fear not for himself, not for his personal safety—but for the woman named Lucy.

The burden had been given, and he did not want it. He did not welcome the responsibility—or the pain—of interceding for Lucy Hoy.

There were already too many other burdens on his heart. And somehow he sensed that this one would require much of him—perhaps much more than he was able to give.

Almost at once, there came the gentle reminder that this new burden, no matter how great or dread-inspiring, was as nothing when compared with the burden of his Savior and Master. Indeed, it could scarcely be viewed as anything more than a small, smooth stone when measured against the burden of the Cross.

Lucy had still not returned. The sickness had passed, for the moment, and now Finola lay, unmoving, her eyes closed against the encroaching darkness.

Again she wished she could pray. But surely God was very angry with her, for her wicked thoughts, her shameful condition.

Did she *dare* approach Him? She was defiled, shamed, in disgrace. . . .

But she could not possibly make such a decision alone, and there was no one else to whom she could confide her fears, her confusion, about so intimate a matter. Except for Lucy.

She already knew what Lucy thought, what she would have her do. . . .

Clumsily, her head spinning with the weakness, Finola pulled herself up. Clutching the bed linen with both hands to keep from falling, she sat on the side of the bed until her head cleared.

Finally, then, she went to her knees, prostrating herself, face down, on the floor.

Assailed by nausea, chilled as much by a sudden feeling of

abandonment as by the cold of the room, she lay, shivering and miserable and frightened.

Please, Lord . . . you know the weakness of my mind—and my faith. I don't know what to think, what to believe . . . what to do. . . .

I have already been such a burden to the Seanchaí—to Morgan—to his entire household! And now there is to be a child . . . oh, my Lord . . . my Lord, what am I to do?

Even as she tried to pray, Finola's thoughts went to Lucy, to the solution she had hinted of.

The babe . . . it was not yet real, was it? Nothing more than a small, unnamed—something—growing inside her. . . .

Seed of wickedness . . . fruit of evil . . . spawn of the devil . . .

An agonized wail of despair tore from her. How could she think such sinful thoughts before the Lord? Had He given her over to wickedness entirely, forsaken her in her shame?

Unexpectedly, with all the terrible clarity of a malevolent portrait against the canvas of her mind, came the terrifying image of a huge dark bird emerging from a forest. So real did it appear that Finola could almost hear the grinding of its vast wings as it mounted upward and began circling and swooping above a lake.

Blackness engulfed her. The floor beneath her became a dizzying wave upon which she rode into a sea storm of nightmares.

In the chapel, Morgan roused, jerking himself upright as if someone had called his name.

Somewhat dazed, he glanced around, realized it was late. The tapers had burned low. No light filtered through the stained-glass windows of the chapel.

He yawned and stretched, then for a moment sat pondering the erratic, disjointed thoughts that often dance in the mysterious valley between sleep and wakefulness.

Without warning, he felt the spark of an idea flicker, then begin to rise deep inside him. It was as if a candle had been lighted in his mind.

Slowly, the webs of sleep began to clear, and he felt a kind of peace born of assurance spread over him. There was no thunderbolt of revelation, no brilliant flash of light or sudden seizure—only a gentle, quiet dawning within his spirit.

But as he sat there, unmoving, in the silence of the chapel, he realized with almost blinding certainty what he could do—what God would *have* him do—to help Finola.

A sudden urgency overtook him to go to her. He whipped the chair around, wheeling himself quickly to the doors, and flung them open with such force that they slammed, vibrating, against the wall.

28

For the Victims of Violence

Come, sweetheart, the bright ones would bring you
By the magical meadows and streams,
With the light of your dreaming they build you
A house on the hill of your dreams.

SEUMAS O'SULLIVAN (1879–1958)

The door to Finola's room stood slightly ajar. Morgan stopped at the threshold for a moment, suddenly aware that it was late and she might be sleeping.

Was he being foolish? He did not yet even know how to articulate the thoughts that had driven him from the chapel in such a fever. Perhaps, after the emotional turmoil of this day, she would not welcome the company of anyone, including him. Perhaps she would prefer to be alone.

No. He would not wait, *could* not wait. Although he did not understand the urgency he was under, not for a moment did he doubt the conviction that had seized him.

Lifting his hand, he tapped lightly on the doorpost. "Finola?" he said softly. " 'Tis Morgan. Might I come in for a moment?"

There was no response. He waited for Lucy Hoy to appear; when she didn't, he repeated Finola's name, then put his hand to the door and pushed it open a bit wider. After another moment's hesitation, he wheeled himself into the room.

When he first saw the empty bed he didn't panic. He looked

about, surprised but relieved that Finola apparently felt strong enough to be up.

The room was dim and shadowed, lighted by only one candle on the bedside table. Despite the immaculate linen and subtle scent of cloves, the cloying odor of illness hung over the room.

It took him a moment to register the fact that there was no sign of Finola or the woman, Lucy Hoy. His gaze went back to the bed.

Where was she?

He felt suddenly chilled. The only sounds in the room were his own shallow breathing and the wild banging of his heart against his chest.

Spinning the wheels of the chair hard, he whipped the rest of the way into the room, coming to a sharp halt before he reached the bed.

"Finola?" he choked out.

With silence his only reply, he veered the chair around to the other side of the bed, screeching to a stop at the sight of her, lying face down on the floor in her nightdress.

"Merciful Lord—Finola!"

Shaking off the panic clutching at his throat, Morgan raised himself almost halfway out of the chair by the sheer strength of his arms. He caught himself just before he pitched forward.

"SANDEMON!"

He had no idea where Sandemon might be, where the woman, Lucy Hoy, had gone. Trembling, he leaned over as far as he could, bracing himself with one hand on the arm of the wheelchair. At last he managed to turn Finola over just enough to reassure himself that she had only fainted and did not seem to be otherwise injured.

Letting go the arm of the chair, Morgan attempted to lift the unconscious girl off the floor, but succeeded only in losing his balance and nearly keeling over himself.

Chafing at his own helplessness, he again called out for Sandemon. He leaned forward, more cautiously this time, and shook Finola gently, trying to rouse her. She continued to lie completely still and silent.

Straightening in the chair, Morgan sat staring at the slender, inert form sprawled on the floor. The longer he sat there, the more furious he grew—with the missing Lucy Hoy, with the accursed wheelchair, with his useless legs. . . .

A thought struck him, and his hand went to his belt. Yanking it free of his trousers, he looped it through the slats of the wheelchair, then fastened it snugly about his middle, anchoring himself to the chair.

Morgan wedged the wheelchair firmly against the side of the bed and again leaned forward. The belt served to give him enough leverage that, this time, he was able to turn Finola all the way over. Grasping her under the arms, he began to lift her carefully from the floor.

––––––––

Lucy panicked when she saw Finola's door standing open. Lifting her skirts, she took off running down the hall and into the bedroom, milk splashing over the sides of the cup as she went.

She stopped just inside the room, gasping at the sight of the Fitzgerald holding Finola in his arms. The girl was draped over his lap like a doll, her long hair nearly touching the floor as it fell free.

He jerked around. Under the burning gaze of those fiery green eyes, Lucy lost her breath.

"Where in blazes have you *been*, woman?" he shouted. "You're supposed to be taking care of her, and I find her on the *floor!*"

His face was crimson with fury, the muscles in his neck knotted like ropes.

Quaking in terror at his anger and the sight of Finola, lying helpless in his arms, Lucy could only stand and gape.

"She must have tried to get up on her own and fainted!" His eyes, still ablaze with anger and accusation, forced Lucy to squirm with guilt.

"I . . . I only meant to be a moment. I went to fetch her some warm milk, to help her sleep!"

"Obviously it took you longer than a moment!" he snapped, his voice harsh with censure.

"But, sir, I *wasn't* gone long, truly I—"

"And where is Sandemon?" he railed, ignoring her attempt to explain.

"I am here, *Seanchai*," announced a quiet, steady voice at the door.

Lucy gulped in a ragged breath of relief at the sight of the black man, hoping his presence would divert the Fitzgerald's attention—and wrath—from her.

Even as he spoke, Sandemon crossed the room and lifted Finola from the Fitzgerald's arms as if she were no more than a young willow branch. With great care, the black man placed her on the bed and covered her.

Glancing down the length of the bed, he met Lucy's eyes. "Some cool cloths, perhaps—"

Lucy jerked to action, hurrying across the room to fetch the basin. But even as she moved, Finola uttered a soft moan and began to stir.

———

"He will discharge me," Lucy muttered to the black man in the hall. They had been dismissed once Finola revived, and now stood at the top of the stairs, whispering.

Sandemon shook his head. "No," he said, "I do not think so. He was only frightened. The *Seanchai* is a reasonable man."

"He is an *angry* man! Did you see the way he looked daggers at me when he told me he would sit with her *alone*?"

The black man might try to reassure her, but Lucy had seen the fury in those fiery green eyes. The Fitzgerald thought her negligent and worthless.

From the beginning, he had only allowed her to stay because Finola wanted her. True, he had paid her a fair wage in the meantime, but Lucy had known her days at Nelson Hall were numbered. She had thought to stay on only until Finola was well.

Now, it seemed even that was not to be. Not that she blamed him. In truth, she *should* have been with Finola, should never have stayed so long in the kitchen prattling on to Sandemon. She should have gone back upstairs immediately. The girl could have been seriously hurt!

"Whatever possessed her," said the black man, his tone thoughtful, "to leave her bed, as weak and ill as she is?"

———

"You gave me a terrible fright, lass!" Morgan said. "Why would you get up, weak as you are? You might have been badly injured, taking such a fall!"

"I didn't fall," Finola murmured. Immediately after the words were out, a stricken look crossed her features, as if she had spoken before she thought.

Leaning as close to her as he could manage from the wheelchair, Morgan frowned. "What happened, then? I thought you fainted and fell."

Abruptly, she looked away. "No . . . I mean, I did faint . . . but . . ."

Studying her, Morgan took in the waxen pallor of her skin, the red-rimmed eyes, smudged with shadows and hollowed by the severe thinness of her face. The effects of prolonged weeping and illness were all too evident.

"Finola?" Uncertainly, he extended his hand, touching hers.

Over the past few weeks, Finola had gained to the extent that he felt free to take her hand upon occasion. They would sit quietly together, talking as friends, although he was invariably the one who made most of the conversation.

While her voice had almost fully returned, her quietness, her faint shyness in his presence, had not changed. But he had begun to believe that she was growing more comfortable with him, was almost at ease in their relationship.

Earlier, when he had heard her sobbing in her room, he'd had all he could do not to go to her. Yet he had instinctively known it would be best to wait, to give her time to absorb this latest shock.

Now, as he sat watching her, his hand barely touching hers, he would have given all he had to gather her into his arms, to try and shield her against her pain. Instead, he was half-afraid she might refuse even the touch of his hand.

To his great relief, he felt her slip her hand inside his. He was careful not to press her fingers too tightly with his big paw, for she seemed as fragile as a reed in the wind.

"Finola," he said shakily, not quite certain how to go on. "I know . . . you have had another shock today."

He saw the tears start, but she kept her eyes fixed on the low-burning candle on the table. His heart aching for her, Morgan started to lift her hand to his lips, then caught himself. "Is there anything I can get for you, lass? Anything I can do—anything at all?"

She blinked, then again shook her head. Morgan didn't miss the obvious effort she was making for his benefit. He could see her fighting back the tears, wished she would simply let go and weep; at least then he could attempt to comfort her.

Struggling not to give in to his own anguish, he said, "I know you must be feeling overwhelmed about . . . everything. Perhaps a bit . . . frightened as well. But this will work out, lass, you will see. I—we will take care of you, Finola. You will stay here, with us. You are not alone."

Finally, she looked at him, and the pain in her eyes caught him like a blow. It was as if her very heart was shattering. The wondrous blue gaze was no longer clear and bright, but instead burned raw with shame and humiliation.

His chest wrenched, stealing his breath. His arms ached to pull her close to his heart. He actually leaned forward, then stopped.

"I didn't fall. . . ."

So faint were the words Morgan wasn't sure what he had heard. He bent his head closer. "What, then, lass?"

He was dimly aware that she was clutching his hand more tightly. "I had . . . I was lying on the floor. . . ." Her words were vague, disjointed. "I only meant to pray, you see . . . I didn't fall. . . ."

Lying on the floor . . . the act of the penitent . . .

Dismay washed over Morgan like a tidal wave. She blamed *herself*! God be merciful, she blamed herself for what had been done to her!

"Finola . . ." he choked out.

Suddenly she was gripping his hand with a strength he would not have thought she possessed. "I'm sorry! I've burdened you so, and now this—I'm so *sorry*!"

Morgan had thought he would never again know such pain. It was the same anguish that had riddled him the morning they carried her into Nelson Hall, beaten and broken, after the attack.

The cry of his heart was silent, but it roared in his ears like rolling thunder as he beheld her torment. "Finola . . . please tell me you are not blaming yourself for what happened! You *must* not!"

But her eyes burned with the undeniable evidence of self-condemnation, shame, and grief.

For a moment he wanted to kill the man who had done this to her! Even as he struggled to control his fury, his mind groped for some bit of reassurance, some word to convince her of the truth. "Finola," he said finally, "do you trust me?"

A startled look crossed her features, replacing the pain. She nodded, slowly.

"Then hear me now. You see the way I am, with these useless legs, bound to this chair—half a man—"

She strained toward him, shaking her head in protest, but he went on. "No, lass," he said gently. "Let me finish. I have told you about the shooting . . . how I came to be as I am—"

She nodded, watching him closely, her eyes questioning.

"Do you believe that I was in any way responsible for what happened?"

For a moment she didn't seem to understand. Then her eyes widened with dismay. "Of course not!"

"You understand and believe, then, do you, that what happened to me was entirely beyond my control? That I had absolutely nothing to do with it? That I merely survived an act of violence committed against me?"

In the silence that hung between them, he sensed her confusion. Her eyes probed his, and he squeezed her hand, gently. "Finola?"

Finally, she nodded. "Aye, you know I do," she murmured.

"Good," he said firmly. "Then so must you understand and believe that what happened to *you* is no different. It is the same for you as for me, Finola."

When she opened her mouth to speak, he stopped her with a shake of his head, saying, "Let me finish. You have survived an attack of violence, just as I did. You were a victim. And just as I have . . . scars . . . of my attack, so will you have your scars. But you have something else, Finola. As a result of that attack, a child now grows beneath your heart."

Leaning as closely to her as he dared, he gathered both her hands in his and gazed into her eyes. "Only God can understand all the reasons for what happened to you and to me, Finola. But I do know this much: if there is no shame, no disgrace, due *me* for the violence that put me in this chair, then there is none due *you* for the violence that left you with child! And I ask you to give me your word, right now, at this moment, that you will never, *never* blame yourself again!"

He saw the tears about to spill over, felt his own eyes burn for her pain.

"Then, the child . . . you don't believe it's . . . evil?" she murmured.

His heart thudded. "What? Of *course*, the child isn't evil! Why would you think such a thing?"

He saw the confusion and uncertainty in her eyes as she answered. "Lucy . . . Lucy said the child . . . that perhaps I should not have—"

Morgan stiffened, not realizing that he had increased the pressure on her hands until, seeing her wince, he quickly gentled his touch.

"Finola? *What*, exactly, did Lucy say?" he asked, his voice tight.

Finola's gaze was stricken, as if she suddenly realized she might have brought trouble on her friend. "She only meant to help me," she whispered, looking away. "Please don't be angry with Lucy."

With great effort, Morgan managed to bank his rage. He would settle with Lucy Hoy later.

"Finola—please look at me," he said, still clinging to her hands.

Finally, she turned back to him.

"There is something I would suggest to you . . . if you are strong enough that I might stay for a bit. Something I think might help us both."

When she nodded her assent, he plumped the pillows behind her shoulders, then again took her hand and began to speak what was in his heart.

29

Sacrament or Sacrilege?

Till her eyes shine,
'Tis night within my heart.

RICHARD BRINSLEY SHERIDAN (1751–1816)

Morgan's mouth felt dry, lined with lint, as he attempted to speak. While the turbulence of Finola's emotions had seemed to subside for now, his own feelings roared like a firestorm in his heart.

Clasping her hand, it occurred to him that, for a man reputed to be most eloquent in the Irish . . . and in the English, too, for that matter . . . he seemed to be a hopeless failure at this sort of speech. "Finola—there is something I would say, but perhaps I should apologize beforehand, in the event I happen to offend you. I assure you, my intentions are the best."

A small frown appeared on the pale forehead, but she said nothing.

Another thought struck Morgan, this time having to do with the fact that he had never, before now, seriously considered the idea he was about to set forth. Feeling very much the green *gorsoon*, he forced himself to continue. "Please understand, lass, that I am looking for no response from you this night. Take as long as you need to consider your decision."

Leaning slightly forward, he added, "And know this, Finola: there are no conditions, no expectations on my part for anything other than what I am proposing. None whatever."

The frown deepened, but her gaze held his, never wavering.

With his voice sounding thick and unnatural in his ears, Morgan went on. "Do you remember, Finola, that night I asked you to come and stay here, at Nelson Hall?"

She nodded, her lips trembling as if she found the memory painful.

For just an instant, Morgan's gaze went to their clasped hands, hers so white and frail, engulfed in his big, thick-knuckled paw. "Even then, I think, what I am about to suggest was in the back of my mind. In time, perhaps," he said, deliberately avoiding her eyes, "I would have found the courage to speak."

He knew there was nothing for it now but to say it all. "I am asking you, Finola, if you would consider . . . becoming my wife."

His face felt suddenly hot, his hands clammy. When he finally lifted his gaze to hers, he thought for a moment she had not heard him, or, at the least, did not understand. So still did she lie there, staring at him in silence, that she scarcely seemed to breathe.

"Please . . . let me explain," he said awkwardly, clearing his throat. "I know how I must appear to you: a middle-aged cripple, vying for a lovely young woman's hand." He scowled at the image his own words conjured up.

"Even before the wheelchair, I was never the great prize. Now—" He gave a resigned shrug. "Now, I am what I am. No doubt you find such a proposal outrageous, and I don't blame you at all. But if you will be patient with me, hear me out, perhaps it will seem a bit less . . . improbable to you."

He stopped, half expecting her to yank her hand away, to shrink from him. She did neither, though her eyes had now gone wide with incredulity.

"Finola," he began again, "do you know that, before tonight, I have never asked a woman to be my wife?" He tried unsuccessfully to smile. "I was always too much the rake, the roaming fool, to settle down and provide for a family. Some claimed I was wed to this terrible island and her troubles. I wonder if it wasn't more that I was her *prisoner*. In any event, I was too selfish entirely to love a woman, to take a wife."

He swallowed down the taste of bitterness swelling in his throat. "I have changed, Finola. Partly, as you might imagine, because of the wheelchair. Partly . . . I hope . . . because I have grown a bit wiser. I am still bound to Ireland, I admit, but now it is more a bond of loyalty and affection than one of desperation. In spite of that, I find myself wanting, even eager, to have a family . . . a wife, children. I have reached a point in my life where, I think, I can love something besides this island."

He was dimly aware that tears had formed in her magnificent eyes. But, with a sense of having been caught up in a raging current, he knew he could do nothing but finish what he had started.

"Lest you misunderstand what I am suggesting, lass, I assure you that I would never . . . force my attentions on you. That is not what I am about. We would live as friends—good friends, companions. I would care for you; I would be a father to the child. You would lack for nothing, I promise you. And I swear to you as well that I would *ask* for nothing."

He was saying it badly, the words spilling out like worthless coins dropping through a hole in a pouch. Finola seemed to have gone paler still, her eyes red and glazed.

He could not stop now. She would hear it all, every bit and piece of it, no matter how much the fool he might appear.

"I'll not deny that I have . . . affection for you, of course," he said, lowering his voice. "No doubt you know that by now. But, Finola, I would never put a hand to you . . . with the wrong intentions." Glancing over his blanket-draped legs, he added dryly, "Not that I am considered much of a threat."

"Morgan—" His name on her lips was little more than a choked whisper. He could not fathom the thoughts behind those wondrous blue eyes, eyes that made all other lights dim in comparison. Yet, she did not let go of his hand. Indeed, she was clinging to it, straining to raise herself up from the bed, her entire body trembling with the effort.

He moved to stop her, putting one hand to her shoulder. "No, lass! You need not say a word in reply. Do not even *try* to answer me yet, please! Just . . . think about what I am suggesting . . . take as long as you need. I know this is a selfish thing entirely on my part, but try to understand that I also have your well-being in mind—"

"There is nothing selfish in you!" she cried, again straining toward him. "But you can't possibly think I would allow you to bind yourself to me . . . and to a nameless child . . . in such a way—"

He cut off her words by gently putting a finger to her lips.

"No! Not nameless. The child—*our* child, Finola—will have a name: *my* name. As for binding myself to you—ah, Finola . . . if only you will have me, I will exult in it!"

He saw the doubt brimming in her eyes as he gently, but firmly, pressed her back onto the pillows. "Don't look at me so, lass— it's true! Sure, and you do not think I would propose such a thing from any misguided sense of selflessness or nobility?"

He smiled at her, smoothing a strand of flaxen hair away from her face. "I fear nobility is not a trait common to my kind," he said wryly. "No, lass, this is much more for my benefit than for yours."

Morgan ignored the quick shake of her head, the soft protest of disbelief. "Now, that's the truth, Finola; don't look at me so! I cannot imagine this gloomy old dungeon without the light of you, I swear I can't! And I would have you understand one thing more, about the child: it will be the same to me as if it were flesh of my flesh. In fact, unless you wish it otherwise, the child need never know but what *I* am its natural father."

At her gasp of astonishment, Morgan moved to convince her. "You've seen my affection for Annie, how I delight in the girl, how dear she is to me. Can you believe me when I say she is as much mine as if my blood ran through her veins?"

Her eyes searched his. At last she nodded, saying softly, "Aye, there is no denying it."

"Then think on this, Finola: Annie, too, is the child of . . . undesirable circumstances, a child rejected and unwanted. Why would I find it any more difficult to love *your* child than Annie?"

"But, why should you—"

Again he silenced her protest. "They will be my children, Finola, I *promise* you. Annie and your babe—and you—will be my family."

The weeping had stopped, but she had gone ashen, and so dark were the shadows smudging her eyes that he felt a pang of remorse. "I've exhausted you! I should go now, so you can rest. We will talk more tomorrow."

Unexpectedly, she grasped his hand, clinging to it with an almost fierce desperation.

"Ah, lass," he murmured, awkwardly wrapping one arm about her shoulders in an attempt to reassure her. "I don't mean to cause you further distress. I want only to help, Finola."

"I know," she said in a strangled voice. "But your kindness . . ."

"Don't talk of kindness!" he blurted out. "This is not *kindness*! I want this for *myself*—not just for you!"

Again the slender shoulders heaved. Morgan cupped her face between his palms. "Don't cry, lass," he pleaded softly. "Please, don't cry. You destroy me entirely when you weep. I want to see an end to your tears at last. I want to make you smile again."

He paused. Then, his voice brisk, he said, "Now, then, you must rest. Tomorrow, when you're stronger, we'll talk again, eh?"

Morgan held her gaze until she gave a small nod. Still, he stayed with her, making no move to leave the room until at last, her hand still clinging to his, her eyes closed in sleep.

He ached to brush his lips over her pale cheek, but he would not take even such a small liberty as this. It was enough to feel her hand in his, to know she was safe beneath his roof and close to him.

God help him, he would never ask for more.

————

His nerves were far too taut for sleep. Wheeling himself to the lift, he went back downstairs, to the library.

The day had seemed so long that he felt it must surely be past midnight. He was amazed to hear the clock in the entryway strike ten. So early!

At his desk, he tried to read, with little success. He fingered through the pages of Joseph's journal, but quickly gave it up, not trusting his concentration. He was relieved when, after a moment, Sandemon knocked, then entered.

"I sent Lucy Hoy back to Miss Finola's room," the black man said by way of greeting. "I assumed you would not want her left alone."

"That didn't seem to make any difference earlier," Morgan snapped.

Sandemon came to a stop on the other side of the desk. "That was my fault," he said quietly. "I came to explain. The woman came into the kitchen to get some warm milk and a sleeping potion for Miss Finola. I . . . detained her with my questions."

"Don't excuse her! She was negligent." Morgan was quickly discovering that, although the hour was not as late as he'd ex-pected, his nerves were stretched to the limit, his body as weary

261

as if he'd been up for days. "We'll find a replacement for her. I don't care for the woman in any event."

When there was no reply, he glanced up to find the black man regarding him with a troubled look.

"Say it, then!" Morgan commanded. "You obviously disagree."

"It might be a mistake," the other said carefully, "to send her away just now. She is devoted to Miss Finola—who obviously relies on her. I don't think you should dismiss her."

Morgan studied the implacable features. "Tell me you've not gone sweet on the woman. You know what she is!"

For the first time since the West Indies black man had arrived at Nelson Hall, Morgan saw a flash of temper. The broad nostrils flared, the midnight eyes went hard.

"Because I am asking you to be fair, you accuse me of such a thing?"

Already, Morgan regretted his rash accusation. "I'm sorry—I didn't mean that. It's just that I want Finola to have someone dependable, that's the thing."

"I don't mean to presume, *Seanchai*," Sandemon said quietly, "but I believe Lucy Hoy is altogether trustworthy . . . at least in this regard. I also think that you might risk . . . doing her great harm . . . if you were to send her away just now."

Morgan stared at him. He hadn't the faintest notion what the man was getting at—but, then, he seldom did. Nevertheless, he had learned to trust Sandemon's instincts.

"All right, then, she can stay," he said grudgingly. "But only until Finola no longer needs her."

The black man inclined his head, then turned to leave the room. Morgan gazed at the broad back, the powerful shoulders. The West Indies Wonder *was* a wonder, and that was the truth. He never ceased to amaze Morgan with his perception—and his compassion. In that instant, as Sandemon walked toward the door, Morgan realized that he should—indeed, that he *must*—tell his friend of his plans to marry Finola.

"Sandemon?"

The black man paused and glanced over one shoulder. "Yes, *Seanchai*?"

"Wait a moment, if you please. I have something I would discuss with you."

Sandemon turned, his expression puzzled.

"You'd best sit down," said Morgan. "This will not be brief."

The black man pulled a chair to the desk opposite the desk and sat down, his gaze fixed intently on Morgan's face.

As Morgan struggled for the best way to begin, it occurred to him that what he wanted most from his friend was not necessarily his understanding . . . but his blessing.

———

Once Sandemon was out the door, Morgan turned back to the journal in front of him. Even with his eyeglasses on, however, the words seemed to run together, indistinguishable.

Fatigue, no doubt. He was about to give over and go to his bedroom when a discreet knock sounded, followed by Sister Louisa's appearance in the doorway.

He motioned her in with some reluctance. Obviously, no one else in the house was as tired as he was.

She stopped a respectful distance from the desk. "Sandemon said you had just left the girl. I thought I'd inquire about her."

Morgan indicated that she should be seated, but she chose to stand. "Finola is . . . resting," he answered. "She was sleeping when I left her."

With a relieved sigh, the nun clasped her hands in front of her. "Poor girl. She's had so much—and whatever is she to do *now*?"

Morgan looked at her. "Because of the child, you mean?" he asked bluntly.

He'd give the woman her due. Most nuns would have gone red and stammered. Not Sister Louisa. She merely nodded and repeated his words. "Because of the child."

He hesitated only a moment. "I've asked her to be my wife," he said evenly.

The nun looked about to strangle, but said nothing.

"She hasn't given me her reply yet, of course, but I'm hopeful."

He was entirely unprepared for what came next.

"You *can't* be serious!" she burst out. "Such a marriage would be—" She stopped, obviously aware that she had overstepped the bounds of propriety.

Removing his eyeglasses, Morgan glared at her. "Would be *what*, Sister?"

He should have known she was far too brash to hold her

tongue. Still, she *was* a nun. He would give her the respect her office implied. "Go on," he said wearily. "You might just as well have your say."

Bristling, she said, "Such a marriage would be a sin."

Nun or not, Morgan flared. "Now *just* a moment—"

"Forgive me!" she burst out, obviously flustered. "I understand what you're trying to do, but—"

"*Do* you, now?" Morgan grated, clenching his hands on top of the desk to resist pounding it. "Why don't you tell me what it is I'm trying to do, Sister?"

A crimson flush spread over the nun's face. "Your motives are admirable, *Seanchai*, but such a marriage would be a lie before God, not a sacrament!"

"I seem to remember," Morgan pointed out nastily, "that you've been known to take issue with some of the sacraments."

"You would be doing the girl a terrible disservice! Binding her to a loveless marriage, a hopeless union—"

The last of Morgan's composure snapped. "It would not be a lie, nor would it be loveless! Not that it's any of your affair—but I happen to *love* Finola . . . very much."

His blunt admission stopped her, but only for a moment. The nun, Morgan had learned, was remarkably quick at regaining her composure.

"Still," she said, her voice shaking, "you would be compromising the sacrament if you wed, knowing there can be no real union—"

A look of horror settled over her sharp features. Had he not been so angry, Morgan might have been amused by her sudden discomfiture.

"I repeat, Sister Louisa, that this is none of your affair. But since it seems you have taken it upon yourself to act as my spiritual advisor, let me assure you that I am altogether capable of a real . . . *union*. My legs may be paralyzed, but I am still a man."

She stared at her feet, at the floor, at the window behind him—everywhere but at him. "I'm terribly sorry . . . I didn't mean—"

"I know what you meant, Sister," Morgan said heavily. "And you are quite in order to be protective of Finola. But let me explain something: although I am capable of being a husband to her . . . in every way . . . I have no intention of forcing myself on her."

He sighed and rubbed a hand across his eyes. "Finola has been hurt—deeply hurt—and her healing will take time. But I intend to afford her every protection while she is recovering. Both she and the child will have my name, and I will do all within my power to shield her from further humiliation."

Sister Louisa slanted a glance at him. "But what," she ventured, "if Finola finds that such a marriage is not enough for *her*?"

Morgan squeezed his eyes shut, then opened them again, his gaze boring directly into hers. "I don't have to tell *you*, Sister, that a wedding which is not . . . consummated . . . can be annulled by the church. If the time ever comes that Finola desires to be free of me, I will not seek to hold her to her vows. But in the meantime, I intend to be a faithful husband to her—and a father to her child."

He paused and looked at the nun, who stood speechless before him. "In *my* mind, Sister Louisa, this is *not* simply a 'marriage of convenience,' nor is it a lie or a sham. I will be a true husband to her, as long as I live—or as long as *she* desires it."

He cut her protest short with a wave of his hand. "If Finola accepts my proposal, her child will have a name. And Finola will have a home—as well as the financial security that comes with being my wife. Now, then," he said, pushing himself away from the desk, "if you have no further admonitions for me this night, I believe I will go upstairs."

Drawing herself up to her full height, the nun looked him in the eye. "I apologize," she said with apparent sincerity, "if I offended you."

Morgan sighed. "No offense taken, Sister," he said wearily. "Good-night."

30

Honorable Ambitions

There is always hope for all who will dare and suffer;
Hope for all who surmount the Hill of Exertion, uncaring
Whether their path be brighter or darker,
smoother or rougher;
. . . There is always hope for those who,
relying with earnest
Souls on God and themselves,
take for their motto, "Labour."

JAMES CLARENCE MANGAN (1803–1849)

New York City
Early March

"I do wish you felt up to g-going today, Nora," Evan said, allowing her to fuss over his neckcloth at the last minute. "I wouldn't have committed the b-boys to sing at this affair if I'd known you couldn't be there."

"Don't be foolish, Evan! You were exactly right to agree." Nora smoothed his stiff white collar once more before sitting down on the edge of the bed. "Besides, even if I'd been feeling perfectly fine, I'm showing enough now that I'd not want to be seen in such a public gathering."

With a sigh, Evan sat down beside her and took her hand. "I confess," he said, "that I simply d-do not understand why women

266

in the family way are expected to stay out of sight. It doesn't seem right to me. N-not at all."

Glancing down over herself, Nora touched her abdomen and smiled. "I expect we make others uncomfortable," she said. "Especially the menfolk. And the larger we get, the more uncomfortable we make them."

Silently, Evan recognized that his discomfort had nothing to do with Nora's appearance; it stemmed solely from his concern for her well-being. Aloud, he simply uttered a short acknowledgment of her reasoning.

"Besides," she went on, "it's not as if none of the family will be there. You'll have Johanna and Daniel John."

"That's true. It was good of D-Daniel to ask Johanna along."

Tucking a small wisp of hair behind her ear, Nora said, "The boy has always been the one to think of others. And even though Johanna won't be able to hear the music, she'll enjoy an outing. The poor girl spends too much time entirely, cooped up in the house helping me."

"Johanna loves you very m-much." Evan pressed a quick kiss to her cheek, then, getting to his feet, helped her up. "It appears to me that she's only too glad to help." Fingering the buttons on his suit coat nervously, he said, "I suppose we m-must be going, or we'll miss the ferry. That wouldn't d-do at all—not today!"

"Everything will go wonderfully, Evan—I know it will! Just you remember—I'll be praying every moment!"

He kissed her one more time. "I'll be counting on that! I've never d-done anything like this in my life, and I *d-do* want the boys to feel g-good about their performance!" He stopped. "You're *quite* sure you'll be all right, with no one here b-but Tom?"

Nora laid both hands on his shoulders and smiled into his eyes. "Ach, will you stop your fretting, man, and get on with you! I will be fine, and your boys will be grand! But not if their director doesn't show up because he missed the ferry!"

Michael looked so handsome!

Sara Farmington Burke beamed as her husband concluded his speech from the podium in the ballroom. Convincing him to visit her father's tailor had been almost as much struggle as coaxing him to speak. But the result was a splendid black suit that emphasized his broad shoulders and enhanced his dark hair—and made her the wife of the most dashing man in the room!

Sara felt about to burst with love and pride as she watched her handsome husband woo the crowd—a crowd made up of some of the wealthiest and most influential members of New York's society. The upstairs ballroom, spacious and elegant, gleamed like a jewel, its stained-glass windows ablaze in the afternoon sun. The silver and enamels had been polished to a dazzling sheen, and mosaics and fine paintings splashed the room with a myriad of colors.

As Michael fielded questions from his listeners, Sara became keenly aware that his appeal to the audience wasn't due solely to his good looks and charm—although certainly he had more than his share of both. No, while there was no denying the fact that he was almost arrogantly good-looking, he obviously had something more, some unidentifiable quality that had caught the interest—and apparent respect—of the crowd on a much deeper level than charm and good looks ever could.

Sara felt guilty in admitting, even to herself, her initial surprise at the crowd's reaction to her husband. She hadn't quite known what to expect; at the back of her mind had lurked the unsettling possibility that she had coerced Michael into doing something that might work against him.

She knew most of these people, knew many of them quite well. She felt sure that the majority of them were good Christian people with a sincere desire to help others. Just as certainly, she knew there were others among them who had come simply out of a perverse sense of curiosity, or merely to socialize. The idea of expending either effort or financial resources to aid the tenement dwellers was the furthest thing from their minds—especially when most of those tenement dwellers happened to be *Irish*.

But overall, the coterie had surprised her—and so had Michael. He'd proved himself more than equal to the crowd, indeed had actually ended up in control of it.

Among the men and ladies milling about the podium were some of the stiffest shirts in New York. Yet, apart from a few sour-faced holdouts, Michael seemed to have won the respect of the group.

Darting a look at her father across the room, Sara saw that both he and Simon Dabney, the big, elegantly attired lawyer beside him, seemed to be as intrigued with Michael as everyone else.

————————

"Your son-in-law is rather a surprise," Simon Dabney observed, not taking his eyes from the Irish policeman at the podium.

"Really? In what way?"

Dabney glanced at Lewis Farmington. "Actually, I'm very impressed with him, Lewis. I'm also a little curious about him. What kind of ambitions does the man have, do you know?"

"Michael?" Farmington's gaze returned to his son-in-law. After a moment, he gave a rather curious smile. "I doubt that you'd understand the ambitions of a man like Michael Burke, Simon. I doubt that very much."

"I don't suppose you're going to elaborate on that?"

Still smiling, Farmington crossed his arms over his chest. "How many uncompromisingly honest men have you known, Simon? Any at all?"

"Lewis—you insult me," said Dabney in a cheerful tone of voice, not in the least insulted. "Let's see now—I assume you mean present company excluded—so that would narrow things down considerably."

Lewis Farmington laughed. "As I thought. You admit the world of politics is populated with less than noble characters."

"Actually, the New York world of politics is rapidly becoming populated with *Irish* characters—as I'm sure you know. And," Dabney added with a simulated sigh, "I'm afraid their record for honesty doesn't rate any higher than anyone else's."

"No doubt you're right," said Farmington. "But you may take my word for it, Simon: Michael Burke is a thoroughly honest man. I would say, even, a *noble* man. As to his 'ambitions,' however, I wouldn't know, although I believe maintaining his integrity would rate high on the list."

"He's Catholic, I suppose?" Dabney inquired nonchalantly.

"No, as a matter of fact, Michael is Protestant."

"Interesting."

"He's an interesting man." Farmington's dark eyes, always dagger-sharp, now probed even more intently than ever. "Why so curious about my son-in-law, Simon? As you may have deduced by now, Michael's chief interest lies in the area of immigrant problems: their abominable living conditions, and the crimes being perpetrated against them. I don't recall your being particularly fired with social conscience in the past."

"Actually, Lewis, I've heard some intriguing things about Captain Burke. Most intriguing. He seems to have earned quite a reputation for himself among the more . . . common elements of the city. Sterling police record, compassionate cop—that sort of thing. An exception, you must admit."

"No doubt."

"As it happens, the party's looking for a likely candidate for assistant alderman—as well as a man worth grooming for better things." Dabney turned an engaging smile on the other man. "I don't suppose you'd know if Captain Burke has any political aspirations?"

Farmington again hiked a dark eyebrow. "I thought I mentioned that Michael is an honest man."

"Exactly what we're looking for."

"A new movement in politics, surely?"

"Lewis, Lewis . . . you can be the most dreadful cynic at times. Though I won't deny the present board of aldermen might be a bit overloaded with a few, ah, questionable individuals."

"Thieves' Row, I would say."

"Perhaps." Dabney sighed. "Seriously, we're not looking for just another crafty politician. We have an ample crop of those already. We're hoping to find someone a cut above the rest. An intelligent man with integrity, a man to help clean things up a bit in the city before moving on to state government—or even higher. As you know, we like to have our own man in Washington. Considering the captain's reputation, and after watching him charm the carriage trade this afternoon, I'm more than a little interested in having a talk with him. You'll introduce me, I hope?"

"Correct me if I'm wrong, Simon, but I don't believe the position of assistant alderman includes a salary, does it?"

"That's true, but I'm sure we could arrange a paying position for the captain somewhere else while he's serving his constituents. As you know, Lewis, this would be just the first step. Alderman, next, then—Congress, perhaps? First, however, we have to find a loyal man whom we can support all the way."

"Quite frankly, Simon, I'm not at all sure I'd want to see a member of my family involved in the political scene. The whole business tends to leave a bad taste in my mouth."

"Nonsense, Lewis! That's just your blue blood interfering with the rascal in you. Why, even the best of families have a politician or two among them these days."

Even before he finished speaking, Simon Dabney turned his attention back to the Irish police captain. His imagination was already measuring that dashing figure for a tall silk hat and an ivory cane.

———

Michael had no time to take stock of how he was doing, but he did register a note of surprise at the sheer volume—and variety—of questions that had been coming from the audience.

Even more surprising was the ease with which he found himself answering those questions. Until today, he hadn't realized just how engrossed he had become in the immigrant settlements and their problems, and it was a bit of a revelation to find out that he knew more than he thought he did.

Not that he was comfortable with what he was doing, standing up here in front of these pillars of society as if he belonged. Yet, his years on the force served him well; if there was one thing a policeman learned almost from the start, it was how to take the measure of a crowd. Another was how to control it.

This particular gathering, of course, could not be compared with any of his previous experiences. Nevertheless, he had discovered early in the day that there were some very decent, genuine people in attendance. There were also, he reminded himself, a number of fools.

Such as the long-nosed aristocrat near the front of the gathering, just to Michael's right. A youth with smooth yellow hair and an elaborate waistcoat, he seemed bent on proving his ignorance each time he opened his mouth.

"You would have us to believe, then . . . ah, *Captain*—" he said, making Michael's rank sound like an ethnic slur, "that the Irish populace of Five Points has been . . . victimized by the city's more fortunate classes? But surely that's an exaggeration! It's a well-known fact that the Irish have *always* lived in squalor, even before they came to America! Why, from what I've read, the entire country of Ireland is just another Five Points slum!"

Yellow-Hair turned a look of utter contempt on Michael, who

resisted the urge to grind him to powder. Baring his teeth in the semblance of a good-natured smile, he replied, "Well, sir, it would seem that you've been reading the British press. That being the case, no doubt you've also discovered that the Irish rose directly from the bogs, having circumvented the Creator's divine plan."

Michael caught a breath, and was surprised to hear a few discreet chuckles among the crowd. "No matter," he went on with equanimity. "The sad truth is that Ireland *is* a wretched, devastated island these days, a condition for which the English can take, if not full credit, at least a healthy share of it. That would be the same English, by the bye, which we Americans licked a few years back when we'd had quite enough of their exorbitant taxes and decadent laws."

Ignoring a smattering of applause, Michael went on. "The Irish came across expecting a bit better from these United States, you see. They'd heard tell that the Americans value their freedom every bit as much as the Irish themselves, and that the country was being built upon the principle of liberty for all.

"Perhaps," Michael added, his tone a bit more harsh than he'd intended, "you can imagine their surprise to learn that that principle apparently applies to everyone else but the Irish."

Suddenly impatient with the lot of them—even those fashionably dressed matrons beaming in his direction—Michael gave a short word of encouragement that they continue their efforts on behalf of the immigrant slum dwellers. Then, with a curt nod and a forced smile, he left the podium.

———

More than half an hour later, Sara was still waiting for Michael to tear himself away from her father and Simon Dabney. Overwhelmed with curiosity, she had occupied herself by making the rounds of the refreshment tables, sampling a variety of desserts.

"Mrs. Burke?"

Sara turned toward the opposite end of the cake table. At first she didn't recognize the woman with the shy smile standing there, alone. Dressed to the nines in a violet silk dress and tulle-trimmed bonnet, Alice Walsh looked younger and more sophisticated than Sara remembered her.

Although she vaguely recalled that her first meeting with the woman had been at another mission bazaar, she was still surprised to see her here today. Somehow, the idea of Patrick Walsh's wife displaying an interest in the plight of New York's immigrants seemed incredibly ironic.

Sara managed a small smile and a civil greeting. Only then did Alice Walsh approach, her expression uncertain, her movements hesitant.

Even knowing how much Michael detested Walsh himself, Sara could not bring herself to treat this sweet-faced woman with anything less than courtesy. As she watched her draw near, she felt an inexplicable softening toward the woman, a feeling bordering on sympathy. It was the same response Alice Walsh had evoked in her that day on Staten Island when Sara had gone to visit Tierney.

After a moment, they began to make polite—and utterly trivial—conversation about the bazaar. The entire time, Sara sensed that Alice Walsh had more than small talk on her mind. It seemed, however, to be taking considerable effort for her to get to the point.

"Mrs. Burke . . . I wonder . . . I wanted to inquire . . ."

She had an aura of uncertainty about her—a shyness, coupled with a kind of urgency. Sara warmed to this lack of confidence almost in spite of herself. Again, she found herself puzzling how such a woman had come to marry a scoundrel like Patrick Walsh.

"I've been thinking . . . that I might be of help in your work . . . your mission work in the slum districts, that is." Now that the woman had finally gotten the words out, she seemed almost desperate to explain herself. "I have a great deal of free time these days, you see, and I should really like to put it to better use! I'd do anything that needs to be done." Abruptly, she put a hand to her mouth as if taken unawares by her own boldness.

Sara was surprised, but interested. They were in dire need of help for the slum missions, the kind of help most difficult to find. Donations of money and material goods were steadily increasing, but it was another story altogether finding workers—workers with the time and willingness . . . and courage . . . to venture among the "untouchables" of the city.

"I'm afraid what we really need, Mrs. Walsh," Sara said directly, "are people with strong hearts—and strong constitutions. People who are willing to go into places like the Five Points and work among the people. However," she was quick to add, "the conditions there are offensive—indeed, they're downright revolting. To be perfectly frank, some of us who have been working in the Five Points for years still have all we can do not to scream and run every time we go in."

Alice Walsh blanched but, to her credit, didn't shrink. "Still, Mrs. Burke . . . I should like to try. I believe I can manage."

Sara wasn't overly tall, but she had to look down to meet the woman's eyes. "Did you have any particular kind of . . . work . . . in mind, Mrs. Walsh? Are you, ah, skilled in anything specific?"

An expression of embarrassment pinched the other woman's features. "Skilled? Oh . . . no . . . I'm afraid not," she stammered, red-faced. After a moment, though, she straightened her shoulders a little and said, "The truth is, I can't do much of anything at all but play the piano. But I'd be willing to do whatever is needed." She paused, then added, "And I . . . I don't swoon easily."

She gave a small, uncertain smile. Searching that clear blue gaze, Sara saw an unexpected glint of determination and strength. She smiled back, saying, "Perhaps you could call at my home next week, Mrs. Walsh. Tuesday would be good; I have two other ladies coming to discuss work projects that day."

A look of gratitude broke over Alice Walsh's face, and it occurred to Sara that she might grow to like this woman very much.

"Well?" Sara tapped her foot impatiently as she watched Michael scoop a huge piece of Esther Parrish's apple cake onto his plate.

Intent on his dessert, he waited until he sampled the first bite to answer her. "Well, what?"

"What did Simon Dabney want?"

He took another bite. "Your father was just introducing us. You know him, I imagine?"

"Of course, I know him! Everybody knows Simon. He's one of the most ruthless lawyers in the state." She paused. "And one of the most successful. He's also very influential in politics."

"Indeed," he said without much interest, looking idly around the room as he continued to savor his cake.

"You were with him for more than half an hour."

Finally, he looked at her, his dark eyes dancing with amusement. "For such a well-bred young lady, Sara *a gra*, you can be unfashionably—direct."

"And impatient."

He grinned. "There's that. Ah, well, I expect I shall have no peace at all if I don't tell you. Mr. Dabney's curiosity," he said, eyeing the last bite of cake with regret, "would seem almost as dogged as yours."

Sara gave her most severe frown, watching him lift his fork to his mouth and slowly down the last of the cake.

"For example," he finally said, touching the napkin to his mouth, "he seems unduly interested in my plans for the future."

"*What* plans for the future?"

He nodded. "Exactly. I tried to explain that I haven't formulated any plans for the future just yet, but he insisted that I *must* have higher aspirations than the police force."

"He actually *said* that?" Sara knew Simon Dabney could be outrageously rude at times, but he ordinarily confined it to fellow politicians.

"Not exactly," Michael replied, his mouth tightening somewhat. "But he implied it."

"What was he getting at, do you know?"

He regarded her as if he weren't quite sure how to answer. "According to your father," he said with a slight edge in his voice, "Mr. Dabney is sniffing about for a, ah . . . 'a man with prospects.' For some reason," he said dryly, "he seems to think I might be such a man."

Sara stood staring at him for a moment. Finally, understanding dawned. "He wants you to consider *politics*? Good heavens, Michael, what did you say?"

He shrugged, and again the eyes twinkled. "Didn't I explain to the man," he said in exaggerated brogue, "that I might be a bit too busy at present for such matters?" He turned back to the cake table with renewed interest. "Mr. Dabney did indicate, however, that he would be in touch."

Abruptly, his expression sobered. "Was that Patrick Walsh's wife I saw you talking with?"

Realizing that he was not about to tell her anything more at the moment, Sara nodded. "Yes. She's really quite a surprise, you know. I'm not sure but what—"

"What's she doing here?" he said shortly.

"Why . . . she belongs to one of the member congregations, I believe. She also wanted to inquire about helping out in the Five Points, and—"

He surprised her with a sharp utterance of disgust. "The gall of the woman!"

"No, Michael, I think she's completely sincere! She said she'd do anything at all, that she has a great deal of free time on her hands and wants to put it to good use."

"So she means to salve her conscience by turning her hand to some of the misery her husband has helped to create?" he countered, scowling.

This was a new thought to Sara, and a disturbing one. "I can't believe that. In fact, I'm convinced Alice Walsh is completely in the dark about her husband's . . . activities."

He looked at her, his expression openly skeptical.

"I mean it, Michael. As a matter of fact, I . . . like Alice Walsh. And what's more, there's something about her I respect." Wanting to break the tension, Sara tucked her arm through his, saying, "Besides, we're almost desperate for workers. *My* conscience would bother me if I didn't at least give her a chance."

He was silent for a time as they strolled about the room, taking in the various exhibits and displays. When he finally spoke, he sounded a little less skeptical. "I suppose it's possible that Mrs. Walsh might not know the truth about her husband. God help the woman if that's so."

Sara felt a stirring of uneasiness when she saw the grim set of his mouth.

Meeting her eyes, he said, "She's sure to find out eventually, Sara. It's inevitable. And if she's as much the innocent as you believe, it will be a bitter thing entirely when she learns the truth."

———

When Jess Dalton strode briskly into the room, he brought a draft of cold air with him. A number of hard looks and, in some cases, openly hostile stares were directed toward the big pastor, who appeared oblivious to it all.

Chester Pauling and the insufferable Charles Street, along with a few others, huddled closely together like a gaggle of cold geese, eyeing Dalton with undisguised animosity.

Sara watched them, feeling a sudden surge of anger at the chain of events this group of prosperous, influential . . . bigots . . . had set in motion.

They weren't alone, of course. Successful businessmen all over the city opposed abolition, as did most journalists. Even the majority of the clergy sided with pro-slavery—after all, their salaries were paid, their churches built, their pews rented by the city's wealthy.

Because of this, the members of the abolitionist movement were often seen as crackpots or foolish visionaries. There was some truth in that charge, Sara knew; with so many of the ministers, merchants, and members of the press opposed to the entire movement, fanatics and undesirables soon filled the ranks.

Ever since 1831, when the radical William Lloyd Garrison first published his Boston periodical, the *Liberator,* the antislavery movement had been fraught with upheaval and dissension. The militant blocs antagonized the more moderate element, and those who clamored for a variety of humanitarian causes, such as equal rights for women and prison reform, managed to alienate those who would restrict their efforts to freeing the slaves.

There was an indisputable lunatic fringe that advocated outright disregard of the nation's laws and even violence to achieve their ends. But northerners, for the most part, revered the Constitution, and when extremists—like Garrison himself—resorted to burning copies of it, or urging slaves to murder their masters in their beds, they tended to view the abolition movement as no better than an organization of madmen.

Now, years later, the hysterical antics of Garrison and his extremist following still overshadowed the efforts of the more moderate abolitionists. Nevertheless, men and women who believed in the essential cause—freedom of the slaves—continued to work for a peaceable, reasonable solution by educating the public and influencing the government.

Jess Dalton was one such man, and it was the very worst sort of unfairness to relegate him to the category of a fanatic. As a minister and a champion of the rights of the oppressed, he labored as a rational, compassionate man of God. What a small group of petty Pharisees were attempting to do to him was nothing short of sinful.

He was aware, of course, of the scheming against him. Already there had been an informal reprimand regarding his activity with the abolitionist movement, and his taking the black boy, Arthur Jackson, into his home.

Watching him now, Sara thought that, at first glance, the big pastor seemed himself: relaxed, cheerful, and confident. A closer look, however, revealed a deepening of the lines webbing out from his eyes, and an uncharacteristic air of distraction.

"I wonder why he's so late," Michael said, beside her. "And where's his wife?"

"She's not feeling well," Sara said. "I talked with him this morning, when we were setting up the exhibits, and he told me that Kerry had taken cold and wouldn't be able to come." She caught her lip between her teeth for a moment. "He seemed worried about her."

"I'd like to throttle that bunch in the corner," Michael said harshly.

"Oh, Michael—it's so unfair!" Sara said. "Jess Dalton is such a *good* man—he works so hard for the church and for the missions—for the entire city! There must be a way to stop what they're trying to do!"

"There is no stopping that kind, Sara, short of a total change of heart." He turned to look at her, his eyes hard. "And no one but the good Lord can bring about such a—"

He broke off, turning toward the doors as the crowd stirred and murmured. The instant Sara saw what was coming, she caught her breath.

Nervously, she scanned the incredulous faces among the crowd as Evan Whittaker and his Five Points Celebration Singers trooped solemnly into the ballroom.

31

Songs of the City

How sad!—to hear a song of mirth
Sung in the homeless street,
By one in melancholy dearth
Of clothes, and food to eat.

WILLIAM ALLINGHAM (1824–1899)

The two journalists in attendance began to scribble furiously when the choir of black and Irish boys from Five Points marched into the ballroom.

The older of the two reporters, Jerry Tanner, could scarcely believe what he was seeing, even as he wrote. He couldn't wait to get back downtown and file his story.

They were sharp-looking lads, for the most part: scrubbed and neat, though in some cases their clothing was tattered. Tanner noted that despite the cold March day, some were barefooted.

From the appearance of things, the one-armed director had the lot of them well under control. *Whittaker* was the Englishman's name, Tanner recalled from the information given to him by Mr. Farmington: *Evan Whittaker.* No doubt about it, the discipline of the youngsters seemed impressive. They filed in like a group of little soldiers, turning toward the crowd as one, then standing ramrod straight with all eyes on their slender, bespectacled director.

Griggs, a rookie from the *Journal,* shot Tanner a bug-eyed look.

"You believe this? How do you suppose they wangled their way in here?"

Tanner shrugged, his eyes scanning the crowd to gauge their reaction. "Dunno. But I doubt anybody's going to question Lewis Farmington on his choice of house guests."

Tanner could have almost predicted the response of some among the crowd. Old Chester Pauling, for example, looked about to strangle on his own Adam's apple, and his sidekick, Charles Street—the senior partner of Street, Storey, and Black—was wagging his jowls like a flustered turkey. Some of the women thinned their noses as if they smelled something bad, and two or three actually turned and led their husbands out of the room.

"They're *black*!" he heard one observant matron choke out to her stricken companion. "*Black* and *Irish*." The friend, whose jaw seemed locked half open, could do nothing but gape and nod.

For the most part, however, people simply stood quietly, staring back at the frightened black and freckled faces. Some folks even smiled—but not many. Lewis Farmington's daughter and her Irish policeman husband were beaming, as was the thin-faced little red-headed girl standing close to the two of them.

When the boys began to sing, Tanner just about forgot the crowd; he even had to remind himself to take notes! Oh, this was something, all right! First, a couple of traditional hymns, then some patriotic melodies before launching into what sounded like something entirely new. A mixture, Tanner thought, an appealing kind of blend of black music—spirituals—and songs from other countries, all wrapped around each other and packaged into something that sounded like—well, like *America*.

The music had a rhythm that made it hard to stand still. Even the less lively numbers had a certain effervescence, a catchy rhythm, that made you want to at least clap your hands or tap your foot.

Glancing around the room, Tanner grinned at the sight of bluebloods like Lewis Farmington and Jason Milhorne nodding their heads and tapping their toes with the best of them. He dashed off a few more descriptions in his notes, then turned his attention back to the boys.

This was something, by gosh—something to write about! That Englishman stood up there, a baton in his one hand, his back as straight as a flagpole, doing little more than nodding his head every now and then or giving a short snap of his wrist. And those boys sang their hearts out for him!

And they sang *well*! No doubt about it, this was a story! Tanner grinned until he thought his face would crack, only vaguely aware as he scrawled his remarks that his own foot was tapping along with everybody else's.

———

From his place in the back row of the choir, Daniel looked out and winked at Johanna, who was standing with Miss Sara and Uncle Mike. She smiled back at him, and he winked again.

Immediately Evan caught his eye, and Daniel sobered as he went on singing.

Evan, Daniel decided, looked about to burst out of his stiff white collar. His eyes behind the spectacles were bright and glistening with approval.

The thought made Daniel smile and sing a bit louder. He was more than a little surprised when an elderly couple at the front of the crowd smiled back at him.

———

Sara stood watching Evan's choir with one hand on Johanna's shoulder, her free hand squeezing Michael's fingers.

Had she not been a lady—a lady in the midst of a public gathering—she thought she might have cheered.

It was sheer delight to see what Evan had accomplished with these boys! Nora had told her how some of them couldn't even read! Yet here they stood, their voices blending almost as one— like one triumphant instrument of an orchestra, for heaven's sake!—singing a mix of music the likes of which Sara had never heard before.

And Evan—why, you'd have thought the man had been doing this all his life!

For a moment, the image of Evan Whittaker as he'd looked when he first stepped off the ship, along with Nora and the others, slipped into Sara's thoughts. Not quite two years ago, the slight-framed Englishman had stood on the dock, gray and emaciated from a botched shipboard amputation. Yet in spite of his weakness and obvious ill health, he had clearly appointed himself Nora's protector.

And now—now they were married, with a child of their own on the way. To think of all that had happened in so brief a time . . .

"Can you believe this?" Michael said, grinning at her. "I can scarce take it in that that's Whittaker up there!"

"It's so exciting! And the music—Michael, Nora says Evan arranges most of it himself! He spends hours every week at the church piano, working on it. Who would have ever imagined it?"

Michael grinned even wider. "Aye, for an Englishman, he's a bit of a wonder, I must admit."

"He's remarkable! But I do think we should find a way to provide shoes for those barefoot boys of his—and I must see about arranging a piano for him at home as soon as possible. Nora says he argues against leaving her now, except to go to the yards. He worries about—"

She stopped, watching as two youths stepped out from among the other singers and walked to the front. In a decidedly nervous tone of voice, the taller of the two boys began a recitation on how "The Star-Spangled Banner" came to be written by Francis Scott Key as he watched the British fleet's bombardment of Fort Mc-Henry in Baltimore Harbor. The tune itself, the youth went on to explain, raising a few eyebrows, was actually that of a popular English drinking song, which the composer borrowed for his lyrics. Immediately after he finished his reading, the entire boys' choir burst into what had to be, Sara was convinced, the most enthusiastic rendering she had ever heard of that somewhat somber piece.

Halfway through, when the group gave way to a solo by the little freckle-faced boy at the front, an awed hush fell over the ballroom. Sara held her breath, and a chill skated all the way down her spine, as the youth's clear, glorious voice seemed to lift and soar above the group.

So true, so pure, were those high, echoing tones that the entire ballroom all at once seemed filled with the sound of bells.

The song ended. There was a moment of absolute silence. Then the room exploded with vigorous applause.

Sara looked around, thrilled to see that a number of familiar faces in the crowd—faces which ordinarily reflected little if any emotion—were now creased with smiles—*enthusiastic* smiles. There were some frowns of disapproval, of course; she would have been astonished had that not been the case. But they were few, and, as best she could tell, seemed to be going entirely unnoticed.

Clearly, Evan Whittaker and his Five Points Celebration Singers were a success on Fifth Avenue. Just as clear was the evidence of what one caring heart and the power of God could accomplish in the face of almost impossible circumstances.

————

Within an hour after the performance of the boys' choir, Sara had managed to find Evan not one piano, but two.

Michael could only shake his head in wonder at this wife. It seemed that both Lydia Huntington and Margaret Smythe had pianos in their parlor "collecting dust." Evan Whittaker could have either one for the price of hauling it away.

Hauling it away would be free—and quite easy, Sara quickly explained to the astonished Whittaker. Since Margaret Smythe lived in Brooklyn, they would simply have one of the men at the shipyards load the piano onto a wagon and deliver it to Evan's house.

She was in the process of offering the mission committee's help with one of his other projects—the reading lessons he'd initiated for some of the boys in the choir—when Jess Dalton joined their little group.

"Careful, Pastor," Michael cracked as he walked up. "Sara's on the hunt. She's likely to talk you out of your office furniture if she catches you unawares. So far, she's collected only pianos and books, but there's no telling what she may set her sights on next."

"Pastor Dalton already gives more than enough," Sara said, her expression all seriousness, "with his time and efforts. He's one of the few who is quite safe from my meddling."

"Never meddling, Sara," said Jess Dalton. His voice was quiet, his smile tired and, Michael thought, a little forced. "Not you. If only we had more who cared as you do. Actually, though, I did come over to offer my help in another area." He paused, then looked at Michael. "The boy you told me about in the Bowery—Bhima—and his friends at the dime museum? If you have time to show me where to go one day next week, I'll make the visit you requested."

Michael moaned silently as Sara turned an inquisitive look on him. "What boy is that?"

When he didn't answer, but simply looked from her to Jess

Dalton, she said again, "Michael? Who on earth do you know in a dime museum?"

"Ah . . . just a lad," he muttered, shifting from one foot to another. "A lad who could use a bit of help."

Before he could say more or Sara could press, Jess Dalton innocently offered further information. "More than a bit, from what you've told me," he said, shaking his head. "What a bleak existence those people must live down there."

"What people?"

One thing about Sara, Michael realized anew, she was nothing if not tenacious.

"The people at the dime museum," he said through clenched teeth.

"You've probably heard them referred to as 'Freak Shows,' " Jess Dalton added with a touch of bitterness in his tone. "Michael's met an unusual boy from one of them. *Most* unusual, right, Michael?"

Sara's smile was sweet, her gaze blade-sharp. "Is that so? Well, you'll have to tell me all about this . . . unusual boy, Michael."

Knowing he would undoubtedly have to do just that before the day came to an end, Michael gave a small sigh and a reluctant nod.

He was relieved when Evan Whittaker brought about a change of subject. "M-Miss Sara—"

Sara turned to him, smiling.

"I—I want to thank you again for the piano. There's no expressing how grateful I am—"

Sara made a dismissing gesture with her hand. Michael understood her discomfort; the last thing Sara would want from this rather remarkable Englishman was gratitude.

"After everything you've already d-done," he went on, "I'm . . . reluctant to ask, but there *is* one thing m-more that would be of im-immeasurable help to the boys and me."

At Sara's encouraging nod, he went on to explain. "There's an old piano in the public house downstairs of the rehearsal room— it's not in b-bad shape, as a m-matter of fact—and the proprietor said we could use it for our practices if we like. I've been thinking that if we had someone who was willing to play for rehearsals, it m-might be m-much easier for the boys to learn the music."

Michael watched, puzzled by the smile that broke slowly over Sara's face. "Evan," she said, clasping both hands beneath her chin for an instant like an excited girl, "come with me, do! There's someone I'd like very much for you to meet!"

32

Light of Grace, Wings of Hope

What word of grace in such a place
Could help a brother's soul?

OSCAR WILDE (1854–1900)

Evan had first noticed the ugly bruises on the Hogan lad the week after the city mission bazaar.

It had been a warm, sun-sweet day, more like May than March, and their first rehearsal since the performance at the Farmington mansion. The boys had come out in short sleeves, some in undershirts, all free of sweaters and jackets.

As was his practice, Evan had been moving among them, one at a time, listening to each individual pitch and tone. When he reached Billy Hogan, he slowed considerably; that glorious voice coming from such a little fellow never ceased to amaze and move him.

He noticed the bruises on the boy's arms, the small cuts near the mouth, right away. At the time, he wasn't overly disturbed. Boys, after all, would be boys: climbing about, playing roughhouse with one another—most boys sported some bruises now and then.

Today, two weeks later, the cold temperatures had returned, forcing the boys to again don their winter coats—those fortunate enough to own one. Billy's arms were concealed by the shapeless jacket he wore, but Evan was sure the gash beside the lad's upper lip and the angry purple bruise next to his right ear were new.

A sense of foreboding nagged at him all the way through rehearsal. Acting on impulse after he dismissed the group, he stopped Billy at the door. "What happened, son?" he asked the boy directly. "Take a fall, d-did you?"

At first the boy simply gave him a blank look. When Evan motioned to the bruise on his cheekbone, his eyes took on an almost furtive expression.

"Aye, a fall, sir, that's what it was," he muttered quickly—a bit *too* quickly, Evan thought.

"I see." When the boy refused to meet Evan's eyes but simply stood, looking down at the floor, Evan hesitated, then asked, "And where d-did you fall?"

The lad looked up, then immediately glanced away. "At . . . home, sir. On the stairsteps, it was."

Evan studied the bowed head, the thatch of flaxen hair that seemed to grow in all different directions. It struck him that the boy was lying. But why?

"Yes . . . well, then, I hope you weren't hurt too b-badly."

"No, sir." The reply was mumbled, the thin little shoulders still hunched as he stood, staring down at the floor.

Evan felt an inexplicable twinge of protectiveness for the boy as he put his hand to the wheat-colored hair. "You b-be careful on the way home, Mr. Hogan. Take care."

He stood watching as the small figure cleared the stairs and ran out the door on a gust of cold air.

Behind him, Alice Walsh cleared her throat, saying, "He's such a little fellow for his age, isn't he?"

Evan turned, still troubled. "Yes, he certainly is. I hope he's healthy enough. No d-doubt, things have been very hard for him and his family. They only came across recently, you know."

His new accompanist nodded as she proceeded to collect the music off the top of the piano. "They all make me wish I could take them home," she said with a sigh, "and give them a good meal and a new set of clothes." With the music in her arms, she turned to Evan. "I want to thank you again, Mr. Whittaker, for asking me to help with the boys. I'm enjoying it immensely!"

Pleased by the woman's undisguised enthusiasm, Evan smiled. "I'm the one who's grateful, Mrs. Walsh. I can't tell you how m-much you've helped.

At the door, she hesitated, "Mr. Whittaker?"

Evan turned as he shrugged into his coat.

"The little Hogan boy..." she said uncertainly. "Did you notice his face?"

Evan nodded, tugging at the collar of his coat. "He said he'd fallen. On the steps at home."

Alice Walsh nodded uncertainly. "Yes, I heard." She hesitated, then opened the door. "Well . . . I must go. I'll be back next week."

As soon as she was gone, uneasiness again swept over Evan. He had recognized the doubt in Alice Walsh's eyes, and it only served to heighten his own concern.

What he was unable to identify was the *root* of that concern, the intuition that made him think the Hogan lad had lied.

————

A weak, gray weeping of afternoon light came through the only above-ground window in the room, doing little more than to prevent total darkness.

While Michael and Jess Dalton arranged chairs in a neat row, Sara stood near the door, appraising their surroundings with a critical eye and making mental notes of possible improvements. The bare wood floor was rough and splintered, and not overly clean. The room itself was damp, the walls smelling of mildew, stale beer, and tobacco smoke. But it was more than large enough for their purposes—a weekly Bible study—and, best of all, free of charge.

She couldn't imagine how Jess Dalton had convinced the surly owner of the dime museum to allow use of the room once a week, rent free. Something in Michael's tight little smile when she had questioned the arrangement made her wonder if he hadn't had a hand in the whole business.

Pastor Dalton had made just one trip to this dime museum in the heart of the Bowery, accompanied by Michael, before declaring that an occasional visit would never do, that instead he would start up a weekly Bible study. "We need to take some light into that dreary place," he announced the same day. "More to the point, we need to take *the* Light into that place."

Earlier today, when Sara commented on the speed with which he had gotten things done, the pastor had simply laughed and said, "From the looks of things, Sara, I may be needing a new pulpit in the near future. Who can tell? Perhaps this will be the start of my next congregation."

He had made the remark offhandedly, as if in jest. But Sara had felt an instant of dark foreshadowing at the thought that his words might prove prophetic. If men like Chester Pauling and Charles Street had their way, this dismal cellar room might turn out to be the only pulpit in the city left available to Jess Dalton.

The thought enraged her, and at the same time made her want to weep. If it should come to that, she thought, if things could actually reach such a shameful pass, she was not at all certain she could ever again trust in any sort of human decency.

Hearing voices at the top of the stairs behind her, she stepped farther into the room, waiting. Her stomach knotted with apprehension as she stared at the open doorway, and she was appalled to realize just how anxious she was about this meeting.

Michael had spared no details in describing the deformities of the "museum's" residents, determined that she not be caught unawares, once all his efforts to dissuade her had failed. Quick to reassure him that she wouldn't be at all put off by these poor outcasts from society, Sara found herself wondering now if she mightn't have been a touch too brash.

True, she managed to deal with the atrocities and misery of Five Points well enough these days, but it had taken months of grueling experience to do so. And unless Michael had exaggerated, there was nothing in Five Points to prepare her for the residents of the dime museum.

Now, as she heard the strange slide-and-bounce sounds on the steps, followed by murmurings and one or two shrill laughs, she could only hope she wouldn't do something awful and embarrass her long-suffering husband . . . and herself.

———

Michael thought he had never loved the woman more than he did at this moment. Watching her with Bhima and his friends, seeing her natural wit and generosity of spirit win them over, he wondered that he had ever questioned her ability to handle the situation.

From the night of the bazaar, when she'd first coaxed him into telling her about the unusual boy named *Bhima* and the other residents of the dime museum, nothing would do the indomitable

Sara but to make a visit to the Bowery.

Today, as the inhabitants of the museum shuffled into the room, Michael realized there was a great deal of skepticism and nervousness on their part. They entered slowly, with obvious reluctance: Bhima, the Tattooed Man, the tall, thin albino, the Strong Man with his arms like oak trees and neck like a giant bull. There were others as well—nonresidents of the museum, but outcasts, all the same: a man with no arms, a one-eyed sailor, his face horribly disfigured by burn scars, and, to Michael's astonishment, the dwarf, Plug—Roscoe Brewster's wee, fierce bodyguard.

Jess Dalton was splendid with each one of them, of course, with his big, genial laugh, his hearty handshake, his unmistakable kindness. But it was Sara—his Sara—who created the magic right from the first, putting them at ease with her irresistible charm, her winsome smile, her quiet compassion. And it was Sara—the remarkable Sara—who managed to create a sense of belonging for these undesirables of society, giving them what might well have been their first real sense of welcome.

Throughout the afternoon, he watched it happen, this amazing event that somehow worked to give these unwanted souls a measure of acceptance, even self-respect. They had come into the room a defeated, abandoned group of misfits, their eyes downcast, their bodies hunched as if to hide their differences from those within.

But before they left, most were making eye contact—at least with Sara—and some even shook hands with Michael and the pastor.

In Bhima, Michael saw the most moving effects of Sara's gentle gifts of grace and caring. She drew him out of his shyness, out of himself, fielding questions, comparing their preferences in newspaper columnists—even teasing him a bit. Little by little, the boy's reserve and uncertainty seemed to fall away in her presence.

His smile was almost beatific when Sara took his hands and leaned forward to say goodbye. With Fred, the albino, waiting nearby with Bhima's cart to help him upstairs, the boy looked from Sara to Michael. "Captain, I do thank you. We asked you for light—and you brought us the sun."

His heart aching with love for her, Michael studied his wife.

"Aye," he said softly, smiling at Sara. "It would seem so."

———————

Heart pounding, Billy Hogan raced down Mulberry Street toward home.

He shouldn't have stopped to shoot marbles with Tom Breen. Rehearsal had run over as it was, and then he'd gone and dawdled another hour away. He was late—again. It would soon be dark, and if he'd been at the drink, Uncle Sorley would be in a rage.

Billy dreaded nothing else as he dreaded his uncle's drunken fits of temper. Uncle Sorley was big, he was, and mean clear through when he'd had too much—so mean he thought nothing of throwing Billy against the wall. Yet, to try and dodge him or defy him might cause him to take out his spite on one of the wee wanes. So Billy suffered his thrashings without challenge.

Uncle Sorley thought the singing a waste of time, the reading lessons *raimeis*—nonsense! "Like throwing shillings down a well!" he would snort if Billy forgot and talked to his mum in front of him.

What Billy counted on was that, so long as he did his chores and sold his papers, Uncle Sorley would let the singing and the reading go, would forget them entirely.

For in this foul swamp called the Five Points, in the airless, gray despair of his existence, the music and the books were like the first fresh winds of morning to Billy. At last, his life held more than the younger tykes crying, his uncle swearing, his mother sobbing. More than peddling his newspapers and taking out slops and struggling from one day to the next to stay alive.

Now there was the profound and utter beauty of words riding his mind, dancing on his tongue like pearls in a silver stream. And there was the inexpressible joy of the music. It was like flying, flying free above the ugliness of tenement houses and garbage-strewn streets, out of reach of Uncle Sorley's rages and his mother's unhappiness.

Some nights, after a particularly painful buffeting, Billy would lie next to Patrick, awake, on his straw-filled cot, listening to the drunken snoring of his uncle across the room and feeling almost overcome by the hopelessness of his life. But then a word would come to his mind, a musical word like *Jerusalem* . . . or *bluebell.* He would silently repeat it, over and over, like a promise. And it would comfort him.

Sometimes a song would come, one of the songs Mr. Whittaker was teaching them, and he would sing it to himself, inside his head, like a lullaby, until the throbbing and stinging of his body ebbed enough that he drifted off to sleep.

Reaching the sagging tenement where they lived, Billy ran inside, taking the steps two at a time. On the upstairs landing, the door to their rooms flew open in his face.

Billy stopped short, the fire in his belly blazing high. Uncle Sorley, his face flushed and mottled, his shirt stained with the whiskey, towered above him. Swaying slightly, he jabbed a pudgy finger in Billy's face. "Didn't I warn ye about bein' late for your supper again, boy? *Didn't I?*"

Attempting to sidestep him, Billy gulped out, "I'm sorry!" But Uncle Sorley yanked him inside by the neck, shoving him into the middle of the room.

Billy twisted, struggling to shield his head. Instead, he only managed to put himself square in the path of Uncle Sorley's fist as it came crashing down on his shoulder with a blinding pain.

———

After an early dinner, Sara went upstairs, admitting that their unusual day had exhausted her.

Michael, too, found the idea of a quiet evening alone together appealing. But first, he made his usual quick inspection of the downstairs rooms to be sure the lamps were extinguished, doors locked, and windows securely fastened. He'd been too many years on the force, he thought with a sigh, to be anything less than cautious to the extreme.

Entering the library, he stopped just over the threshold. The oil lamp on the desk flickered brightly. Sara's grandmother, in her dressing gown, turned toward him.

"Grandy? Is something wrong?"

She smiled faintly. One hand gripped her cane, the other held a thin volume. "Actually, I'm feeling a bit restless tonight. I came looking for a book—" She indicated the one in her hand. "I decided on Mr. Poe."

Michael raised an eyebrow. "Not what I'd call relaxing reading for a lady."

She grinned at him. "Because he's so gloomy?"

"Demented," offered Michael.

"Unhappy, perhaps," she said with a sigh. "Poor man. He's had a rather tragic life, I think. Small wonder that he'd be . . . morose."

"They say he's more than a little fond of the drink. And his opium."

"Oh, bother '*they*!' " she retorted, waving the book in her hand. "He has a ghastly reputation, of course, and perhaps he deserves it all. But I happen to know a good deal about one or two of his more vicious critics, and I can tell you they're far worse reprobates than Mr. Poe. In any case, I get dreadfully bored with some of our more 'respectable' authors; they tend to lecture or preach, and I've never felt that literature is the place for either. Mr. Poe is . . . refreshingly different."

Her eyes took on a glint of amusement. "Sara disapproves, you know. She finds his work morbid and disturbing."

"The little I've seen of it, I'd have to agree."

"Yes . . . well, Sara, bless her, wants everyone to be happy."

Michael grinned. "She does indeed. She was wonderful today," he added, sobering. "You should have seen her with those people—Bhima and the others. They adored her."

Grandy nodded, her eyes warm. "Sara is very special."

Michael was aware of Grandy Clare's good-natured scrutiny as they stood, saying nothing, for a moment. Sara's grandmother often gave him the unsettling sensation that she could read his thoughts—and everybody else's. Yet, she was so wholly generous about the foibles of others that no one ever seemed particularly bothered by her perception.

"I'm so glad you changed your mind, about taking Sara along to meet the people at the dime museum," she said, tucking the book under her arm. "I was afraid you wouldn't."

Rubbing a hand across the back of his neck, Michael gave a frown. "Well, I didn't much like it, you can be sure. It's an evil place entirely down there. There's something so . . . corrupt about it that it seems to hang in the air. You can almost feel it still clinging to your back when you leave." A cold shudder swept through him and he added, "It's not the sort of place a man wants to take his wife. But you know how she is, our Sara."

Grandy nodded. "It's a fine thing to be protective of your wife,

Michael. A woman like Sara *ought* to be cherished and safe-guarded. But I'm glad you also have sense enough to realize you can't protect her to the extent of interfering with God's will for her life. That can be a very grave mistake, and one we often make in regard to our loved ones."

Michael studied her, still frowning.

"My late husband—Sara's grandfather," she said with a sigh, "did everything but lock me up in a box during the early years of our marriage. At first it was rather flattering; I suppose I even reveled in it. It made me feel . . . treasured—and special. But after a time, I began to feel as if I were suffocating from lack of air. There were things I sensed God calling me to do, things I began to suspect might be a part of His plan for my life. But Samuel was so protective that, somehow, he just kept . . . getting in God's way."

She shook her head as if saddened by the memory. "We can do that, can't we? In our desire to shield those we love from the ugliness or the pain or the danger of the world, we actually end up thwarting God's better purpose for them, perhaps even keeping them from becoming all He intended them to be."

She looked up, met Michael's eyes with an unwavering gaze. "I'm so relieved that you aren't like that, Michael. Letting your son have his freedom as you did must have been very, very difficult for you. But it was probably the best thing for you and the boy, at least at this time in your lives."

Michael hoped the pain he felt at her reminder of Tierney was well hidden. For the truth was, he seldom thought of his angry, rebellious son without wanting to weep. As for giving him his freedom, he had no illusions about that: it had been more an act of desperation than anything else. In truth, there had seemed no other choice. He was tempted to voice the fear that was never far from his mind, the nagging dread that, by giving Tierney his freedom, he might have only hastened the boy's undoing.

"You're wonderfully good for Sara, Michael." Grandy's quiet voice tugged his thoughts away from Tierney. "I'm so thankful she married a man who's wise enough to give her all the room—the 'air'—she needs, in order to grow into the person God intends her to be."

Looking away, Michael swallowed down his impulse to deny her affirming words. Surely she had seen his dogged determination to insulate Sara, to provide, as much as humanly possible, a fortress of his love and protection around her as a way of keeping her safe from all the ugliness and fearful things the world might inflict.

"You do understand what I'm saying, Michael?"

He met her gaze and found her regarding him with an odd little smile. *Of course, she had seen! This was her inimitable way of telling him she had seen, and warning him, in love, of the possible consequences.*

For a moment Michael stared back. "Why, I expect I do, Lady Clare," he finally said, meeting the faint twinkle in her eyes with a rueful smile of his own. "I believe I understand exactly what you're saying."

33

An Absence of Conscience

The hands that fail to halt the knife
Are stained with the same blood
As those that hold the knife.

ANONYMOUS

Alice Walsh hadn't realized she was so preoccupied with her own thoughts until Patrick observed to the children, "I do believe your mama isn't feeling well this evening." His eyebrows lifted as he glanced across the dinner table at her. "Another headache, dear?"

While his words were solicitous, his tone was somewhat sharp. Hurt, Alice was tempted to point out that she seldom had headaches at all, and certainly not often enough for him to make such a remark. Just as quickly, she decided that *she* was the one being unfair. Obviously, her husband was just showing his concern.

"No, I'm quite all right, thank you, Patrick." Picking up a bowl of fruit, she passed it to Henry. "I'm sorry if I seem distracted. Something's been troubling me since choir rehearsal this afternoon."

She waited, but Patrick neither inquired about the reason for her distress nor showed any real interest. Setting his cup very carefully onto the saucer, he said, "Alice, it seems to me that this business with that . . . choir is becoming too much for you."

When Alice leaned forward and would have protested, he si-

296

lenced her with an upraised hand, going on. "No, now hear me out. It's all very well to do your good deeds and give to charity. You're very generous with yourself, and I commend you for it. But you know you're not overly strong, dear. Frankly, Alice, you've been more than a little . . . strange this evening. You're worrying me and the children."

Alice glanced at Isabel, who was eyeing her with a disapproving frown, then at Henry, who seemed wholly engrossed in dissecting his apple. Neither looked in the least worried about their mama.

Anxious that he not insist on her giving up the choir, Alice forced a smile. "I'm sorry if I've been negligent, Patrick," she said, choosing her words with care, "but playing the piano for Mr. Whittaker and the boys takes almost no time at all, and very little effort. Actually, I believe the experience has been quite good for me. It's just that there's a little boy I've been somewhat concerned about."

The memory of the little Hogan boy, the thin, freckled face . . . the bruises . . . the cuts . . . slipped into Alice's thoughts, stirring a pool of concern. "I'm afraid something might be wrong," she said softly, more to herself than to her husband.

She looked up when Patrick pushed away from the table. "That's too bad, dear," he said vaguely, getting to his feet and pushing his chair in to the table. Coming around behind Alice, he gave her shoulders a brief squeeze. "I'm sorry to rush off like this, but I've a meeting at eight. Now, I want you to be sure and turn in early tonight. You're obviously exhausted. Isabel—Henry—see that Mama minds."

Alice watched him stride smoothly from the dining room, not looking back. Crumpling her napkin into a ball, she was pierced by another stab of pain.

At first, Patrick's utter lack of interest in what he referred to as her "good deeds" hadn't bothered her. It wasn't that he was uncaring, after all. Naturally, she couldn't expect him to add her concerns to his own. The man hardly ever had a free moment the way it was, what with his seemingly endless business involvements.

Still, some peculiar petulance made her wonder if he couldn't have shown at least a polite curiosity about the choir in Five Points—or about her personal concern for little Billy Hogan.

The sudden awareness of anger surprised her. She never, *never* felt anger toward Patrick, and for good reason: he never gave her *reason* to be angry. Oh, he could be cross at times, but not often, and he was never unkind.

She understood, however, that she could test his patience. They were vastly different, after all. Her mind worked slowly and deliberately, whereas Patrick's wits were sharp and mercurial. Often, things had to be explained to her, while Patrick seemed to grasp the most complicated of ideas with no prompting whatsoever. She tended to be precise and methodical; Patrick was given to whims and an adventuresome spirit.

Small wonder if he occasionally grew impatient with her. She was being shamefully unfair, Alice thought guiltily, and she must stop. Pushing herself away from the table, she stood and smiled at the children. "Your papa's right; I've been neglectful this evening. Let's all go into the parlor and we'll have a game of whist."

As it happened, Isabel had lessons to do, and Henry preferred to spend time with his telescope. So Alice spent the rest of the evening alone, just as she usually did.

———

In Rossiter's small office at the midtown hotel, Patrick Walsh stood looking out the window.

There was nothing to see but a night with no moon and a few dim spots of light from other windows. Waiting for Hubert Rossiter, the hotel's bookkeeper, who also served as middleman in a number of Walsh's other business ventures, he found his thoughts going to his wife and her odd behavior of late.

Seldom did he feel the inclination to think about Alice one way or another. His wife usually required no more of his attention than a routine peck on the cheek, a brief conference about some rare infraction or problem with one of the children, and, rarer still, an uninspired night in her bedroom. Alice was a dutiful, if dull, wife. Her efforts to keep him comfortable and happy were, for the most part, admirably successful. He had little complaint with her, even less interest in her.

Lately, however, she was beginning to get on his nerves. She seemed different, somehow, had for days now. He couldn't quite put his finger on what it was—he thought it might be a touch of a new confidence he'd detected in her. And, more peculiar still, a bit less attention to *him*.

The changes were scarcely noticeable. But ever since she'd started that silly piano playing for the Englishman, he'd sensed a certain distraction, a cheerfulness, about her that had no apparent connection to him or the children.

Whatever it was, he was losing patience. As a matter of fact, he was growing more than a little tired of hearing about her new "interests"—that "fine Christian gentleman, Mr. Whittaker," for example, and his "amazing accomplishments with his boys."

Walsh almost snorted aloud. "Mr. Whittaker" was a one-armed stick of a man who had apparently wangled himself into the good graces of one of the wealthiest men in the country—the shipbuilder, Lewis Farmington. Obviously, the man was simply a clever parasite who happened to fancy himself some sort of missionary.

As for "his boys," they were merely a bunch of raggedy immigrant and Negro scalawags who apparently had nothing better to do than fritter away their time singing songs.

Bracing a hand on the wall beside the window, he began to tap his fingers in agitation. He supposed he had both the Englishman, Whittaker, and the high-and-mighty Sara Farmington Burke to thank for Alice's involvement in this Five Points business.

Sara Farmington Burke. Walsh curled his lip and cursed aloud. He'd had reason enough to despise the woman before: in spite of her being the only daughter of Lewis Farmington, she'd gone and married that bloodhound police captain, Burke—who for some reason seemed to have made Patrick Walsh his own personal quarry. Bad enough that she was the wife of his nemesis, but now she'd involved *his* wife in that do-gooder nonsense for which the Farmingtons were legendary.

Alice, of course, had no way of knowing that one of his two most lucrative businesses was built on the squalor of the Five Points district. Still, he didn't much like her being down there every week. It didn't seem right somehow. *His* wife should have no part in that filthy slum.

He liked even less her involvement with Sara Farmington— Sara Farmington *Burke,* he corrected himself sourly. Every time Alice mentioned the woman's name, he ground his teeth. He was going to have to put a stop to all this foolishness before it went any further.

But at the moment, he had bigger fish to fry. Turning away from the window, he sat down at Rossiter's desk and began to thumb idly through the papers in front of him. When the door opened, he looked up, nodding to the bespectacled Rossiter, then to Tierney Burke, who stood just inside the door behind the book-keeper.

Walsh leaned back in the chair, his fingers playing over the papers on the desk. "Come in, Tierney," he said, smiling.

"You sent for me, Mr. Walsh?"

Rossiter stood at a respectable distance on the other side of the desk, but Tierney Burke drew closer.

Walsh studied the boy in silence. The good-looking face bore no sign of the severe beating he'd endured several months ago, except for the thin, angry scar that ran along the side of his left eye. The ice-blue eyes, slightly hooded and always defiant, stared back at Walsh with something akin to disdain.

Lately, the boy tended to put Walsh on edge. There was no sign of the deference due a generous employer, no real indication he even respected the man who paid his wages. In fact, the more he drew the young rascal into the business, the more keenly he felt Tierney's arrogance.

Yet this one was worth half a dozen others in boldness and daring alone. The boy had proved himself absolutely reliable time and again.

Walsh reminded himself that Tierney Burke had a couple of weak spots. For one thing, he was known to drink. Not regularly, it seemed, but often enough that the men had noticed it on him now and then. Walsh himself had detected a slight slur to the young rogue's words on more than one occasion, and at times, like tonight, those intense blue eyes seemed to hold an even brighter glint of defiance than usual.

Then, too, Walsh despised that unresolved zeal and Irish patriotism of his. Although the boy seldom spoke of Ireland, almost never referred to his political leanings, he'd opened up just enough early in their acquaintance that Walsh knew him to be a rebel at heart. A fanatic on the subject of Ireland.

Since Walsh had spent most of his adult life burying his own Irish roots—burying them so deeply that even *he* tended to forget them—he had little patience for what he thought of as Ireland's national madness. As for the drinking—he viewed it as a definite character flaw, one that continued to consume and destroy the Irish immigrants by the score.

Still, whether the boy turned out to be an authentic fanatic or a rolling drunk really wasn't his concern. As a matter of fact, either tendency, or both, might just prove to be of benefit if the boy got too independent for his own good.

Walsh's smile brightened still more as he regarded young Burke. "Tierney, I've been giving some thought to your request about taking on something else, in addition to running deliveries and messages—something more ... lucrative. I thought you might want to sit in on my conversation with Hubert here this evening."

Amused, Walsh saw Rossiter flush with undisguised annoyance. It was common knowledge among the men and messenger boys that the nervous little bookkeeper disliked Tierney Burke immensely.

Patrick Walsh thought it more likely that Rossiter feared the boy. And it wasn't all that difficult to understand why.

———

The conversation between Walsh and Rossiter had gone on for over an hour, and Tierney was becoming more and more impatient. Impatient, and a bit uneasy.

He had caught the drift of things after the first few minutes. Walsh had himself a kind of slave trade in the works, right here in the city. It couldn't be much slicker. Negro kids, both boys and girls, were rounded up from the streets and alleys and herded off to the Bowery, where they were delivered to their "new owners" for a prearranged purchase price. Of course, in many cases, there was no previous owner; a number of the pickaninnies were children of free Negroes. On the other hand, as many others probably had parents on the run, hiding from the slave catchers, hoping they'd never be caught in a city as large as New York.

What Walsh was doing was illegal, at least in the North. It was also, his father would say, immoral.

Tierney immediately dismissed the thought of his father's disapproval. Still, he didn't much like what he was hearing. There was no telling what kind of scoundrels bought up these black

301

kids, no imagining what their plans were once they got hold of them.

But the fact remained that the city was becoming overrun with Negroes—Negroes who took jobs from the Irish. They'd work for almost nothing, and that was the truth. In a city that was papered with signs reading NO IRISH NEED APPLY, the blacks *did* apply—and were often hired.

After a while, feeling somewhat dull from the whiskey he'd had earlier, Tierney banked his sympathy for the black kids and began to ask questions about his part in the operation. Including how much it was going to be worth to him.

34

Feed My Sheep

And this is the Christian to oversee
A world of evil! a saint to preach!
A holy well-doer come to teach!
A prophet to tell us war should cease.

JOHN BOYLE O'REILLY (1844–1890)

No doubt, thought Kerry Dalton, if any of the straitlaced, ponderous pillars of the Fifth Avenue congregation were to see their pastor at this moment, there would be still another fuss about "Mister Dalton's questionable behavior." Casey-Fitz and Arthur had him trapped in the middle of the parlor floor, the three of them roughhousing like a litter of frisky pups.

From the rocking chair by the hearth, Kerry smiled and put down her mending to watch. This was Jess's favorite part of the day, a time he looked forward to and, inasmuch as possible, arranged his hectic schedule to ensure.

The sight of him, in his shirtsleeves on his knees, tumbling about the floor like a boy himself, brought a sudden, unaccountable touch of sadness to her heart. Lately, Jess seemed to have so few times like this: lighthearted times in which he could simply shrug off the daily problems he faced and, at least for a while, escape the encroaching storm that now seemed to threaten his ministry.

Kerry's smile waned as she watched him. Every day there seemed to be a new sprinkling of silver in his hair, a few new lines about his eyes. The startling blue gaze that could still melt her heart now looked out on the world with what appeared to be a permanent sorrow, as if somewhere deep within his soul there smoldered an unspeakable pain.

With her, he was never less than gentle, always considerate, tenderly teasing and affectionate and thoughtful. But Kerry knew that a part of him often drifted off, away from the haven she had tried to create with her love. Even here, in this deep-cushioned, warm, friendly room that had become so much a refuge for them all, she would often sense his thoughts slipping away into troubled waters.

She knew he wasn't sleeping, although he was careful not to disturb her when he left their bed during the night. All too often she would awaken and hear him moving about downstairs. Obviously, he was trying to keep his restlessness from her, so she worried in silence.

It seemed to her that Jess's heart was breaking, slowly, quietly, one piece at a time. Her gentle giant was a man whose wounds were many, wounds inflicted by the cruelty, the wickedness, the apathy of a world at war with itself. Like the grieving prophet, Jeremiah, her Jess was a God-driven man, tormented by the brutality and oppression all around him, a man unable to compromise the Truth he had been given, a man often accused of fanaticism or foolish idealism . . . a man whose very spirit bled for the agony of the world.

And yet he was also a man who had managed to turn his anguish into sacrifice, his personal pain to a kind of triumph. For through it all, he had clung to the faithfulness of a God who had promised to one day redeem and repay and reward.

Abruptly, Kerry looked up, yanked out of her dark reverie by a sense of being watched. Flanked by two bright-eyed boys, Jess stood in front of her. His grin and the glint in his eye spelled nothing but mischief.

"It seems to me that Little Mother looks entirely too comfortable. What do you think, boys? Shouldn't she join in the fun?"

"Ladies," she said firmly, anchoring herself to the chair with both hands, "do not indulge in horseplay."

Jess looked at each boy, then cocked an eyebrow. "Is that a fact, now?" he challenged in a brogue that would have done Kerry's father, God rest his soul, more than proud.

"What do you say to that, lads? Shall we unseat the grand lady from her throne?"

Before she could squeal out a protest, Kerry found herself pried loose from the chair and lifted into her husband's arms. For a moment, he pretended to consider tossing her to first one boy, then the other. Finally, at her indignant demands—highly feigned—he laughed and set her to her feet. With obvious reluctance, he declared an end to the playtime.

———

Later, when the boys were in bed and the house was finally quiet, the two of them sought the privacy of their bedroom. As was his practice, Jess pulled up a chair behind her at the vanity and began to brush her hair.

Kerry smiled at his reflection in the mirror as he worked intently to bring order to her stubborn red curls. "Watching you with the boys downstairs," she said, "I decided your favorite time of day is when you're down on all fours with the two of them. I believe there's still a great deal of the boy in you, Mr. Dalton."

He slowed the brush, meeting her gaze in the mirror. "You're right about that, I confess." He paused, then added, "But not about my favorite time of day, Mrs. Dalton."

"Indeed?"

He nodded, meticulously unwinding one copper curl from around the bristles of the brush. "Indeed."

Carefully, he replaced the brush on the dressing table and put his hands to her shoulders, slowly turning her about to face him. "As it happens," he said, pulling her into his arms, "my favorite time of day is just beginning."

———

Long after Kerry had fallen asleep, Jess tucked the blankets snugly under her chin, then eased himself from the bed. Slipping into his dressing gown, he left the bedroom and went downstairs.

It was late enough that he was the only one up and about, but he closed the library door behind him anyway. He needed the quiet, and he craved the solitude.

He sat at his desk, his head in his hands as he pored over the Scriptures. Outside, a steady, beating rain had begun, and, born on the rising wind, lashed the roof and the sides of the house. The lamp on the desk flickered in the draft.

The minutes turned to hours. Still, Jess read and prayed. At times he stopped and sat, scarcely breathing, a feeling of anticipation rising in him, then ebbing.

For more than a week now, he had caught a sense of God endeavoring to break through the turmoil of his days. In the midst of the clamor of the hourly responsibilities and problems crowding in on him would come a gentle stirring in his spirit. Sometimes, awash in the turbulence of his thoughts and rioting emotions, he would be engulfed by an unexpected hush, a sudden stillness. Just as quickly, a heaviness would center in his chest, weighing in on him like a knot of dread at some impending disaster.

He was determined to spend the rest of this night alone, in the silence, waiting. Waiting for whatever it was that God wanted to make known to him. And praying that he would be given the strength for whatever might be required.

At last, though, the recent succession of sleepless nights and wearying days began to take their toll. Exhausted, he slumped over the desk and, resting his head on his arms, fell asleep.

———

Arthur wasn't sure what had awakened him. Maybe the rain beating down on the roof that jutted out past his bedroom window.

He raised up in bed and listened. Other than the rain, there wasn't a sound to be heard, but somehow he knew that Mr. Jess was having another wakeful night.

Night after night lately, he had heard him. The stairs would creak under his weight, and after a while Arthur would hear him pacing the downstairs hall or moving quietly from room to room.

There was trouble. Bad trouble, even though nobody was saying much about it. It was that business at the big church again. Mr. Jess was in trouble, sure enough, with the people that ran things over there. And all because of *him*—Arthur Jackson, a runaway slave boy who didn't belong here in the first place.

A mixture of sick fear and anger set his stomach to churning as he thought about what was happening to Mr. Jess. And what it would mean to Miss Kerry and Casey-Fitz. Oh, Casey-Fitz kept on insisting that most of the trouble had to do with his daddy's being an—an *abolitionist*. But Arthur knew the boy was just try-ing to make him feel better.

He also knew what he had to do. It would mean breaking his promise to Casey-Fitz, and now that he was a Christian, he re-alized that was a wrong thing to do. But right now, keeping Mr. Jess and his family out of trouble seemed a lot more important than a promise.

Besides—he was the only one who *might* be able to help. He'd brought this trouble on Mr. Jess, after all, so he reckoned it was up to him to put an end to it.

Ignoring the chill of the room, he slipped out of bed and dropped down to his knees. Two weeks ago, he'd decided for him-self that what Mr. Jess had been teaching him about the man named Jesus had to be the Truth. There was no other way that man could have done the things He did—raising dead people up out of the grave and making those leper people clean—and, the most amazing thing of all, forgiving those hateful folks that nailed Him up on the cross.

So, with Mr. Jess helping him, and Casey-Fitz and Miss Kerry laughing and rejoicing, he'd become a *Christian*—baptized and everything!

Mr. Jess said that one of the most important things a Christian should do was to pray. That, even though there was no explaining how the Lord could hear everybody praying at the same time and still work out answers for all of them, the fact was that He did it.

So ever since then, Arthur had been practicing his praying each night, with the help of Mr. Jess, and sometimes Casey-Fitz. He thought he was good enough at it by now to try some praying on his own, so, squeezing his eyes shut and taking a big breath, he asked the Lord to make him brave enough to do what he knew he had to do.

And to please let Casey-Fitz forgive him for breaking his prom-ise.

————

The desk beneath his arms had become a pulpit . . . the pulpit at the Fifth Avenue Church. Solid and sturdy oak, softened and aged by the oil of human hands throughout the years—preachers' hands. . . .

No longer did Jess sit in the library, at his desk. Now, in this strange dream that he somehow knew to be a dream, he stood at his pulpit in the sanctuary, speaking to the congregation. . . .

The pews were crowded with people. His people. The flock placed under his shepherding care. His to teach, to guide, to comfort. To shepherd.

Streams of morning sunlight flooded the sanctuary, bathing the heavy oak doors, the pews, every corner—even the ceiling— with light. Golden light, as warm as a touch.

With his Bible at his fingertips, Jess opened his mouth to preach the Word, the Good News that they were a beloved people, beloved of the Father God, the sheep of His pasture.

He felt, rather than saw, the light shift. The radiant, golden hues began to spiral, as if tossed by a sudden wind, to the rear of the sanctuary, where they writhed and gathered until the light became a dense, pewter smoke.

As Jess watched, the smoke began to drift and coil, wafting forward, coming to settle over the people in the pews like an ominous, undulating cloud.

In the second row, a hawk-faced Chester Pauling shifted restlessly, tugging at his brocade waistcoat as the smoke engulfed him. Jess peered through the gray haze and saw, to his amazement, the brocade fabric take on the look of flesh—living flesh, adorned with color and design. His eyes snapped up to Pauling's face . . . but it wasn't Pauling at all—it was the Tattooed Man from the dime museum!

The smoke drifted and hung in a wreath around Charles Street, who sat glaring up at Jess. As Jess watched, the man's arms and chest began to swell like a balloon, bursting the seams of his coat and snapping his collar stays. The haze moved on, and Jess found himself looking into the eyes of the Strong Man.

Down in front and to the left sat a small boy, his legs tucked under him on the pew. Once more the smoke descended, completely obscuring the lad's small form. When it lifted again, in the child's place sat Bhima, the Turtle Boy, gazing up at Jess with his gentle, sorrowful eyes.

On and on it went, a succession of chilling, unaccountable changes, until the entire assembly had been transformed to a sea of faces from the Bowery . . . and Five Points . . . and Shantytown.

Gripping the pulpit with both hands, Jess saw the smoke lift and slowly retreat to the back of the sanctuary. Slowly, it began to thin, brightening and rising until again the sunshine bathed the sanctuary like a golden benediction.

He came awake to a gentle whisper, a voice so deep within himself that it seemed to abide in his very spirit, repeating over and over: *"These are your people . . . and Mine . . . beloved of the Father. These are the sheep of My pasture. Feed My sheep . . . feed My sheep. . . ."*

With the whisper still sounding deep within him, Jess stirred. Early morning sunlight streamed through the library window. Blinking, he lifted his head and turned around to face the light.

PART THREE

DREAMS FULFILLED

—

New Tomorrows

You know with all your heart and soul
that not one of all the good promises
the Lord your God gave you has failed.
Every promise has been fulfilled; not
one has failed.

JOSHUA 23:14

35

The Princess and the Blackbird

And to one is given a beauty rare,
Like a star of heaven's isle . . .
And to the other is given the star of Erin
And heaven in her smile.

MORGAN FITZGERALD (1849)

Dublin
Early April

Morgan sat, staring with satisfaction at the papers in front of him one last time. After another moment, he tucked them safely back inside a large envelope and locked it in his desk.

These were only copies, of course; Guinness had already filed the originals. Still, he wouldn't want to chance them accidentally reaching Annie's eyes. Despite the child's brave efforts to pretend otherwise, he sensed that her mother's rejection had caused her grievous pain. To see the woman's signature on a document, whereby she irrevocably abdicated all rights to her daughter . . . well, it could do nothing but increase the girl's feelings of abandonment.

As he sat drumming his fingers on the desk, a mixed tide of emotions washed over him. So, then . . . he was to be a father at last. Legal father to Annie, and, eventually, to Finola's babe.

The astonishing turn his life had taken in less than two years was almost more than could be comprehended. The inheritance of his grandfather's estate, the move to Dublin, the shooting that had left his legs paralyzed. . . .

Most significant among all the changes, of course, was the advent of those whom he had come to think upon, with great affection, as his "family." First, Sandemon, the West Indies Wonder . . . then Annie Delaney, his wee, fey child from Belfast . . . Finola, beloved of his heart . . . even Sister Louisa, the radical nun who had somehow brought order to their lives, as well as to the school.

Morgan shook his head, smiling faintly. He could not help but think that many of the events of his life made for classic evidence that God could change grief to glory, could, indeed, just as the Scriptures promised, turn evil to good.

Most astounding of all, he would be a father. And two weeks hence—a husband. Such a succession of events was enough to weaken the knees of even the stoutest man. Ah, but *his* knees, of course, were unaffected, seeing as how they were already useless.

Turning his thoughts back to Annie, he pondered how to tell her the news. It should be a special occasion, he decided, a meaningful time for the child—an "event."

Taking a small green velvet box from his desk, he opened the lid and sat staring at its contents for a moment before sliding it inside his vest pocket.

He removed his eyeglasses, then rang for Artegal. When the white-haired footman appeared—Artegal never *entered* a room, but rather seemed to *materialize*, like the pale specter he looked to be—Morgan dispatched him upstairs. "Tell Miss Annie to dress for dinner, that we will have a special family meal together. And tell her," he added, "that she should be prepared to help Finola as well, if she's able to come down. Oh—and send Sandemon to me."

The footman inclined his head, his disapproval all too evident. Morgan wondered again why he did not simply discharge the man, whom he actively disliked and vaguely mistrusted.

True, Artegal was efficient to a fault; efficient and unobtrusive. Yet he bore an air of superiority, of unspoken condemnation, toward every member of the household, except perhaps toward Morgan himself—and when it came down to it, Morgan wasn't at all sure that *he* was exempt.

He shrugged, and, as was his habit, relegated his dissatisfaction with Artegal to the back of his mind. There were more important things to think of this day.

———

Perched on a stool in the sewing room, with Fergus napping beside her, Annie pricked her finger with the needle for the third time. With a fierce scowl, she flung down both fabric and needle, suppressing a great howl and a curse. The wolfhound lifted his head and gave her a questioning look.

For the most part, she had given up her former habit of cursing. But at times like these, it was tempting to take it up again. She hated the sewing with a vengeance, she did! But Sister said she must learn, that needlework was a necessary part of her education.

TROUBLESOME NUN, Annie thought, grinning to herself. These days she seldom thought of Sister with anything less than affection—except when she bullied her about things like the sewing and proper *de-portment* and ladylike behavior.

Still, Sister knew very well that Annie preferred almost anything else to the sewing. Her "Favorite Things to Do," of course, included working in the stables with the horses, feeding the other animals on the estate, and practicing her sketching—in which Sister Louisa herself was instructing her.

But "young ladies," Sister said, needed to acquire a "vast variety of domestic skills." Bah! So far as Annie could tell, these domestic things were of no great account at all except to the maids.

Of course, there *was* the possibility of sewing for Finola's baby. Sister had hinted that if Annie showed progress in her skill with the needle, she might be allowed to sew some garments for the wee wane.

Annie glanced down at the hateful material at her feet. Finally, grudgingly, she retrieved it and started it again. Perhaps she *should* make the effort so she could be of help to Finola.

The thought of the baby spurred her on. These days the entire household was in a continual whirl of haste and confusion: a wedding to plan, a baby to prepare for—so much work, and in such a brief time!

Even Sandemon, ordinarily so unhurried and serene, seemed to move with a new spring in his step and speak with a bit more urgency. As for Artegal the Ghost—Annie screwed up her mouth with distaste—the sour old footman's nose appeared even longer than usual, his eyebrows pulled up in a constant expression of disapproval. Artegal, of course, disapproved of everyone and everything; no doubt he was only concerned about the fuss and bother a baby would bring.

For her part, Annie could scarcely wait. The baby would be a fine thing! And she would be a *good* big sister, she would, the very best! She would help to feed the babe and rock it to sleep and play with it—if she were allowed, that is.

Abruptly, she stopped sewing. She *wanted* to be the baby's sister, wanted it fiercely! And as the *Seanchai*'s adopted daughter, she *would* be, once he and Finola were wed.

But only if she were adopted . . .

Nobody spoke of the adoption of late. All during Finola's recovery, the *Seanchai* had barely said a word about the matter, and Annie feared that he might have forgotten about it altogether, what with worrying over Finola. It took everything Annie had not to ask at least once a day. But she didn't, for fear of being a nuisance.

Each morning she would awaken, her mind clamoring with the same excitement of the night before, stirred and revitalized by the prospect of another day about to begin. And in spite of her firm intentions not to think about it, almost immediately she would wonder if today might be the day . . . the day she would be adopted.

But it never came, that news for which she had prayed so long and so fervently. She was sure that by now the Lord must be growing impatient with her incessant pleas. Hadn't she pestered Him for months with her prayers?

Yet no answer came. Nothing changed.

What if it never did? What if, for any number of reasons, it did not work out? Then, she wouldn't be *anything* to the *Seanchai* or the rest of his family—not his daughter, nor the baby's sister. She would simply remain what she was now.

And what was that, then? A nobody. A nobody who did not really belong . . . to anyone.

The threat of disappointment hovered at the edge of her mind, just waiting for a chance to edge its way into her thoughts and spoil her happiness.

She leaned over to put a hand to Fergus's great head, seeking comfort from his warmth. "We must be very, very good, you and I, Fergus," she said, her voice low. "And very *helpful*, as well. To everyone. Not just most of the time, but *all* the time. Perhaps then, even if we're not adopted, we'll still be welcome."

She swallowed hard against the knot in her throat. "I couldn't bear the hurt if we had to leave, Fergus, and that's the truth. There wouldn't be enough tears in the whole world to wash away such a hurt!"

Her heart pounding, Annie took a big breath. "But you're not to worry, mind! The *Seanchai* would want us to stay with him, even if for some reason we're not adopted. He would. Sure, he would."

She looked up to find old Artegal the Ghost hovering in the open doorway. His nose was pulled down almost to the top of his thin upper lip as he glared at them. Annie was struck with a terrible fierce urge to stick out her tongue at him. But he would tell, and then she'd get a scolding from Sister for certain.

"The master instructs that you . . . dress . . . for dinner," he announced stiffly. "And that you assist Miss Finola, if she, ah . . . is able to come downstairs."

Strengthened by her new resolve to be good at all times, Annie actually managed to smile. A foolish, ladylike smile, she expected. Not that she cared. "Why, thank you very much, Artegal," she said sweetly, pleased when he shot her a suspicious look.

After whisking herself into the only dress she really favored— a vivid, green-striped tarlatan—Annie hurried to Finola's room, only to find that Lucy had already helped Finola complete her toilette.

Somewhat impatient with the round-faced Lucy—who was, Annie had privately declared to Sandemon, a bit shifty-eyed— she insisted on dressing Finola's hair by herself. This was another of her "Favorite Things to Do," for Finola's hair was a glory, and that was the truth.

With Lucy dismissed to take her meal in the kitchen, Annie had Finola to herself, except for Small One, who lay on the bed eyeing Fergus with a suspicious stare. Poor Fergus, as usual, was made to wait just outside the door, looking in; he and the cat simply could not agree, and had to keep their distance from each other.

"You look beautiful, Finola." Annie stood behind her at the vanity, brushing the heavy, flaxen waves into spun gold. "Like a princess."

Their eyes met in the reflection of the mirror, and Finola smiled at her. "I think you've been reading the faery stories again, Aine," she said softly. "Sure, I'm no princess."

Finola was the only one who seemed to consider Annie grown up enough to be called by her birth-name, *Aine*, and she preened at the sound of it.

Finola had a voice like rarest silk, she did. A voice as golden as her hair, sweet and flowing. Annie felt, when she opened her own mouth, like a squawking bird in comparison. Indeed, looking at herself and the fair Finola in the mirror, it was like gazing on an ungainly blackbird and a swan.

"You are a princess to me, Finola!" she blurted out. "And to the *Seanchai*! He is the prince of Nelson Hall, and you are his princess!" She stopped, the brush suspended in her hand. "Sure, he treats you like one, and that's the truth!"

The reflection in the mirror sobered as the faintest hint of pink touched Finola's cheeks. "He is . . . kindness itself to me. I . . . I can't think how I shall ever repay him for all he is doing."

Surprised, Annie stared at her. "Why, Finola—the *Seanchai* wouldn't expect you to *repay* him! He does what he does because—" Annie stopped, not wanting to embarrass Finola. "Well, because he cares for you."

The flush on Finola's pale skin deepened still more. "His heart is large," she said. "It holds much compassion. Perhaps too much."

Annie studied the lovely, troubled face in the mirror. "What is it, Finola? What makes you so sad?" She blurted out the question before thinking, then wondered if she'd been too forward. Still, they *were* friends; Finola said so herself. Indeed, Finola treated her more as a sister than a bothersome child.

The thin shoulders slumped, and Finola lowered her head as if in dismay. "I never meant to be a burden to him," she said miserably, the wondrous voice naught but a whisper. Annie had to lean forward to hear. " 'Tis the last thing I would be to him. I shouldn't be letting him do this thing . . . making me his wife, giving my child his name ... but I don't know what else to do. He is such a great man, a noble man ... and because he is, he has burdened himself with me ... and the child ... a child he doesn't want, a child that is nothing to him. ..."

Dismayed, Annie saw tears track slowly down the hollowed cheeks and fall onto the soft blue dress. She put the brush down and gripped Finola's shoulders with both hands.

"Oh, Finola, *no*! You're wrong, you are! Dreadfully wrong! You're not a burden to the *Seanchai*! He truly cares for you ... why, he *cherishes* you! Don't you see it, in his eyes? Everybody else sees—don't *you*?"

Finola began to shake her head in protest, but Annie caught a glimpse of something else, something that made her think Finola *wanted* to believe.

"And as for the babe," she hurried on, "it isn't true at all, that your babe is nothing to him! The *Seanchai* wants to be the father, he does!"

Still looking at Finola's reflection in the mirror, Annie saw the uncertainty in her eyes. She was being bold, perhaps even offensive, but somehow she had to make her understand! Finola was wrong—ever so wrong—about why the *Seanchai* was marrying her!

"He adores you!" she burst out. "He has, from the very first! It's the truth, Finola, and you must mind it! And as for the babe—" Annie stopped, her mind fumbling wildly for a flash of inspiration that seemed just out of reach. "It's—it's just as Sister told me, once, when I was fretting about not being the *Seanchai*'s real daughter.

" 'Annie Delaney,' Sister said, 'a man is not a father because of a legal document, or even because of the blood tie. A man is a father by a choice of the will and a ... a commitment of the heart.' " Gulping in a huge breath, Annie rushed on to finish what she felt an urgency to say. "Don't you see, Finola? The *Seanchai* has made a choice of the will and a commitment of his heart—to you, and to your babe. He wants you *both*, now that's the truth!"

Their eyes met and held in the mirror's reflection. And as Annie looked into Finola's startled blue gaze and thought about the words she had spoken so boldly, the first light of morning began to dawn, somewhere in the very deepest part of her. A warm, comforting awareness washed over her, and she knew, in her heart of hearts, that, even if life should take a cruel turn and somehow prevent her from being adopted by the *Seanchai*, nothing—*nothing* would ever prevent her from being his daughter, from belonging to him.

In his heart. And in her own.

———

Waiting for the others to come down to dinner, Morgan read Frank Cassidy's letter again. He found it as intriguing the second time through as the first—intriguing, and, in some respects, maddening.

Frank was, of course, doing his utmost to carry out the burdensome task with which Morgan had entrusted him. Cassidy was as faithful as the sunrise and loyal to the death. If the truth of Finola's past could be found, then he would find it.

But he was having the time of it getting started, or so it seemed. It had been a month now since Morgan had set him to the search, a search that had begun right here in the streets of Dublin. Early on, however, after just coming upon a possible source of information, he'd been forced to abandon his assignment and leave for Galway, where his recently widowed daughter was having landlord problems.

At last he was back on the job, which, according to his letter, had taken him to Drogheda:

> Although the information given me by the gleeman— Christy Whistle—could only be, at best, considered questionable, I'm inclined to follow it through. This is going to take some digging and some wandering about, I fear. I know you are anxious, but try to be easy, for you've my word that I'll not quit on you. I do think I may at last have found the beginning of a worthwhile trail to pursue.

Drogheda. He couldn't imagine what Cassidy had learned from the street minstrel that had led him to the old city, but the mere fact that he had gone there was enough to make Morgan hope something would come of it.

Yet, perhaps it was best that it was going to take some time, as Cassidy had indicated. Determined as he was to uncover anything in Finola's past that might help her, Morgan uneasily acknowledged that whatever lay buried among her forgotten memories was more than likely unpleasant, possibly harmful. She had enough—more than enough—to deal with for now. Anything else might turn out to be too much. What was important for her now was a time of healing.

Hearing voices on the stairs, Morgan glanced up, then folded the letter and put it back in the desk. Quickly, he wheeled himself across the room and out into the hallway.

Looking thin and too pale by far—but with a faint smile for him—Finola stood at the bottom of the stairway, Annie and Sister Louisa on either side of her. Morgan's heart gave a great leap: now the evening would be even more special than ever.

———

It was a fine evening, and that was the truth—the finest Morgan could remember in a very long time. Although Finola had come down for meals three or four times before tonight, this was the first time she had taken more than a few indifferent bites, the first time she did not seem to distance herself from the rest of them.

He found it difficult to keep his eyes from her. Her flaxen hair was shining, her eyes more alight than he had seen them for months. It was, of course, impossible not to notice the slight trembling of the hand when she lifted her cup, the occasional sadness that darkened her gaze when she thought no one saw, the faint color that crept across her face when he happened to catch her eye.

But she was here. She would sit at his table, eat at his side. She would share in this happy time for him and Annie, and he would be blessed by her nearness, her grace, her golden hair, her gentle smile. It was more than enough.

———

Annie had known from the moment she saw the vast dining room table, lavishly spread as if for a banquet, that something was afoot. Something was different. Something special.

The table was set with the best crystal goblets, the most delicate of the china, the silver all polished and gleaming in the candlelight. Sister Louisa, who usually took her meals with the students in the Academy, was seated at the table, smiling at Annie as she walked in.

Annie began to rack her brain. Had she overlooked an event of some sort? Neglected a birth date or an anniversary? An important guest?

By the time the dessert was served—her favorite, cream custard—she was fairly wild with curiosity and pent-up excitement. Finally the *Seanchai* tapped his goblet lightly with a spoon. Annie had all she could do to stay in her chair. Obviously he was about to make a statement of some importance!

At first, she could not take in what he was saying. "A momentous occasion," he declared. He had been given "a gift . . . and a precious responsibility" . . . it had taken "long months," but now "all was prepared," and it was time . . . "time to make known . . . time to declare . . .

"Time to formally acknowledge . . . my new daughter. The papers have been finalized, and all that awaits is the addition of your new name—or your present name, as you so choose. Annie?" He extended his hand. "Come here, lass."

Annie's eyes bugged. Her mouth went slack. She looked from the *Seanchai* to Finola, at his left . . . then to Sister, bright-eyed and smiling beside Finola . . . then to Sandemon, whose face seemed about to crack as he lifted his eyebrows at her, beamed, then rose to his feet and gave a grand, low bow.

Annie went round the table, approaching the *Seanchai* with stiff, slow steps, determined not to bounce and run, as she would have liked. He took her hand and coaxed her to his side, searching her eyes for a very long moment. Then, releasing her hand, he reached into the pocket of his fawn-colored vest and produced a small velvet box of forest green.

"This is for you, *alannah*," he said quietly, handing her the velvet box. "To remember this day. I commissioned it weeks ago to make certain it would be ready for this occasion."

Annie's hands shook as if she had the palsy, but at last she managed to tip the lid of the box and peek inside. She gasped, her eyes locked on the treasure within: a brooch, made in replica of the *Seanchai*'s own minstrel's harp, set in what appeared to be purest gold, the neck studded with three small emeralds.

"Oohh . . . my . . . you don't mean it's for me!"

The *Seanchai* laughed softly. "Take it out, child. Turn it over."

With trembling fingers, Annie freed the wondrous treasure, turning it over in the palm of her hand. Engraved on the back, in the Irish, were the words: "To the daughter of my heart."

Annie stared. Bit her lip. Sniffed. Swallowed hard.

"Here, child," the *Seanchai* instructed gently. "Stoop down here and let me pin it on you."

Immediately, Annie dropped to her knees beside him, waiting. His big hands fumbled, his smiling gaze held hers as he pinned the brooch carefully in place at her throat. Then he took her by the shoulders, saying, "What name shall we sign to the papers, *alannah*? Will you take my name, then?"

Annie nodded fiercely, then managed to choke out, "Aine Fitzgerald shall be my name . . . if you please, sir."

His slow smile drew her into his heart, even as his sturdy arms drew her into his embrace. "Tonight," he whispered against her temple, "I am a proud man, Aine Fitzgerald. A man blessed, to have you as my daughter."

36

Distant Dreams and Ancient Burdens

I will my heavy story tell
Till my own words, re-echoing, shall send
Their sadness through a hollow, pearly heart;
And my own tale again for me shall sing,
And my own whispering words be comforting,
And lo! my ancient burden may depart.

W. B. YEATS (1865–1939)

Late that night, after Sandemon had helped him into bed, Morgan settled back against his two massive pillows, gesturing that the other should stay.

After Sandemon had pulled a chair close to the bed and sat down, Morgan said, "I've heard from Joseph. He sent his regrets, but will not be able to officiate at the wedding. He didn't admit it, of course—I have never known Joseph to complain—but I think he's ill. Perhaps gravely ill. The letter was brief, and his hand was nearly illegible."

Sandemon nodded, his expression sad. "Father Joseph has exhausted himself for his people. And he is no longer a young man, after all."

"Aye, I'm worried for him," Morgan said with a sigh. "And

324

disappointed. I had hoped he would offer the wedding mass. It would have meant a great deal to have him here."

Again the black man gave a nod. "Would you like me to speak with one of the priests from the cathedral? They were most kind about coming here when you didn't feel up to attending."

Crossing his arms over his chest, Morgan studied him for a moment. "Perhaps," he said vaguely. "The young Father Hugh— the one who looks to have stuffed walnuts in his cheeks—has been most agreeable." He paused. "There is something I would ask of you."

"Of course, *Seanchai.*"

"I'd like you to assist the priest and perhaps offer the benediction."

The instant the words were out of his mouth, he saw the black man tense. The broad shoulders stiffened, and his expression went bleak. "You know that I cannot do that, *Seanchai,*" he said, his voice low.

"I know no such thing," Morgan said evenly, his eyes meeting Sandemon's midnight gaze. "Perhaps I understand why you *think* you cannot, but I disagree. And I very much want you to do this for me. You will be my one close friend in attendance. Joseph cannot come; Smith O'Brien still languishes in gaol. It would mean much to me if you would take part in the ceremony."

He had not anticipated the look of pain that crossed the black man's features. Immediately, Morgan regretted asking. He would not intentionally cause this good man pain for any reason.

"Please, *Seanchai*—please do not ask me again." Sandemon's tone seemed strangled on a note of sorrow, and Morgan chose not to press.

With a slight wave of his hand, he gave over. "All right. All right, then. But you will at least do me the honor of standing with me as my man?"

With a look of great relief, the black man quickly nodded. "I would be most proud."

Morgan raked one hand down the side of his beard. "I want this day to be perfect for Finola," he mumbled, more to himself than to Sandemon. "But it seems that each idea I've had for the wedding turns out to be as unlikely as my foolish dream."

"What dream is that, *Seanchai*?"

Morgan hesitated, then repeated with some embarrassment his recurring dream of standing like a man to meet Finola at the altar. It had plagued him almost nightly of late. He realized that it undoubtedly reflected an entire multitude of hopeless longings, yet the dream never moved past the elation of Finola's smile as, approaching, she saw him free of the wheelchair, standing tall as he awaited her.

Almost immediately, Morgan regretted his candor and tried to make light of it. "Ah, well," he cracked, "at least the dream enables me to stretch my legs now and again."

Sandemon smiled in exchange, but Morgan did not miss his thoughtful scrutiny.

Silence hung between them for a moment. Then Sandemon asked, "What else can I do for you, *Seanchai*? For the wedding day, I mean?"

Morgan shrugged. "Thanks to your usual efficiency, I can think of nothing."

The black man glanced away for just an instant. "What about Miss Finola's rooms? Shall I move . . . her things?"

Heat stole over Morgan's face. "I believe I explained the . . . arrangements of the marriage to you," he said, his tone sharper than he'd intended. "Finola will not be sharing my rooms. I thought you understood."

At once, Sandemon shook his head, lifting one hand. "Forgive me, *Seanchai*. Of course, I understand. I only meant to suggest that you might want her belongings moved to the other connecting room. Because of the delicateness of her . . . condition, I thought you might want her as close to you as possible."

Morgan frowned briefly. "A sensible idea."

"Then I will see to it," said Sandemon.

Sister Louisa finally had to apply great firmness to remove Annie from Finola's bedroom. The child had followed Finola upstairs and, even at this late hour, continued to bombard her with a running stream of excited chatter.

Fearful that she would exhaust Finola, Louisa stepped in. "The seamstress is coming first thing in the morning for a fitting of your gown—and Finola's. Now, then, no more delays, young *Aine*—to your bedroom at once."

The child scowled. "I *detest* dress fittings! There's nothing more boring than being prodded and probed and pricked! And Mrs. Dowling is rough and heavy-handed entirely!"

Sister Louisa turned a long, warning look on her. "And will you disappoint Finola, then, and not participate in the wedding?"

The child darted a glance at Finola, who was sitting silently on the side of the bed, looking extremely weary. "Of course, I won't disappoint Finola," she muttered, stalking off to the door. "But that doesn't mean I will enjoy the fitting."

"Such a stubborn child," Louisa said, watching her stamp on down the hall, the faithful wolfhound trotting along beside her. Turning, she studied Finola, who still sat, her gaze downcast, her hands clenched in her lap.

Louisa went to her, putting a hand on her shoulder. "Lucy should be right up with your warm milk. Aren't you feeling well, child?"

The girl looked up. As always, the clarity and depth of those wounded blue eyes caught Louisa off guard, piercing her own heart. "What is it, then?"

Finola pulled at the material of her nightdress, and as Louisa met her gaze she felt as if she were staring into a vale of despair.

"The wedding gown," murmured Finola. "I know you and the *Seanchai* . . . that you insisted it should be of white satin, but . . ."

Wringing her hands, she again looked away. Sympathy, raw and painful, twisted through Louisa. The poor, lovely child, so wan and thin in the voluminous blue nightdress, her expression embarrassed and despondent, seemed scarcely older than Annie.

Sitting down beside her on the bed, Louisa pried one white-knuckled hand free of the other and enfolded it gently inside her own. "Why don't you tell me about it?"

"The white dress . . . I don't think . . . I should wear white. . . ."

Louisa had to lean closer to make out the whispered words. Appalled, she put both hands to Finola's shoulders, turning her about and making the girl face her. "But, of *course*, you should wear white!" she said. "Why would you think otherwise?"

Finola shook her head slowly, with a look of great sadness. "I am not pure," came the faint reply.

Louisa was suddenly angry—not at Finola, but at the terrible injustice that had been wreaked upon her. She chose her words carefully. "Finola, what happened to you is not your fault—you must believe that. In God's eyes, you are chaste—as pure as if it had never happened at all."

The girl looked at her in surprise.

She truly did not understand, Louisa realized with dismay. "Oh, child, child—listen to me! Purity is a matter of the *heart*—a heart in right relationship to our Lord! His love wasn't changed or diminished by the awful wrong inflicted upon you! You are not . . . stained or unclean in His sight."

Desperately, she searched for just the right words to comfort the girl. "You must never forget, Finola, that you belong to God; you are His beloved. He sees you only in the light of His love, and you are pure and undefiled in His eyes."

With some difficulty, Louisa forced a note of cheerfulness into her voice. "The white satin, Finola, is perfect for you—truly it is. You will wear it in beauty and in grace. You will be radiant, and the *Seanchai* will be pleased." Her voice faltered for an instant; then she added, "As will our Lord."

———

Annie could not sleep. Countless times her mind danced through the events of the evening, savoring them over and over again, determined to store for a lifetime each moment. And with each recollection, her happiness grew, her excitement swelled, her smile broke wider.

For the second time that night, she scrambled out of bed and plopped down on her knees. On the opposite side of the bed, Fergus stretched and lifted his head just enough to peer over at her.

Apparently he was growing accustomed to seeing her in this position, for he merely gave a great yawn and went back to sleep. Lazy wolfhound!

Repeatedly, Annie gave thanks, praying aloud. Somehow, speaking in a normal tone of voice made it seem more likely that the Lord was right here, in this very room, keeping company with her.

She thanked Him . . . again . . . for her adoption, for the approaching wedding, the babe to be born, the new joy that now seemed to be permeating Nelson Hall.

"Oh, and before I go to sleep, Sir—though in truth I do not see how I shall ever sleep this night—but just in case, I want to ask you once more to please bless my mother. The *Seanchai* says it was the loving thing she did, giving me this opportunity."

Annie stopped, feeling her happiness begin to recede and determined not to let it. "The *Seanchai* doesn't think I know the truth, Lord. He would have me believe that Mum gave me up because she loves me and wants what's best for me. He wouldn't like knowing I understand the true way of things, that I was always just a bother to her and Tully, that she never really wanted me at all."

She pressed her lips together, determined not to let anything darken this shining night for her. None of it mattered anymore, not a bit. No longer would she waste time feeling sorry for herself and contemplating a bleak future outside Nelson Hall. She was now the . . . the *legitimate* daughter of Morgan Fitzgerald himself.

Pressing her face into the palms of her hands, she breathed in another deep sigh of happiness. She thought she understood why the *Seanchai* didn't want her to know the truth.

"It's because he really loves me, isn't it, Lord?" she whispered into her hands, smiling. "He truly, truly, truly loves me! And I am going to make him proud, I am! I will be the very best daughter he could imagine." She paused, thinking. "Although I expect I'll be bothering you even more, from now on, Sir, for as you know, my good intentions are usually better than my behavior."

Still smiling, Annie touched the brooch that she had fastened to the neck of her nightgown. "Well, I expect I should try to go to sleep now and let you attend to some other prayers. I know you're busy, and you've already done more than enough for me. So . . . good-night, Sir. And thank you again."

———

Much later, while the household slept, Sandemon, still dressed, paced the bedroom.

He had been restless throughout the last hour, had even found it difficult to concentrate during his prayer time. Then the idea had come, only moments ago, and now it would give him no rest.

It could work, he thought. It *would* work, with careful planning. But the time was short before the wedding, and his hours were already filled with much to do. Still, he required little sleep. He would use the two hours before dawn, when the *Seanchai* slept most deeply.

And, later, he would enlist the help of the child. He smiled. No doubt the *Seanchai*'s new daughter would be pleased and eager to combine efforts in the creation of such a very special gift—a wedding gift. They had succeeded in keeping a secret once before, had they not?

Yes, and they would do it again.

Eager to begin, and knowing sleep to be impossible, he decided to go to the stables and take stock of his supplies. After looking in on the sleeping *Seanchai*, he put on his shoes and, closing the door quietly behind him, started down the hall.

———

On her way to the kitchen, Lucy Hoy tried to avoid the chapel doors, as she always did. Somehow, even the thought of the holy place made her feel dirtier and more vile than ever.

For a time after Finola's tragedy, with Gemma's place and the life of the streets behind her, she had attempted to overcome her feelings of defilement. She had hoped that this new life, so far removed from the drunken sailors and her wicked past, would eventually bring about a kind of cleansing, even enable her to forget her shameful yesterdays.

Instead, her self-disgust and hatred had grown more intense. This separation from the past, instead of distancing her from her sin, had only seemed to increase her awareness of it. At the same time, the slightest contact with something holy—like the chapel—chilled her blood and made her want to turn and run away.

Yet, inexplicably, she could not seem to approach it without stopping to peer inside. After a moment, she cracked the doors and stood staring into the dark sanctuary, shuddering at the holy hush within. Finally she started to back away, as if some heavy, unseen hand had warded her off.

———

The woman's back was to him as Sandemon turned the corner and started down the hallway.

He stopped, watching her. With one hand on the chapel door, which was partially open, she stood staring inside.

It was a familiar scene. Any number of times, he had seen her, standing just like this, staring inside the chapel—but always safely outside the doors. Evidently, something about the chapel itself drew her, as if she were fascinated, yet unwilling to enter.

Clearing his throat so as not to startle her, Sandemon said, "You may go in, you know. The chapel is for everyone."

She whipped around, letting the door swing shut. A hand went to her throat. "No—I—no, I don't want to go in. I was just—curious, is all."

Sandemon nodded. "Still, remember that it is always available to you as a member of the household."

She made a weak attempt to jest, her chin trembling as she said, "Sure, the timbers might fall in, were a sinner such as myself to enter."

Sandemon smiled at her. "I think not. This is a very old house. I'm sure far worse sinners than you have walked through those doors over the years."

The woman said nothing, but simply stood, looking acutely embarrassed and miserable.

"You are troubled," Sandemon said. The words came unbidden, and he felt an instant of surprise.

She made no reply, but he had a sense of some overwhelming conflict raging within her. He saw the anxious, evasive glances, the slight tremor of her hands. The woman was in pain.

She was also frightened.

To be pursued by the Ancient of Days, the Holy God, could be a terrifying thing.

He remembered.

Suddenly, she looked at him and blurted out, "They will ask me to leave soon!"

Sandemon frowned, but she hurried on before he could protest. He heard the fear behind the rush of words. "They will! He doesn't approve of me, you know it's true! He will hire a nurse—a regular nurse—for Finola, and then he'll send me packing, you just see if he doesn't! He doesn't think I'm good enough to take care of her—or the child! He looks at me as if I'm—diseased!"

So that was it. She had reached the point where she imagined her own hatred for herself reflected in the actions of others. "The *Seanchai* would never condemn you. He is not that kind of a man. He might have been impatient with you once, for what he thought was a minor negligence. But I explained that I was at fault, and he has never mentioned it since that night."

She wasn't listening. Shaking her head, she said again, "He will send me away. He will!"

Studying her, Sandemon felt a great pity overwhelm him. "And where would you go?" he asked softly.

Slowly she raised her head and looked at him. "I've only one place to go," she said dully. "Back to Gemma's."

A sense of her despair shuddered through Sandemon. "But you would not choose to do so?" he questioned gently. "That is not what you want?"

Slowly, she dragged her gaze back to his, and the agony in those world-weary eyes pierced his heart. "I would rather die," she said flatly. "When I look back on that time now . . . it is like a memory of hell."

Sandemon nodded, understanding all too well. "I know," he said softly, to himself. "I know."

Abruptly, her eyes blazed. "You do *not* know! A man of God— what could you know about hell?"

The knife twisted even more deeply. "I am no man of God," he answered quietly. "I am only a man *saved* by God. And I have my *own* memories of hell, Miss Lucy."

Her eyes widened, questioning.

The urgency inside Sandemon swelled to a thunderhead, and he knew that it was time. Once again, the time had come to break the silence, to unseal the tomb of the past.

All that was light within his soul seemed to flicker and go out. For one terrible moment, a keening rose up inside his spirit, like the wailing of the damned, and he longed to flee: flee the woman, Nelson Hall, and his memories.

Instead, he simply gave a heavy sigh and, resigned, said quietly, "I will tell you what I know of hell. Perhaps then you will understand what I tried to tell you once before, that there is nothing in this world so wicked that God cannot redeem it." He paused. "Perhaps then you will finally understand that all the legions of evil cannot stand against the army of heaven."

Then he turned and started for the kitchen, the woman following him.

37

Dark Dragons

I see black dragons mount the sky,
I see earth yawn beneath my feet—

JAMES CLARENCE MANGAN (1803–1849)

In the kitchen, Lucy sat down at the table. The black man, however, went to the window and stood, unmoving, bracing the palm of each hand on either side of the window frame as he stared out into the night.

A storm had blown up over the past hour, and now the wind howled and whipped the rain against the house with a vengeance. Lightning streaked across the window, flaring and leaping in a frenzied, eerie dance to the night.

Always nervous in a storm, Lucy jumped as a chain of thunderbolts seemed to tear the heavens open, pummeling the house and rattling the windows. The familiar sense of confusion and intimidation the black man evoked in her only added to her growing anxiety.

Without turning, he finally began to speak. The ease of his posture, his calm demeanor and quiet voice struck a direct contrast to the wildness of the stormy night and the darkness of his words.

"You spoke of memories—'memories of hell' you called them." He paused. "I think you cannot imagine the reality of such words, of a life lived altogether in the shadow of hell."

A roll of thunder silenced him for a moment. When he spoke

again, his voice was so low it seemed to shudder and vibrate with the storm. "For years I spoke of my past to no one—you will see why. So hideous, so painful, are the memories that lie buried deep inside me that, to this day, I cannot call them forth without a most deadly anguish.

"The *Seanchai* knows, of course," he said, glancing over his shoulder at Lucy. "It seemed . . . deceitful, somehow, not to tell him the truth. But apart from him—and, now, you—I keep silent about my yesterdays. It was a very long time ago, and God has given me a new life. The old one is best forgotten, as much as possible. I tell you this only so you will understand what I was, where I came from—and the supreme act of deliverance it took to rescue me."

He turned back to the window. "I am a freed slave," he said. "My people were slaves—generations of them—taken from Africa to Barbados to work on the sugar plantations. As is so often the case with an oppressed people, we sought solace in superstition and magic. Our religion was *vodun*—voodoo. Do you know of it?"

Again he looked at her. Lucy was bewildered by the raw pain . . . and something else, something that looked very much like dread . . . in his eyes. She nodded. "The sailors sometimes talked of it."

Lowering his head, he turned back to the window. "Followers of *vodun* believe our world is filled with demons. Demons and gods and spirits of the dead. There is much magic—dark magic—in *vodun*. Charms and spells, sacrifices, secret ceremonies—all these make up the magic," he explained.

"Many years ago, when I was still a young man, I became the *houngan*—a *vodun* priest, a person with the magic, and of great influence among the people."

Lucy caught her breath in astonishment. As she watched, the black man's entire countenance seemed to go taut, as if set in marble. A muscle at the base of his jaw tightened, and his shoulders visibly tensed.

"The *houngan* is a person of great power . . . and of great evil. He is looked upon as a kind of physician, but he is much, much more. At times he acts as a kind of intermediary between his people . . . and the Evil One. Among other things, he supervises ceremonies whereby they become possessed by demons of darkness—or in which they make pacts with Satan."

He stopped, drawing in a long breath. When he continued, his words were tinged with unmistakable sorrow and much pain. "I did terrible things, dark, evil things—demonic mysteries—which seemed only to increase my powers. I applied the secret poison that turns the living into the walking dead—*zombies*. I presided over brutal animal—and human—sacrifices. I participated in the secret chants and strategies whereby the demons are called forth to possess beasts and human beings. And, perhaps most damning of all, I initiated any number of young people into the rites."

Unexpectedly, he turned and faced Lucy full on. She put a hand to her mouth to stop a gasp of dismay at the bleak anguish burning from his eyes.

"Know this," he said in a terrible voice, "your worst nightmares could never hold even a part of the evil which consumed my life! I could tell you things . . . that would drive you mad, things so vile and unbelievable your mind could not begin to take them in."

Once more he turned away from her, and Lucy found herself relieved to escape the torment in his eyes. He went on then, his words drumming out in a dull, plodding monotone, as if he were merely repeating a sequence of memories and images that had come, unbidden, to his mind.

In a voice so low Lucy had to strain to hear, he resumed his story. And even though his eyes were turned away from her, Lucy shivered under the conviction that she was hearing things—hidden things, secret things—which were best left concealed by the darkness. . . .

———

His mind followed the dark path back to the past . . . back to that night, just after the priests came, when he had been forced to look upon the reality of his own evil. . . .

Like a brief, terror-filled moment, when something vile rises up out of the darkness to be suddenly and brutally revealed by a flash of lightning, that night he had looked in horror upon a scene emblazoned by firelight . . . and beheld things depraved, an evil that seemed to permeate his brain, his senses, his entire body.

It had been a night very much like this one, without rain, but with a savage storm gathering in, preparing to assault the island.

Thunder threatened to rend the earth, and dangerous lightning seared the darkness.

Around the fire on the beach, the people were dancing and chanting to the beat of the drums. The drums. Always, the incessant, bewitching seduction of the drums. Enticing the people, calling forth the powers of darkness, the rulers of the night. Sounding the ancient rhythm of the dance of hell.

His power had been very great that night. Many of his people had become hosts or had received new visions; countless pacts had been made, and the Prince of Darkness was pleased.

But suddenly, as if borne on a mighty gust of wind, the fire had blazed up, furious and out of control. Startled, Sandemon whirled around, looking up to the gentle rise only a short distance away. Two black-cassocked priests stood, unmoving, framed against the horizon by the glow from the raging fire.

One, a small man with a sorrowful countenance, turned his face toward Sandemon, impaling him with his piercing priest's eyes.

Sandemon stood, breathless, feeling himself stripped, not only of his outward clothing, but of his pride—which was great—and his deceits—which were many. His feet, bare upon the sand, felt as if he were treading on hot coals, yet so violent was the chill that shook him that his entire body began to tremble.

When he finally managed to tear his gaze away from the priest, he saw in the angry red flames what appeared to be a vast number of faceless shadows, monstrous silhouettes, writhing and snaking upward from the blaze. A blood-tinted glow sprayed the beach, where his people crouched and rolled, danced and wailed. And in their midst, two little girls ... so small ... lay dead. Slaughtered ... mutilated ... sacrificed by their own friends and families. An offering ... to the Prince of Devils.

The rhythm of the drums went on, louder and faster, more frenzied and demanding, as the people swayed and leaped and screamed.

Again Sandemon traced the ascent of the shadows, the dark dragons rising and mounting the air, then swooping down, their loathsome forms mingling among the people, transforming familiar faces into the heads of beasts or hideous demons. Unable to stop himself, he turned once more to look at the mournful-eyed priest. And suddenly, he felt his evil self wracked and torn asunder as if the very armies of darkness and light were deadlocked in a battle for his soul.

As quickly as it had begun, it was over. The fire flickered and waned to a struggling flame. Rain began to fall. The sacrifices were disposed of, and, finally exhausted and depleted, the people groaned and slowly began to creep away. Some went on all fours like weary animals, others stumbled, dazed and drugged from the magic.

Sandemon was left alone, standing in the rain on the darkened beach, staring out at the sea. For the first time in his life, he questioned the magic, wondering what he had seen and what it meant.

From then on, things began to change—at first in subtle ways, then more dramatically. The priests—Father Ben and Father Eric—came among the people, teaching and ministering, healing and loving. Rumors circulated of powerful prayer meetings, meetings where people were delivered from possession and spirits were bound and banished.

Sandemon began to feel his own powers blocked, as if some unseen, unknown presence were tying his hands. Some followers fell away; others *ran* away—and disappeared entirely.

He knew that extraordinary powers were at work, that something exceptional was happening. And he knew it had to do with the priests. So he went to them, angrily confronting them with his accusations that they were interfering with the people—his people—and with his magic.

The reply had shaken him, badly. The quiet-voiced Father Ben, a man scarcely half Sandemon's size, simply gave him a steady look, saying, "Indeed, we are, *houngan*. We are doing just that. We are binding the evil source of your powers through prayer and the intervention of God's holy angels. And we will keep right on doing so, for your wickedness is plunging these people into the very pit of hell!"

Furious, Sandemon swore to circumvent their claims of "binding." Yet every attempt he made to remove these priestly obstacles availed him nothing. He began to feel impotent, a failure.

One day, his owner came looking for him in the stables with astonishing news. He had been hired out—to the priests! Trained in blacksmithing and carpentry, he would be of great assistance, his owner explained, in helping to build a new chapel.

The black man turned toward Lucy now, and she saw that his face was contorted in a futile attempt to smile. "An irony, yes?" he said. "God's men setting one of the devil's own to building a house of worship for Him."

Leaning back against the wall beside the window, he crossed his arms over his chest and continued. "For weeks, then months, I worked alongside these two godly men. The entire time, they were praying for me—they told me so! They would even pray within my hearing. 'Doing battle for my soul,' they called it.

"By this time, many of the people had begun to come to the priests, asking them to teach them of the one true God. Little by little, I found myself listening, along with the others. My owner had taught me to read when I was still a boy, and I began to sneak looks into the Holy Bible they left lying among the lumber."

A ghost of a smile relieved his grave expression as he went on. "One evening, on my way back to the plantation, I found a small, worn copy of the Scriptures—a different copy—tucked into my pack. Right there, alongside the path, I sat down to read. I read so long I was late reporting back and got into trouble with my owner," he said, still smiling at the memory. "I simply could not put the book down.

"As the days wore on, and I worked side by side with the priests, listening to their teaching, witnessing their love for the people, all the while aware of their prayer efforts in my behalf, I began to ask questions about their faith—their God. And, at last, I was brought into a direct confrontation with the Truth."

The smile vanished as he continued. "At that point, I became utterly and terribly overwhelmed by the enormity of my sin, the depths of my wickedness. At first I thought to run, to flee the relentless, searching love of the God I now knew to be pursuing me.

"Instead, I went to Father Ben. And this good man, with his infinite patience and gentle kindness, led me very carefully, one step at a time, into the Light. Although for days I seemed to be living in the middle of a battleground, with angels warring against the demons of hell for my soul—for my very life—eventually, thanks to the intercession of the priests and others among the people who had turned to Christ, I was delivered safely into the sheltering arms of the Savior."

He stopped, raking both sides of his face with his hands for a moment before looking at Lucy. "For a long time after, my life was good. I married a lovely woman who worked in the plantation house, and we had a little daughter—Maya. During that time, I tried, as best I knew how, to make up for some of the evil I had done to my own people. I went among them, with the priests, to teach the Truth and do battle with the darkness for their souls. It did nothing to alleviate my grief at the knowledge that I was the one responsible for their evil enslavement, but it was the only way I knew to give back even a fragment of the love and forgiveness my Savior had given me."

He was silent for a moment, and his wide shoulders sagged a bit. When he looked at Lucy, she saw that his dark eyes were now glazed with a terrible despair.

"It was no simple matter to come out of the darkness," he went on. "The new *houngan* had become enraged by my activities with the priests. He began to fight me with all the magic at his disposal, threatening me and my family, humiliating me in every way possible—he stopped at nothing in his efforts to destroy what the priests and I were trying to do.

"Then one evening . . ." The black man's voice faltered. When he finally recovered his composure, his voice sounded strangled. "One evening, I returned late from the work on the chapel. It was dark by the time I reached the plantation. My wife . . . and my little girl . . . they were gone."

Hugging her arms to herself, Lucy held her breath, waiting.

"I found them later," he said, his voice hoarse and unsteady, "on the beach. Slain. Mutilated."

Lucy moaned aloud at the agony in his eyes, the sorrow spilling over in his words. Appalled, she saw tears glaze his eyes, then fall slowly down his cheeks, unchecked, as he went on.

"I thought I would go mad. I meant to kill the *houngan*, to kill myself—" Again he broke off until he recovered. "But the priests and my people stopped me. For days I lay abed, unable to stand upright like a man, unable to do anything but lie weeping for my loss."

As Lucy stared at him in stunned silence, he straightened. "I have had to live long years with the consequences of my sin," he said, brushing away the tears with the back of one hand. "For there is no denying the painful truth that sin *does* bring consequences, often tragedy—to the life of the one who has sinned . . . and sometimes to his loved ones as well.

"I had been a thoroughly evil man," he continued in a steady voice, "and it does no good to say that I did not realize the extent of my depravity. While it is true that, for a time, like many of my people, I was almost entirely ignorant of all that was good, even in my darkness I was somehow aware that there was a better way, a way of light and honor and goodness.

"Yet, I would most assuredly have remained as I was . . . a man completely without hope . . . had God not made me face my own wickedness—and His goodness.

"By forcing me to confront the evil in my soul, and by allowing me to come in contact with the reality of His love, He changed my heart . . . and my life."

He inclined his head slightly. "Perhaps now you can see, Miss Lucy, why I am so utterly convinced that my Lord is the God of new beginnings, the God of new life. Like the great apostle, Paul, I have cried out in the night, *'O wretched man that I am! Who will deliver me?'* And, like Paul, I can declare that *'Christ Jesus came into the world to save sinners—of whom I am chief!'* "

He paused. "I will admit to you, Miss Lucy, that you cannot change your past. You cannot undo whatever bad or harmful things you may have done. Nor will I deny that there may well be consequences, painful ones, as a result of your past."

He stopped, lifting his chin slightly, looking at Lucy with an expression that was both kind and knowing. "But I can tell you this much: you *can* change your future. You . . . and God . . . can put the past behind you and start over. You can have a new beginning . . . a new life. Like me, you can be forgiven. Made clean. Changed. I lost my family—a terrible loss, a grief from which I will never be wholly free. Yet, in His mercy, God has given me a *new* family, here at Nelson Hall, to help ease the pain, to fill and bless my life."

He nodded, slowly, his eyes soft with great kindness. "You can make new memories, my unhappy friend, that will, in time, enable you to live at peace with the old ones."

Outside, the thunder had receded to a distant rumble. The lightning had weakened, coming in sporadic flashes. The only sound to break the silence in the room was the gentle patter of rain on the roof and in the trees.

For another moment, the black man stood watching her, his eyes grave. Then, like a storm clearing away from the land, his gaze brightened, until the faintest hint of light smiled out at Lucy.

"Do you know what I think, Miss Lucy? I think that if the chapel timbers do not cave in when Sandemon enters, it is not likely that they will give way for you."

With a small nod, he pushed himself away from the wall and started to cross the room, stopping when he reached Lucy. For a moment he solemnly searched her face. "You need to know that the battle for your soul has already been won. It is left for you only to claim the victory."

Without another word, he straightened his shoulders and swept out of the room.

————

Lucy sat, weeping quietly, for what might have been hours . . . or only moments.

As if in a dream, she heard the rain, saw the candles burning low on the table, tasted the salt of her tears. She spread her hands before her in a gesture of helplessness, then moved to hug her arms to herself to keep her heart from shattering inside her chest.

She stared at the candle nearest her, entranced by the flame. Outside, the wind wailed, causing her to shiver and grip her shoulders even more tightly. The darkness inside her spirit tugged at her mind, her heart, trying to entangle her, suck her into the night . . . the night inside her soul. But she kept her eyes on the flame, unable to look away.

Slowly, she freed a hand and reached for the candlestick. Staring at the flame, rising and flickering in the draft of the room, she lifted the candle, rose, and started for the door.

As if buoyed by an invisible wind, she walked out of the kitchen and down the hall, stopping at the doors of the chapel.

For a long time she simply stood, staring at the massive closed doors. Then, with the candle held aloft, she reached for the chapel door with her free hand and slowly opened it.

Inside, all was hushed and cool and serenely peaceful. Still, Lucy stood listening, waiting. Finally, she lifted her eyes above, to the roughly hewn timbers that crossed the ceiling.

The candle shook in her trembling hand, the flame flickering precariously. But after a moment it steadied, and a faint smile slowly curved her lips as she stood, unmoving, breathing in the quiet and peace of the chapel.

"You need to know that the battle for your soul has already been won. It is left for you only to claim the victory. . . ."

With her eyes on the light of the candle and Sandemon's words echoing in her heart, Lucy stepped out and began to walk down the aisle toward the altar.

38

In the Shadow of Five Points

I was the moon.
A shadow hid me
And I knew what it meant
Not to be all.

RHODA COGHILL (1903–)

Sometime in the night, Kerry Dalton came awake with a chilling sense of impending tragedy.

As she lay listening to the silence of the house, she shuddered, wondering what sort of dream had shaken her so violently from her sleep.

As a Christian, she had forsaken the old superstitions, no longer placed any credence in the mythic world of legend and faery lore that had been a part of her childhood in Ireland. Yet, lying here in the darkness, the shadows of night hovering about her, she could not help but remember the ancient tales of the *Banshee* and her dread visitations to keen one who is about to die.

Kerry's family—the clan of O'Neill—ranked among those of Gaelic nobility to whom the *Bean Sidhe*—the Banshee—would appear in the depths of the night. It was a faery tale, of course— one of the myths of preternatural beings that had evolved from the dark, unknown recesses of time's beginning.

Kerry instinctively moved closer to Jess's large, solid warmth. Shivering, she forced down any further thought of unwelcome

344

night visitors. Even so, sleep was a long time returning.

Thoughts of their recent troubles coursed through her: the reality of Jess's resignation from his Fifth Avenue pastorate, the hard feelings of parishioners they had once called their friends, and the somewhat frightening unknown of the future.

Yet, Jess was convinced he had done what he must, and after learning about his disturbing dream, Kerry had no doubts but what he was right. God was calling him away from a ministry to the affluent, commanding him to go to the unwanted of the city.

It was somewhat intimidating, yet at the same time, exciting. To Kerry, it was but one more evidence that the Lord had great faith in her husband, to entrust him with such an enormous challenge.

Jess seemed encouraged. His spirits were brighter than she'd seen them for weeks. For her part, however, Kerry thought it would take a long time before she would completely forget the pain of the past.

———

It was dark when Arthur sneaked away from the Daltons', but by the time he reached the Five Points, the sun was beginning to come up.

In the first weak light of dawn, the slum looked even uglier than he remembered. Broken bottles and rubbish littered Paradise Square. Pigs rooted through the garbage piled high in the streets, ignoring those drunks who lay sprawled in front of doorways. Already, a few homeless children darted in and out of the alleys, heckling the few honest workers who made their way across the square, heading for the factories.

With the smell of the streets already filling up his nose, Arthur stood, delaying his return as long as possible. He had hoped never to smell the rotten odor of the Five Points again. But he had to stay somewhere, and this was the only place he knew to come.

It occurred to him that Mr. Jess would be waking up just about now. How long would it be before they realized he was gone? By breakfast time, for sure, if not before. Miss Kerry always made him and Casey-Fitz eat their breakfast before going to school.

The thought of them all—even Molly, the sharp-tongued housekeeper and her husband, Mackenzie—made his eyes sting. For a moment, he was tempted to turn around, to take off running as fast as he could and not stop until he reached the Daltons' house.

Instead, he pulled himself up a little straighter, swallowed down the lump in his throat, and started walking again. He couldn't go back. He had done enough harm, brought enough trouble on Mr. Jess and his family.

All the hateful things that had been said, the mean way they'd been treated—it had all been because Mr. Jess had defended the Negroes and wanted to help them. Arthur guessed taking *him* in must have been the last straw.

Now Mr. Jess had resigned from the big church as their preacher and was setting up what he called a "mission pulpit" in the Bowery, and another one here in the Five Points.

Oh, he and Miss Kerry had talked a lot about it being "God's will," and that he'd had a "call," but Arthur was pretty sure that if it hadn't been for him, things wouldn't have come to such a sorry place.

Now the family would have to move out of the parsonage and find another house. They'd be leaving the big church and their neighborhood—why, Casey-Fitz might even have to change schools!

And all because of him. Arthur Jackson, a runaway slave boy.

Nossir, he wouldn't go back. He'd done enough damage. He had made do down here in Five Points before, and he'd make do again.

Hiking his stick a little higher on his shoulder, Arthur jumped across a mud puddle and started toward Cow Bay. He'd go back to the Old Brewery, where he'd stayed before. There, one more darkie would never be noticed.

Casey-Fitz's heart raced as he stood in the middle of Arthur's bedroom. There was an air of finality about the neatly made bed and the orderly condition of the room's furnishings. The drapes were still closed against the early morning sun. The pine rocker was bare: no trousers or shirt hung across its back, no shoes or socks rested beneath it.

With his pulse throbbing in his ears, Casey went to the wardrobe and opened the double doors. For a moment he stood appraising the contents.

Arthur seemed to have taken scarcely anything with him. Most of the things they had bought for him still hung in place. The Sunday shoes sat, black and gleaming, right in front, directly under the good gray suit. The freshly laundered shirts and trousers hadn't been touched. But on the peg inside the door hung a red nightshirt, like a warning.

He was gone.

Not quite able to get his breath, Casey turned away from the wardrobe, his gaze again sweeping over the silent bedroom. He had been afraid of this very thing.

But Arthur had *promised*, had given his word that he would not leave. With a sinking feeling, Casey-Fitz remembered his own promise of some months ago: *"God and Dad will take care of this,"* he'd told his friend. *"The two of them will handle everything, you'll see. . . ."*

He had believed it then, and, although it was getting much more difficult as the days went on and the trouble mounted, he believed it now. Dad had tried to explain to them all that his resignation was by choice, that he felt good about his decision—"the Lord's persuasion," he'd called it.

But Arthur blamed himself. Casey-Fitz had seen it in his averted gaze, his sober expression, his sudden silences.

Slowly, he walked to the door. With his hand on the doorknob, he stopped, turning back to survey the room one more time. Finally, he stepped into the hallway.

Downstairs he heard his parents in the dining room. Any moment now, Little Mother would come to the bottom of the stairs and call him and Arthur to breakfast—the "second and last call," she would declare.

With heavy steps and an even heavier heart, he started down the stairs, slowly at first, then faster until at last he broke into a run.

———

When they had found no sign of the boy by midday, Jess Dalton began to feel the first stirrings of fear.

He had been so certain they would find him in the Five Points. That was where he would go, of course; it was the only place Arthur knew, except for the parsonage.

But they had been searching for over three hours, with still

347

no sign of him. Both he and Casey-Fitz had scoured the tenements, trudged through the tramps' nests, among the blind beggars, the hungry children, the derelicts. They had crossed Paradise Square at least five times.

Jess was grateful he had brought Casey-Fitz with him to the Five Points before today. At least the boy had grown used to the squalor, the filth, the abject misery all around them. Nothing they encountered on their door-to-door search was likely to shock him.

They had enlisted some help along the way: Skipper Jones, an unemployed Negro hod carrier, and a Catholic priest known in the area simply as "Father John." So far, however, no one had come upon the slightest trace of Arthur.

With Casey gripping his hand, Jess led the way across the square. He couldn't stop the memory that flashed through his mind as they walked. This was where Arthur had first come into their lives. On a bitter November day, an angry Irish striker had shot him down, right here, in Paradise Square. Jess had taken him home to recuperate—and Arthur had stayed, to become a part of their family.

A tug on his hand called him back to the present, and he glanced down at his son.

"I'm sure we'll find him, Dad." The boy's voice sounded anything *but* sure.

Jess studied the thin face, the solemn green eyes. "Of course, we will, son," he said, squeezing the boy's hand. "We'll keep searching until we do." He paused. "You're quite certain Arthur didn't say anything—anything at all—that might help us know where to look?"

Casey-Fitz shook his head. "No, sir. Nothing. I could tell he blamed himself for our troubles, and I know he fretted about your resigning—even after you explained. But I don't have any idea where he might go." His voice faltered. "I should have watched him more closely, I expect."

Again Jess gave his hand a gentle squeeze. "No, you couldn't possibly have known what Arthur was thinking. Don't blame yourself, son. There's no blame in this for anyone."

"But Arthur thinks there is," Casey-Fitz said softly. "He blames himself. That's why he's gone."

Having no answer for the boy—or for himself—Jess remained silent. "Let's go get the buggy," he finally said. "I think our next stop ought to be the police station."

———

When Evan Whittaker walked into the rehearsal room, he knew at once that something was amiss. The boys were huddled together, heads down, and everyone seemed to be talking at once. From the looks of their grave expressions, Evan concluded that whatever had happened was not good.

They broke apart with obvious reluctance when he rapped his baton. Without waiting for permission to speak, Billy Hogan blurted out, "Mr. Whittaker, sir, Arthur Jackson is missing!"

No more were the words out of his mouth than Daniel spoke up. "Uncle Mike and Officer Price were just here, asking if we'd help with the search. They think Arthur ran away to the Five Points because of all the troubles Mr. Dalton has been having."

Evan stared at them with dismay. He had developed a real fondness for the spunky young black boy. Arthur was one of his most dependable choir members and was showing real promise in the reading classes.

He glanced at Mrs. Walsh. She was sitting on the piano bench, her features troubled, her hands clenched in her lap.

"Of c-course, we must help," Evan said distractedly. "Mrs. Walsh, we won't be rehearsing t-today. Is your d-driver waiting?"

She stood, saying, "He'll wait as long as necessary. I'll go with you and the boys to help look for Arthur."

"Oh—n-no . . . I d-don't think that's—no, you mustn't d-do that! I'll see you to your carriage. . . ."

"No, Mr. Whittaker, I'm going to help," she said firmly, putting on her gloves. "Please don't be concerned about me. I'll be quite all right."

When she continued to override his protests, Evan reluctantly gave in. Before they left the rehearsal room, he pulled Daniel to one side. "D-don't let Mrs. Walsh out of your sight. I can't very well insist that she not g-go, but she can't possibly have a thought as to what it's like down here."

"Aye," Daniel nodded, glancing over at Alice Walsh. "But I think she's the sort of woman who will manage."

"Let us hope," Evan said tightly. "Let us hope."

———

Alice realized that the search through Five Points might well give her nightmares for weeks. Yet, she felt compelled to accompany Mr. Whittaker and the boys, knew an unexplainable need to subject herself to this vale of misery.

Nothing could have prepared her for her first close-up encounter with the wretchedness of Five Points. She had read about it, of course, but even the newspapers seemed somewhat guarded in their chronicles of the notorious slum, as if words alone were not enough to convey its horror. The women in her mission aid society spoke of the area mostly in whispers, with downcast eyes.

Up until now, Alice had arrived for choir rehearsals safely ensconced in her buggy, quickly delivered and collected before the taint of the slum could rub off on her well-tailored suit. Not once had she walked into the festering alleys to confront the suffering quartered therein. What lady *would*?

The rotting buildings with their broken windows, the streets teeming with garbage and pigs, the slatternly women, some scarcely covered by their tattered dresses, the drunken men with their abusive language and hate-filled eyes—Alice had neither seen nor imagined even a small part of the area's squalor.

But as she moved through the streets, well-protected by the police escort and the solemn-faced Mr. Whittaker and his boys, she felt a peculiar sense of satisfaction to be here. Far too long had she been sheltered from the reality of the world she lived in. For too many years she had managed to skirt most of what was unpleasant or painful. It was, she admitted grimly to herself, time for her to grow up.

Their search went on throughout the remainder of the afternoon and into the evening. And the deeper into the Five Points they went, the more Alice's shame increased.

How had she managed to live so long . . . and so well . . . ignorant of the fact that thousands upon thousands of people existed in such an abject state of poverty and degradation—like animals? She had not known, had never realized, the appalling conditions under which human beings could actually survive.

Guilt at her own ignorance and apathy overwhelmed her. She lived in a mansion twice the size her family actually needed, pampering her already spoiled children, indulging herself with rich food, piano playing, and church teas—while an entire community only moments away existed in a veritable nightmare.

Ignorance was no excuse, she thought grimly. But even if it were, it didn't apply to Patrick. He *knew* about this place and its people. He could not *help* but know, with his involvement in business throughout the city. She had heard him—and her father—discuss Five Points, the Bowery, and other slum areas of New York, where the immigrants—especially the Irish—lived in misery.

Why, Patrick was Irish himself, although he didn't appreciate being reminded of it! They could have been doing so much, could have been taking measures to help alleviate the suffering in places like Five Points. Instead, Patrick just went on accumulating more and more wealth, while she continued to squander her days as an indulged, indifferent child, salving her conscience by giving money and playing the piano a few hours a week for Evan Whittaker's boys' choir.

Self-disgust washed over Alice, and right there, in the middle of the abominable stench rising off the littered streets, she promised herself . . . and her Maker . . . that she would no longer live such an isolated, wholly selfish existence.

She did not know where she might begin or what, exactly, she could do. But she would do *something*—and she would begin right away. And she must make Patrick, too, realize the—the *sin* of their indifference. He worked hard for the money that provided their luxuries, but surely she could make him see that they must not go on living entirely for themselves, as they had in the past.

In the meantime, however, she must concentrate on her reason for being here in the first place: Arthur Jackson, of whom there was still not so much as a sign.

———

Arthur heard them before he saw them—Mr. Jess and Casey-Fitz, the two of them following Captain Burke up the rickety stairs. They were making their way up to the second floor of the Old Brewery, while Arthur stood beneath them, squeezed inside a dark, concealing alcove.

He was close enough that he could have reached out and touched the big preacher's foot as they ascended, had to choke off a cry when he saw his tall form reach the landing. It was all he could do not to call his name.

Instead, he slipped out of the building through the Murderer's

Alley entrance, crouching in the shadows until he could no longer hear their voices.

They would never find him as long as he stayed in the Old Brewery. The place was a shadowland of dark and winding passages that ran throughout the whole building, with any number of alley entrances and hiding places deep within.

Arthur knew it was one of the favorite means of escape for the thieves and pickpockets that infested Five Points. A body could get lost in here for months without being found, if he had a mind to.

As he huddled behind a stack of rags in the fetid darkness, deliberately trying not to identify the rustlings and muffled sounds around him, Arthur knew a moment of the most shattering pain he had felt since leaving the Daltons' that morning before daybreak. A terrible, aching loneliness assailed him with all the violence of a blow, doubling him over until he thought he would be sick.

So intense was the hurt that he bit his lip until it bled. Suddenly, the sound of a muttered oath and the strong, sour smell of unwashed bodies loomed over him.

Caught off guard, Arthur lifted his head, trying to make out faces in the darkness.

"Here's another'n!" An agonizing kick in the small of his back sent Arthur sprawling to his belly. He gasped for breath, choking as he was roughly yanked to his feet from behind.

"He's a *big* one! I got him now—hold his arms!"

Stunned, Arthur twisted to free himself, squinting into the darkness at the two hulking forms that had him trapped.

He tried to bring his arms up, but a rope slipped down over his head, almost strangling him when his attacker hauled it tight.

He lunged, charging with his head, screeching like a cornered wildcat, until the rope cut off his air and a fist slammed into his face, silencing him.

39

The Warehouse

Alas! it is a fearful thing
To feel another's guilt!

OSCAR WILDE (1854–1900)

Word about the missing Negro boy from Pastor Dalton's household reached the Bowery late that night.

Bhima and two of the other residents of the museum—the Strong Man and Plug, Brewster's bodyguard—were huddled in the shadows behind the warehouse.

"The pastor is fond of the boy," Bhima told them. "He speaks of him with much affection."

"Then we should help find him," said the Strong Man. His massive frame was encased in a loosely knit sweater and flapping trousers instead of the circus tights he wore on stage. "With all the preacher is doing for us, it's only right that we do what we can for him."

"But not until after tonight," Bhima reminded him.

"You're sure the captain is coming?" growled Plug, the dwarf. "One of the newsboys said he was still in the Five Points earlier this evening, helping search for the Negro boy."

"He will come," Bhima said with confidence. "And we will be waiting."

The other two nodded their agreement. Plug touched the deadly looking brass knuckles on his right hand reassuringly.

The Strong Man again stretched to peer inside the grimy win-

353

dow, while Bhima and Plug waited impatiently.

————————

Just after midnight, Michael and his men entered the abandoned warehouse across from the dime museum.

A faint light drifted in through the sooty windows from the streets outside, enough for Michael to see that he didn't like the looks of the place. Not at all.

Here and there around the warehouse, upended barrels and boxes littered the splintered wood floor. The heavy scent of mold and dirt and cleaning fluid hung in the air. In a rough semicircle around the far end of the deserted building, packing crates and deteriorating bolts of fabric, stacked nearly the height of two men, formed a natural barrier between the east wall and the main doors.

"All right, then," Michael whispered, "spread out. Into the shadows, every man of you—and keep a sharp eye on the door. Remember—don't move until I give the signal." He motioned Rourke and Price and the others into place with a final warning: "There will be children with them, don't forget. So take care!"

Michael crouched into a dark shaft of shadow between two boxes to wait. Bhima had come through, after all, with the information he'd been trying to get for months. Tonight, Walsh's men were scheduled to ship out more than twenty of the homeless black children who roamed the streets of the slums . . . children who would more than likely spend their remaining years in slavery.

Unless he and his men could stop them.

A bitter bile rose up in his throat as he considered the terrible fate that awaited the children if they should fail them this night. Nervously fingering the handle of his nightstick, he told himself again that they would not fail. There was too much at stake, more, even, than the lives of the children.

Walsh, of course, would not show his face or dirty his soft hands with such a mean job. He was too slick . . . too *respectable* . . . to risk his neck at a slave exchange. But his henchmen would be here, and once they were safely put away, Michael hoped to convince at least one of them to save his own skin by squealing on his elusive employer.

Yet, whatever else happened, the children must come first. He would not endanger them just to get Walsh, no matter how much he wanted to put the snake away.

In the silence of the warehouse, Michael's heart hammered against his chest as he went on waiting.

————

Somewhere in the distance a clock struck one. Michael jerked to attention. He had lost track of time. How long had they been inside the warehouse, waiting?

His legs ached from crouching down in the same position for so long. Shifting, he tried to straighten and stretch, then stopped, holding his breath.

From near the main doorway came a thump, then a shuffling sound. The door swung back with a creak and a groan, and the shuffling drew nearer.

Total darkness, total silence, except for the shuffling and an occasional soft sob. Then the door grated shut, and Michael heard the thud of a bolt being thrown. A muffled voice issued what sounded like a warning, and the sobbing stopped.

Peering around the stack of boxes that concealed him, he could see little of anything, except a huddle of small, dark shadows, surrounded by a circle of larger silhouettes.

He smelled the sulfur before he heard the match strike. Someone lit a torch, then two, then another, and in the eerie, flickering glow he saw a sight that chilled his blood.

Bhima had been wrong. These were not twenty black children, rounded up to be sold as slaves. Instead, there were close to a *hundred* lined up, grouped together, their eyes wide with terror in the torchlight, their small faces frozen in frear.

And not all the faces were black. . . .

Rage flared in Michael as he saw the frightened faces of four little white girls illuminated by the wavering light. After a moment, he scanned the men holding the torches, recognizing at least four of Walsh's men—thugs who might, to make things easier on themselves, spill what they knew about their employer's dirty business dealings.

Another man stepped into the light, this one smaller than the others. *Rossiter!* Michael's heart raced. Of course, the weaselly little bookkeeper would be here, no doubt to make sure no one double-crossed his boss!

In the darkness, Michael gave a grim smile and nodded. This was more than he'd hoped for! If he could take Rossiter . . . and his books . . . it should give him enough evidence to finish Walsh!

But his first job was to rescue those children.

As he watched, Rossiter balanced one end of a ledger against his chest and began to write. Just then, a knock sounded on the warehouse door: two raps . . . pause . . . three raps . . . pause . . . then one more.

A signal.

One of Walsh's men handed his torch off to another standing next to him, then slid the bolt. The door opened just a crack, enough for a man to enter, and a tall shadow eased into the flickering circle of light.

Michael stared. A sick heaviness settled over him, taking his breath. For an instant he squeezed his eyes shut, then opened them.

There was no mistake. It was his son. It was Tierney.

Tierney Burke took the distance between the door and Rossiter in three long strides.

Looking around, he locked his gaze on the bookkeeper. "You can't do this, Rossiter!" he threatened.

"Now you just hold on one minute, Burke! You knew what you were getting into when you agreed to do the job. And you're being paid well—*too* well, in my estimation."

As always, Rossiter's high, shrill voice grated on Tierney. Scowling, he took a step toward the bookkeeper, who stumbled backward.

"I knew about the *blacks*," Tierney pointed out. "But nobody told me about *them*!" Without looking, he gestured over his shoulder to where a small group of white girls—some with red hair and freckles—stood huddled in unmistakable terror. They looked to be no more than twelve or thirteen years old; even clad in rags, with dirty faces, they held the first faint promise of budding Irish beauty.

Rossiter sneered. Out of the corner of his eye, Tierney saw two or three of Walsh's henchmen move in closer to him and the bookkeeper.

"Why, the market's just as good for your little Irish biddies as for the pickaninnies, Burke," the dome-headed Rossiter said with an ugly smile. "Maybe better. Their skin is white, but they're every bit as dumb as the darkies."

Anger erupted into a furious rage inside Tierney. His teeth clenched until his jaw ached, and his hands trembled at his sides.

He pressed his face close to Rossiter's, close enough to catch the scent of the man's fear. "Walsh wouldn't *allow* this! He's Irish himself!"

Backing up, Rossiter forced a laugh. "Who do you think dreamed up the entire scheme?" He reached to straighten his spectacles. "That's right: *Walsh*," he said with evident satisfaction. "Your boss and mine, boy. Walsh, who sets the runners onto the ships to swindle your dim-witted cousins from the . . . 'ould country' as soon as they dock. The same Walsh who owns those fine boardinghouses in the Five Points, where your countrymen live in high style."

Fury blurred Tierney's vision, and for an instant Rossiter's detestable face receded. It was all he could do not to slam a fist into him, but he knew Walsh's men would jump him if he tried.

He dragged in a long breath and tried to think. Since the only thing Rossiter understood was money, he decided to meet him on his own ground. "I'll take care of the girls, then. How much?"

Rossiter stared at him, then snorted. "You're not serious? *All* of them?"

Tierney glanced at the girls, then back at the bookkeeper. "There are only four. I'm good for the money—you'll have it by midday tomorrow. Besides," Tierney added with a shrug, "what do you care? My money's as good as the next man's. Just give me the paper, and I'll take them off your hands."

The bookkeeper hesitated. "I don't know . . . they're already spoken for . . . Mr. Walsh wouldn't like it. . . ."

Tierney lifted an eyebrow. "Come on now, Rossiter. We both know Mr. Walsh thinks I'm a fine fellow. He'd be the last to begrudge me a bit of fun."

Hoagland, a big man who was missing one ear, gave a laugh. "Go on, Rossiter. The boy's right. Give him the girls."

Rossiter looked from Hoagland to Tierney. With a grudging nod, he handed him a paper. "Get them out of here, then. Take them outside before the buyers get here. And you be sure to bring me the money no later than tomorrow!"

Banking his anger, Tierney snatched the paper out of Rossiter's hand and started toward the girls.

———

Michael was too far away to hear the exchange between Tierney and Rossiter, but when he saw Tierney herd the four white girls outside, he breathed a sigh of relief.

He watched as the men with torches now encircled the other children. Rossiter stood to one side, his books open, his glasses glinting in the reflected torch fires.

The men separated the children into groups one by one, pushing them roughly, as Rossiter stood making his notes. When the smaller ones had all been counted, Walsh's men began to herd the older boys forward.

"Got some big ones this time," said the man with a missing ear. "Good for the field work, I expect."

As Rossiter glanced at the next in line, Michael narrowed his eyes. The torchlight distorted the boy's face, but there was something familiar—

"You ain't gonna get away with this!" the boy said, his voice unsteady. "Mr. Jess and Captain Burke, they looking for me! Soon as they find out—"

Michael's head snapped up as one of Walsh's goons backhanded the boy across the face. The black boy fell, immediately pushing himself up on his hands, then rolling over to glare up at his captors.

With a sinking heart, Michael recognized Arthur Jackson.

All day, he and Dalton and Evan's boys had been searching for the missing lad, and had come up empty-handed. Now he knew why: Walsh's men had found Arthur first.

His breath shallow, his mind spinning like a fury, Michael tried to think. With Rossiter and his books, there should be enough evidence to convict them all—including Walsh. Tierney was outside, out of danger. Rossiter would be no problem, but there were at least ten of Walsh's thugs here—undoubtedly armed.

But *he* had twelve men and the element of surprise. If he acted now.

His decision made, Michael pushed himself up. Without a word, he moved out from behind the boxes, then lifted a hand to signal his men.

358

Tierney hurried the four girls away from the warehouse to the edge of the Bowery district, where he gave them a stern warning. "Go home, now—all of you! If you don't have a home, go to one of the police station lodging houses. You've seen what can happen to you on the streets!"

They were all crying by now, sobbing and nodding their heads as they huddled together. Finally, one of them—the tallest and the prettiest of the four—wiped at her eyes with the back of one hand. "But what about the others?" she asked, her voice tremulous.

Tierney stared at her. "What others?"

"The others like us," she persisted. "The ones what was caught—the black ones. They'll sell 'em, they will—sure, and, they told us so right out."

The others like us . . . the black ones . . .

Tierney tried to swallow down the sour taste in his mouth. "Go on," he said grudgingly, "get away! I'll see what I can do."

As the girls scattered into the darkness, Tierney turned and stared back toward the warehouse. *The girl doesn't know any better,* he thought, *she doesn't know the difference between the blacks and the Irish. . . .*

But maybe he was the one who didn't know any better. He had seen for himself what Patrick Walsh was capable of, after all. Had he really thought a snake like that would differentiate between Negro and Irish—him, who disavowed his own Irish blood?

His own blind spot made it worse. That, after all this time, he could have been naive enough to expect anything but consummate evil from a man like Walsh was nothing short of foolishness on his part.

Da had been right about Walsh all along. . . .

He had sensed Walsh's wickedness, his depravity, right from the start. That's why he had been so set on exposing him and putting an end to his rotten dealings. Da wouldn't have been the least surprised to learn the extent of Walsh's corruption.

The thought of his father only served to deepen his anguish. It would destroy him to know his only son had been a party to tonight's bad business. It would break his heart entirely. Da, who made no distinctions between Negro or Irish, black or white, rich or poor . . . who would give his life just as quickly for a black person as a white . . . who would believe anything of a man like Walsh . . . but not of his son.

Da . . . oh, Da!

Sick with shame, Tierney squeezed his eyes shut. He was unable to think of anything else but his father, yet the thought made him want to weep.

Finally opening his eyes, he stood staring at the warehouse. After a moment, his heart pounding, he took off at a dead run.

40

Trial by Fire

It seemed life held
No future and no past but this.

LOLA RIDGE (1883–1941)

Arthur Jackson, still dazed and stinging from the slave catcher's blow, heard everything the man called *Rossiter* said to the tall boy with the scar above his eye.

Burke, the bald-headed man had called him. Tierney Burke. Arthur knew the name. Tierney Burke was the captain's son, wasn't he?

But what was he doing *here*? He couldn't be one of the slave catchers, could he—with his daddy a policeman?

Still, Captain Burke was an Irishman. And those people did hate the colored folk something fierce.

Arthur wondered if anybody in this city liked anybody else. Or were they mostly all like the people at the big church, fussing and feuding and making trouble for the few really good folks, like Mr. Jess?

Nothing was fair in the city, it seemed. Captain Burke, he seemed like a pretty good man, yet he had a son working for the slave catchers.

And Mr. Jess—well, they didn't come any better than that man, and just look at all the trouble he was in!

For that matter, how about himself? He'd run away to help Mr. Jess, and because of that, he had a rope around his neck and

361

was going to get sold—maybe even sent back to Mississippi.

A shivery chill, like the kind that came with a sickness, trickled down the back of Arthur's neck, all the way down his spine.

Any boy with a lick of sense knew that Mississippi was one of the worst places for a slave to end up. Mississippi and Alabama were as close to hell on earth as a slave boy could get.

Oh, Lord . . . please, Lord, don't let me end up back in Mississippi! If I got to go back to the South, couldn't I maybe just go to Virginia, or somewhere else, somewhere that's not quite so bad for colored boys?

A sudden movement in the back of the warehouse caught Arthur's eye. He looked over the bald man's shoulder, into the shadows. There was something shiny back there. Something like a flash of light. A flash of light from a badge. A policeman's badge.

Locking his eyes on the badge shaped like a star, Arthur began to smile.

———

Hubert Rossiter glared down his nose at the arrogant young buck in the center of the torches. He was a feisty one, all right. The kind who would have brought top dollar at a regular auction. Too bad the price had been set at so much a head. Quantity, not quality, was what counted tonight.

Already, he regretted letting Tierney Burke make off with the Irish girls. His first thought was that the high and mighty boy wonder would get in trouble with Mr. Walsh—would finally hang himself, and good riddance! But the more he mulled it over, the more he began to question his judgment. Walsh seemed to favor the young pup, in spite of his cheek. There was never any telling how he'd react to the boy's insolence. More than likely, Burke would walk away from this episode smelling like a rose, as usual.

Rossiter turned his anger on the black boy, wondering how it would feel to slap that defiant face. Then he saw the dark eyes lock on something behind him. At the same time, a faint smile began to creep over the Negro boy's features.

The skin on Rossiter's forearms tightened. In the split second it took for him to realize something was wrong, one of Walsh's men charged forward with a curse, only to be stopped by a low voice.

"Drop your weapons, boyos. It's all over."

Tierney reached the warehouse, heaving from the exertion of his run, only to find the main door bolted from within. He sagged against the door for a moment, then turned and made his way around the building, pulling on every door he passed.

In the back alley, he tried the last door in vain. Leaning his head against the splintered wood, he choked down an oath of frustration.

"Over here!" a voice whispered.

Tierney lifted his head, looked around, but saw no one.

"Here!" hissed the voice, louder.

Tierney glanced down. Coming toward him out of the darkness was a dark-haired, dark-eyed . . . something . . . on a wooden cart.

He squinted, then realized what he was seeing. The legless "Turtle Boy" from the dime museum. He had seen him on stage a couple of times, had passed him on routine trips to the Bowery, riding about the streets on his little cart.

"What are you doing here?" he said, forcing back a shudder of revulsion as he eyed the boy.

The Turtle Boy stared up at him, his expression unreadable in the darkness. "We thought Captain Burke might need some help," he said matter-of-factly, raising one hand to gesture over his shoulder. Two shadowed forms entered the alley from the other side: one, a huge, muscular youth, almost grotesque in size, and the other, a mean-looking dwarf.

"I'm his son," Tierney said, studying the three of them. He shifted uneasily, realizing how differently he responded to these people than his father would. What Da would call their "differences" made him feel uncomfortable, almost fearful.

"Yes," the Turtle Boy replied shortly, "I know. I heard part of your conversation with Walsh's man inside."

Perched on his cart, he regarded Tierney with an unsettling mixture of what looked to be pity and suspicion. "Have you perhaps changed your mind about your employer tonight?"

Immediately defensive, Tierney frowned. "What do *you* know about my—employer?"

"Being without legs doesn't mean I can't see and hear," said the Turtle Boy curtly. "Patrick Walsh is well known in the Bowery." He paused. "At least, by reputation."

Before Tierney could ask further questions, the boy went on. "There's no time for this now. Do you see that hole, there, in the side of the building?" He pointed to a large, gaping hole just above the foundation of the warehouse. "I'm going in and unlock the back door. You come in with them," he said, motioning toward the dwarf and the big, heavy-shouldered youth.

Tierney nodded dumbly, standing aside as the legless boy flipped himself off his cart, then scooted easily through the hole in the wall.

After another moment, he heard the bolt slide free. Soon, the back door cracked open.

As soon as he returned to the alley, the Turtle Boy, using his hands and moving as swiftly as a young seal, hefted himself back onto the cart and started for the door. "We'll have to be very quiet," he warned.

Tierney followed the others into the dark warehouse, stopping just inside. At the far end, toward the front door, he could see a circle of men holding torches.

His eyes went to Rossiter, who seemed frozen in place as he stared at—what?

Tierney squinted, then caught his breath. There, silhouetted against the torchlight, was the unmistakable form of his father, advancing on Hubert Rossiter with a gun.

Michael held the gun on Rossiter as he continued to move forward. Keeping his eyes on the bookkeeper, he jerked his head toward the children. "Stay back!" he told them, still closing in on Rossiter.

He glanced to see them backing up, eyes wide with fear. "Now," he said to Rossiter, his voice low, "you'll just be giving the book to me—and very carefully."

Extending his left hand toward the bookkeeper, he spied a movement by one of Walsh's henchmen. "HOLD IT!" he shouted, swinging his gun around.

But he was too late. With a mighty heave, the goon hurled his torch straight at Michael.

He ducked, and the torch bounced across the floor toward the opposite end of the warehouse.

His men scattered, flinging themselves out of the way as the torch landed at the base of a stack of crates. Boxes and packing crates blazed up like dry tinder, illuminating the warehouse in an exploding flash of light.

Walsh's men, swinging torches and clubs, piled into the policemen. Michael lunged toward Rossiter, but was too far away to reach him.

Running at a crouch, he shouted, "DON'T SHOOT!" to his men, but the warning came too late. Gunshots echoed off the walls of the cavernous building. Abandoned containers of cleaning fluid exploded as bolt after bolt of discarded material shot up into flames.

Dense, black fingers of smoke snaked upward, slithering around the rafters as the fire gathered momentum. Michael could already feel the heat. His throat burning, he whirled around, signaling his men to move forward. "HURRY! YOU MEN IN THE BACK—GET OUT OF THERE! NOW! GET THOSE CHILDREN OUT OF HERE!"

Turning back, he saw Rossiter at the main door. With the ledger securely tucked under one arm, he was struggling with the bolt on the door.

"NO!" Michael screamed, taking off at a run toward him. "DON'T OPEN THE DOOR!"

The bookkeeper whipped around, his eyes wild as he stared into the fire. Without warning he hurled the ledger across the floor into the blaze. Then, turning back, he jerked the bolt free and threw the door open.

The blaze exploded with a roar. Men screamed, windows shatterd, and chunks of the ceiling let go as the flames whooshed over the walls, a raging ocean of fire.

Rocked by the backdraft, Michael stumbled, righted himself, and again dropped to a crouch.

The ledger! It was his only evidence against Walsh! He had to get the ledger. . . .

His eyes burned, his lungs struggled for air as he lurched toward the fire. His men came staggering past him, herding the children toward the door.

Denny Price, with a little boy on each arm, tried to stop him, but Michael pushed him away, shouting, "KEEP GOING! GET THEM OUT OF HERE!"

Spying the ledger, which had landed near a barrel, Michael pitched forward, losing his balance and floundering. The fire came racing toward him across the splintered wooden floor, coiling and rolling like hell unleashed.

His chest exploding from the smoke, his heart thundering with panic, he gave one strangled gasp and flung himself full-length across the floor, grabbing for the ledger.

The fire met the barrel. Michael saw a blinding flash of light, then nothing more.

———

Trying to stay clear of the smoke, Tierney saw the explosion coming before it happened.

"DA!" he yelled, his voice lost in the roar of the blaze and the clamor of shouting and shrieking children. "NO, DA! DON'T! GO BACK!"

He made a desperate, futile lunge toward his father, falling just as one of the ceiling timbers gave way, pinning his right leg to the floor. Dazed with pain and smoke, Tierney writhed and twisted, struggling to free his leg. Smoke billowed around him, nearly blinding him. The heat seared his skin, his eyes.

He knew he was losing consciousness, fought against it.

Suddenly, the weight was released from his leg.

Almost blinded by the dense smoke and gasping for breath, he felt himself lifted from the floor and carried toward the open door, away from the inferno.

He heard the sound of wheels whirring past him, and a small, shadowy form scooted by, toward the center of the fire.

Choking, Tierney fought for air, but found only smoke. Then the merciful darkness closed in around him.

———

Prodded along by one of the policemen, Arthur Jackson was on his way outside. Something made him slow his steps to glance back over his shoulder. At that instant, he saw Captain Burke dive toward the fire, his arms outstretched.

Arthur didn't think. Breaking free of the other children milling toward the open door, he charged back, toward the fire, head down, to help the captain.

His head snapped up when he heard the explosion. At the same instant he leaped into the wall of fire, throwing himself between the captain and the flaming barrel.

His last conscious act before the blinding light sucked him inside was to give the policeman a hard shove with both feet.

———

When Michael came to, a light drizzle had begun, misting his face. He coughed, heaved, then shook his head, clenching his teeth against the pain.

He forced his eyes open, but they wouldn't focus; all he could see was a mass of colors and distorted shapes. He started to drift off again, into the blackness. Suddenly it all came rushing back to him: the warehouse . . . the children . . . the fire . . . Tierney. . . .

Tierney!

At last his head began to clear. Again he choked and coughed, clutching his throat, which still burned with a vengeance.

He looked up, and found himself staring into the concerned face and gentle eyes of Bhima.

"*Bhima*? How . . . where's my son?"

He tried to push himself up, but a dizzying rush of pain sent him sprawling onto his back again. He squeezed his eyes shut, then flung an arm over them.

Bhima's soft, consoling voice spoke out of the darkness. "Your son is fine, Captain. But you must not try to get up just yet. You had a very close call. . . ." The boy's words drifted off as Michael once more gave in to the momentary comfort of darkness.

When he again opened his eyes, Tierney hovered over him, studying him with a worried gaze.

"Da? It's over now. You're all right, Da."

For an instant, Michael forgot his sick despair at his son's involvement in the evil of this night. "You're not hurt?"

The boy shook his head. "Took some bruises on my leg is all. "I'm fine."

Staring at him, Michael remembered what he had seen. "You left—"

"I came back." Tierney's voice sounded strangely harsh and unsteady.

Michael searched his son's eyes but could read nothing in the hooded gaze. "Was it you who got me out?"

Tierney shook his head. "No," he said, and Michael saw a faint trembling of his lip. "It was the—the one you call 'Bhima.' He and his friends—" His voice faltered. "They . . . brought both of us out."

"Bhima—" Michael again tried to push himself up. "Where is he? Where did he go?"

"He's with the children, Da," said Tierney. "He and the others went to help the children. You'd better lie still now. You took an awful lot of smoke."

A thought struck Michael, and he gripped Tierney's hand. "Rossiter! And the ledger—what about the ledger?"

Tierney glanced away, saying nothing. He got to his feet when Denny Price walked up, backing away to make room for him.

Dropping to one knee, Price wiped a hand across his smoke-blackened face, waiting until Tierney walked away.

"The ledger's gone, Mike. In the fire." He hesitated, then added, "Rossiter's dead. We got two of the other goons, though. They're already in custody."

Michael looked away, his gaze scanning his surroundings. Across the street, the warehouse was still burning, lighting the night sky with a gold and crimson glow. A firewagon was there, in front of the building, and some of the Bowery residents had formed bucket brigades. The smell of smoke was almost overpowering.

"They've got it under control," Price said. "The rain should help finish it."

Michael drew in a ragged breath, immediately choking and gagging when his lungs rebelled. His throat was tight, his eyes burning, not so much from the smoke as from the bitterness of defeat.

"We were so close," he muttered. "We almost had him."

Glancing across the street, he saw Tierney. The boy was standing at the west wall of the dime museum, one arm braced against the building, his head hung low, his eyes downcast.

Heavyhearted, Michael looked away, turning his gaze in the opposite direction. In the middle of a vacant lot, directly across the street, stood a tall, powerful figure of a man, who seemed to be staring down at something near his feet.

Jess Dalton. As soon as Michael recognized the big pastor, he pushed himself up on one arm, catching his breath at a fresh wave of dizziness. His head cleared, and as he watched, he saw Dalton, in his shirtsleeves, his dark hair damp and tousled, bend and carefully scoop something into his arms.

The drizzle had increased to a light rain, and a cheer went up from the firemen.

Michael was only vaguely aware of Denny Price's low voice beside him. "We lost Scanlan tonight, Mike. Bill's gone. . . ."

Jess Dalton had started walking in their direction, and Michael pushed himself up even further.

As the pastor came closer, Michael saw that he was carrying a blanket-draped form, limp and still, like a broken doll. . . .

". . . and the Jackson boy . . . he didn't make it either. . . ."

Jess Dalton kept walking. He was close enough now that Michael could see his eyes, glazed with anguish, and his face, wet, but not with rain . . . with tears. . . .

". . . the poor little fellow, he hadn't even got a good start on his life, such as it was. . . ."

Michael fought not to strangle on the painful lump in his throat. "How?" he choked out. "What happened?"

Price didn't answer right away. When he did, Jess Dalton had almost reached them, the burden in his arms seemingly weightless as he cradled it against his massive chest.

"Rourke saw him run in after you, when you went for the ledger." Price paused, then added softly, "Bhima and his friends, they brought you and Tierney out . . . but the black boy was the one who saved your life. . . ."

Jess Dalton stopped in front of them. The rain was falling steadily now, and as Michael looked up to meet the stricken gaze of the pastor, he felt his own tears spill over and mingle with the rain.

A great sorrow clouded his spirit, and Michael knew, beyond a shadow of a doubt, that tonight heaven itself wept over New York City.

41

Sons and Heirs

Behold what manner of love the Father has bestowed on
us, that we should be called children of God!

1 JOHN 3:1 (NKJV)

Arthur Jackson was buried on Good Friday. Because he had helped to save the life of a New York City police captain, he was given a hero's funeral, along with Officer Bill Scanlan, who had also perished in the warehouse fire.

As Daniel Kavanagh stood at the graveside with Evan Whittaker and the boys' choir from Five Points, other deaths . . . too many others . . . passed with wrenching clarity befor him. He closed his eyes against the pain, remembering. . . .

So many partings, his heart whispered . . . *so many good-byes.* His father's face, strong and good, rose in his memory. Then Ellie, his little sister, dead of the famine fever before her seventh year. Tahg, his gentle-natured older brother, buried at sea before their ship of escape ever left Ireland. And Katie, his childhood sweetheart . . . dead, after only a few months in America. Thomas, her father. Catherine, her mother. Gone. All of them gone.

And now Arthur. A runaway slave. A boy whose only dream had been to live free, to live like a human being instead of an animal. Also gone, just like the others.

Daniel opened his eyes, scanning the other mourners at the grave. With a fresh twinge of sadness, it occurred to him that Arthur would have been more than a little surprised at the mixed

370

crowd who had gathered to pay their last respects to him.

People like Bhima and his friends from the Bowery—the Strong Man and a dwarf named Plug. Lewis Farmington and Evan's Aunt Winifred. A small band of black laborers from the pipe factory. Mrs. Walsh. Miss Sara. Uncle Mike. Even Tierney.

And what looked to be the entire New York City police department.

Daniel's throat tightened, and tears scalded his eyes as a kilted piper from the police force, standing on a gently sloping green hill nearby, began to play.

After a moment, the boys' choir, of which Arthur had been such a proud and loyal member, added their voices to the wail of the pipes. . . .

Amazing grace, how sweet the sound
That saved a wretch like me!
I once was lost, but now am found—
Was blind, but now I see.

Through many dangers, toils, and snares,
I have already come;
'Tis grace has brought me safe thus far,
And grace will lead me home.

When the last words of the hymn died away, Evan Whittaker stepped back to stand with his boys, between Daniel and Casey-Fitz.

For a moment, his mind went to Nora, who waited at home for him.

Thank God for Nora . . . the light of his heart, the joy of his life. When everything else seemed darkened by shadows, Nora's love still came shining through to warm his world. Even now, in the midst of another tragedy, her love buoyed him on. . . .

He glanced at the little fellow at the end of the row. Billy Hogan was crying openly for his friend. The sorrow of the day only deepened in Evan as he saw yet another new bruise on the boy's cheek.

He must not . . . he would not . . . let this child end up as one more tragedy. As soon as possible, he would talk with Michael Burke about his suspicions. Somehow, he was going to help that little boy, or, God forbid, he might end up like Arthur Jackson . . . another statistic, another child in despair . . . or worse. . . .

Evan looked at Jess Dalton, standing at the head of the burial plot, his wife weeping quietly at his side. The Daltons, he realized with some consolation, had, at least for a brief time, been the light . . . and the joy . . . of young Arthur Jackson's life. They had given the homeless boy refuge, provided him with a greater sense of freedom than he'd ever known in his short lifetime, filled the emptiness of his world with love and caring.

For a time, however fleeting, Arthur Jackson had known the shelter, the haven, of a home.

And now he would know the eternal security of a heavenly home. . . .

"ARTHUR JACKSON HAS GONE HOME. . . ."

Jess Dalton's resonant voice soared above the graveside like a trumpet call. Surprisingly steady in spite of his own private pain, the big pastor's words brought Evan's heart an unexpected gift of hope and comfort, reminding him that in two days it would be Resurrection Sunday. . . .

"I AM THE RESURRECTION AND THE LIFE; HE WHO BE-LIEVES IN ME, THOUGH HE WERE DEAD, YET SHALL HE LIVE. . . ."

The pastor went on, his voice growing stronger as his words echoed across the springtime afternoon. . . .

"God says that once He has put the Spirit of His Son into our hearts, we are no longer slaves—but sons. We are sons and heirs of the Father himself, through Jesus Christ.

"Arthur Jackson was born a slave, but he dreamed of freedom. He ran away from the only home he'd ever known to come here . . . to New York City . . . in search of his dream, in search of freedom."

Tears fell freely down the big pastor's face as he lifted both arms toward heaven. In a voice that rang, not with grief, but with exultation, he proclaimed:

"ARTHUR JACKSON IS NO LONGER A SLAVE! HE IS A SON, BELOVED HEIR OF THE FATHER. AND HE HAS FOUND THE FREEDOM OF WHICH HE DREAMED. ARTHUR IS FREE . . . FREE AT LAST!"

Evan bowed his head and, with an aching heart, began to pray . . . *Lord, let this boy's death not be in vain . . . let it be a new beginning, for all of us . . . from this time forth, let us strive all the more to bind up the wounds, to bridge the differences, to tear down the walls. Oh, Lord . . . make your people one in you. . . .*

Early Saturday morning, Tierney Burke stood with his father and Sara on the docks, waiting to board one of Lewis Farmington's new packets, the *Land of Canaan*.

Until today, he would not have believed that the thought of sailing for Ireland could bring him anything but sheer joy. Instead, his heart seemed caught up in a storm of conflicting emotions, not the least of which was the unexpected pain brought on by the thought of leaving his father.

"You have the letter for Morgan?" Da asked again.

Tierney had lost count of how many times he had repeated the question. Touching his shirt pocket, he said, "I do, Da. It's right here."

His father's face was tight and strained, and when he chanced to meet Tierney's gaze, he quickly looked away. "Aye . . . well, I'll be sending him a letter as well. Right away."

Tierney nodded, not knowing what to say.

The three of them jumped when the ship's horn blasted.

"Well, then," his father said awkwardly, "you'll be leaving soon. Here it is . . . your dream at last."

Again Tierney nodded. He glanced at Sara, shaken by the depth of kindness and understanding in her eyes. He had her to thank for getting him passage so quickly. Her, and her father.

"Sara," he said, his voice sounding thin and unnatural in his ears, "thank you again for . . . everything."

She smiled at him, and Tierney was dumbfounded to see tears in her eyes.

"You've already thanked me, Tierney. Just . . . take care. And write to us. You *will* write?"

He nodded, unable to meet her gaze any longer. "Da. . . ."

"This is what you always wanted," his father broke in, repeating the same words he had said often throughout the morning. "You've waited a long time for this day."

"I . . . that's true . . . but I hadn't thought it would be like this. . . ."

"Aye . . . but it would seem the only way now," said his father gruffly.

It seemed to Tierney that Da looked older this morning than

he had ever seen him. Older and sad and strangely unsure of himself.

"By now Walsh knows about your freeing the girls," his father was saying. "And how you came back to help the others. There's no telling what he'll try." He paused, then added in a slightly stronger tone, "Especially if he learns you've filled us in on all his illegal—businesses."

"I hope I gave you enough to help, Da."

"Everything helps. The time will come when there's enough," his father said grimly. "It will come."

Again the three of them stood, not speaking, each glancing about the docks as if they hadn't already inspected the entire harbor several times during the past hour.

"I expect we'll miss you!" his father suddenly blurted out.

Tierney turned a startled look on him. The hurt in Da's eyes arrowed right to his heart, and for one terrible moment he thought he would burst into childish tears.

He would miss him, too. *Oh, Da . . . I will miss you more than you would dream . . . more than I would have believed . . . until now. . . .*

As if he had read his thoughts, Da suddenly reached for him, pulling him into a fierce embrace. Tierney's voice strangled on the unshed tears caught in his throat. He heard Sara give a small sob, which only made it harder.

"Tierney . . ." Da choked out, his arms still wrapped tightly about him, "I hope you find what you're looking for. I hope Ireland doesn't disappoint you."

Knowing in another moment he would fly apart entirely, Tierney eased himself back, out of his father's arms. Forcing a weak semblance of a smile, he said, "It'll be grand, Da. I've no doubt about it. Ireland's for me, all right."

His father glanced down at his hands, as if wondering what to do with them. "Well . . . but you know you can always come home. I'll get things fixed up here in no time at all, so you won't have to worry about coming back . . . when you're ready."

"Oh, I know, Da. I know you will. And I'll be back. . . ."

He could not bear another moment of this, could not endure his father's anguished gaze. "Well . . . I expect I should go aboard now, don't you?" he muttered, looking neither at his father nor at Sara.

Without another word, he turned his back on the two of them

. . . and New York . . . and, slinging his jacket over his shoulder, started up the gangplank.

When he reached the deck, he went to the rail. They were still standing there, watching him. Sara waved, then Da.

Tierney lifted his hand to wave. There was enough distance between them now that they couldn't see the tears he could hold back no longer. His vision blurred as he smiled and waved good-bye.

And so at last, he was on his way to Ireland.

42

Gifts of the Heart

He'll meet the soul which comes in love
and deal it joy on joy—
as once He dealt out star and star
to garrison the sky,
to stand there over rains and snows
and deck the dark of night—
so, God will deal the soul, like stars,
delight upon delight.

ROBERT FARREN (1909–)

Dublin
April

The night before the wedding, Sandemon and Annie were still hurrying to complete the last details of the gift which might, at least in part, fulfill a certain dream.

The two of them were hard at work in the stables, their heads bent low over the project. The wolfhound sat nearby, watching their efforts with a skeptical, though polite, expression.

Intent on her part in things, Annie bit her lip almost to bleeding as she held the last part of Sandemon's invention in place to be hard soldered.

"This . . . should . . . do . . . it," said Sandemon, easing back from his work at last to appraise the finished product.

Annie also contemplated the results of their efforts, imitating the black man's solemn nod of approval. "A fine job," she said, glancing at Fergus as if to say, *I told you so.*

"Only if it works," cautioned Sandemon. "It remains yet to test its effectiveness with the *Seanchai*, later tonight."

On her knees beside their creation, Annie refused to even consider failure. "Of course, it will work, Sand-Man! You *said* it would!"

Raising his head, he nodded distractedly. "We must take it into the house now. Later, I will present it to the *Seanchai* and help him experiment with it."

Annie would have liked very much to see the *Seanchai*'s face when he beheld their creation, but the hour was already growing late—and Sister had given strict orders that she report to her yet tonight for some last-minute instructions.

No doubt she intended to "do something" with Annie's hair. Sister tended to become a bit wild-eyed about things like clean hair and clean socks and clean fingernails.

"You must tell me every word the *Seanchai* says when he sees it," she reminded Sandemon.

He lifted an eyebrow. "Even if it's a total failure and he thinks us demented?"

"If it's a success, he will think we're quite wonderful," she pointed out.

Helping him to wrap the culmination of two week's work in paper and canvas, she changed the subject. "I'd like your opinion on something, Sand-Man."

Straightening, he wiped his hands on his trousers. "A rare occurrence, surely."

Annie frowned at him. "This is important. I've been thinking a great deal about it. Now that I am truly the *Seanchai*'s daughter, what do you think I should call him?"

The black man put a hand to his cheek, considering her question. "You're wondering if you should no longer call him *Seanchai*, is that it?"

Annie nodded. "What do you think would please him most?"

"The *Seanchai* knows," he said after a moment, "that you held a great affection for your birth father, God rest his soul, and, certainly, he does not intend to usurp that affection in any way. I believe he also understands the depth of feeling you hold for him.

So, then, it is my opinion that, however you choose to address him, he will be pleased . . . for the devotion in your eyes, child, names him 'Father' with every look."

Annie beamed at him. "You are very wise, Sand-Man."

He smiled at her, and Annie blurted out, "I'm awfully glad you're a part of our family!"

"Thank you, child," he said softly, still smiling. "I am greatly blessed to be among you."

———

In her bedroom, Sister Louisa inspected her gift with a sharply critical eye, hoping all the while that she had not been presumptuous in the planning. There was no denying the fact that it was somewhat . . . unusual.

True enough. But, then, so was this wedding. Neither the groom nor the bride could be considered . . . conventional.

Indeed not. She smiled a little, pausing in her appraisal of the gift to remember the upbraiding she had received from the *Seanchai* the night she dared to question the marriage. For one so obviously intimidated by nuns in general, he had certainly put her soundly in her place.

Lest her examination of the gift give way to vanity, she put it away, taking care to conceal it from curious eyes.

At a sudden hard hammering on her door, she realized her caution had been well advised.

"Come in, child."

"How do you always know it's me, Sister?"

Louisa studied the braids, askew as always, the grease-smudged face, and the eager wolfhound, who, at the moment, looked far more presentable than the child.

"It is *I*," she corrected automatically. "And I always know it is *you* because you announce yourself so . . . vigorously." She glanced again at the dog, who walked in, tail wagging, and immediately plopped down at Louisa's feet.

"He's looking quite handsome," she observed to them both.

The child grinned and preened. So did the wolfhound.

"I gave him a bath first thing this morning. For the wedding."

Sister Louisa regarded her with suspicion. "I do hope you're not planning to take the dog into the chapel."

The wolfhound lifted his head, grinning hopefully as he looked from one to the other.

"Certainly not!" said the child, tossing her braids. "Fergus will be attending the door."

"By whose consent?"

"Sand-Man and the *Seanchai* both agreed," declared the child, with obvious delight.

Sister Louisa lifted her eyes heavenward, marveling not for the first time at the foolishness of grown men who really ought to know better.

"What is that?" asked the sharp-eyed child, spying the gift propped up in the corner.

"That," said Louisa firmly, "is private. Now come here. We really must do *something* with your hair. We'll start with a thorough brushing."

The child scowled. The wolfhound sighed.

Louisa prevailed.

———

Finola had expected to feel painfully awkward with Morgan this night, on the eve of their wedding. But after a few moments alone with him, she forgot her own discomfort in an attempt to ease *his*.

At least three times since having her things moved earlier in the week, he had inquired if she was comfortable, if she was pleased with her new rooms. Tonight he went through the same explanations once again, as if he could not reassure her often enough that his intentions were entirely honorable.

"Morgan, these rooms are beautiful," Finola said, again trying to reassure him. "You see? Even Small One has given her approval."

Morgan glanced toward the massive bed, where the black and white cat, utterly contented, was curled up in the center of the coverlet.

At the sound of her name, Small One opened one eye and looked at Morgan. Then, slowly, she stood up, yawned, stretched languidly, and stalked to the head of the bed, where she made two circles before settling down on the pillow and shutting her eyes again.

Morgan did not seem convinced.

"These were my grandmother's rooms," he repeated for the fourth time. "I had them freshly decorated just for you." Once more he pointed out that he meant for her to have the largest and finest bed chamber—and the one with the most expansive view of the grounds. He admitted to wanting her near, especially with the child coming and what with Lucy now having a room of her own, albeit adjacent to Finola's.

"Is she still so terrified of me, by the way?" he asked somewhat gruffly. "The woman fairly quakes every time I enter the room."

Finola had been standing at the window, gazing out at the moon-dusted grounds below. She turned, smiling a little at the grudging tone of his voice.

"Perhaps not terrified," she said. "Perhaps . . . only mildly panicked."

He drew a long breath. "I have been kindness itself of late. I don't suppose she's mentioned that."

Again, Finola was struck by how ill at ease he seemed, despite his obvious attempts to be casual. "In fact, she *has* told me. And she's most grateful. Oh—and she likes her new room very much. She thinks it's quite grand."

"You've only to say so, you know, if you want her things moved back," he reminded her. "I just thought that, since you're feeling some stronger now, you might like a bit of privacy."

She nodded, coming to sit down in the rocking chair opposite him. "This will work out well, I think. Lucy needs some privacy, too. She's had little time to herself, since . . ."

She let her words drift off, still unable to give voice to the ugliness of what had happened.

As always, he seemed immediately sensitive to her thoughts and quickly moved to change the subject. "I don't suppose you've learned anything more about what went on, to bring about this remarkable change in her."

Brightening, Finola shook her head. "Only what I've told you. Apparently she and Sandemon talked. She says he 'showed her the Light.' I do know she is much changed. She reads the Scriptures like a starving soul at a banquet—and she spends much time in the chapel. She loves the chapel."

Morgan nodded. "The man is truly a wonder," he said, smiling to himself. "Though a stern taskmaster with me," he added wryly. "He's waiting for me now—it seems there is something we are to do yet tonight. I did remind him that tomorrow is my wedding day, but he was unmoved. He said he would wait."

For a time they were both silent. An awkward silence. Now and then he would glance at her, or Finola at him, each quickly looking away when the other smiled.

Finally, he cleared his throat. "I told you that I would present you with the wedding ring tomorrow," he said stiffly.

Finola nodded, wondering if he was having second thoughts.

"Yes . . . well, I hope you'll be pleased with it. I had it designed especially for you."

"I'm sure it is lovely," Finola said, studying her hands with great concentration.

Again, silence. Then, "Finola?"

She looked up, and he wheeled his chair a bit closer to her. "I . . . wanted you to have this tonight. It is my wedding gift for you . . . and there is something I would say."

Studying his dear, strong face, now taut with uncertainty, Finola watched him withdraw an ivory-colored case from inside his coat.

"I would be pleased if you would wear this . . . tomorrow . . . for the ceremony," he said, handing her the case.

Again he cleared his throat. The brilliant green eyes looked everywhere but at her for a moment, then returned to rest on her face. Holding the still unopened case in her hand, Finola thought she could not bear the tenderness in his gaze.

As always, his voice was gentle when he spoke to her. "I would like you to know, Finola, that I am infinitely grateful to you for agreeing to become my wife."

Startled, Finola stared at him and would have protested, had he not gone on. "You cannot imagine how proud it makes me that you are willing to wear my name. You are giving me a priceless gift, and I am thankful beyond all words. Please," he said, gesturing to the case in her hand, "open it."

With trembling fingers, Finola slipped the latch on the smoothly polished case. She gasped, putting a hand to her throat when she saw the exquisite treasure within: a finely carved pendant of purest ivory, in the graceful shape of a swan, suspended on a thin, delicate gold chain.

Her eyes filled with quick tears as she traced the outline of the swan with one finger. "Oh, Morgan! It is quite the loveliest thing I have ever seen!"

He smiled into her eyes as if her words gave him great pleasure. "You will wear it, then?"

"Oh, of course, I will wear it! I . . . may I put it on now?"

"Please," he said.

When her hands continued to tremble so badly she couldn't release the clasp, he took it from her, wheeling his chair around to her side and slipping the chain over her hair as she dipped her head.

Finola straightened, touching the pendant at her throat.

He was staring at her in the strangest way, his hand on hers, his eyes somewhat glazed. "Even ivory," he said softly, "seems a poor thing in the light of your loveliness."

He leaned toward her then, and Finola held her breath. "May I?" he whispered. Finola's heart leaped when he touched his lips to her cheek, so lightly she almost thought she had imagined it.

He backed away immediately, again reaching inside his pocket. "This is meant to accompany the pendant," he said, pressing a piece of folded paper into her hand. "But I would ask that you not read it until later, after I leave you." He paused, then added lightly, "Which I will do now. You must rest, and the West Indies Wonder awaits my presence."

Finola caught his hand. "Morgan . . ."

He waited, smiling uncertainly.

"There is something I, too, would say. I . . . want you to know that I think you are . . . quite wonderful. And I . . . am more than pleased . . . I am overwhelmed . . . to wear your name. And this lovely gift."

He left her then, wheeling himself quietly from the room with one last glance as he said goodnight.

After he was gone, Finola sat for a moment, fingering the ivory pendant. At last, she opened the paper he had placed in her hand. For a moment she had difficulty making out the words, for she was forced to read through a mist of gathering tears. Finally, she saw that it was a poem . . . a poem written by one called *The Singer* . . . for one named *The Swan*. . . .

It was a wondrous piece of writing, an enchanting prose-poem composed of love and light and promise. When Finola reached the final lines, she was breathless at the beauty of the words, in awe of the power of Morgan's gift . . . and utterly and overwhelmingly moved, to know that she was to be the wife of such a man. . . .

> "Now life's lake is full of loveliness,
> The sky filled up with splendor,
> And my heart can only measure joy
> By overflowing founts. . . ."

43

Wonder Upon Wonder

For the stars will sing a love song,
And the angels add their voices,
As the gift of love is granted
To the Singer and the Swan. . . .

MORGAN FITZGERALD (1849)

In the vestry off the chapel, Morgan Fitzgerald subjected himself to the strong arms and capable hands of his attendant.

Fidgety as he was in these last moments before the ceremony, he was nevertheless mindful of the ways his brawny black friend had changed his life—and all for the better.

The West Indies Wonder's most recent stroke of genius was finally in place, and well concealed. It had actually taken less than twenty minutes to secure the iron braces over Morgan's legs—a rather impressive record, considering that their initial efforts the night before had engaged more than an hour.

Now he sat fixed in his chair, legs sprawled straight out in front of him, as he watched Sandemon make one last inspection of the crutches—odd-looking contraptions, designed with broad, platform tips, and reinforced with iron rods running the length of the bows.

Although his iron-encased limbs were discreetly covered by his trousers and a lap robe, Morgan was keenly aware of his awkward condition.

"I feel for all the world like a trussed turkey," he muttered.

The black man glanced at him. "A well-dressed one, at least."

Not amused, Morgan glared. "You are absolutely certain this will work?"

"There are no absolutes in life, *Seanchai*," Sandemon answered mildly. "You, of all people, surely know that." After another moment, he gave a small nod of satisfaction and braced the crutches against the wall of the vestry. "We do know that it worked last night, and very well." He paused. "If you are unwilling to risk it, there is still time to remove the braces," he added gently.

Morgan gripped the arms of the wheelchair. He had already decided it would be worth the risk. "We will proceed," he said with far more confidence than he felt. "What is the worst that can happen, after all?"

A rare look of uncertainty crossed the black man's face, driving Morgan's own doubts to a new high. Clenching his jaw, he waved a dismissing hand. "Ah, well ... the chapel floor is of rugged construction," he cracked, managing a sickly grin. "At the worst, I will make a great crash."

Sandemon chuckled. "Like thunder from heaven."

Unwilling to consider the possibilities too closely, Morgan moved to change the subject. "Who knows about all this?"

His companion turned and looked at him. "You told me to use my discretion. I thought it best if most of the household knew, so early this morning I mentioned the surprise to Artegal." The ghost of a wry smile curved his lips. "Always a sure way to spread news. Still, it seemed best. Otherwise, by tomorrow the city would be rife with rumors that wonders and miracles are occurring at Nelson Hall."

"I am not sure the rumors would be greatly exaggerated," Morgan said softly. "Since you came to me, my friend, I have seen definite signs of Divine intervention at Nelson Hall."

The black man looked at him. "Still," he said, lifting one eyebrow, "I think it wise that the people know today's wonder to be ... undergirded, at least in part, by human effort."

Morgan looked at him, then burst out laughing. "Well put, and no doubt you're right. I'd as soon not have pilgrims traipsing through the rooms of Nelson Hall in search of a miracle."

Leaning forward, he examined his legs once more. "You left instructions that no one enters the chapel until the doors are opened?"

Sandemon nodded. "The wolfhound is standing sentry over the doors. Sister Louisa is also to come down early."

"Mm. Yes . . . well, for my part, I'd rather go up against a wolfhound any day than a nun."

"Especially *our* nun," Sandemon remarked.

"Indeed."

———

On her way down the stairs, Sister Louisa could see that the doors of the chapel had already been opened. With no one in sight, she assumed that most of the household had been seated by now.

Soft harp music came drifting out the open doors, and the mixed fragrance from lavish sprays of flowers reached even the stairway.

Hurrying the rest of the way downstairs, she started toward the chapel, stopping short at the incredible sight that greeted her.

Decked out in a stiff white shirtfront—obviously hand-made by someone whose stitches were large and shamefully clumsy— the wolfhound sat just outside the chapel doors. He seemed enormously pleased with himself, as, no doubt, was his sponsor, the *Seanchai*'s daughter.

Louisa shot a glance heavenward, heaved a resigned sigh, then bent to give the wolfhound a quick pat of approval. He grinned happily as if to say he was having himself the fine time of it.

Returning to the landing, Louisa stood, hands clasped at her waist to stop their nervous trembling, as she waited for a glimpse of the bride and her young attendant in the upstairs hallway.

———

Inside the chapel, there was a rustling among those awaiting the commencement of the ceremony.

Eyes widened and necks craned as the *Seanchai* himself entered the chapel from the vestry, the West Indies black man right behind the wheelchair, carrying a pair of oversized crutches.

The *Seanchai* was resplendent in a fawn-colored suit and bronze silk ascot, his full head of hair brushed to a blazing copper sheen.

Interest piqued even more as the black man handed the *Seanchai* the crutches, then returned to stand behind him.

There was a collective intake of breath as, gripping the master under his arms, the black man slowly . . . very slowly, and with obvious care . . . raised him from the wheelchair to his feet.

Once he was upright, with Sandemon still supporting his weight, the *Seanchai* braced the crutches under each arm. His eyes still locked on the black man, he leaned slightly forward to balance his weight, then gave a nod.

A hush fell over the chapel as Sandemon slowly released his hands and took a step backward.

There was a long silence, then a collective sigh of relief. Some wept and made the sign of the cross. Others gaped at the master's height, nearly forgotten after so long a time in the wheelchair.

All thrilled to see the smile that swept his strong features as he turned his face toward the doorway of the chapel.

────────

Morgan flinched, nearly losing his balance, when a blast from the organ heralded the approach of the bride.

Sandemon was right beside him, lending confidence to his racing heart, his trembling arms. Although they had rehearsed this over and over, until late into the night, he had not realized . . . could not have imagined until this moment . . . the dizzying, overwhelming sensation of standing upright once again, like a man.

Even with his legs devoid of feeling and wholly confined in the iron braces, he fancied he could feel the floor beneath his feet, could almost believe that he might step out at any moment and walk. It was exhilarating—and terrifying.

As he watched, Annie appeared in the doorway, and with a stirring of great excitement, the congregation stood.

Morgan gaped at his new daughter.

Was it possible? Could this delicate young beauty in green satin truly be the imp with the smudged face and gap-toothed grin who had haunted his hospital room in Belfast, following him all the way to Dublin City?

With her cheeks flushed from excitement, her riot of dark hair caught up in an emerald-green bow and the elegant harp brooch at her throat, Annie . . . his Aine . . . was nothing short of lovely!

A wonder, and no small one at that!

He saw her smile falter for only an instant as her black eyes anxiously scanned the congregation, then came to rest on him.

Her smile strengthened, and she stepped out, head up and eyes shining. Down the aisle she glided—another wonder . . . Annie gliding!

And behind her . . . Finola.

She followed Annie, her eyes downcast, a pale vision in delicate ivory lace and satin. She took the aisle with hesitant steps, and Morgan could almost feel the trembling of her heart as she approached.

His eyes locked on her loveliness, the breathtaking gown, carefully draped to conceal any evidence of her condition, the swan pendant at her breast, the flower-trimmed veil. For a moment he knew a sharp pang of sadness for his young bride. He was painfully aware that this day fell far short of the wedding she must have dreamed of as a young girl. It grieved his heart that this occasion, which should have been, at the very least, a continuous joy, had been clouded by a tragedy beyond all understanding, marred by the fact that, at best, it was only an arrangement.

Then, during that brief instant of regret, she raised her head. Despite the veil, Morgan felt her startled gaze lock on him. He saw her stumble, sway slightly, then recover.

Suddenly, he forgot the braces on his legs, forgot the crutches that held him upright. He forgot the gathering in the chapel and even his friend at his side. He forgot the reality that within a short time he would return to the wheelchair, that this was but a momentary grace and could not last.

He forgot everything . . . everything except the wonder of Finola . . . the most splendid wonder of all.

At last she was at the altar, by his side, touching his arm with a trembling hand. Even the veil could not conceal her glistening eyes, her incredulous smile, her radiance.

As they stood before the priest, Morgan silently thanked God for this wondrous shining moment, when he once again could stand upright like a man, his bride beside him.

Then, in glorious fulfillment of his old, recurring dream, he heard her whisper his name. . . .

"*Morgan* . . ." she breathed, lifting her face to meet his eyes. Her hand tightened on his arm, and Morgan vowed to himself . . . and to his God . . . that, somehow, he would love her enough to make up for her own lost dreams and abandoned hopes.

Epilogue
A Family Portrait

Come to this hallowed place
Where my friends' portraits hang and look thereon;
Ireland's history in their lineaments trace;
Think where man's glory most begins and ends,
And say my glory was I had such friends.

W. B. YEATS (1865–1939)

The wedding banquet was a gala affair, with the entire household invited. Mindful of the famine conditions throughout the country, the *Seanchai* had chosen not to spread an extravagant feast at table, but instead had ordered distributions of food to numerous poorhouses and famine hospitals in several counties.

Nevertheless, there was a generous meal for all, and the servants were invited to attend the opening of the gifts that had been arriving for days.

Now relaxed in the wheelchair at table, his legs freed of the iron braces, the *Seanchai* laughed a great deal and smiled often at his bride, who everyone agreed, was quite the loveliest young woman in three counties.

One gift after another was presented to the bride and groom, each receiving keen attention and vigorous applause. At the very end, Sister Louisa stood to present her gift to the happy couple.

With uncharacteristic hesitancy, she brought forward a large canvas completely draped with a dark cloth.

"I thought this might be appropriate for the occasion," she said, her eyes averted.

A hush fell over the room as she pulled back the covering to reveal a portrait . . . a *family* portrait, exquisitely rendered and striking in each likeness. In the center sat the *Seanchai* himself, holding his minstrel's harp and looking altogether pleased and quite proud. Behind him, at this left, was his new bride. She stood with one hand on her husband's shoulder, a small black-and-white cat tucked in her other arm.

Behind the *Seanchai*, to his right, towered Sandemon, the West Indies Wonder. Regal in purple shirt with flowing sleeves, the black man's expression was both affectionate and serene.

Perched on the floor beside the *Seanchai* sat his young daughter, Annie—Aine. One hand clasped her father's as she beamed her newly found happiness for all eyes to behold.

And at the very front, at the *Seanchai's* feet, sat the great wolfhound, a magnanimous smile on his friendly face as if to indicate how pleased he was with them all.

The *Seanchai*, visibly moved, admired the portrait for a long time, proclaiming it a wonder and a most splendid gift. His bride agreed, and went to embrace the smiling Sister Louisa.

In the midst of all the admiring comments, however, the *Seanchai* loudly cleared his throat, saying, "Sister Louisa? There is one thing I would point out to you, if I may." His face solemn, he went on. "I fear there is a serious omission in the portrait."

Sister Louisa's eyes widened, then narrowed, and she flushed slightly. "An omission?" she repeated, her voice somewhat strained.

"Aye," said the *Seanchai*, watching her carefully. "You seem to have forgotten a member of the family—a most important member, at that."

Clearly flustered, the nun lifted a hand to her throat as she peered at the portrait. "I'm afraid I don't—".

"*Yourself*, Sister!" put in Annie Fitzgerald gleefully, bouncing from one foot to the other. "Don't you see—you forgot to include *yourself*!"

With a glint in his eye, the *Seanchai* laughed and nodded, "Indeed, Sister," he said. "The portrait is splendid, but hardly complete without you."

Principal Characters

IRELAND

Morgan Fitzgerald:
(the *Seanchai*)
Poet, patriot, and schoolmaster. Grandson of British nobleman, Richard Nelson. Formerly of County Mayo. Dublin.

Sandemon:
(the "West Indies Wonder")
Freed slave from Barbados. Hired companion and friend of Morgan Fitzgerald. Dublin.

Annie Delaney:
Belfast runaway given refuge by Morgan Fitzgerald. Dublin.

Finola:
Mysterious Dublin beauty with no memory of her past.

Sister Louisa:
Nun employed as teacher by Morgan Fitzgerald for his new Academy. Dublin.

Lucy Hoy:
One of the women at "Gemma's Place," Friend of Finola. Dublin.

AMERICA

THE KAVANAGHS AND THE WHITTAKERS

Daniel Kavanagh:
Irish immigrant, formerly of Killala, County Mayo. Son of Owen (deceased) and Nora. New York City.

Nora Kavanagh Whittaker:
Irish immigrant, formerly of Killala, County Mayo. Wife of Evan Whittaker. Mother of Daniel Kavanagh. New York City.

Evan Whittaker: British immigrant, formerly of London. Assistant to Lewis Farmington. New York City.

Johanna and Thomas (Little Tom) Fitzgerald: Irish immigrants, orphaned children of Thomas (Morgan Fitzgerald's deceased brother). Adopted by Evan Whittaker and Nora. New York City.

THE BURKES

Michael Burke: Irish immigrant, New York City police captain, formerly of Killala, County Mayo.

Tierney Burke: Rebellious son of Michael Burke. New York City.

THE FARMINGTONS

Lewis Farmington: Shipbuilder, Christian philanthropist. New York City.

Sara Farmington: Daughter of shipbuilding magnate, Lewis Farmington. New York City.

"Grandy Clare":   Sara Farmington's widowed grandmother. New York City.

THE DALTONS

Jess Dalton: Pastor, author, and abolitionist, former West Point chaplain. New York City.

Kerry Dalton: Irish immigrant, formerly of County Kerry. Wife of Jess. New York City.

Casey-Fitz Dalton: Irish immigrant orphan, adopted by the Daltons. New York City.

THE WALSHES

Patrick Walsh: Irish immigrant, formerly of County Cork. Crime boss. New York City.

Alice Walsh: Wife of Patrick, mother of Isabel and Henry. New York City.

OTHERS

Arthur Jackson:	Runaway slave, formerly of Mississippi. Given refuge by Jess and Kerry Dalton in New York City.
Billy Hogan:	Fatherless Irish immigrant. New York City.
Bhima: (the "Turtle Boy")	Resident of New York City dime museum.
Winifred Whittaker Coates:	Evan Whittaker's widowed aunt, formerly of England. New York City.

A Note From the Author

When I first began to research the idea for the first book in this series, *Song of the Silent Harp*, I discovered a strong religious thread throughout the history of Ireland. I hope I have communicated to my readers a clearer understanding of how Christianity influenced the lives of some of America's Irish ancestors.

During those years of study and writing, I became aware that it is virtually impossible to separate the past from the present. The struggles and successes, the trials and triumphs of our forebears, make up not only a rich heritage but also contribute in immeasurable ways to what we—and our world—are today. Like young Daniel Kavanagh, I believe that, from God's perspective, yesterday, today and tomorrow are one vast *panorama*, a continuing epic which our Creator views in its entirety, from the dawn of time through the present to eternity.

Further, history *does*, indeed, repeat itself. Most experiences of the past continue to happen. The horrors of famine and hopelessness that surround many characters in An Emerald Ballad still exist. Month after month, year after year, the innocent victims of war, disaster, political indifference and oppression go on suffering and dying, just as they did in Ireland during the Great Famine.

Government programs and private charities cannot begin to meet the escalating demand for worldwide assistance. I believe the Christian church should be at the very front of international rescue operations, for it is the *church* that bears the responsibility—and the privilege—of giving love to a world that needs it.

I invite you to join me in finding practical ways to help. I have selected World Relief Corporation, but there are many organizations that provide an opportunity to put faith and love into action. One person *does* make a difference.

B. J. Hoff

At the author's request, a percentage of her royalties for *Land of a Thousand Dreams* are paid directly to World Relief Corporation, the international assistance arm of the National Association of Evangelicals (NAE). Founded in 1944, World Relief attempts to meet the physical and spiritual needs of people on every continent.

World Relief is a church-centered ministry of compassion, offering help and hope to victims of war and disaster, famine and poverty. In addition to their international projects, they assist with the resettlement needs of refugees in the United States. Information on World Relief can be obtained by writing to:

World Relief Corporation
P.O. Box WRC
Wheaton, IL 60189